DALRIADA
EDGE OF THE BLADE

DALRIADA
EDGE OF THE BLADE

CHRISTOPHER H. CONNOR

Book II

Copyright © 2019 Christopher H. Connor.

Interior Image Credit: Susan Curtis

Fifth Edition: February 2018

This is a work of fiction. All of the characters, names, incidents, organizations, and dialogue in this novel are either the products of the author's imagination or are used fictitiously.

Archway Publishing books may be ordered through booksellers or by contacting:

Archway Publishing
1663 Liberty Drive
Bloomington, IN 47403
www.archwaypublishing.com
844-669-3957

ISBN: 978-1-4808-7339-1 (sc)
ISBN: 978-1-4808-7338-4 (e)

Library of Congress Control Number: 2019900741

Print information available on the last page.

Archway Publishing rev. date: 12/04/2023

This book is dedicated to my wife, Gina G. Connor,
who has loved me with a deep and abiding
love and has taught me how to do the same.

"The two most important days in a husband's life are the day he marries his bride and the day he realizes how much he loves her." — C. H. Connor

ACKNOWLEDGEMENT

SEVERAL PEOPLE WERE KIND ENOUGH TO READ *The Dawn of a King* and *Edge of the Blade* as the books moved through the lengthy editing process. I cannot express the full measure of my gratitude for these individuals and their willingness to give their time, passion, energy, and feedback to refine and strengthen the story you now hold. Without these generous souls, this novel would not be the work it is today.

Specifically, I'd like to thank my good friend and work colleague, Chris Williamson, for his glowing reviews, his effervescent praise, and his winsome encouragement to would-be readers that they should, "pick up and read." Thanks, Chris, for your unending support.

Finally, in some manner, beyond that which my mind can conceive, I hope that my mighty Lord and kind Savior, Jesus Christ, is glorified through the story of Alpin and his courageous sons, Coric and Kenneth.

Soli Deo Gloria.

Hooah!

Britannia, 820 A. D.

PROLOGUE

WHAT BEFALLS A MAN THAT HIS HEART WOULD
CHANGE?

CHAPTER 1

THE SUN SAT HIGH IN THE DALRIADAN SKY. ALPIN and Coric rode lead. Laise and Ronan rode close behind. Their mission was singular. They would find their people—Kenneth, Aiden, Nessa, and the other captive Scots. And in Alpin's heart, he was prepared to pour upon his enemy all measures of fury, cunning, and might needed to extract those he loved from the clutches of the Vikings, regardless of the cost.

As they rode, few words were spoken. Their minds were occupied, and their hearts were steeled.

The path north carried the four along the western rim of Loch Lomond where the gradual crests and sloping dips of the rolling woodland draped the placid body of water like a skirt, descending and shaping its basin.

The landscape had once been idyllic. Yet now, the once tranquil vista had lost its beauty. Its innocence was gone, thrashed and pummeled. The Viking army had moved through the region like a herd of savage beasts ripping at the land and leaving a tortured path in its wake, a path trampled with hoofprints and wheel ruts. Among the ruts lay discarded waste and countless mounds of horse manure, littering the landscape and exuding a pungent odor that hovered like an invisible cloud in the hot sun.

The four Scots moved quickly down the decimated path. They pressed across the high plateau of the loch where the trail leveled and cut through a grove of yellow aspens. The trees' golden foliage quaked quietly under the gentle gusts of the autumn breeze, a stark contrast to the rumbling of the Viking horde that had passed only a day earlier.

Beyond the aspens the trail straightened for a hundred yards, cutting a course through a pair of twin pine rows lining either side of the path. The towering evergreens loomed above the trail like giant sentries, dwarfing the riders and casting their shadows upon the path as the western sun pushed against their arm-like branches.

"Whoa, whoa," Alpin called out, sighting a large obstruction in the path ahead. He tugged his reigns and slowed.

"What is it?" Ronan asked, lagging the pack.

"Seems to be a horse," Alpin replied. "A dead one."

The four paced forward and found themselves amid a choking, putrid odor wafting from a decomposing horse carcass.

"The arrow in its shoulder must've brought it down," Alpin noted as he dismounted. Slowly, he circled the swollen corpse and stooped beside it. His eyes combed over the body of the fallen creature and locked on the bloody puncture in the animal's chest. "Judging by this wound, I'd say someone put it out of its misery."

"Then where's the rider?" Coric asked.

"No saddle, no reigns ... seems odd," Alpin said. "Maybe the rider took'em."

"Or maybe someone else did. Look here." Coric pointed to two sets of footprints leading away from the horse.

Alpin stood and studied the trees. "Split up," he said. "Look for signs of struggle or signs of Kenneth. This may have been his horse. If it was, he may be near."

Coric rode a short distance ahead, past the pines and rounding a curve. He dismounted and scanned the overgrowth on either side of the path. Then he stepped through a small gap in the underbrush and teetered between two prickly blackthorn bushes. Suddenly a new scent invaded his nostrils. Coric waved his hand in the air to push away the odor as he pressed through the thorn bushes.

Clearing the brush Coric glanced down and halted. On the ground in front of him lay the body of a dead man. Black flies roosted on the bloated corpse, scurrying over their host, coming and going in sporadic flight. Coric's stomach wrenched. He convulsed and turned away. Then he eased his eyes back to the body and noted the man's brown leather garb. He had seen it before. It was the same he'd seen on the dead Vikings in Renton. "Father, come here!" he yelled.

Coric circled the corpse and prodded the body with his sword. He pushed the tip of his metal blade against the man's distended belly, and an irritated fly emerged from the man's mouth and departed in flight. Coric grimaced, then startled as Alpin appeared through the brush.

"Good Lord!" Alpin exclaimed, gasping at the stench and gaping at the corpse. His eyes drew narrow. "What's a dead Viking doing here?"

Before Coric could offer a response, Laise and Ronan materialized through the bushes, bumping Coric in the back and sending him stumbling over the body.

Ronan's eyes widened. "Dang! Quite a shot!" he said as he caught sight of the arrow protruding from the man's neck.

Laise stooped beside the dead Viking. He carefully examined the arrow's shaft and fletching. "Crossbow. Looks Dalriadan."

Coric crouched beside him and extracted the arrow. He peered up at his father. "It's a Dalriadan arrow, but nothing Kenneth would possess, nor anything I've seen in Renton."

"Somebody wanted the man dead," Alpin said. "Keep looking, we may find more clues."

The four divided and continued the hunt.

Coric finished searching the brush and stepped back to the path. "Find anything?" he called to Ronan.

"Nothing," Ronan replied. "How about you?"

"Nothing."

"Coric, Ronan, come here," Laise shouted, standing forty yards away at the edge of a large field. He waved his arms and motioned for the two to hurry. "Your father found something!"

Alpin remained occupied in the middle of the large field, an expanse that stretched across a rolling terrain and found its boundary at the western bank of Loch Lomond. The field was empty and uninhabited, save its knee-high grass and a single ancient oak.

"Father, what is it?" Coric asked as the three approached.

"Appears to be someone's home, or what is left of it. Seems Renton wasn't the only place the Vikings struck." Alpin crouched and lifted a piece of blackened wood from the abandoned ash pile. He inspected the wood and then gazed forward toward the loch. "I suspect the arrow in the dead Viking came from the people who lived here."

"Wonder where they are now?" Coric said.

Ronan kicked a charred piece of wood. "They could be far gone."

"Or dead," Coric muttered. He knelt and ran his hand through the charred remains of the small home. "Father, there is nothing here. We should move on. Kenneth may be ahead ... Aiden and Nessa, too."

"Agreed," Alpin replied. "Our time is short. We should go."

The four departed the ash heap and returned to the path. They mounted their horses and headed northwest—never noticing the spying eyes watching from the distance.

◎

The late-afternoon sun shined its rays down upon the four Scots. Coric lifted his hand to his brow to shadow his eyes, and he peered into the distance. He wondered if the sun's light was playing tricks on him. "Do you see that?" he shouted to the others.

Alpin squinted. "It's a cart, with some sort of cage." He kicked his heels into the ribs of his horse and spurred the animal past Coric.

A wooden cart sat deserted in the middle of the path. Its frame stood tilted on three wheels, and the cage mounted to its frame held no prisoners.

The four Scots approached and dismounted beside the abandoned cart.

"An army must have been here," Coric said, staring at the prints surrounding the cart. He lifted his head and pointed to the empty prison-like cage. "Looks like they unloaded and left the cart … Aiden and Nessa could have been inside."

"The wheel was snapped clean," Ronan said, standing beside a tree at the path's edge, furtively inspecting the stray wheel with his fingers.

"Father, they can't be far. They may have been a couple of days ahead, but if they're on foot now, they'll be moving slower."

"We don't know for sure. They may have more carts. We don't know how they're moving, only that they have one less cart," Alpin muttered.

Coric surveyed the ground and examined the footprints at the rear of the cart. Then he stepped to the front, continuing to scan the muddy path and working to decipher the disarrayed prints of horse and man. "Here, more footprints leading away … people walking." He moved alongside the path, tracking the steps. "Here, there's more. Two rows of prints, side by side. They're walking, Father! We can catch them!" Coric hurried to his horse and pulled himself up. He shook the reigns and turned his horse west. In moments, Coric's steed was galloping, kicking splatters of mud on the others as he rode away. "Hurry, let's go!" he yelled back.

Ronan and Laise mounted their horses and flew after him.

Alpin lingered as the three departed. He ambled to the cart and tied a small black leather strap to a post on the empty cage. He gazed south toward Renton. "Luag, come quickly," he whispered. Then he mounted his horse and followed his son.

⟁

The Scots arriving in Renton took camp outside the village. The men from Cashel had been the first to appear with several additional clans from the west arriving not long after. In total, their numbers swelled to over four hundred men, young and old. Clan by clan the groups arrived, each finding themselves in a state of disbelief when first glimpsing Renton's destruction. Many aided the decimated villagers, helping to sort through the burnt buildings and salvage those items that had survived the fires. Of the dozen or so structures in the village, all but four were reduced to rubble and ashes, and even those now appeared pitiful and tattered.

With Alpin absent, Luag and Constantine were in charge. The two called for the clan leaders to assemble, but the group could no longer gather in Renton's meeting hall. The memorable hall had been one of the first casualties of the Viking attack. Instead, the cloistered men congregated under a circle of oaks where a large canopy had been erected to shelter the men from the random spells of drizzle and rain.

Latharn arrived in the late afternoon with nearly eighty men from Milton. His heart sank when he saw Renton's devastation. After conversing with a local villager who had survived the Viking attack, Latharn hurried to find Luag and Constantine. Renton's fall troubled him, but it was the news of Laise's departure with Alpin that troubled him most. Spotting the canopy in the distance, Latharn left his men and marched toward the assembly.

"Is it true?" Latharn said, stepping under the tent and catching Luag's attention. "The Vikings did this and my son has left with Alpin to chase after them? And where is Ceana?"

"Yes, Alpin has left—"

"Could he not have waited another day?" Latharn interrupted. "I don't like this. Where is Ceana?"

"Latharn, your daughter is alright. Ceana is with Ena. As for Alpin, he waited as long as he could. We think Aiden and Nessa were taken in the raid. Alpin had no time. He had to go after the Vikings. They took several captives when they attacked and the other clans had yet to arrive in Renton, leaving Alpin no choice but to pursue them."

"And Laise went with him?"

"Yes, and my son as well," Luag added. "Coric too."

"But in waiting a day, he would've had hundreds of men behind him. Now he has three to fight the Vikings! What will he do if he finds them?"

"I understand your concern, Latharn," Luag lamented. "I have no simple answers. Was he to stay and let the Vikings vanish? He only had two choices, and neither was promising. Latharn, you know Alpin. You have always trusted him … trust him now."

"I trust him," Latharn answered, "that's not the point."

"Then respect that he knows the dangers and has weighed the cost. His children and many others were taken by those savages. I can't fault his decision."

"Alright, enough," Latharn granted, lifting his palms in the air, "I concede." He lowered his hands and folded his arms across his chest. "But I still don't like it."

Dusk began to fade as the last trace of the sun sat on the horizon. The men finished their plans and agreed to leave at sunrise. They would depart Renton and head north along the western shores of Loch Lomond. As the group readied to disassemble, a voice called from the distance.

"Gentlemen," Guaire shouted, ambling forward to join those congregating below the canopy.

The gaze of the assembly locked on Guaire.

"I see that Renton has been hit hard, and I hear that Alpin is now off on his own." He paused and peered at the stone-faced audience staring back at him. "That leaves *us* to decide the fate of the Dalriadans and choose how we shall protect our people and our land."

"Our plans need no deliberation," Luag said gruffly as he moved through the assembly and stepped face to face with Guaire. "Our plans have not changed since we settled them ten days ago."

"Everything has changed! How can you say there is no change? Everything has changed."

"The men have gathered, Guaire. Alpin has instructed me to take the men west of the loch and meet him. Together, we will fight the enemy and save our people!" Luag insisted, not hiding his irritation.

"Alpin may have wished for you to follow him, but the men here see what this enemy can do. I'm sure they don't intend to chase a ghost in hopes that he's still alive and able to lead."

Constantine stepped between the two. His eyes locked on Guaire. "There are no wishes and no ghosts here. Our men will leave in the morning. We will find the enemy and fight them." Constantine held his gaze for a long moment, then moved past Guaire and departed the tent.

The others followed and left for their respective camps. Only Guaire and Luag remained. The two stared at one another, though neither spoke. Luag hesitated briefly and then shook his head and walked away.

As the meeting under the canopy ended, another meeting began not too far away.

"I need to speak with you," Searc said, stepping from the shadows. He nervously glanced over his shoulder, ensuring the two were alone. "It's about Oengus."

"Forget Oengus, what the hell happened here?" Taran said, pointing in the distance at Renton.

"The Vikings raided. They stormed the village and burned it! They took Alpin's son and daughter, Aiden and Nessa, and several others. Taran, they've taken them as slaves!"

"I don't give a damn about the people they've taken—they're gone. We have to focus on keeping the rest of Dalriada alive," Taran said. "Where were the Picts? Didn't you go to Oengus? Wasn't he supposed to be here to speak to the men?"

"Taran, that's what I'm trying to tell you. I did see Oengus—I've seen him twice. I've just returned from Perth, and Oengus may be a part of all this."

"What do you mean you've been to Perth twice? That Oengus may be a part of this?"

"Taran, as we agreed, I went to Oengus after the men met in Renton's hall to tell him that the clans of Dalriada would assemble in Renton to fight the Vikings. I said that he should come to see them, and speak to you and your father."

"So what happened?" Taran asked. "Did he agree to come?"

"He said he had given Alpin his chance—"

"Dammit, Alpin will be the end of us," Taran groused.

"But Taran, that's not all. Only a few days after I told Oengus of our plans, the Vikings attacked Renton. That's why I returned to Perth. At first, I wanted to tell Oengus of the Viking attack and convince him to join us. But

Taran—he's determined to kill Alpin. And I think he may have even been behind the Viking attack on Renton."

"Oengus devised the attack on Renton?" Taran said. "Searc, you've lost your mind. Oengus needs Dalriada as much as we need Pictland."

"No, Taran, you don't understand. He may have called for the attacks—he speaks in riddles! I don't trust him. He means to kill Alpin, with or without the Vikings."

Taran began to pace. His mind spun in a maze of thought. "Is Oengus willing to speak with my father, to someone who sees something better for Dalriada?"

Searc could feel his nerves unravel as he listened to Taran's words. "Taran, don't you hear what I'm saying. I don't know that we can trust Oengus. I fear—"

"I don't care what you know or don't know! Much less do I care of your senseless fears! You brought this attack on us, and your fears will be better spent looking for a way out!" Taran exclaimed, then he lowered his face close to Searc's. "You'll start by paying Oengus another visit."

Searc's heart sank. "Taran, don't send me back. I can't go back."

"You will go back and you will tell Oengus to meet with me and my father!" Taran locked eyes with Searc. "I'm certain Luag and the others would be quite interested to hear that you've befriended the Pict," he muttered in a calm, callous whisper.

"But what if Alpin returns?"

"Forget Alpin! There is no more Alpin. He won't survive the Vikings."

The meeting ended as quickly as it began. And in Taran's heart, he steeled his vision for Dalriada—and it did not include Alpin.

CHAPTER 2

THE AIR WAS THICK AND MOIST. THE DARK summer clouds dimmed the fading light of the sun as dusk fell upon Alpin and the three younger Scots. They had trailed the Vikings for miles, but remained behind them. How far behind, they did not know. The path had led them north out of Renton and had turned west at the far end of Loch Lomond.

Alpin rode beside his son. A light drizzle began to fall. Alpin turned his head to look back at Laise and Ronan. He paused for a moment and then called to the two, "We'll find a place to rest for the night."

"Yes, someplace dry would do," Ronan responded.

Alpin glanced at Coric and then peered back a second time, turning farther in his saddle and scanning the path to the rear. "Follow me, be quick about it," he said. He snapped his reigns and raced ahead of Coric, abruptly veering right and leaving the path.

Alpin's sudden departure alarmed Coric, and he hurried after his father. Laise and Ronan trailed close behind.

Alpin steered his horse through the timber line and into a small creek measuring twenty feet across at its widest point and four feet deep in the center. Patches of brush and saplings lined either bank, tucked here and there below the sprawling branches of the occasional willow.

Alpin and the three pressed against the creek's steady current and rode a fair distance upstream before cutting to the opposite side. Reaching the far bank, the group followed the creek west for several hundred yards before stopping at the base of a craggy hill. There, five large boulders sat in a disjointed half circle.

"Are we camping here?" Coric asked.

"We'll see. We are not alone—"

"We're not alone!" Coric exclaimed. "What do you mean?"

"Someone was behind us on the path." Alpin dismounted and wedged his horse's lead into a crack in the rocks.

"What makes you say that, Alpin? What did you see?" Laise asked. He dismounted, grabbed his bow, and began to seat its string.

"Men on horseback, they were trailing us in the distance. I don't know who they were, but I'm not taking any chances. That's why we moved through the creek. It may have thrown them off if they were following us."

"Could it have been my father and the men?" Ronan asked.

"The group was too small. I would have known if it was them. What I saw appeared to be a couple of riders … but we can't be sure if they're friendly," Alpin said. He untied his leather water sack from his horse and took a drink to wet his throat. "Coric, you and I will head to the creek again. We will cross over on foot and watch the path to see if the riders pass. Laise and Ronan, you two take cover between the rocks. Listen with your ears, your eyes will do little good with night upon us."

Coric grabbed his crossbow from his horse. He followed his father, who had disappeared into the bushes at the edge of the creek. By the time Coric broke through the brush, his father was standing waist deep in the slow-moving water. With the sunlight gone, Coric could only see the outline of his father's figure. Coric stepped into the creek and waded to his father. The two remained still for a long moment, standing like stone statues in the black current, scanning the woody world around them.

"We say no more ... every sound will betray us," Alpin whispered. He turned and crept silently across the creek to the far side.

Coric followed.

At the opposite bank, the two lowered to the ground and crawled through a narrow gap within a copse of wild laurels, continuing on their bellies until they cleared the brush. With even a trace of light, they would have been able to spy the coming riders on the path. But in the darkness, they could only listen. The two crouched next to one another, waiting and listening over the soft sound of the trickling creek.

Without a word, Coric eased an arrow onto the shaft of his crossbow and set the trigger.

Alpin startled when the arrow engaged. "Don't be anxious. Let them come to us," he whispered.

"I want to be ready."

"You're plenty ready ... we'll hear them coming well before they reach us."

The two remained in the silence of the trees, motionless. The sprinkling rain came and went. No sounds of approaching riders. No hoofbeats. No murmuring voices. No clatter of swords against buckles or belts, only an empty darkness and the trickle of the creek.

Alpin tapped Coric's shoulder. "We've been here long enough. They're not coming this way, not tonight. We'll go back."

The two snuck back to the creek, waded through the water, and crossed to the opposite bank. Lifting from the water, Alpin raised his hands to push through the brush at the water's edge.

Coric grabbed his father's arm. "Father, don't move. Wait a moment." Coric lifted his hand to his mouth and made the hooting sound of an owl, *whooo, whooo, whowho*. He paused and listened. *Whooo, whooo, whowho,* he heard in response. He tapped his father. "All clear, let's go," Coric said and smirked, though the darkness veiled his grin. "Thought I should warn them we're coming before we get an arrow between the eyes."

Alpin nodded and the two pressed through the bushes.

"Anything?" Laise asked in a low voice as Alpin and Coric emerged and approached.

"Nothing ... nothing at all," Alpin said. "How about here? Anything?"

"Nothing," Ronan replied, holding his knife ready in his hand. He glanced down at his belt, found his sheath, and replaced the weapon.

"Something doesn't feel right. I know there were riders behind us. Maybe they turned back or lost our trail. Either way, we'll have to stay alert."

The four made camp beside the boulders. After watering the horses and consuming a ration of dried venison, Alpin set a sleep rotation for the night. Two at a time were to remain awake on watch. Alpin claimed the first rotation and volunteered Ronan to join him.

Coric and Laise took to their bedrolls and tried to sleep.

Ronan relieved himself behind the boulders before setting out his bedroll and taking a seat. He faced west. Alpin sat a few feet from Ronan, able to glimpse Ronan from the corner of his eye. He faced east, staring into the trees twenty yards away.

The two watchmen sat in the darkness fighting the weight of exhaustion. Their eyelids grew ever heavier as sleep beckoned their submission.

"You awake?" Alpin asked.

Ronan replied with a slow nod.

The night hours slowly passed and the clouds began to separate in the black sky. At times, the moon broke through, full, bright, and round. The small camp remained quiet with the dull hum of silence, stirred only by the soft noise of the creek and the occasional croaking of a restless frog.

Alpin glanced at Ronan. The young Scot sat half-slumped on his bedroll, his head bobbing up and down as he breathed. Alpin inched toward Ronan. He placed his hand on Ronan's shoulder and pushed. Ronan's body crumpled to his bedroll, and he muttered unintelligibly yet never woke.

Alpin let the boy lay. He turned from Ronan and sat up straight with his arms folded in his lap. He sighed heavily and gazed into the night sky. Thoughts of his family filled his vision.

God in Heaven, where are my children? The question haunted him. He hated the Vikings. He hated them for their arrogance and savagery. Somehow, they believed it was their birthright to oppress and enslave. Alpin prayed for Nessa and his sons, wondering if he could ever save them. The thought of them as captives unnerved him and drove him mad. He had to find them.

Alpin could sit no longer. Forcing his stiff legs to rise, he stood and began to pace, yet the wrenching in his heart refused to fade. He glanced at Coric, asleep on his bedroll. His mind drifted back, recalling times not long past of him and Ena caring for their young ones—Drostan sleeping beside Nessa and Coric, they were just babes. But those times were gone. They were now only faint memories, memories that he could never know again.

Alpin remained still, staring up at the heavens. The full moon above hung in the sky as if it were the white iris of God looking down upon him. *Why? Why do You let us live and give us breath for each day? Yet, does not every day bring more misery than the one before? You say there is hope, the clerics tell us of Your hope, but where? Where have you hidden it? Why have you taken it so far from us? You tell us to walk, and yet Your burdens hardly permit us to crawl.*

Alpin shook his head, angry at himself, angry at the night, angry at God.

He would not give thought to the days ahead or the days behind—both had their pains. He tried to fill his mind with better things, yet emptiness surrounded him as the hours passed.

Midway through the night, the clouds vanished and the moon sat high in the southern sky. It was then that Alpin realized he was no longer alone.

"Coric," Alpin whispered, nudging his son. "Coric, stay as you are." Alpin paused, his lips hardly moving as he spoke. "There are shadows moving in the trees to the east. They're near, watching us."

Coric's heart jumped in his chest, instantly awakened by his father's words. "How many?" he whispered.

"I've seen two, but it's hard to say. Listen carefully. I will go to the creek as if to fetch some water. One of them will likely follow. Wake the others when I'm gone … we must not let them corner us. We have to split up and divide them."

Coric nodded his head.

Alpin stood. He stretched his arms lazily and picked up his leather water sack. He ambled nonchalantly toward the creek. As he walked, he glanced at his bow and sword leaning against the rock near his bedroll. He passed them both.

Alpin slipped into the shrubs at the edge of the creek. In the thick bushes, he stooped to a crouch. He peered back at the three—they were lying as he'd left them under the moonlight.

Coric lay unmoving, staring back at his father.

Alpin nodded and disappeared into the creek. He dipped below the surface and submerged himself in the dark water. Below was a deeper darkness. Alpin's hands became his eyes. He pressed his fingers in the mushy creek bottom and crept downstream.

Coric remained still on his bedroll, facing the trees, taking in every noise and shadow. Then, among the distant trees, he saw movement. *Branches blowing in the breeze or the figures of men?* he questioned.

There! There it was again—a figure, a man in the darkness moving through the trees toward the creek.

Coric rolled over and pulled himself to the others. "Ronan, Ronan!" he whispered loudly. "The riders, they're in the woods."

"Wha—"

"Shhh!" Coric shoved his palm over Ronan's mouth. "The men my father saw, they're in the trees to the east."

Ronan's eyes sprung open, wide and round.

"There, the shadow moving under the trees, by the creek," Coric said.

"I don't see anything, Coric," Ronan replied. He peered again, shifting and sitting up on his elbows for a better view.

"Wake Laise," Coric said. "We need him up."

"I'm awake," Laise growled in a hushed voice. "You two need to settle down. If they're out there, then they'll see you looking for them. They need to think we don't know they're here … and we need to get our weapons and find cover."

"Agreed, but we have to split up," Coric whispered. "My father went to the creek, through that gap over there. I'm going to follow him." Coric nodded his head in the direction of the opening in the bushes, then gazed back at the two. I'm certain I saw someone moving toward the creek, but there may have been others … I don't like this."

"Alright, you stay with your father," Laise replied. "We'll post as lookouts behind the rocks."

"I'm leaving. Find cover. Ronan, signal me if you see anyone—but don't overdo it." Coric peered into the eyes of his friends. He paused a moment and then turned and hurried to the creek.

Alpin's legs scraped a fallen tree buried in the creek. He twisted and grabbed hold of the sunken trunk and then surfaced and sucked air into his lungs. With only his head above water, he sighted the trees along the north edge of the creek near the spot where he'd earlier seen the moving shadows. His eyes slowly combed the forest.

Nothing.

He peered downstream. A large willow tree protruded out over the water from the north bank. Its branches hung over the surface of the creek like long, crooked fingers.

Seeing nothing, he submerged and vanished.

"Ronan, I'll get my bow, and then we've got to get behind those rocks," Laise said, pointing to the large boulders to his left.

Ronan nodded, then he jumped from his bedroll and scampered like a fox. He snatched his sword and disappeared behind the rocks.

Laise grabbed his bow and quiver and followed Ronan. Something rustled in the distance as he reached the rocks. "Ronan," Laise whispered in the darkness as he rounded the rear boulder. "Ronan?"

A hand clasped Laise's shoulder.

Laise spun, his fist ready to punch.

It was Ronan.

"Don't do that!" Laise exclaimed. "I heard something in the trees where Coric said he saw movement." Laise peered around the rock, trying to scan the trees, but the other boulders blocked his line of sight. He turned back to Ronan. "Let's move over there," Laise said, motioning toward the far rock.

The two crouched low and moved forward from one boulder to the next until they reached the fifth and final boulder. Together, they peered over the large mass of granite and stared into the forest.

"Anything?" Laise asked.

"Nothing," Ronan said. "But see those two big rocks beside the tree line?"

"The two side by side?" Laise replied.

"Yes. If I run to them, can you see well enough to cover me?"

"I think so—there should be enough light to see."

"You think, or you can? I'm not running out there for you to test your eyesight!" Ronan exclaimed.

Laise looked down at his bow and then back at Ronan. "Sure … as long as you run fast."

Alpin's nose lifted above the water's surface. He had maneuvered downstream and was now beside the large willow tree. Its lanky branches hovered overhead.

Alpin surveyed the banks of the creek. Nothing—no moving men, no moving shadows. He turned and peered upstream, again facing the grove of trees where he'd seen the shadows earlier. Feeling his way along the creek bottom, he slowly inched forward, his nose levitating above the water and his eyes scanning for his enemy.

"Alright, get ready. I'm going and I'm not looking back," Ronan said. "You can do this, right, Laise?"

"Yes, run like a rabbit. I'll shoot anything that moves."

"Except me, right?" Ronan said, his voice tense. He lifted from his crooked stance and peered over the rock. "I'm going—"

A buzzing arrow suddenly soared past Ronan's head and he dropped to the ground. "What the hell was that? Can they see us?"

"That was too close, Ronan. Don't get yourself killed."

"How can they see us, but we can't see them?" Ronan said, not expecting an answer. He waited several moments and then inched up over the rock again.

Swoosh. A second arrow passed overhead.

"Laise, who is shooting at us? Why can't we see them?" Ronan said, glancing down at Laise in the moonlight.

Laise was lying prone on his belly, peering around the side of the rock. "It's the big tree in the middle. That's where the last arrow came from. See that long thick branch … I think he's standing on the one below it."

"Well, I'm not running to those rocks. We need another plan," Ronan said.

"I have one, but you may not like it."

"I don't," Ronan said.

"Listen for a moment, it's not hard … maybe dangerous, but not hard."

"You're a real comfort, Laise," Ronan muttered.

"It's simple. You stand up again—"

"Stop there," Ronan whispered and held up his hands to quash the idea.

"Only for a moment, then you'll drop down quickly."

"Not dead, I hope."

"No, not dead. Now listen, once you stand, he'll shoot."

"Don't you think I know that?" Ronan quipped. "That's what he's been doing."

"Calm down … when he shoots, I'll see where he is. Then I'll shoot."

"I don't know, Laise, what if there are two out there?"

"Well, then we'll start over and you can stand up again," Laise prodded. "This will work … but you'll need to stand and drop quickly."

"I've got the 'drop quickly' part."

"Let me get ready," Laise said and he inched toward the side of the rock. Then he set his arrow and drew back his bow. "Alright. When I say 'go,' you stand."

"Why am I the one standing?" Ronan murmured under

his breath. He crouched behind the boulder with his forehead pressed against its rough surface, and he mouthed a silent prayer. When he finished, he gazed down at Laise and said, "I'm ready, say 'go' when you are."

"Go!"

Ronan popped his head above the rock. An arrow rushed toward him as he dropped to the ground. Then he heard a thump in the distance. "What was that?" he whispered.

"That, my friend, was a hell of a shot," Laise boasted.

"You got him?"

"Yes, I got him … did you think I'd miss? Have some faith."

"Better him than me … are there more?" Ronan asked.

"Maybe you should stand up and find out," Laise said as he set another arrow in his bow.

Alpin crept back upstream in the center of the creek. With his body immersed below the surface, only his head was visible, appearing as a turtle shell floating on the water under the light of the moon. He slowly drew even with the cluster of trees where he had first seen movement in the darkness.

Where are the boys? Had they taken cover? Alpin asked himself.

He turned toward the opposite bank, and his eyes combed across several bushes, a fallen log, and a few small saplings. He glanced downstream. He saw only the large willow and its eerie finger-like limbs hanging over the water. Slowly, he rotated his head upstream, studying the overgrowth along the bank between the willow and the collection of trees beside him.

His heart jumped when he heard the sound of a crossbow cocking. His eyes swept to the far bank.

A man stood ten feet away, hidden among the spindly trees lining the bank. The man was robed in black. His sleeves were long, extending to his wrists, and he wore a black scarf-like wrap covering his neck and head. Alpin had seen the black garb before. He had seen it at Ae.

The man was staring upstream.

Something wasn't right.

Why was he setting his bow? The boys!

Alpin leapt from the water, his knife clutched in his hand.

The man startled and turned.

Alpin threw his knife with force to kill. The weapon spun end over end and hit with a thump, burying its blade into the man's chest.

The man's eyes fell to the knife. He lumbered and dropped to the ground.

Alpin rushed from the water and hurried to finish his work, but there was no need. He pushed the man with his foot, and the man twitched and then stilled. As Alpin bent to reclaim his weapon, he heard the click of a second crossbow. He froze, his hand hovering two feet above the handle of his knife.

A man, draped in the same black garb, stepped from the shadows of the forest.

Alpin straightened and peered at the man.

The man leveled his bow. "Now you are the one who will—"

"DIE!!!" Coric's angry voice erupted from the darkness. He leapt forward and wrapped his limbs around the man's frame, clutching him like a spider to a fly.

The man dropped his bow and stumbled under Coric's weight. He tottered several more steps before the two crashed to the ground at the creek bank with Coric landing on top.

Coric pushed on the man's chest and righted himself, pinning his enemy below him. Coric released a torrent of blows and beat the man's face over and over, punching furiously with both fists. Blood oozed from Coric's knuckles.

With one arm wedged below Coric's knee, the man wrestled to free himself. He grabbed a large stick and struck Coric on the side of his head above the ear.

Coric rolled halfway off and tore the man's sleeve as he fought to right himself.

Again, the man struck Coric with the stick.

Coric tumbled sideways into the water, ripping away the man's sleeve as he fell.

The man rolled and grabbed for Coric.

Coric dodged, then grasped his opponent and pulled him into the creek. With a firm grip on his shoulders, Coric spun the man and plunged him into the water. He pushed his enemy deep below the current, extending his arms and pressing his knee against the man's chest.

The man fought, kicking and clawing, madly searching for anything to lift himself from the suffocating water. In a matter of moments, the fight was over.

Coric rose and loomed above the water, staring down at the man's bloated face below the surface. The moon's light illuminated the dead man's skin and captured Coric's reflection on the water's surface. A chill pulsed through Coric's body. He pulled the man from the creek and dragged him to the bank. Then Coric turned to his father.

Alpin hunched beside a tree, struggling to hold himself

upright while trying to push past the pain of the arrow protruding from his thigh.

"Father! You've been hit!" Coric yelled in a panic and rushed to his father.

"It went all the way through," Alpin said. His fingers scanned the tip of the arrow extending out the back of his leg. Blood streamed from both sides of the wound. Coric exploded with rage and ran to the dead man on the bank. He began kicking the man over and over, cursing with each blow.

Laise and Ronan suddenly appeared, and Ronan grabbed Coric in a bear hug. Coric wrestled to break free, but Laise grabbed his arms to settle him. "He's dead, Coric. He's dead," Laise shouted.

"Stop, stop … let go of me!"

The two released their hold, and Coric raised his hands in surrender.

Laise turned to Alpin, "Are there any more?"

"There are two here. Did you see any?" Alpin replied, his voice weakening.

"We killed a third not far from where we slept," Laise said. "We found three horses down past the trees on the far side of the bank. Maybe we got'em all."

"Let's hope," Alpin said, then he grimaced and clutched his thigh.

Coric gazed down at the man he'd beaten. He studied his frame and leaned over his body.

"Coric, let it go!" Alpin said.

Coric ignored his father and knelt beside the man.

"Coric!"

"Father! These men are Picts!" Coric lifted the man's

arm and pointed to the painted black patterns etched on the man's skin.

"They can't be Picts!" Alpin exclaimed. His eyes narrowed as he stared at the markings. "These men are Briton mercenaries. Their black garb is the same we saw at Ae." He pushed away from the tree and limped toward Coric. After a few steps, he stumbled. Laise grabbed him and helped him to balance.

"I'm okay," Alpin said, and he brushed away Laise's hand. Then he continued his hobble toward Coric while Laise shadowed him from behind.

Alpin neared and studied the man's arm. "Oengus wouldn't send these men after us. We're his only ally against the Vikings. He knows he needs us. If this is a Pict, he must have defected from Oengus some time ago. He's wearing the black garb of a Briton mercenary." Alpin lifted his eyes and gazed at the three. He paused for a moment and took a gulp of air. "However, it's hard to believe the Britons would have sent men this far north. They must be mercenaries, possibly working for the Vikings—hired to track and kill us."

"Father, I don't trust Oengus," Coric said. "They could be his men."

"I don't trust him either, but he's not foolish enough to fight against us. He is more clever than that. He'd have no help to fight the Vikings if he turned against the Scots," Alpin said, his voice weakening. "No, not even Oengus, in all his pride, would be so unwise ..."

Alpin's voice failed him and he fainted where he stood.

Laise caught Alpin and eased him to the ground at Coric's feet.

"Father!" Coric exclaimed. "Are you alright? Father?"

Coric tugged his father's arm, attempting to rouse him. "Father?"

Alpin's eyes opened. He blinked several times before he found Coric.

"Father, you fainted. You're losing a lot of blood. We need to stop the bleeding."

"I'm alright," Alpin said with a half-hearted voice. Then his eyes rolled back in his head and his eyelids shut.

"Father." Coric grabbed his father's shoulders and shook him. "Father!"

"We have to stop the bleeding, Coric. We can't stay here," Laise said. "We have to get help."

CHAPTER 3

KENNETH WOKE IN CHAINS.

His last glimpse into Aiden's cold eyes still pierced his heart. The gaze had burned an indelible image upon Kenneth's soul—an inescapable, haunting image.

Gone. He was gone. Never again would Kenneth see him, hear him, touch him. How could he have lost his brother—the boy who lived to wrestle, race, and watch the stars shoot by in the dark summer skies? Together, they had grown from boys to men. Though death was no respecter of age, surely eighteen was too young to die.

The pain in Kenneth's gut was real, tearing at his soul, as if he was rotting from the inside out. The ache was incurable. *How could this have happened?* Kenneth asked himself countless times over. There was no answer. There would never be an answer.

Kenneth had been with Aiden nearly every day of his life. He was always the first person Kenneth saw at sunrise. He could see his brother's dark head hiding from the light, trying to steal another moment of sleep before their father called them to chores. Now he was dead. Kenneth could not piece together all that had happened. Seeing his brother standing on the edge of the cliff and accepting death was more than Kenneth could bear. His brother's expression had held no hope except the expectation of being released from pain. Kenneth reasoned with himself that it was his brother's burns that overtook him, that the pain must have pushed him beyond his will to live.

A deep sadness tore at Kenneth, stifling his strength, and even his desire, to move forward.

Did it matter? What was left to lose? What was left to gain?

Kenneth gazed at his chains and thought of his father. He had already lost two sons—would he soon lose a third?

God, why? Where is Your Christ? Your messengers speak of hope, and of Your great might. I know of neither.

The simple life he had known as a boy had left him, fleeing far away from where he now stood. The muddy path he would soon march, the path to captivity, the path to hell, was now before him. The Viking chains that bound his hands and feet bound his soul as well. They were a terrible reminder of all he had lost.

⟡

Four men on horseback arrived at the bank of a large river that cut through the northern mountains of Dalriada. A warm orange sun hung to their backs in the eastern sky. The retreating rains of summer had caused the river to recede, exposing much of the earthy river bed. From the distance, the men on horseback were not able to discern what they were viewing on the muddy bank ahead. Though it was common for fallen trees and branches to collect on the banks, the object appeared more like a person than a log.

The four riders moved up the bank to gain a better view.

There, they dismounted their horses and tromped halfway across the soft, mushy bank on foot toward the mysterious object. When the mud grew ankle deep, the four men stopped, still unable to identify the mangled mass. Then one of the men called to their leader, "Grogan, what do you want to do?"

"I say we head back to the horses," one man replied.

"No, we're not heading back to the horses," Grogan replied. "We're going to see what it is." Grogan was a muscular man with a ruddy complexion and an overgrowth of stubble that ran the length of his neck. He was also notably older than the other men.

Grogan left his men and approached the figure. His feet sunk deeper into the mud with each step. As he moved, he scanned the river, combing his eyes up and down its banks as if expecting to glimpse something, or someone.

Nearing the twisted heap, Grogan gazed at the form and realized what it was—the body of a young man clutching a broken log. Grogan surveyed the far river bank a second time and glanced at his men. The three were standing still with swords drawn, gawking back at him.

The ruddy-faced Grogan stooped next to the body and turned it with his thick, tattooed arms. The body separated from the log and remained unmoving on the bank.

Grogan winced and turned his head at the sight of the burnt flesh hanging from the young man's face. The boy's white and shriveled skin was detaching from his cheek. The burns extended down his neck and across his left shoulder.

Grogan called to the others, "It's a Scot."

A second man slopped across the muddy bank. Reaching Grogan, the man stepped to the body, placed his foot under the tattered mass of skin and bones, and pushed. The lifeless

frame rocked in place and settled back into the mud. The
man gaped at the young man's ruined face. It was somebody
he didn't know, and if it was a Scot, it was somebody he
didn't care to know. His eyes fixed on the dead flesh along
the boy's upper body and the grotesqueness of the burns
mesmerized him. Slowly, the man bent down and studied
the boy's brow and cheek. Then he noticed a mud-covered
charm tied around the boy's neck. He grasped the charm
and rubbed away the mud. A grin eased over his face, and
he tightened his palm around his new prize.

"It's not yours," Grogan muttered.

"Why not? He's dead!"

"If he was dead, then that silver charm would belong to
Oengus. But the boy appears to be alive. Watch his chest,
he's still breathing."

The Pict let go of the necklace and rose to his feet. "He'd
be better off dead," the man murmured. He twisted his
sword in his hand and peered at Grogan with a smirk.

"Put it away, we'll let Oengus make that decision. Get
him on your horse. You have the honor of carrying him back
to Perth. Just make sure he doesn't die along the way."

⑥

A large raven soared overhead in the otherwise empty
skies of northwest Dalriada. The ominous black bird perched
on a dead branch of an aging oak and crowed mockingly at
the wretched procession below.

Kenneth cursed the creature under his breath. He
had enough misery to suffice. The iron shackles had worn
blisters on his ankles, making every step more miserable
than the last. His wrists were equally blistered, and the

constant rubbing drove him mad. He stared ahead at the next hill. *How long would this march continue? How far to this pending hell?* A heavyset Viking riding past Kenneth yelled something unintelligible and disappeared over the hill—a hill that hid the answers to Kenneth's questions.

One by one, the prisoners in front of Kenneth reached the hill's crest. Each gasped when they saw the other side.

When Kenneth reached the hilltop, his eyes beheld a sight he had never seen. The structure was monstrous. The image stole the air from his lungs and he then understood the prior groans of the captives preceding him.

The fortress in the distance stood like a grinning giant eager to devour him. Its walls rose fifteen feet in height, formed with massive tree trunks sunk side by side in the earth. Columns of mud and stone formed the corners of the fort and stood as high as the neighboring walls. The ground in front of the fortress extended far and wide with a thick muck that had been trampled and beaten under the weight of a thousand hooves.

A scan of the structure quickly revealed that its construction remained ongoing. Kenneth now realized why the Vikings had taken captives—more labor to complete the work.

The fort's front wall faced east. It was half-finished and served as the entrance to the fort. Slaves, as well as Vikings on horseback, moved in and out of the entryway like busy ants. Several stacks of fallen timber lay piled in front of the fort. A dozen men heaved axes, stripping the timber, while others discarded unwanted limbs onto a nearby heap. Along the south wall of the fort, a small army of slaves slogged forward in a single-file line. Some toted large stones in their arms, while others hoisted shoulder sacks filled with smaller

stones. Guards bearing whips and swords stood watch over
the prisoners as they migrated through the fort entrance,
burdened under their heavy loads.

As Kenneth approached the structure, he took special
note of the slaves. They were haggard and exhausted. Their
clothes were tattered from wear and their flesh bore the scars
of scourging. One particular man, piling discarded limbs
from the downed trees, caught Kenneth's attention. The man
had no eye in his right socket. The side of his face drooped
and he carried his head with a tilt. Kenneth noted another
man walking with a severe limp. A distinctly swollen knee
caused him to favor the bad leg each time he stepped and
hobbled forward. The large stone he carried didn't help.

As Kenneth neared the lame man, a muscular barrel-
chested Viking yelled at the man, scolding him for falling
behind.

Again, the guard yelled at the man, "Move it!"

The man's steps quickened and he labored to keep pace
with the moving line.

Suddenly, a long leather whip snapped through the
air and cracked across the man's back. The man dropped
his stone and tumbled, his face smacking hard against the
ground.

Kenneth froze beside his fellow captives.

The Viking hovered over the man and began shouting.

Kenneth glanced at the captives beside him, waiting for
a reaction, hoping for a reaction.

No one moved to aid the fallen man. Kenneth brooded
in anger. He felt the urge to do something, anything. *That
Viking bastard! The man needs help, but I can't help with
these chains. What if I had no chains—would I help him*

then? His answer shamed him. He knew, too, that it would shame his father.

A Viking on horseback approached and abruptly passed. He yelled at the line of fresh captives, and the progression moved forward into the fort. Kenneth's head hung low as he ambled behind the others. He passed the Viking and the lame man and then heard the Viking curse again. And again, he heard the sharp crack of the whip.

Inside the walls of the fort, Kenneth slowed and peered at his surroundings. Several prisoners were filling sacks of dirt dug from a hole in the corner of the fort where the front wall met the north wall. The hole appeared roughly eight feet wide and deep enough to bury a man. Kenneth couldn't see the men digging, only buckets of dirt being lifted with ropes. From the length of the ropes, he guessed the hole was nearly ten feet deep. Several skinned tree trunks lay next to the hole. With the fortress sitting beside a small river, Kenneth wondered why the Vikings were digging a well—if it even was a well.

The captives continued their progression into the fort until they were commanded to halt at its center. A dozen Vikings encircled them and corralled them like sheep in a herd. The two carts in the procession were pulled into the circle, and the imprisoned captives were released and made to stand with Kenneth and the others.

Kenneth's gazed swept over his fellow captives. They were the people of his village. They looked different now, doomed and hopeless. They showed no emotion, save fear—a fear that filled their eyes and gripped their hearts.

A sharp jab suddenly struck Kenneth's backside.

"Forward!" Kenneth heard a loud voice behind him.

Kenneth turned to see the butt of a Viking spear leveled waist high.

"Forward!" the man repeated.

It was one of the many guards who had ridden beside the captives over the last day and a half, and the same guard who had plagued the captives with a perpetual barking. Kenneth gazed long at the man and wished him dead.

Kenneth turned and inched forward, pressing together with the others in the center courtyard of the fort. In total, the captives numbered nearly three dozen. Most were men, all older than Kenneth. They moved without vigor in a comatose state, staring at the ground in a dispirited stupor. Only Gavin, who had earlier helped Kenneth save Aiden and Nessa, made eye contact. The young Scot's glances shifted to and fro, peering at the Vikings and then at Kenneth.

The Vikings tightened their circle around the captives. They began jeering one another and wagering which Scot would be the first to die. Several pointed at the Scots and taunted them, shouting, "For you, logs!" and, "For you, stones!" Others cracked whips for amusement.

Kenneth gazed down at his chains. He was the only captive bound in irons. He knew why he was chained, and he remembered Aiden.

A whip suddenly snapped beside Kenneth's ear, and he startled and jumped. Then Kenneth spun and peered at the guard holding the whip, watching as the man ran his hand along its woven leather strands.

The Viking glared at Kenneth, wearing a smug grin as if daring him to fight. The man was of medium build for a Viking, yet he likely drew his smugness from his handsome features and his tangled blonde hair that hung just below his shoulders.

Kenneth's blood boiled. His chest bowed outward and his fist tightened. Then the shifting crowd of captives pressed against Kenneth on all sides, and he slowly turned away. Once enveloped within the mass of bodies, Kenneth lifted high on his toes and peered over the others. He reckoned that Jorund would be nearby, and that it would be best to know of the large Viking's whereabouts. He wanted to know two other things: where their leader was located, and what part of the fortress was most vulnerable. With the fort yet to be completed, certain areas would be easier to breach than others. Finding them soon would be wise.

Being no taller than most of the Scots and a few inches shorter than the majority of the Vikings, Kenneth found standing tiptoe improved his view. He slowly turned his frame and surveyed the area while trying not to draw attention to himself. He scanned the courtyard for Jorund. The lumbering giant would surely have a score to settle.

As Kenneth's eyes combed the grounds of the fort, he spotted several Vikings exiting a long wooden structure built into the north wall of the fort. Likely barracks, Kenneth presumed. The outpouring Vikings moved to the center of the courtyard and formed a row in front of a six-foot-high platform sitting square in the middle of the fort. Moments later, Kodran ascended the platform stairs.

A hush entered the fort, and every eye turned to the elevated structure. Jorund and two other men followed behind Kodran. The four men stood proud, peering down at the captives below, as if they were gods or guardians of a god. It was then that Halfdan climbed the wooden stairs and stepped to the platform's center. He stood amid the four men, two to his left and two to his right, while a backdrop of gray clouds filled the distant sky behind him.

Kenneth recognized the man in the center. Kenneth had seen him when Aiden and Nessa were tied and marching in a line, yet he hadn't seen him since he'd regained consciousness after his fight with Jorund on the cliff. Kenneth could only assume the Viking leader had seen him unconscious, or at least had been told about him. Either way, he was certain this man was the one who gave the orders for his chains.

Kenneth lifted his shackles eye-level. He stared at the cold metal bands and then shifted his gaze to the man on the platform. He already hated the man—without a doubt, he was the head of the snake.

Standing on the elevated platform above the crowd of Vikings and Scots, Halfdan gazed forward, indulging himself and basking in his conquest. He smirked, and pride oozed from his countenance.

The Viking leader then focused his eyes on the filthy, half-starved captives standing below him. "People of this land, you were once your own. That has changed. You may have had kings or lords. You may have served them in pleasure or disdain, but now … you will serve me. You now belong to me." He raised his arms in the air as if welcoming their reception. "I am Halfdan the Black, son of Gudrod the Hunter. We come from a distant land. We are the Norse people … and as you can see, we are a strong people. My fathers visited this land many years prior. We have learned that you are a stiff-necked people, but we have found, with the right coaxing, you can be taught to serve … and serve well."

Halfdan began to move back and forth along the length of the platform. "My servants! Make yourselves comfortable here. As you can see, we are working to finish this great fortress that stands as a beacon of Norse strength. Much work has been done and much work remains. And those who have come before you have grown weak." He gestured toward the prisoners gathered along the south wall of the fort. "Your strength is needed. We have many trees to drop and many stones to move. Consider this your new home. I encourage you to make the most of it." His men laughed at the insult. "If all goes well, you will live out your lives here … if things don't go well, your lives will quickly end here."

Kenneth's rage swelled like a tidal wave. With every word the man uttered, he hated him more. He flexed his arms and pulled against his iron clasps. When they refused to release, he cursed them.

Thunder roared in the distance. Night was coming and bringing with it a summer storm. Halfdan continued, "You will begin your work to finish this fortress starting tomorrow. You will bring logs and stones as required to fortify the walls. When the structure is complete, we will move deeper into your heartland, and you will begin the process over again. Slowly but certainly, you and your clans will build a host of fortresses for the Norse people. Today, I am your lord … and in time, I shall be your king. Your people have only heard with their ears of the terror of the Vikings, now they shall see it with their eyes!"

Halfdan heralded his words like a self-proclaimed deity. And with every passing moment, Kenneth wished more earnestly that his father would crest the eastern hill with a thousand angry Scots, descend upon the arrogant maniac, and send him to hell. Kenneth took a deep breath and promised himself that he would not live to see the completion of the fort. He would either see to its destruction or die destroying it, but he would not take part in the overthrow of his people. Of this, he was certain.

Thunder rumbled once more in the western sky.

Halfdan glanced upward before continuing, "Men of Dalriada, you have the freedom to walk and move about as you please … within the confines of your apportioned lot." Halfdan gestured again, this time toward the large, prison-like area that was bound by ten-foot posts sunk in the ground and tied together in the fort's southeast corner. "But I warn you, disobedience, insurrection, or any attempt to escape will be met with grave consequences. You will lose any trace of freedom and quite likely your life."

Halfdan turned toward the guard at the base of the stairs. "Where is the one in chains? Bring him forward."

When the words hit Kenneth's ears, a wave of shock jolted through his body.

Four guards pressed through the crowd and parted the captives, forming a gap between Kenneth and the platform. A shove came from behind and Kenneth stumbled forward. A second shove followed. Kenneth tripped, then regained his footing and moved toward the platform. He was twenty feet from the wooden structure when he stopped and met eyes with Halfdan.

"So, this is the man who sought to be a hero … and yet he is merely a boy," Halfdan mocked.

His Vikings cheered.

Halfdan glared at Kenneth and chided, "Courage? You think you possess it, yet you mistake it for foolishness—for you are a fool! You dare to pry my possessions from my hands? And what did you gain … a dead Scot and a life in chains! You will regret your foolishness. Your irons will be a reminder to you and your people, that those who aspire to bravery, those who wish to challenge, will be brought low. Know this, everything you once possessed has been taken from you, and anything that remains is now mine!"

Halfdan glared over the dismal faces of the broken captives.

Not a soul spoke a word.

"Take away the prisoners," he uttered with a stone face. "See them to their lot." He strode across the platform, descended the stairs, and departed toward his quarters at the rear of the fort.

Kenneth could not remove his eyes from the man. He had seen for himself the face of evil. Rain suddenly began to fall, and Kenneth remained where he stood while a heavy drizzle soaked into his garments. Within moments his entire body was drenched.

The guards moved among the captives and prodded them like animals, pushing them through the pooling puddles toward the entrance of the prison. One by one, they filed inside behind its wooden posts.

A Viking guard shoved Kenneth, rousing him from his trance. Kenneth moved forward, shadowed by the guard, until he found himself behind the prison barrier. The few pieces of tent cloth that hung overhead did little to protect the captives from the pouring rain. Of equally poor benefit was the scattered straw strewn throughout the pen. It provided no great relief from the saturated, muddy ground.

Though the prison pen was filled with Scots, including those from Renton, Kenneth spoke to no one. Solitude was all he sought—and solitude was all he found.

He sat down at the base of a large post that served to anchor the prison wall. He ignored the pool of water below him. He recalled the last time he saw such heavy rain. It was not so long ago, yet now the memory seemed like a distant time and place. How quickly it all had changed.

CHAPTER 4

ARABELLA RODE THE OVERGROWN PATH TO Renton. She needed the company of Ena and Ceana. The main route through the village would be filled with Dalriadan men, including her father. He'd likely be upset for her leaving Cashel, but she couldn't stay there any longer.

Arabella's path opened to a field that once boasted a bounty of golden barley. She stopped. The remains of Kenneth's home sat ashen gray in the distance. The smoke had ceased, but the charred remains of the black wooden heap lay as a reminder of all that was lost. She recalled Kenneth wandering through the rubble, his pitiful countenance overcome with loss. She remembered his empty stare and how it was filled with a thousand questions—and how she had no answers to offer.

She covered her mouth as tears welled in her eyes. She thought of Kenneth standing at the edge of Renton, then she fought to keep herself from imagining something worse.

Arabella turned her horse toward Coric's small home that sat across the field. She wiped her eyes and rode forward, anxious to find Ceana. She needed her friend.

Her anxiety grew as she approached, her emotions twisting with hope and sadness, relief and fear. Smoke rose from the small chimney that poked through the modest thatch roof. Arabella found comfort in the sight. She dismounted her horse and walked to the door. Standing there, she wondered what she would say—and who she would see.

She opened the door.

"Arabella!" Ena dropped her half-peeled potato onto the counter.

Arabella ran to Ena and clutched her in her arms. "Thank the Lord!"

"Arabella!" Ceana lowered a log beside the hearth, hurried to her friend, and swallowed her in a hug.

"Oh, Ena, Ceana, I was so scared for you. I am so sorry all this has happened."

Ena's brow furrowed, and she searched for a smile. "Darling, I was so glad to hear you were safe." Like a mother, she brushed back Arabella's hair. "I'm scared for Nessa and the boys. I think about them every moment. I cannot sleep, I—"

"They'll be alright, Ena. The men will find them and bring them home," Ceana interrupted her mother-in-law, trying to be hopeful. "Coric and Alpin and the others will find them. They're out there and they'll find them."

"Is my father with them?" Arabella asked. "Have they left to face the Vikings?"

Ena pulled off her soiled apron and laid it on the table, fretting and laboring at the same time to temper her emotions. "Alpin and Coric took Ronan and Laise with them. They went to find Kenneth, Aiden, and Nessa," she said. Trying to busy herself, she grabbed a handful of potatoes and placed them into a pan. "Coric wanted to go after Nessa and the boys without waiting, but Alpin insisted they wait for the other men … they waited as long as they could, but then the four left alone." Ena glanced at Arabella. "The whole thing is so awful. Donald is not himself. His father is gone. His brothers and sister are gone. He's hardly spoken a word since all this happened."

Arabella stood in a stupor, wanting to say something helpful, something encouraging. She knew Donald's fears, his confusion, his anger. She had faced the same in her own personal tragedy, one that no child should endure. "Where is Donald now?" she asked with a tinge of reticence.

"I sent him to gather some wood," Ena replied. "Seeing you will lift his spirits." She stepped to the hearth and removed a loaf of bread baking over the hot flames. Lost in thought, Ena pressed the top of the loaf with a single finger then gently placed the loaf beside the hearth to cool. "After they left, the others began arriving in Renton. The village is now overrun with men. They're everywhere. Your father said they were going after the others—even leaving today, but some of the men from Dumbarton, Guaire and his son, Taran, caused a stir insisting they reconsider. There is talk that Guaire wants to seek help from the Picts. Luag and your father are furious."

Ena glanced about the room, as if searching for another item requiring her diligent attention. She paused, gazed at Arabella, and then briskly passed by her. In an attempt to hide her agitation with the men, Ena further distracted herself by wiping the table and straightening the surrounding chairs. Satisfied, she turned and stared at the cooling loaf of bread. "Ceana and I have given the men as much bread and stew as we can muster. I suppose we have more to offer them now." She half smiled and gently pressed her finger a second time onto the crown of the warm loaf, fighting to ignore the emotions welling inside her. "I don't want them to leave for battle ... but neither do I want Nessa and the boys to be prisoners in the hands of those animals! Arabella, they were awful, awful men."

Ena turned from the bread, and her gaze fell upon the girls. She cupped her palms over her face and rubbed her eyes.

Ceana drew a chair and prompted Ena to sit. Ena hesitated before slowly lowering herself into the seat.

Deep down, Arabella couldn't help but empathize with the fragile woman that sat before her, a woman broken in spirit and soul. Arabella stirred in anger, even hatred for what the Viking savages had done. A desire for strength, a desire to fight, surged deep within. She kept her poise and stepped in front of Ena. A moment passed before she broke from her gaze and offered a sympathetic smile. Then she bent to hug Ena. "It's going to be alright. Your boys are brave. Kenneth will find Nessa and Aiden, and he will help them," Arabella said with a calming, reassuring voice. She stood and faced Ceana. "And Coric and the others will help Kenneth find them." Arabella then paused, momentarily struck by a thought. "My father thinks that I am in Cashel. If he and the men are still in Renton, then I will go to him." She hesitated. "He will be upset that I've come, but I will speak to him. He will listen to me. I know it won't be easy, but he'll listen because he'll see that I'm only trying to help him. I'm certain I can to convince him that we can't lose any more time, that we have to search for the others now. Our men are strong, they can defeat the Vikings." Arabella knelt beside Ena. "I will speak to my father."

Ena had hardly heard a word. She remained despondent

and numb, grimacing. "Arabella, I'm afraid of what lies ahead. When the Vikings attacked our home, Aiden fought against them ... he saved me. He fought so bravely. But there were too many! They wrestled and fell into the fire, and I heard him scream. It was awful. The fire was burning him. These men ... they are murderers, they are heartless murderers, they—"

"Don't say anymore," Arabella blurted out. Her hands shot upward, pleading for Ena's words to cease. "I saw them fight Kenneth in Renton. I know they're awful. But we must trust our people will be protected. What the men can't do, we must trust God to do. I trust He is watching Kenneth right now, protecting him," Arabella said, struggling to reassure herself as much as the other two. "We have to hope that they'll escape, or survive until our men reach them. We must pray for that."

෧

"Place him on the bed," the old man said as he hurried into the room behind the others. The man, a physician of sorts, carried a worn basket filled with medicinal herbs and several jars of ointments varying in color and consistency. He stepped to the far side of the bed as the four men with painted arms placed their patient on the straw mattress. "Tell Oengus about the Scot," the old man said. "But tell him I'm not certain the boy will make it."

"Alright, I'll see Oengus. But Mathe, try to keep him alive," Grogan replied, as he and the others departed the room.

The old Pict physician was a wiry man of medium height. The back and sides of his head were donned with stringy, unkempt gray hair, while the top of his skull remained quite barren of any locks at all. He squinted when he worked and had an odd habit of sniffling and rubbing his nose. As for his dress, his clothes were much like that of the servants in the Pict castle, yet his appearance differed in that he didn't bear the body paintings of the others.

The old physician leaned toward his patient and began to inspect the burns along the young man's face and neck. The wounds were severe and extended from his cheek down to his left bicep. Mathe lifted the young man's eyelids, but the pupils showed no response. Then he placed his ear on his patient's chest and listened for a heartbeat. The rhythm was steady, but weak.

Mathe sorted through his collection of ointments, eventually finding his desired concoction. Grabbing the round, fluted jar, he carefully poured the viscous ointment, dripping it slowly onto the burns of his unresponsive patient. The milky drops formed small puddles as they settled onto the tortured skin.

"What have we here?" Oengus called out as he entered the room.

"My lord, the men have found a young Scot, though I fear the boy is waging war against death itself—a war he may lose in the end."

Oengus approached the bed and peered down at the patient. His lip arched into a snarl at first sight of the burns. Then his gaze traced over the swath of festering blisters, and his eyes locked on the silver cross around the boy's neck. He stepped closer and placed his hand on the boy's head, turning it to see the unburned side of his face.

"Oengus, what are you doing?" Mathe exclaimed.

"Only looking at the boy, Mathe. Relax." Oengus peered

closer at the boy's face and grinned. "Mathe, this boy may be worth more to me than you are, even if you are my physician … if he dies, you may not be far behind. Make sure he stays alive. I need him." When Oengus finished admonishing the old physician, he turned to leave. "I expect to hear of his recovery soon," he called back as he exited the room.

"Yes, my lord," Mathe replied to an empty doorway, his voice carrying an unhidden quiver. He spun and scurried about until he found the broad cloth he was searching for. Ripping the cloth into strips, he laid the strips flat and coated them with the milky ointment. Carefully, he applied the strips to the boy's burns. Then he wrapped the remaining cloth over the bandaging strips, enveloping a sizeable portion of his patient's shoulder, neck, and face.

Once finished with the wraps, the old physician returned to his basket and removed the only elixir that held any promise of reviving the boy—assuming the boy would ever wake to drink the fluid.

CHAPTER 5

THE SUN DISAPPEARED FROM THE AFTERNOON sky and hid behind a blanket of clouds, leaving the damp, tepid air heavy with moisture. Below the thick clouds lay the crippled village of Renton, its small, frail structures blackened and burned. Yet the men gathered there were far from crippled and frail. Indeed, peace and security had been torn from them, but their anger was fresh and raw, fueling a deep hunger to exact their revenge.

The army of Scots remained ready in Renton, bustling about the village like agitated bees on a battered hive. They spent their time swapping supplies and conjecture, sharpening both their blades and tongues alike. The growing gathering of sweaty men and soiled horses gave off a noticeably pungent, earthy scent that filled the air. The odor hung like a fog, rife with the smell of campfire smoke, urine, and manure.

The men were irritable and itching to move. It would be wrong to expect otherwise. The contemplation of war plagued their spirits and tormented their hearts, rekindling the old warrior adage, "War imperils the mind, yet waiting for war imperils the soul." The saying was true, and the men could feel it deep in their bones. For in the silence of waiting for battle, they could sense, even hear, Death's taunting whispers, beckoning them, "Come."

⊚

When Arabella reached Renton, the sight of the multitude overwhelmed her. She could not recall a gathering of soldiers so large. Their sheer numbers portended the awful days to follow. She coaxed her horse forward and approached the crowd of men, purposing to be strong and confident.

Weaving through the clustered clans, she searched for her father. Halfway into the crowd of bodies, she recognized a group of men from Cashel. She cued her horse and trotted toward them.

"Pardon me, gentlemen. Is my father with you?"

"Arabella?" one of the men uttered, surprised to see her. "Your father said you were home in Cashel. Why are you here?"

"Yes. That was my father's wish … but I had to come. I must speak with him. It's urgent. Is he here?"

"He is. He's speaking with the other leaders," a second man said. The man glanced at his comrades before saying more. "I should warn you, your father is a bit upset. Some of the men from Dumbarton have complained to him. They're angry that Alpin's gone. There have been more than a few heated arguments over the matter. Some are saying to leave for battle, but others want help from the Picts."

"That is why I wish to speak with him. Where can I find him?" Arabella replied, raising her head to see over the pockets of men and horses.

"Do you see those large oak trees?" the first man

responded and pointed in the distance where a handful of men had gathered. "He's over there."

"Thank you," Arabella said, giving a slight nod. She departed the men and coaxed her horse toward the large oaks.

Taran's eyes fixed on Arabella the moment he glimpsed her riding toward him. He gaped at her long brown hair, watching as it fell wide across her shoulders. Her beauty struck him no less than it had the last time he had seen her. He brushed off his shirt and ran his fingers through his dirty red locks.

An expanse of men stood between Arabella and the oak trees. She dismounted her horse and led the animal by the reigns, weaving through the crowd.

"You look lost," a voice said. Then Taran suddenly appeared beside Arabella's horse.

Arabella gasped and stopped where she stood.

"Absolutely beautiful," Taran remarked, ignoring Arabella's surprise. He cupped the side of the horse's snout with one hand and brushed its large jaw with the other. "She's an absolutely beautiful animal," he concluded with a grin.

"I don't want you near me."

"You're not still upset from the evening at the meeting hall?"

"I said, I don't want you near me," Arabella repeated.

"Alright, I admit that the ale got the best of me that night. But for a lady as lovely as you, is it right to hold a grudge against a man who simply wishes to talk?"

"You weren't simply 'talking' that night!"

"As I said, the ale got the best of me. Allow me to personally ask your forgiveness. I assure you, I meant no harm."

"You tried to have your way with me and then you fought Kenneth and his brothers. You were drunk!"

"Drunk, no … silly, maybe," Taran said, donning a disarming smile. "I meant you no harm—are you not willing to forgive?"

"I shouldn't," Arabella replied.

"But you will?"

"Taran, I just want to find my father."

"I'll take that as a 'yes.'"

"Take it as you please," Arabella snipped. "I simply would like to find my father. Can you tell me where he is?"

"It would be my privilege. Your father is with my father. They are over there, beside those trees," Taran said. He pointed to the small group of men standing by the oaks. "I believe they are speaking of the Picts and how we should unite with them." Taran grinned. "My father and I have nearly convinced them."

"Have they spoken with the Picts?"

"No, not yet. But we will once your father and the others agree."

"Taran, we are running out of time. The Vikings have taken our people. Kenneth is gone, and he is out there, somewhere, trying to find them. Alpin is gone, too. We can't wait any longer."

"Waiting isn't the problem. Having the men to fight the Vikings is, and Alpin's leaving didn't help matters. Don't you see? We don't even know how many Vikings there are. We need Oengus and his men. We need the Picts, we'll be stronger with them."

"We don't need the Picts to save us. Our men are able and ready. We should find the others now!" Arabella exclaimed, unashamed of her defiance. As she finished her words, she recalled how she'd fought with Kenneth on this very point—but now she was on his side. She closed her eyes and sighed.

"Why is it that you trouble yourself with this matter? Let our fathers settle it." Taran kept his tone even and calm.

"Settle? Our people are prisoners. We have to help them. We have to save them!"

"We have to save Kenneth. Isn't that what you mean?" Taran corrected.

"This is not about Kenneth. Our people were captured by the Vikings. We must save them!"

Taran eyed Arabella, his demeanor growing more brazen. "Have you not heard of the bodies scattered about this very village? They took what they wanted and burned the rest. This place is an ash heap! The savages who raided Renton will not give up and simply surrender when we find them. They could have a thousand men ready to fight, ready to crush Dalriada. We would be wise to unite with the Picts if we hope to defeat them. Only a fool would run head first into such an army and expect victory—and Alpin tried it with four men!" Taran finished and awaited a response.

Arabella only stared at him. She said nothing.

"These animals kill simply for the thrill of it. They're not cowards who turn from a fight. They'll seize Alpin and the others, rend them limb from limb, and leave their bodies to rot for the birds to feast upon. You don't understand this enemy, they take pleasure in destruction. We must join the Picts … there's no other way."

Arabella had no reply. The cold reality struck hard. Memories of the slaughter of her parents returned. Flashes of Kenneth and the Vikings in Renton rushed through her mind and tore at what was left of her fragile hope. She recalled the sunset she'd shared with Kenneth. How the rain had come, driving the two to their rock shelter on the hillside. She remembered falling asleep beside him, protected from the rain and the world. Her thoughts shifted to Renton's thick gray smoke and the silhouette of the man she loved. She saw Kenneth with Renton burning behind him. His distant promise of return still echoed in her ears.

Arabella felt as if she would cry. But she wouldn't. The muscles in her gut tightened, and she clamped the side of her lip in her teeth. Kenneth disappeared from her mind. "I must see my father," she said, now glaring at Taran. She extinguished her gaze, tugged the reigns of her horse, and stepped to move past him.

Taran extended his hand in a bow, smiled, and permitted her to pass.

"Father," Arabella shouted over the buzz of the men as she moved toward Constantine.

Constantine lifted his eyes without halting his conversation with Luag and two others. He briefly glanced in her direction before pausing to look again. "Arabella, it's you. What are you doing here?"

"You seem unhappy to see me," she said as she approached.

The furrow on his brow faded, and he worked to form a smile. "Darling, I'm always happy to see you. But I thought we agreed you'd stay in Cashel. Is everything alright?"

Arabella frowned. "Well, nothing is alright. But I am not hurt or ill, if that's what you mean. I know you wanted me to remain in Cashel, but I couldn't stay any longer—not alone.

I couldn't stop thinking of Kenneth and the others. I had to come and see Ena and Ceana."

"I know it's hard, darling. And I agree, it's not good for you to be overwhelmed with worry, especially not while you're alone," Constantine replied. "Maybe it would be best for you to stay with Ena and Ceana."

"There's more, Father."

"More?"

"I see the men and I hear them talking, but Father, aren't we going to do something? What about Kenneth and Aiden? What about Nessa and the others? Shouldn't we go after them?"

Constantine took Arabella by the arm and stepped away from the oak trees and the noise of the men. "Arabella, this is a difficult situation, surely you see that. I assure you, we are taking the matter very seriously. I know you are worried about Kenneth and the others—so am I. But Alpin has left with Coric, Ronan, and Laise. We are waiting for—"

"That's my point, Father. We keep waiting!" Arabella interrupted. "I saw Ena. I saw how this is tearing her apart. We have to do something!"

"Arabella, you don't understand. It is not that simple! Half of these men are determined that we should join the Picts. We are working to find agreement, we—"

"But Father, what about Kenneth and his family? They are our family, too. Can't you do something?"

"That's enough, Arabella." Constantine insisted. His anger swelled, yet his heart broke as he stared into his daughter's eyes and saw her hopelessness. "Darling, I've tried to reason with you, but you're letting your feelings for Kenneth cloud your judgement. That is why I wanted you to stay in Cashel."

"I'm not a child anymore, Father! Stop treating me as one."

"Well, maybe you should—" Constantine stopped himself.

"I should what, Father? I should stop acting as a child?"

"No, Arabella, it's simply …" he hesitated.

"It's what, Father?"

Constantine took a deep breath. "I was only going to say that I understand how you feel. I understand the pain of losing someone you love. Arabella, we lived through this together when we lost Senga."

Arabella shuddered when hearing her father's words. She stared at Constantine, the man who saved her life, the man who brought her back to life. His love for her was unconditional—he'd proven it. She gazed at him as a stirring sadness hung in his eyes.

"I'm sorry, Father. I guess down deep there is still a young girl inside. I'm sorry."

Constantine's cheek lifted and a fragmented smile formed on the side of his mouth. "I know that none of this is easy. I'm … I'm glad you came—it's good to see my little girl."

Arabella hugged him. "I love you," she said.

"I love you, too."

Arabella lifted her gaze and searched her father's eyes. She paused. "Now can I ask if you are going to search for Kenneth and the others?"

Constantine smirked and shook his head in disbelief. "My Arabella, always the strong-willed one. Why don't you visit Ena and Ceana and let me work with the men to find the others. You have to trust me."

Arabella nodded. "I do, Father. I do."

◎

Kenneth opened his eyes. The late afternoon rain had passed, but Kenneth's hollowness remained. The muscles in his back throbbed as he sat pressed against the hard wooden post of the prison. He rubbed his face to wake himself. As he moved, his chains clanked and the sound stirred a visceral ache in his gut. He peered at his hands and then at the irons clasped around his ankles. *How long can this go on?* The thought echoed in his head. Pushing his hands against his knees, he rose to his feet.

The sound of activity and the chatter of voices hummed behind Kenneth. Just beyond the wooden prison, two fire pits blazed, each sporting a full-size buck roasting over the open flames. A small army of Vikings sat nearby, arrayed on a row of short stumpy logs lined beside several long wooden tables.

From appearances, the Vikings were eager to feast. The men at the tables were joined by a constant flow of brutes streaming into the fort from a horse corral on the far side of the courtyard. The aroma of the meat cooking over the fires seemed to call to the horde like a dinner bell.

The alluring scent of roasting venison bathed Kenneth's nostrils and made his stomach rumble. He could not remember the last time he'd eaten. At the moment, he was willing to eat anything—and a serving of venison would be nothing short of a delicacy.

Kenneth sidled along the wall of the enclosed pen, staring between the wooden posts at the men at the tables. He envied them as they pulled the meat from the deer's hindquarters and devoured the meal without a thought. To Kenneth, even the leftover scraps would have been a feast.

Glancing at the pitiful frames of the resident captives, he realized he wasn't the only one in want of food. Certainly, they would have to be fed if they were expected to haul logs and stones for any period of time—if that was what the Vikings truly intended.

Kenneth glanced toward the entry of the pen. Outside the gate-like door that sealed the prison, two guards sat muttering to one another. Neither appeared too concerned about the meal. They'd likely already had their fill.

Kenneth gazed back toward the fires and the deer cooking above the flames. At that moment, a particular Viking pushed away from his table and ambled toward the fire. Kenneth reckoned the man was his father's age. He was of average height and build for a Viking and carried himself like a seasoned warrior, rugged in appearance. His head was bald and on his scalp, above his left ear, was a large reddish-brown birthmark. The discolored splotch was roughly the size of a man's palm and bore the resemblance of a fox head.

Kenneth watched the man as he moved toward the fire. There, the man pulled a knife from his belt and stepped beside the roasting deer. He inspected the meat and cut a second helping for himself. A group of men at a nearby table grumbled, and the bald man returned their groans with grunts of his own. No one responded. The man strode back to his stump, carrying his slab of hot meat with the tip of his knife.

As much as Kenneth tried, he couldn't pull his attention from the feasting. He resented the men, gaping at them as they devoured their food and fed their gluttonous bellies. They ate like wolves, suspiciously glancing at one another as they tore into the meat, hardly swallowing before they ripped off another bite. Grunting and chewing, chewing and grunting, they rarely spoke. When they did speak, Kenneth couldn't understand a word. It was gibberish to his ears, and he wondered how they were able to speak Dalriadan when they desired to do so. He realized there was more to the Vikings than he knew, and that the stories he'd heard were true—this wasn't their first encounter with Dalriadans. Studying the savages, he noticed their tendency of shoving one another and making brief challenges as a show of stature. If a man did speak, it was apparently to deride another. The exchanges were often followed by others joining in, mocking and chiding, while the ridiculed victim responded with insults of his own.

Kenneth stirred from his daze when three women appeared in his line of sight. They emerged from behind a curtain that filled the doorway of a small, hut-like structure built into the wall of the fortress. The women were captives and appeared to be Dalriadans, though Kenneth had never seen them before.

The women carried pitchers of water and moved among the tables to serve the men. When the women found themselves caught between the tables, a game began. Each time the women would bend to pour water, the men would grab at them. When the women pulled away, the men would erupt in laughter and lure them back to pour again.

Kenneth brooded behind his wooden prison posts. His blood pulsed in his veins. He hated the men. Then he thought of Nessa and how she could've been one of the women. And he hated the men even more.

Kenneth continued to watch as two of the women poured the last of their water and hurried back through the curtain into the safety of the hut. When the third woman finished, she twisted through the maze of tables and headed toward the shelter. Being alone, she was easy prey. And being young and comely didn't help. Her strawberry-blond hair crowned her head and curled down either side of her shapely chest, accentuating her figure and arousing the testosterone-filled brutes.

Weaving through the last of the tables, the men's advances became more ravenous. The woman dodged their predatory palms and she quickened her pace. Passing the final table, a thick beast of a man with hairy arms and a bush-like beard turned in his seat to meet her. He reached for her and clutched his arms around her waist. As he pulled her to him, she slapped at him and tried to break free.

The men catcalled with excitement.

"She likes you, Magnus," one man yelled to the brute.

More cheers erupted.

Kenneth's muscles tightened and he wanted to fight.

The man called Magnus squeezed the young woman against his chest. Then he stuck out his tongue and tried to lick her cheek as she wrestled to escape.

Kenneth clutched the wooden posts of the prison, his knuckles whitening in his grip. He tugged on the posts. They didn't budge. "Stop! Stop it!" His shouts fell like whispers on his enemies' ears.

The hairy man held his trophy tight in his hands, pinning the woman's arms to her side. He shouted to the others, "Magnus has found a wife!"

A ruckus of jeers and howls echoed from the tables.

Humiliated, the woman pried at the man's hands to free herself, yet she labored in vain. Refusing to surrender, she arched her back and lifted her leg. With a sudden thrust, she plunged her knee into the Viking's groin.

Magnus gulped for air. Stooping in pain, he released his

prize. Then he stumbled backwards and fell, knocking over a table on his descent.

The men roared. "Magnus the Fallen," a man shouted.

Magnus rose to his feet, glaring at the feisty redhead. "You shouldn't have done that little lady," he growled. Then he lunged for the woman—but never reached her.

The bald man with the fox birthmark had interceded. The overturned table was his, and his meat now lay soiled on the ground. Clutching Magnus' shoulder, the bald man yanked and turned him. In a blink, the rugged man landed a hard punch to the face of the bearded brute—and the mighty Magnus fell like a sack of flour.

The men rushed from their seats and circled the two, hooting and yelling for Magnus to stand.

He didn't.

The bald man muttered, spat on Magnus, and sauntered away.

Kenneth witnessed it all. He studied the victor as he departed, staring at the man's unusual birthmark. He would call the man "Fox."

Fox vanished through the crowd of men and disappeared from Kenneth's sight. Kenneth turned to search for the woman, but she was gone.

"Damn bastards!"

The angry burst came from Kenneth's left. Kenneth spun and there beside him stood a large, thick man tugging at the posts of the pen. The man grasped the wooden bars and bent his head toward the ground like a bull ready to charge. He spat and began to mumble to himself. Kenneth watched the man as he carried on with his cursing.

After finishing his tirade, the big man peered at Kenneth. Kenneth said nothing.

The man released his grip of the posts and continued to stare.

"You know the woman?" Kenneth asked, unsure if he wanted an answer.

"I'll kill'em. One day I kill'em!" the man growled.

The large Scot looked to be ten years older than Kenneth and was several inches taller. He had a scraggly beard, thick along the sideburns and chin, but thin and patchy on his cheeks and neck. His hair was brown and wavy and matched the bushy eyebrows that framed his sunken eyes.

Kenneth glanced over his shoulder at the men dispersing from the tables, then he gazed back at the large man in front of him. "Is this what they do to our women … whatever they please?" Kenneth asked.

"They won't if I can stop'em," the man said. "If God grants me the chance, one day I'll kill'em." His tone was firm and resolute.

"You're angry … I feel the same. What's your name?" Kenneth asked.

The large Scot stepped toward Kenneth. He extended his arm. Kenneth raised his chained wrists to return the greeting.

"I am Dorrell, son of Beathan, from the north region of Dalriada."

"I am Kenneth, son of Alpin of Renton, from the land south of Loch Lomond … I wish I were there now," Kenneth replied. His chin dropped and his eyes lowered as he remembered what was left of his home. "We were devastated … worse, I lost my brother to these pigs!" Kenneth blurted out. He wasn't sure he wanted to speak of Aiden, but his words came without thinking.

"Sorry to hear that," the large Scot replied. "Our village

was destroyed as well. People close to me died … many in the attack and some later on as they brought us here. The three women you saw, they are from my village. The one they were after is my cousin, Rhiannon. Her father and brother were both killed protecting her. I promise you, I will kill any man who hurts her … or I'll die trying." Dorrell glared at the hut where the women were housed, and he shook his head.

Kenneth eyed the large man. He seemed to have meant what he'd said. Kenneth figured he had little regard for his own preservation—possibly he didn't fear the Vikings, or he didn't fear dying, or both.

Kenneth's anger had dulled enough for his hunger to return. "Do they feed us here … or are we supposed to eat each other?" he asked.

"We only get what they pass over. Bread and potatoes … usually we get'em when night comes, at dark. Beans at times, but not often. We've had meat only once. They feed us just enough to keep us from falling dead."

"I saw several captives working when they brought us here. I suppose they use us as slaves?"

"To them, we are nothing but slaves. For you, it will be either rocks or trees," Dorrell said.

"Rocks or trees?"

"You will either be taken to the rock quarry to carry stone or sent to the forest to cut and haul trees. You'll do it from sunrise 'til sundown. And you'll need every bit of bread and potatoes that you can eat just to stay alive."

Dorrell studied Kenneth, sizing him up and down. "Based on your build and age, I'd say they'll have you work the trees." Then Dorrell gestured toward Kenneth's chains, "You won't be able to use an axe with those, so maybe I'm wrong. Maybe they'll work you in the rock quarry instead."

Kenneth stared at the shackles binding his wrists.

"Why the chains for you? None of your other people have'em," Dorrell asked.

That was a hard question, one Kenneth didn't care to explain. With reticence, Kenneth spoke. "I tried to save my brother. But I couldn't." Kenneth shook his head, angry with himself. "It was my fault he was captured … I tried to free him … everything went wrong, it should've never happened." Kenneth turned from Dorrell. He'd lost interest in talking.

"You know this isn't over. You lost your brother, but you can't give in."

Kenneth didn't respond.

"You and I are still alive. We can't let it end here." Dorrell said.

Kenneth turned and peered at Dorrell.

"You're going to have to fight to keep your head square," Dorrell said. "No matter what happens, don't lose courage … someday you'll need it."

Kenneth closed his eyes and lowered his head.

Dorrell stared at Kenneth for a long moment then walked away.

Kenneth opened his eyes and gazed through the wooden posts imprisoning him. He grabbed hold of the posts and squeezed them in his hands. He hated the place. Standing in solitude, he made a promise to himself that he would not let them break him. That he would do as Dorrell said—he would hold on to courage.

His thoughts traveled far away to his father, to Coric, and to his family. *Will they find us here, in the middle of God knows where? Will we still be alive if they do find us?*

Can we even defeat these animals? The thoughts passed and no answers came.

He reflected on days long ago, days of growing up with his brothers. As boys, they owned nothing but had everything. Life was free, joyful, and full of hope. They had so much ahead of them, dreams to pursue and adventures to live. Freedom, joy, hope—all gone. Kenneth considered hope—such a precious treasure. It takes much to tear it down, but once gone, only God Himself can resurrect it.

The sun was leaving Kenneth.

The fading sunset stirred his memory of Arabella, sitting with him on the grassy hilltop west of Renton. He remembered that night. It was a night he would never forget. He missed her badly. To see her, to smell her, to touch her— he wanted to hold her. "Arabella, where are you now? Safe below the distant stars?" he whispered in wonder. He prayed she was alright, safe in her far-off home in Cashel, many miles away.

The growling returned to his stomach. His mind cleared, and he stared out beyond the wooden posts still clutched in his hands. He gazed at the dull fire and the picked-over carcass hanging above it.

Surely they would be fed now that darkness was coming?

CHAPTER 6

CAMPFIRES CRACKLED IN RENTON'S NIGHT AIR. The clouds remained thick, obscuring all signs of the late summer moon. Some men had fallen asleep, while others crowded around disparate fires, debating the inevitable battle in the days to come. The conversations vacillated between facing the Vikings alone and adding the Picts, albeit under Oengus' hand. Ironically, the clans neighboring the Picts, those in the north and east, contested an alignment with the Picts, while the clans of the south vied for it.

As the men bantered around the glow of the fires, they paid little attention to the lone horse that moved slowly between the huddled groups. The horse stopped in the shadows and kept its distance from the surrounding campfires. After several moments, the animal nickered and caught the attention of a man from Cashel. The man rose beside his fire and squinted in the darkness at the horse—and the exhausted rider slumped upon its back.

The man hesitated and then jogged to the horse. He gripped the arm of the rider and shook it gently. The rider lifted. It was a young woman. "Get Constantine, have him come quickly!" he yelled. A few men departed and others rose from the fires and hurried to help.

Constantine and Luag were warming themselves by a fire not far away. The two jumped to their feet when they heard the news and rushed to join the gathering of men. Wedging their way through the crowd, they parted the bodies and froze when they saw the rider.

Constantine recognized the young woman, immediately. "It's Nessa!" he exclaimed. "Quick, get her down, and fetch some food and water!"

"I'll send for Ena," Luag added. He signaled two boys to find Ena and bring her.

Constantine gently pulled Nessa from the horse. She roused, only to lift her saddened face and sob.

Constantine held her, letting her cry in his arms. He motioned to the men. They would carry her to a nearby home at the edge of Renton to let her rest.

When Ena arrived, she entered to find Nessa sitting in bed, awake and speaking to Luag. "Nessa. You're alive!" she exclaimed and rushed to Nessa.

"Mother, I thought I'd never see you again!" Nessa leaned forward and hugged her mother. At first, only a single tear fell from Nessa's eyes. Then she broke down. "It was awful Mother, awful," she cried.

"Nessa … Nessa, you're home. Shhhh, you're home," Ena said. She held her daughter, rocking her back and forth.

Not many moments passed before Arabella and Ceana arrived. They stood in the doorway, gaping at Nessa. Luag moved from Nessa's bedside and nodded at the two. Then he stepped aside and left the women to tend to Nessa.

Nessa glanced at Arabella and Ceana and pushed away her tears. She tried to smile and hugged them both. Releasing her embrace, she turned to her mother. "Luag said that Father is gone?"

Ena's eyes combed over her daughter. "Darling, your father left with Coric, Ronan, and Laise to find you. They've been gone several days." Ena tried not to appear frightened as she formed her next words. "Nessa, do you know where Aiden is?"

Puddles pooled in Nessa's eyes. Her lips quivered into a broken frown. Then she shook her head slowly, not uttering a word.

"Nessa, what is it?" Ena asked. "What happened?"

"Mother, he didn't make it," she cried.

"Oh, God, no." The deathly soft whisper fell from Ena's lips like a tear falling into a grave. She stared at the floor in a daze, brokenhearted. Piece by piece she felt her life being stripped of all things precious. Sadness gripped her, suffocating her in sorrow and crushing what little hope remained.

Nessa stared at her mother while agony hung in her mother's eyes. "I'm sorry ... I'm so sorry," Nessa said, sobbing as she remembered her brother. She wiped her face with the front of her blouse, trying to regain herself. She paused a moment and then she spoke, "Mother ... Kenneth, he—"

"Oh please, not Kenneth too?" Arabella interrupted, pleading and praying against the very question she'd asked.

"Arabella, Kenneth saved us. He saved me and Aiden from the Vikings."

"You saw him? He found you? Did he escape?" Arabella begged.

Nessa wiped her hand across her nose and gazed at Arabella. "Kenneth found us and freed us from the Vikings. But when we escaped, he took Aiden on his horse. Oh, Aiden, he was burned so badly, he—" Nessa stopped, paralyzed by the images of her brother falling from the cliff. She shoved the edge of her blouse into her mouth and bit hard, groaning and weeping at the thought of her brothers.

"Nessa. Nessa. We need you, Nessa. We need to know where Kenneth is," Ena said, clutching Nessa's arm and studying her blood-shot eyes.

Nessa took a deep breath and spoke, "Kenneth took Aiden, and they broke off from me. He drew the Vikings away from me. I was able to escape without them following. When I was far enough to hide, I stopped. I had to see if the boys made it, but they didn't. I was standing far away, and I saw Aiden and Kenneth high on a ridgeline with a river below. They were surrounded by six or seven Vikings. Something was happening, but I couldn't see. Suddenly, Aiden and a Viking were at the edge of the ridge, and they fell—Mother, it was awful!"

"Oh, no. No!" Ena cried. She cupped her hand over her mouth and her heart grieved. The grim reality of Aiden's death filled the room, bringing with it a cold, palpable anguish.

Moments passed without a word. Then Arabella broke the silence. "Nessa, did Kenneth survive?"

Nessa's lips pursed and her eyes closed shut. Then she opened her eyes and slowly nodded. "After Aiden fell, Kenneth and those animals were all tangled together. They moved out of sight, and I couldn't see them anymore. I'm sure he was captured. They must have taken him and put him with the others. They're going to make them slaves. They're awful men. They're evil, evil!" Nessa exclaimed.

The fright in Nessa's voice carried a sharp chill that pierced Arabella's heart like a dagger.

⑥

The cool night air would have comforted the soul on most any other night. But not this night. No starry night sky, no cool summer breeze, nothing on earth could comfort on this night. Arabella found a quiet place in the darkness, away from the fires, away from the voices, away from the others. She wanted more than anything to be alone.

Arabella recalled the frightening premonition she'd had the day Kenneth left her in Renton. Since that moment, her heart had lived with the dread that one day she would wake to find him gone forever. And now, she feared, the day had come. Her unspoken prophecy was being fulfilled. She'd returned to Cashel as Kenneth had asked. Yet the unending questions and the deafening silence of solitude had driven her back to Renton. Wanting to renew hope, she'd sought comfort in Ena and Ceana. Now the news of Aiden's death and Kenneth's capture abruptly shattered the only remaining hope she'd held.

After leaving Nessa and the women, Arabella moved through Renton. She passed several campfires, each surrounded by men with bickering tongues. The men's arguing only confirmed her feeling of hopelessness. Their rantings were senseless and irreconcilable, and without Alpin, they seemed helpless to find agreement. Yet even more than the bickering, it was the overhearing of her father's entrenched debate with the men of Dumbarton that crippled her most. In that single moment, she became acutely aware of what little was being done to find Kenneth and the others. Her father was a strong man, but with Alpin gone unity among the men seemed impossible. And sadly, Alpin was now as far away as Kenneth.

"I didn't think I'd find you here," a voice came from behind Arabella.

She knew the voice. "I didn't think I wanted to be found."

"I heard about Alpin's sons. That's a shame."

Arabella wasn't sure how to take Taran's comment, though he'd said it like he meant it. "Yes, it is," she replied, saying nothing more.

"I'm sure Kenneth is still out there. He is a headstrong young man. His stubbornness will suit him well. He has what he needs to stay alive," Taran commented.

He sat down in the grass beside Arabella, far from the campfires. The light of the moon was hidden, making it hard for the two to see one another. Arabella preferred it that way.

"Taran, I'd rather be alone. There is nothing you can do. Aiden is dead and so much has been lost. And from where I sit, it seems that now you and your father are the ones keeping the men from searching for Kenneth and the others."

"I disagree. My father is the only man who seems to see things clearly. The others have blood on their tongues and wish to rush into battle, blind to the strength of our enemy. Pursuing Kenneth with our handful of men is suicide." Taran peered at Arabella, trying to measure her reaction in the dim light. "We could more than double our men if we join the Picts. With Oengus, we'd have twice the strength to fight the Vikings ... and save Kenneth."

"Taran, you say you see clearly, but there are things you're not seeing. Asking the Picts to help us will take time ... time we don't have! Joining them as you say means that we submit to Oengus who wants to be king—king over us." She could almost hear Kenneth mouthing the very words she had spoken. "Are you willing to submit to Oengus and give up what you stand for as a Scot?"

"If unification with the Picts means victory and freedom from the Vikings, then yes, I could be willing."

"Can't we be free without them!" Arabella blurted out in frustration.

"I have said this again and again—but you refuse to accept that we need the Picts. Why won't you listen?" Taran's voice grew louder and carried a tinge of anger. "I assure you of this … you will not see your beloved Kenneth alive again without the Picts fighting beside us. You've seen what the Vikings are capable of doing. You've seen their lust for blood. They inflicted their will upon Renton with ease. Without the Picts, your Kenneth is a dead man."

Arabella lowered her head and covered her face in her hands, not wanting Taran to see. Her back heaved up and down as she cried silently to herself.

"I am not trying to be cruel. I'm trying to help," he said.

Arabella pulled her hands from her face, "Just leave … please, just leave."

Taran lifted to his feet. He stood above her for a moment and then walked away.

Before he had gone far, he glanced back at Arabella. "You would do well to talk some sense into your father … Kenneth's life may depend on it."

Arabella was too removed under the dark sky to bother with the tears streaming down her cheeks. Who would see or even care? She couldn't refute Taran's words. She had seen the Vikings' brutality. She knew the harm they were capable of inflicting.

She didn't like Taran, but that didn't mean he wasn't

right. She could talk to her father, but he would only do as he felt best. Her mentioning the Picts to him would likely be viewed as a young lover's callow attempt to save her betrothed. He wouldn't see it as a shrewd battle plan. Pure Scot blood ran through his veins—like his cousin Alpin, his confidence rested in the Scots alone.

Her aggravation grew at the thought of how such a proposal to her father would be taken as an insult or a show of disloyalty. She tried to dismiss her anger. Her father had only shown her love from the day he found her and took her as his own. He had always trusted her. He had always listened.

She could speak to him—but would the other men force him in a direction he didn't wish to go? She refused to force him to choose between his daughter and his men. Yet she determined, somehow, to find a way to help Kenneth.

She would stop to see Ceana first.

⊚

Arabella knocked on the door and then stepped inside. "Ceana," she called out.

Ceana emerged from the bedroom, "Arabella."

"Where is Ena?" Arabella asked.

"She's in Renton with Nessa. Do you need her?"

"No, I need to talk to you, Ceana."

"Is everything alright? Do you have news of Kenneth or Coric?" Ceana asked. She sat down on a wooden bench beside the hearth and offered for Arabella to sit.

"No, I am fine. I didn't hear any news … and I can't stay long," Arabella replied, nervously. "Ceana, I must go to see Oengus—"

"In Perth?" Ceana exclaimed.

"It's alright, Ceana. I only need to see him briefly. I intend to ask him to join the Scots."

"Arabella, no, it's too dangerous. The ride to Perth, or even entering the Pict castle—it's far too dangerous! You can't do this. You certainly can't go alone. Does your father know?"

"I know it's dangerous. But I have to get help. We need to do something. Kenneth's life—and Coric's—may depend on it. As for the Picts and Oengus, I'll be alright. I am a Pict by birth, and Oengus will respect that. He will listen to me."

"But does your father know, Arabella?" Ceana repeated.

"I want to tell him, but I can't. I want to talk to him, reason with him, and have him send men to Perth. But he won't understand … and even if he did, he may not be able to go against Luag and the others who don't trust the Picts. I can't put him in that position. This is the best way, Ceana. It's the only way."

"Arabella, he'll be furious when he finds out."

"He won't find out," Arabella said, staring straight at Ceana. "All he needs to know is that I am returning to Cashel. I am simply taking a longer route to get there." Arabella paused and then finished, "It's our secret Ceana. Can you do this for me? Please? Coric and Kenneth need us—their lives are at stake."

Ceana nodded. "I will. But promise you'll be safe and hurry back to Cashel as quickly as you can."

"I promise, Ceana. I'll be safe. I'll send a messenger when I arrive home."

"I love you, Arabella," Ceana said. She extended her arms and clasped Arabella's hands.

"I love you too, Ceana. Pray for me … and the boys!"

Ceana nodded and tried to smile. "I will."

Arabella hugged her, and then turned and hurried out the door.

CHAPTER 7

THE AXE HUNG HEAVY IN KENNETH'S HANDS. Torn blisters from the constant heaving of the tool lined his palms. Removing the iron cuffs from his wrists brought relief, but the open sores on his hands and the numbing tightness of his overused muscles offered new pains.

Oddly, it was Jorund who had insisted that Kenneth's cuffs be removed, though he kept the Scot's feet chained. Likely, the beastly Viking understood that cutting trees would carry a heavier burden than the lesser drudgery of carrying stones. The labor of wielding the axe was severe, but for Kenneth, having his arms and hands free was well worth the exchange.

Kenneth swung the big axe hard. Its blade cut deep into the white meat of the pine. The swinging of the iron head provided an outlet for Kenneth, a means to vent his unquenched anger. With each blow, Kenneth cut deep into the trunk, splintering chips of wood from the heart of the tree. The white woody shards piled at his feet like snow atop the knotty roots that fingered outward from the trunk of the pine.

Sweat soaked Kenneth's hair and shirt. His chest heaved in and out as he cut over and over into the tall evergreen. As he performed his mindless, repetitive cuts, he envisioned himself turning the axe on the Vikings and rushing the guards who watched over him. He saw himself in a delirious rage, cutting into every Viking in sight. If it weren't for their crossbows, that covered a greater distance than the axe, he would have done more than simply envision his act.

Kenneth purposed to be patient. He would wait for the right time—either his father would come with an army of Scots, or the Vikings would make a mistake. Either way, he would wait for his opportunity.

Another swing. The tree teetered. The large pine had nearly succumbed to the small axe. The steady blows had carved a deep slot into the wood and now little remained to hold the tree upright. Kenneth's blows came faster. The spindly beast began to tilt. The spine snapped, and a tearing sound erupted from the base of the tree. The cracking grew louder, the branches swayed, and the tree began its descent, crashing through its neighbors and snapping off their limbs on the way down. Its impact against the earth released an echoing boom, along with a certain satisfaction that pleased Kenneth.

Kenneth gaped at the fallen monster, contemplating the finality of the massive beast. He lowered the head of his axe to the ground and leaned on its handle to catch his breath. He glanced at a nearby guard, then gazed down at the barren stump. It was riddled with cuts except for the small ridge of splintered pulp sticking up from where the tree had held to the end. Kenneth heard laughter that sounded something like a grunt. He looked to his side. It was Dorrell. He had stopped to watch the grand tree fall.

Dorrell wiped his brow and grinned at Kenneth.

Kenneth returned a grin of his own. It felt good. Cutting hard and bringing down the tree—indeed, it felt good.

"Move on. Strip the branches and clean it up," a guard grumbled at Kenneth.

Kenneth brushed off his sleeves and rubbed the dripping sweat from his forehead. He looked at the guard, then at his axe, and then back at the guard one last time. Kenneth stepped over the stump where the pine had once stood. He loomed over the fallen tree and began whittling away the remaining branches.

One by one, he would cut them all.

⊚

"Why have you returned, Scot? I assume you come with good news? I will not have my meal interrupted for anything less," Oengus said, sitting erect at the large wooden dining table. He snapped his fingers to dismiss the attendant who'd served him.

"Yes, my lord. I bring you word from Taran of Dumbarton," Searc said, unsure if his news truly was good news. "He and his father, Guaire, are gathered with the men of Dalriada in Renton. There is no sign of Alpin. He has not returned, nor have the three traveling with him. Taran has persuaded the men to remain in Renton and—"

"The Scots are staying back, they have not left to find their people? Have they lost courage? Have they finally come to their senses, now seeing their need of the Picts?" Oengus gloated.

"Well, uh, yes … they are beginning to see, my lord Oengus."

"Your confidence fades from your voice as you speak, Scot."

Searc's gaze fell to the floor. He hated being alone with Oengus. He fumbled for words, "My lord, many do see the wisdom of joining the Picts, but others—"

Oengus sprang from his seat. His chair tipped and crashed to the stone floor. "It is not a matter of joining, they are to pledge their fealty to me! The Scots are to be my subjects! That is their only option. I tire of this game, Searc. Is this Taran unable to persuade these men? You spoke as if he were capable!"

"My lord, he sees that seeking your aid is the only means of survival. He has convinced many of this. With Alpin gone, the men grow restless for leadership. I assure you, they will be persuaded."

"Boy, you are in no position to assure me of anything. I want Taran and his father, Guaire, here … and Constantine. Then I'll be assured they've seen the light of wisdom."

"My lord, this will happen, I'm certain of it," Searc said. His stomach knotted and he wanted to run, but he needed to hear the answer to one more question. He mustered the courage to speak, "Have you heard from your men … have they found Alpin?"

"DO NOT MENTION THAT NAME!" Oengus bellowed. "That is not your worry! My men will accomplish their task. I have spoken on the matter and that is enough!"

Searc trembled like a dry leaf in a winter wind. "Yes, my lord … I, I will go … I will return to Renton and come back with the men you have requested." Searc bowed and inched toward the door.

Oengus ambled to the side of the large table. "Before you

leave …," he said, gazing across the grand dining hall, "I have one more use of you."

"Yes, my lord?" Searc uttered, quivering and wishing at this moment that he was deaf, blind, and mute.

"I have someone I want you to see."

"Someone you want me to see, my lord?"

"Yes."

"My lord, who shall I see?"

"It is the younger son of Alpin," Oengus said.

Searc froze. A single thought raced through his mind—*Aiden*? "My lord, how is this?"

"My scouts found the young man nearly dead—half drowned and badly burnt. They brought him to me. He has little strength, though he is improving. My physician is seeing to his recovery … I should say he doesn't seem fully aware of all that has happened."

Searc glanced at the corridor exiting the hall, weighing his chances of escape. The odds were slim. Sheepishly, he returned his gaze to Oengus. "My lord, what could I say to him that would be of any good?"

"You will tell him the news of his father, that the Vikings seized his father and killed him."

"I can't do that. He will surely ask about his mother and will wish to return to Renton," Searc pleaded. The tenuous exchange with the Pict lord felt to Searc as if he were moving over a vast sheet of fissured ice, never knowing whether it would hold or instantly crack and plunge him deep into its chilling grip.

"You can and will do this. You will tell the boy of Renton's devastation, and how the Scots see no other path than to pledge their allegiance to me. His mother, of course, you will tell him, insists that he stay in my care until he is well. And, too, that she wishes for him to serve under me as a means of goodwill, assuring that our people will unite … a sort of ambassador, if you please." Oengus paused and smiled. "The pledge of Constantine, Guaire, and Taran will further solidify your message to the boy." He mused at his plan to secure the Scots' loyalty, and in time, the Vikings' demise. In the end, all would be well, the Picts—and the Scots—would have their king.

The soft glow of candlelight lit the cool, damp room. Searc stood motionless in the doorway, watching the shadows dance beyond the flickering candle flames. His eyes swept over the stone walls before settling on Aiden. He lay asleep in the bed, breathing in slow, cadenced breaths that lifted and lowered his chest. Searc hesitated and then entered.

A four-foot wrought-iron candlestand stood in the center of the room, fashioning three equally-spaced candles. Their golden fires fluttered as Searc passed. Searc rehearsed his words. He wondered if Aiden would even believe him. He hated himself for being Oengus' pawn and casting deception upon Aiden. Aiden was the one person who called Searc a friend. Yet Searc had ventured too deep into the den of treason. He had no choice but to take the next step. He convinced himself that this lie could be his last, and his debt would be fulfilled.

Searc stepped beside Aiden's bed and gazed over his battered body. Bandages covered much of his face and neck. Those on his shoulder were soiled with the weeping of blisters. Even the uncovered wounds lining the edges of the bandages were grotesque with ooze. Searc could only imagine the hideousness of the sores hidden below.

"Who's there?" Aiden said with a groggy voice, waking

to Searc's presence moving through the dull light. "Who is it?" he repeated.

"Aiden … it's me, Searc."

"Searc," Aiden said, stirring from his sleep. "What are you doing here? I thought Renton—"

"Shhh. Don't try to move, save your strength," Searc said, and he placed his hand on Aiden's shoulder, gesturing for him to keep still.

"I'm strong enough, Searc," Aiden said. He slowly moved his arms and pushed against the bed to sit up.

Searc stepped back and watched Aiden labor to lift himself. "Aiden, I have spoken with Oengus. He tells me that you were nearly dead when he found you, and that you have been in and out of consciousness ever since. You're lucky to be here."

"Searc—how is my family? Are they alive? Are they well, are they here with you?" Aiden said. He studied Searc's face, waiting for a response.

Searc glanced furtively about the room, refusing to find Aiden's eyes. He wished he could vanish. Groping for words, he spoke, "As you know, there is little left of Renton. Many of our people perished in the attack, Aiden. Our village was destroyed, and our people were decimated. Your mother and your brother's wife are alive. They survived the attack. The men have gathered in Renton—"

"My mother, she is well?"

"Yes, she was unharmed. And you should know—"

"Nessa and Kenneth, did they make it home to Renton?"

"I know nothing of Nessa and Kenneth, only that they were believed to be with you," Searc said.

"My father, has he returned from the hunt with Coric, Donald, and the men? Has he seen our home?"

Searc lifted his hand and rubbed his lower lip, wedging it between his forefinger and thumb. He stepped away and turned toward the candles. Their hot flames burned white, puddling pools of wax under the glowing heat. Searc saw irony in the candles—how they lived to burn, yet in so doing, they burned themselves to death. In some ways, he saw Aiden in the candles. In some ways, he saw himself.

"Searc, has my father returned? Does he know what happened?" Aiden repeated.

"Your father returned, Aiden. But he did not wait for the men to come to Renton. He left to find you and the others. He and Coric left Renton with Ronan and Laise. They left alone." Searc stopped, not wanting to finish.

"What else, Searc? There's something else you're not telling me."

"I don't know how to tell you, Aiden. You are like a brother to me—"

"Searc, dammit, tell me!"

Searc lowered his gaze. "Word has come that your father has been ... that he has been killed."

Aiden leapt from the bed and stumbled to keep his balance. "What are you saying, Searc? My father, he is ... he is dead!" Aiden shuddered under the pain of his movement. He began to shake. The room began to spin. He bent and placed his hands on the stand beside his bed. Then he opened his eyes wide and took a deep breath to push away the dizziness.

"Aiden, you mustn't do this. You must rest. Let me help you," Searc insisted, more to assuage his guilt than to offer kindness.

"My father can't be dead. He's going to lead the men against the Vikings," Aiden muttered in disbelief.

"Constantine and Guaire of Dumbarton are leading the

men. They are devising a plan for the Scots in your father's absence," Searc said. He stared at Aiden, watching him labor to stand erect. "Aiden, did you hear me?"

Aiden slowly nodded his head. He lifted upright with a grimace pressed upon his face and then turned to the side and leaned against the bed.

"Aiden, I'm sorry to tell you of your father. I understand your pain … you know I do. I, of all people, know the pain of losing a father." Searc slowly paced the floor. "Aiden, time will bring healing. And … and … you should know, all is not lost. The Scots are assembling now in Renton. They are making plans to defeat the Vikings. They say that aligning with Oengus will bring an end to the Vikings. Aiden, we will avenge your father's death. We will find Kenneth and the others and restore Dalriada." He stepped to Aiden and gazed at him. "I'm sorry, Aiden."

"I'll return with you to Renton. I will help my mother," Aiden said.

"No, you must recover fully, Aiden. You need to stay here and regain your strength." Searc held Aiden's arm and prompted him back to the bed.

Aiden's breathing grew erratic, and beads of sweat formed on his clammy skin. "No, my mother needs me now, Searc. I must return home."

"Aiden, I assure you, your mother wishes you to stay here. She wants you to heal under Oengus' care. His physician can help you. You will be the voice of the Scots here in Perth. You can see to it that our interests are heard. It is best for you to stay here and recover." Searc finished his plea and edged Aiden closer to the bed.

Aiden abruptly turned and pushed Searc. "No, I will return to Renton. Don't try to stop me!" Aiden stepped to move past Searc. Then his legs suddenly stiffened and his knees buckled. Black dots filled his sight before he lost focus and collapsed to the floor.

Searc caught Aiden as he fell limp and lowered into a heap. There Searc paused. He glanced at the door and contemplated his next decision. After a long moment, he shook his head and lifted Aiden to the bed. Upon lowering Aiden's head to the pillow, Searc lifted Aiden's legs and pushed them onto the straw-filled mattress. His eyes combed Aiden's body and the bandages holding him together. "I'm sorry, Aiden, I had no choice," Searc muttered. He lingered a moment and then whispered, "Stay here, Aiden … please, stay here."

Then Searc blew out the candles and left without looking back.

CHAPTER 8

CONSTANTINE SWALLOWED THE LAST BITE OF HIS meal. The food appeased his hunger but did little to relieve his irritation. Across the table sat Luag and Guaire consuming their dry, salted mutton. Though both had much to say, neither spoke. Latharn stood at the window behind the two, staring out at the campsites teamed with men busying themselves under the morning sun.

Constantine's gaze shifted to his half-empty mug of water sitting on the table in front of him. Past debates among the four played over in his mind. *A divided army is a defeated army,* he concluded. He knew the four would have to find resolution soon—Dalriada needed as much.

Constantine rose from his seat. He peered at the three, one by one. "Men, we have no choice but to depart and find those taken by the Vikings—Alpin and the boys included. Our time is up. I am asking each of you, as leaders of men, let us settle this."

Luag nodded his agreement and glanced at Latharn and Guaire.

Latharn turned from his perch beside the window and folded his arms across his chest. "I'm torn. If we find the Vikings, we won't be simply asking them to kindly return our people—we'll be starting a war. And we won't have the element of surprise that we had when this all started. The Vikings will be expecting us ... this whole thing could be a trap."

A frown crept over Guaire's face. He turned to Constantine, "Latharn is right. We want to find the captives. But we would do well just to survive an encounter with the Vikings." He stood and pushed his chair under the table. "We can't lead our men into a trap. Why would we not send an envoy to Oengus and remind him of what's at stake? He doesn't want the Vikings here either, or they'll be coming for him next. Surely he'd agree to supply the necessary men."

"I don't see any good in adding the Picts to our numbers," Luag contested, addressing Constantine. "We don't have time. We've already waited too long—"

Suddenly, a loud knock rapped on the door.

"Sir!" a voice called from outside.

Constantine stepped across the room and opened the door. A single Dalriadan scout stood beyond the threshold. "What is it?" Constantine asked. Then his eyes peered past the scout toward a mass of men moving in the distance. "Where are the men going?"

"I have found Alpin and the three others," the scout replied. "I spotted them and joined them on the north road. They are coming behind me. I rode ahead to bring the news. Alpin has been badly injured—it's his leg. He was shot with an arrow, and he has lost much blood."

"Where are they now?" Constantine asked.

"They're not far behind. They should be entering Renton any moment, sir."

"Very good. We're coming."

Constantine turned to the three, "Let's go!"

"Constantine, I'll have my men find Seamus. He's Milton's physician. He'll be able to help Alpin," Latharn said.

Ronan led the group of four into Renton. Seeing his father pressing through the crowd of men, he called to him, "Father, Father!"

Luag hurried to his son. "What happened to Alpin?"

"He's been wounded," Ronan said. "We were ambushed, and that's when Alpin took an arrow in his thigh. He's holding on, but it's been a long ride home and he's very weak. We need to get him to a bed. He'll need food and water."

Coric and Laise rode abreast of Alpin as the three entered the village fifty paces behind Ronan. Alpin sat slumped forward in his saddle, leaning against the neck of his horse. He lifted as he approached the crowd of men. His face was white and haggard, and his eyes were listless and tired. As he neared the men, he repositioned and sat erect in his saddle. He held up a clenched fist and gave a reassuring nod.

The men cheered at the sight of Alpin's return, glad to see him home alive.

Constantine's spirit lifted when he saw the men's reaction. He and Luag approached Alpin to help him dismount. "So you decided to come back," Constantine remarked, with a tone that promised to encourage Alpin. Then he peered at Alpin's injured thigh and grimaced. "It's good that you didn't use your head to stop that arrow ... we need to get a doctor to look at that."

"Lord knows I didn't want to come back. Having you fuss over me like an old wife ... that's more than I can take," Alpin replied and attempted a grin. He dismounted with a groan and hobbled when his bad leg reached the ground.

Coric dismounted beside his father. "We need to find

him a bed and a doctor," he said. His hair was disheveled, and his face was covered with a grimy film that ran from his ear to his neck, though he had no concern of his appearance. "Constantine, can you send someone for my mother and my wife. They'll be able to help once we get him settled."

Constantine called to a man and gave the order. Then he turned back to Coric, "Let's get your father to that bed. Follow me."

Coric nodded, grabbed a leather bag from his horse, and followed the men as they led his father away.

Alpin's eyes opened and closed. His body gradually relaxed in the comfort of the soft cot, as his mind vacillated between coherency and exhaustion.

"He's lost a good deal of blood," Seamus said, kneeling beside the makeshift bed where Alpin lay. Seamus signaled his handmaid to bring more water and rags.

Alpin attempted to speak and he muttered a string of unintelligible words. After a long pause, his brow furrowed and exhaustion overtook him.

"Seamus, can you help him?" Latharn asked his physician.

"He needs rest. He probably should have died from the blood he's lost. The belt the boys placed around his leg may have saved his life," Seamus commented as he removed the belt. "I need to change the bandage, then I'll reset the tourniquet."

"How long until he wakes?" Constantine asked.

"I can't say, but don't plan on moving him. He needs more strength. He will need plenty of nourishment and rest before he tries anything. His leg is fairly torn up. It'll be some time before he can walk with any real vigor. The arrow seems to have missed the bone, but it got muscle, front and back. It's pretty bad."

Constantine turned to Coric, who was standing at the edge of the bed, mesmerized by the physician and the talk of the men. "Tell me what happened, Coric."

Coric stared at Constantine, his anger resurging. "They were hunting us."

"Who was hunting you?" Luag asked.

"Three men. They followed us for some time as we tracked Kenneth and the others. We were on the trail the Vikings had taken." Coric paused, puzzled by the expression forming on Constantine's face. "What is it?" Coric asked.

"Go on, Coric, tell us about these men," Luag said. "Who are they?"

"You mean, 'Who were they?' They're dead now," Coric replied.

"This doesn't make sense," Constantine said. "Were they Vikings?"

"No, they weren't Vikings. They were trying to conceal their identity. They wore these," Coric said, pulling a black garment from his leather bag and lifting it for the others to see.

"They were Britons," someone behind Coric said.

Coric whirled around to find Taran standing in the open doorway with a half dozen men at his side. Coric stepped toward Taran. "No, they weren't Britons … they were Picts!"

"How could they be Picts, that's the same garb worn by several of the Britons at Ae?" Guaire replied.

"I know they were Picts! I ripped these rags from their dead bodies, and two of them were covered in painted markings. They were Picts!"

Guaire chuckled. "Simply because a man has paint on his body doesn't mean he's a Pict."

"Of course they were Picts. Why are you so quick to dismiss that? Only Picts cover themselves in paint," Luag insisted, peering at Guaire.

"On the contrary, it may mean they once were Picts, or at one time they rode with the Picts. But if they were hunting our men, they were most likely mercenaries, working for any man willing to pay the highest wage. I would suppose the Britons paid these men to kill Alpin. Their black garb seems to suggest as much," Guaire responded.

"I don't buy it!" Coric said. "Britons don't travel this far north. These were Picts ... maybe mercenaries, but Pict mercenaries. Oengus will have to answer for this!"

"So now you plan to start a war with the Vikings *and* the Picts? That's an odd decision when the Picts may be your only chance to defeat the Vikings," Taran said. "I wouldn't be so rash—we may need them."

"I don't need you telling me how to fight and whose hand I should bow to, Taran. Oengus can't be trusted! He would gladly see Dalriada burn to the ground. I'm convinced he wants my father dead, and the bastards with painted bodies prove it!"

Taran didn't blink. He even seemed to enjoy the moment. "The men know we need the Picts to strengthen our forces. They know your father's hatred for Oengus. One man's pride should not hinder the security of the many. These so-called 'mercenaries' are dead. They can't tell of their ties to Briton, but their black garments can. You would do well to put your past with Oengus behind you and consider how we can stop the Vikings."

Taran glanced to his right and left at the men standing

beside him, then he turned back to Coric. "Your time to save your lost brother Kenneth is growing short. We must join the Picts—and soon, if we hope to stop the Vikings."

Mutterings of approval rose from Taran's entourage.

"We don't need the damn Picts, Taran. I'll find my brothers … and my sister and the others," Coric replied.

"Ah, yes, you haven't heard. I will leave that for the others to share with you and your ailing father. But be quick, we must call on Oengus and depart soon," Taran said, and he turned and walked away. The small crowd of Dumbarton men followed.

Coric felt a hand on his shoulder. "Let him go, Coric."

Coric spun, still seething from the encounter.

"Forget Taran. Let's just you and I talk, without Taran," Constantine said, trying to calm his nephew. Constantine glanced at the others in the room and then shut the door.

Ronan and Laise stood beside Coric. Luag, Latharn, and the other men stood silent, waiting for Constantine to proceed.

Coric gazed at Constantine, studying his face and noting his burdened demeanor. "Taran mentioned some news that I 'have not heard.' What did he mean?" Coric asked. "What have I not heard?"

"Nessa is well, Coric. She has returned to us. She is with your mother and your wife. The three of them are fine," Constantine said.

"Nessa escaped? She's here?"

"Yes, she escaped … she says that Kenneth found her and was able to free her."

Coric eased, then tensed. "Kenneth freed her? Where is he? Where are Kenneth and Aiden?" He felt his heart sink as if he knew the answer.

"Coric, Nessa says Kenneth is alive, but that he was captured. Likely, he's being held with the others," Constantine replied.

"She saw him taken alive? Was she the only one who escaped?"

"Yes, she was the only one who escaped. But Coric ...," Constantine paused. He glanced at Luag and struggled to return his eyes to Coric. "Son, Nessa told us ... she told us that Aiden ... that he died. He was killed during the escape."

The words sliced into Coric as though his gut had been ripped asunder. He would have thrown up, had he any food in his belly. "Aiden is dead," he uttered, disbelieving. Coric's gaze moved to his father. He was lying on the cot, his leg wrapped in bandages and his mind oblivious to the news of Aiden—his father would wake to a living hell.

How God, how could this happen? Why did Aiden have to die, I could have saved him! God, my father won't survive this! Anguish flooded Coric's soul. He shut his eyes and stood in silence, seething with rage. His jaw flexed and his teeth clenched tight. Then his eyes shot open. "Oengus! He's behind this! He came into our village demanding fealty. When Father would not submit, he became indignant. He hates the Scots, he hates my father! It was *his* men who tracked and hunted us! He's behind the Viking attack. I know it!"

"Coric, we don't know the mercenaries were sent by Oengus. They could be Britons. And why would he be against the Scots? The Vikings will come after him, too." Latharn said.

"I ask you, were the Pict villages destroyed? Did they attack Oengus' castle?" Coric demanded. "Why did the

Vikings attack south to Renton and then return north without attacking farther?"

The older men stood in a stupor, mulling Coric's claim in muddled deliberation.

"Somebody answer me! Tell me why Oengus and the Picts have remained untouched by the Viking butchery. I'm telling you, he sold his soul to those devils—"

"I believe Coric is right," Ronan said, speaking up and eyeing his father.

Luag's barrel chest surged as he drew a breath under his son's gaze. He folded his arms and glared at Constantine and Latharn. "I've never trusted the Picts. And I don't trust Oengus. I think we should listen to the boys."

Constantine began to pace the small room, tracing his eyes along the wooden planks of the floor. Continuing to amble, he addressed the young men, "I have heard what you've said. I do not fully disagree with the charges you've made. What you have said may be true, but at the moment, we only have suspicions. We mustn't overlook the gap between truth and suspicion—we need proof." He paused and stepped to the window. He stared at the men gathered outside. He was not surprised to see Taran huddled in a group with a dozen others. Constantine shook his head in disgust and turned back to Coric. "Coric, if what you've said is true, then it will have much bearing on what we do next. But before we leap into a war we may not win, we must have real proof—suspicion alone is insufficient. We must know for sure that your suspicions are true."

"There is no other answer, Constantine. I am certain of it," Coric insisted. "What more proof do you need? Wake my father, he knows Oengus. He'll agree with what I'm saying."

"We will wake him soon enough. He needs to rest and

recover. As for your certainty, I know you believe you are right. But I cannot start a battle with Oengus and the Picts while in the midst of a war with the Vikings, especially without proof that Oengus has conspired against us. For now, the evidence is based on circumstances, and dare I say, emotion. We need more facts, Coric. I will not send these men against the blade of two enemies without absolute certainty."

"Proof. You need more proof," Coric fumed incredulously, shaking his head. "Soon enough you'll have your proof." He broke his gaze from Constantine and departed without uttering another word.

CHAPTER 9

HER SOFT CURLS CARRIED THE FRESH SCENT OF A rose as they touched his cheeks and tickled his skin. The thought of brushing aside her fragrant locks never crossed his mind. He rested beside her with his eyes closed. He was happy and content. It had been a long time since he had felt the warmth of her body. He drew her close in his arms and held her.

Since he was a young boy, he had dreamed of lying beside her in the cool afternoon shade, resting in the lush green fields of Dalriada. He felt strong as she rested close to him. His heart, at last, knew satisfaction.

She stirred.

He opened his eyes. Her face was like that of an angel, her skin aglow with an unearthly light, without blemish or flaw. Her breathing was rhythmic and steady. What more could a man desire? Her beauty belonged to him and to him alone. He would keep her and protect her, and she would never know want or sorrow. He would be her provider, her defender. He would fight for her, for her hand and for her honor.

Again, she stirred. Yet this time her breathing was uneven and labored. Her body shook.

He lifted to sit straight.

She began to cough.

He shook her gently to wake her.

Her coughing intensified. She opened her eyes and searched for him, yet her gaze found only emptiness.

"Arabella?" he said. "Arabella!"

But she could not see with her eyes. And she could not hear with her ears.

"Arabella, it's me."

He pulled her closer.

Her coughing came in violent bouts. She broke from his grasp and stood. She gazed about, frantically feeling the air like a blind mother searching the darkness for her lost child. Her chest heaved as she coughed, and she gasped for air. She fought to speak, "Kenneth." His name fell from her lips.

Kenneth tried to stand and reach for her, but his legs would not allow him. His eyes fell to his feet—iron chains anchored him. He pulled himself along the ground, fighting to draw closer, and he stretched out his arms to touch her, but she was beyond his reach.

A smoky fog slowly filled the void between the two lovers. She moved and was lost from sight.

"Arabella!" he called. He could hear her coughing amid the smoky haze.

Her last cry came, "Kenneth ... Ken."

Her voice rang in his ears.

He fought his chains, tearing at the ground, but the chains refused. He stared into the fog and caught a final glimpse of his beloved. And then she vanished.

Her cry echoed in his heart, "Ken ... Ken ... Cawl ... Cawl ... Cawl."

Kenneth's eyes opened to the dreary morning sky. The

dark gray clouds churned overhead, denying any glimpse of the sun's warm light. A large black raven sat perched on the prison wall above where Kenneth lay, watching Kenneth with a singular eye and then twitching its head to spy him with the other eye.

The angry bird stared a moment longer and then crowed again, "Cawl ... Cawl ... Cawl."

Kenneth cursed.

Arabella was gone.

He had never held her. She was never by his side. Every touch, every scent, every image that had captured his heart had been a lie, a curse, a damnable vision that served only to drive him mad.

He stewed in anger. He vowed that he would no longer live his life in such abject misery. He refused to submit another day to the Viking savages. He refused to live as another man's slave.

Rage welled in his heart, and delirium gripped his soul. A plan formed in his maniacal mind—he would have his vengeance, and he would have it now. He would rush the prison wall in a screaming fury. He would rouse the sleeping Vikings from their peaceful slumber, and he would force them to contend with his wrath—even to the death.

He didn't care if he was reckless. He would be dangerous, very dangerous.

A restless strength surged in his limbs, and a fierce anger steeled his heart.

He lifted himself from the ground and stood. He saw nothing, considered nothing, loved nothing. His legs erupted below him, and he rushed the prison wall in a dash of madness.

His steps were quick but few. A tight tug locked his

feet, and his body hurled forward. The sudden impact of his face hitting the ground nearly broke his nose. He lifted his head, and blood trickled over his lips. He glared back at the shackles binding his ankles.

"Cawl ... Cawl ... Cawl." The large black bird leapt from its perch and stretched its wings in flight.

Kenneth watched as the creature rose effortlessly into the air. The bird flew high into the sky and disappeared beyond the tall pine trunks of the fortress wall.

Kenneth lay motionless on the ground. He slowly breathed in and out, and his mind replayed the vision that had graced his sleep moments before.

Then Kenneth made a silent promise to himself. A promise he intended to keep.

⑨

Coric had only moments to linger. He could not stay long. He had convinced Laise and Ronan of his plan, and the three young Scots were anxious—Perth was waiting. The plan was dangerous, but they had no choice. They had agreed they would depart without notice, and they would do so at once— yet not before Coric could be sure *she* was safe and secure.

Coric separated from his comrades on the path east to Perth, promising to rendezvous with them on the road ahead. He left Laise and Ronan to see Ceana.

Coric dismounted his horse two hundred yards from his home. He concealed himself behind a grove of yews. Separating the branches of the thick bushes, he gazed across the field. There she stood, alone in her garden. He watched his young wife as she tended the small patch of potatoes the two had planted in the spring. She seemed at peace in her work.

Her braids sat pinned behind her ears, keeping her curls from her eyes. Coric loved her sandy-brown hair. She dragged a hoe through the soil at her feet, working and turning the tender soil. He wanted to go to her. As a man, he desired to run to her and hold her and tell her that he was going, and that he would soon return. Yet as a warrior, he suppressed his desires. He knew he could not go to her and please her and then leave her again. She would be better off if she were left in her peace, or so he convinced himself.

The moments passed as he watched her.

She paused from her plowing and stood to rest.

Coric lowered his head.

She looked up at the sky and gazed for a long while.

Coric wondered of her thoughts. She was lovely. Maybe he could go to her?

She peered about the field, even pausing as she looked in his direction.

He stared back at her.

She never saw him.

She brushed back a tuft of hair that dangled across her cheek. She rested a moment longer and then returned to her chore.

Coric remained concealed. Going to her would only break her. She wouldn't understand. "I'll return soon, when all this has passed," he whispered to himself. Then he released his grip of the branches, and he left Ceana.

From the distance, he hadn't noticed that his wife's body was changing.

Had he known she carried their child, he may have gone to her.

Had he gone to her, he may have never left.

CHAPTER 10

ARABELLA'S GAZE REMAINED UPWARD. THE guard nodded and then disappeared behind the parapet atop the castle wall. Persuading him to grant her entrance had been more difficult than she had presumed. Yet at last, the castle doors would soon open and she would have the audience she desired.

Now alone in front of the two large wooden doors, Arabella's thoughts spiraled in her head. She wondered if Oengus knew of her Dalriadan father, Constantine, or of her Pict heritage. She wondered if he would be sympathetic to her lineage. She would have remained a Pict, had it not been for that awful day long ago. She thought of Constantine and Kenneth, the two men who had always accepted her and loved her most.

She refocused on the moment. Her lips moved in silence as she rehearsed her words.

The large castle doors slowly opened.

And she prayed for mercy.

"Arabella, did I get it right … it is Arabella?" Oengus greeted her with a welcoming smile as he entered the large dining hall.

Arabella startled and withdrew her hand from the glass vase displayed on the oversized dining table. She turned and found Oengus. "Yes my lord, it is Arabella."

"You may call me Oengus, Lord Oengus," he said and grinned with feigned regard. "How is it that I am graced by such a rare beauty on this fine day? What is it that the Scots wish from me?" Without awaiting a response, he continued, "And I am compelled to ask, who is it that sent you? I confess that they must be most foolish. Is it that they are foolish or simply blind? How can it be that they would allow such a lovely young lady to come all the way to Perth, alone, while the countryside is running mad with savages?" Oengus finished, and his eyes settled on Arabella.

"My lord, I have come of my own accord. My father, Constantine—"

"Constantine?" Oengus' head cocked upon hearing the name. "You are the daughter of Constantine … the adopted daughter? I am right to say 'adopted,' correct?"

"Yes, my lord. When I was a young girl I was—"

"A Pict. You were … you are, a Pict. I know very well of your father's quests through our lands, and how he *helped* a young girl in distress many years ago."

"I wouldn't be alive today if it were not for my father, Constantine," Arabella replied.

"You may not be alive tomorrow because of him," Oengus retorted, disallowing her striking looks to restrain his tongue. "These Viking animals obviously have a hatred for Scots. Traveling such distances alone in times like these is neither wise nor safe." Oengus strode slowly beside the dining table before stopping with only the four-foot-wide tabletop separating him from Arabella. He surveyed her figure and the features of her face and found himself bedazzled, his blood even warming in his body.

"I would travel twice the distance if need be. My coming to speak with you is of grave importance," Arabella said, hiding her trepidation. "You know of the Viking attack on Renton, yes?"

"I do."

"You know that they burned the village and took many captives, leaving few survivors?"

"I do."

"Do you know that Alpin, the one who leads the men of Renton, was not there to fight off the attack?"

Oengus chuckled at her words before stopping himself. "You believe Alpin alone could have stopped those men? They are animals … utter beasts!"

"Yes, he would have found a way to turn them back," Arabella replied.

"He would have died trying."

The Pict's cold, terse tone surprised Arabella. She turned from him and kept her tongue.

Oengus eyed her backside and found a certain pleasure in the awkward, lingering silence. A moment passed, and he quietly folded his arms across his chest with a purposed delay.

Arabella took a deep breath and tightly clutched the fabric of her blouse. Then she faced Oengus. "Some did die trying." Her eyes moistened. "Alpin lost a son in the attack. And I fear he may lose a second if help isn't found."

Oengus' eyebrows lifted in contemplation. "So, he lost a son. I am sorry to hear that. No father should have to endure such misery." He slowly stepped to the end of the table. "Did his son die during the raid?"

"His son, Aiden, was captured in the raid, along with his daughter, Nessa. Their brother, Kenneth, helped them escape. Nessa got away, but her brothers were recaptured. It was then that Aiden was killed and Kenneth was taken captive."

"Kenneth sounds like quite the hero … sorry to hear he got himself caught and his brother killed—"

"He didn't get his brother killed. The Vikings killed Aiden!"

"As you say, as you say," Oengus retreated. "Please have Alpin know that I regret to hear of his loss." Oengus' head tilted as he measured if his truce had been accepted.

"I can't tell Alpin these things. He's gone."

"Gone?" Oengus bluffed surprise. "Has he led the Scots to battle the Vikings?"

"No, he has taken his son, Coric, and two others to find Kenneth and the other captives."

"Well, I certainly hope he finds them," Oengus replied. "And your father, Constantine, did he go with Alpin?"

"No, he remains with the Scots in Renton, or what's left of Renton," Arabella said. "That is why I'm here."

"You are here to tell me your father is in Renton. Alright, I thank you for telling me this." Oengus smirked, amusing himself.

"No, please, you don't understand," Arabella insisted, struggling to regain ground. "I have come to Perth to ask of your aid. I have come to ask if you will fight with my father and the Scots. Together, the two armies can defeat the Vikings and keep them from destroying both our lands. I believe, with your help, our armies could find the Viking camp and rescue Kenneth and the others."

"You seem quite fond of this Kenneth. I take it you were close."

Arabella gazed at the floor, taking a moment to catch her breath. "Yes, I was, I am … we are close."

"So you came here to persuade me to save this Kenneth?" Oengus said. "You realize, I extended my mercy to Alpin, offering him to join me, and in return, I would protect his people. His prideful heart insisted otherwise. It was his own arrogance that brought this tragedy upon his family and his people. Now you want me to risk my men to save him and his son. Young lady, you are beautiful … but even your divine beauty cannot cast a spell strong enough for me to risk the lives of my men to save a fool such as Alpin."

"But my lord, you must."

"No. I will not!"

Arabella gasped. She clasped her hands together and fought to speak, "My lord, won't you reconsider? I will go to my father and convince him that pledging his sword to you will serve both Pict and Scot. My father will listen to me. He knows I have the interests of both in mind. We must come together to stop the Vikings."

"You think that your father would pledge fealty to the Pict throne? Alpin would disown and crucify him if he did such a thing."

"The men in Renton see strength in uniting. My father sees this too. I am certain I can convince him that it's our only choice."

Oengus gazed at Arabella—indeed, she was beautiful—then a thought entered his mind. "I must say, my head tires from these contrivances," he remarked. "The day has grown sufficiently long, and you will not be able to return to Renton by nightfall. Therefore, you shall stay the night here, in my castle. I will see that you are given a hot meal and a warm bed. You will be my guest. We will put aside our differences for the evening and will talk of this again in the morning." Without another word, Oengus snapped his fingers and signaled a servant, then he turned and sauntered from the dining hall.

"But my lord, time is growing short," Arabella called out as he departed.

He never looked back.

⊚

Gray morning clouds brought afternoon showers to the mountains of northwest Dalriada. Kenneth, Dorrell, Gavin, and a dozen others stood among the trees in the drizzling rain. The late summer showers cooled the men as they swung their heavy iron axes. The Scots were expected to fell six trees a day, lest they invite the whip of the Vikings. Six was doable if the thickness of the trunk measured two feet or less. For larger pines with wider girth, felling six was a more formidable task.

During the first weeks, Kenneth had struggled to drop three trees a day. Having worked the axe for some time since, he had learned the art of felling trees—the force of the axe, the angle of the cut, the rhythm of the swing. He was now dropping six to seven a day.

The other men were matching Kenneth's pace, including Gavin, but Dorrell's ability far exceeded them all. Standing three to four inches above his brethren and boasting long, muscular arms and hands that could likely crush a man's skull, Dorrell was built to swing the axe. Though revered for his strength, it was his skill with the axe that set him apart.

He wielded the device like an artisan wielding a sculpting tool. With crafted cuts and powerful blows, his axe easily devoured the tender meat of the white pines. He readily cut two trees for each tree cut by another. On one particular day, he dropped fifteen trees—no other man had dropped more than nine.

The rugged work of harvesting timber became an outlet for the men, an escape, a task to hold their focus, a task to keep them sane. Kenneth found himself favoring the time in the forest, wielding the axe and dropping the trees. It cleared his mind of the miseries of the prison. Too often, the nights within the fort were filled with inedible food and an endless barrage of Vikings mocking, jeering, and fighting one another—or a captive if they were inclined for such sport. But it was not the meager food, or the mocking, or even the threat of whips on his backside that Kenneth dreaded most, but rather it was his dreams of Arabella. Dreams of holding her and loving her, only to have her vanish—these were the dreams that plagued him most. In sleep, he found not rest but simply bitterness.

Often, when waking at night, Kenneth would plead to God for freedom. He would beg God to send his father and an army of ten thousand Scots to crush his captors. The endless nights and days dragged on, but no sign of mercy appeared. Instead, the captives were visited each morning by their cruel and ruthless captor, Halfdan. Before sunrise, Halfdan would walk beside the prison pen with Kodran and Jorund not far behind. He would point at the men who appeared weak or frail and consign them to quarry duty. The other captives, those strong enough to swing an axe, were assigned to cut timber. If a captive appeared exceptionally frail, Halfdan would point to the man and yell something to his men in the Norse tongue. Kenneth noticed that on those mornings, the man would not return to the prison at night. The meals were also served with a ration of meat on those nights. Kenneth never ate on those nights.

It was on such nights that Kenneth found his struggles inescapable. He wrestled with himself and with God. As a young boy, he'd had a great zeal for life and the world, but now that he was older, he saw things not as a boy, but as a man. There were days when he despised life and held a deep hatred in his heart—for the world and even for life itself. Thoughts of Arabella gave hope, yet it was a dwindling hope, chipped away with each passing day. Memories of her brought sweetness for a time, but as the days passed, so did the fondness of his memories.

Kenneth hated his enemy. He hated the injustice of life— that one man could take so much from another.

⟡

Arabella woke and opened her eyes. The morning sunshine beamed through the small square window of her castle bedroom. Specks of dust gently drifted in the bright glow of the sun's light as it formed an elongated rectangle on the opposing wall. The walls of stone had appeared so ominous in the night, yet now they seemed less threatening in the light of the sun.

Arabella's spirit lifted in the warmth of the glow. She rose from her bed and crossed the room to a small wooden table. There she poured a cup of water from a tarnished pitcher on the table. As she set down the pitcher, her reflection emerged on its round metal contour, catching her eye and giving her pause. She examined herself, frowned, and pulled back her hair, combing it with her fingers and pushing it over her shoulder.

Arabella finished her water and returned to her bed. She thought of the prior evening and Oengus' reaction to her request. She was hopeful that the night's sleep had persuaded him to reconsider. For several moments she lost herself in a collage of distant thoughts, envisioning Kenneth's rescue and him holding her again. She suddenly snapped from her trance, and she stood and tidied her blouse. She approached the door and grasped its heavy iron latch. Lifting the latch, she cracked the door and peered into the hallway. It was empty. She stepped from the room and quietly closed the door behind her.

Stepping through the windowless, torch-lit halls, she rounded two corners. Once passing the second corner, her ears caught the faint sound of clanging swords. She quickened her pace and the sound grew louder, echoing through the maze of stone halls. Her mind said *run,* but her heart said *go—go forward.*

She moved forward.

Following the sounds of the clashing swords, Arabella found her way to a connecting hall. To the right, the hallway extended thirty feet with mounted torches spaced along the walls. To the left, the hallway was shorter, and its end was aglow with sunlight.

She turned left. And the clanging grew louder.

At its end, the hallway connected to an open walkway encircling a courtyard below. Arabella peeked over the waist-high wall and looked down. The large square courtyard marking the castle center opened to the wide sky above. Green grass covered the grounds from end to end with a single stone path sectioning the yard in two.

Stepping closer to the wall, Arabella took in the full expanse of the yard—and the company of men brandishing swords and shields.

A voice suddenly shouted below, and the men charged one another in a sort of mock battle engagement. Swords swung, shields raised, metal clanged. Arabella gawked and studied the violent rehearsal of the combatants.

"Do you enjoy watching the men spar? It can be quite sporting at times," Oengus uttered.

"Oh, I didn't know you were there!"

"Well, I hope that you're alright with my being here … after all, it is my castle."

"Oh, yes, it was just that I was watching the … well, I heard noises and I thought … I thought I heard men fighting."

"They are not fighting, they are training to fight. You see, to be a warrior, one must train." Oengus gazed at the men below. "They must gain the skill and confidence required for battle. A man who has not swung a sword before battle is a man who will die holding it when faced with battle." Oengus grinned as he spoke. "This exercise is required for my men. When the day of battle arrives, they will be ready."

"Ready to fight the Vikings?" Arabella asked.

"Ready to fight the enemy," Oengus replied as his eyes took in her womanly form. "Enough of the men, how did you sleep … restfully, I presume?"

"Yes. Yes, I slept well," Arabella replied.

"How is it that you can sleep through the night so restfully and wake to appear so beautiful, as if you never slept at all?"

Arabella acknowledged the comment with a smile, then

coyly turned and peered down at the men as if intrigued by the training.

Oengus gazed at the courtyard and watched alongside, sidling close to her.

It was then that Arabella took notice of a particular man suited with bandages. "What happened to that one?" she asked and pointed. "There, the one with his face and neck bandaged? He is hardly able to swing his sword."

"That young man? He had an accident while helping to douse a fire. He is recovering well." Oengus placed his hand on Arabella's shoulder. "Come, let us leave the men to their sparring and see if our breakfast awaits us."

Arabella glanced back at the young man. Something about him seemed familiar—

"Come, our breakfast grows cold," Oengus insisted.

The bandaged warrior below glanced up at the walkway as the two turned to leave. He caught a glimpse of Oengus and the young woman. The woman seemed pretty, from what he saw of her long brown hair. He had not seen such a woman before inside the castle. Her hair reminded him of someone he knew, someone he knew well.

It couldn't be, he thought.

CHAPTER 11

UNDER A MOONLESS PICTLAND SKY, THREE
young Scots floated across Perth's north river. The water was
cold and the night was black. The river cut through a rocky,
sloped gorge rising from either bank. Boulders, lying one on
top of another, formed the gorge's steep, jagged slopes. The
large rocks extended from the base of the gorge to its crest,
forming a torturous, labyrinth-like maze up the slope and
rendering any route or passageway nearly impassable. The
simplest means of crossing the river along the rear side of
the Pict castle was the north bridge. But the simplest means
wasn't necessarily the safest. The Pict guards ensured as
much.

Positioned at the rear of the castle, the north bridge
spanned the river and the gorge below. The bridge was
seldom used, even by those residing in Perth. Its primary use
was for the disposal of refuse from the castle. The north river
and its gorge were natural deterrents for would-be foes, and
the rugged terrain of the rocky forest beyond the river made
common travel unsuitable. Because the natural defenses of
the surroundings provided sufficient protection, only a small
contingent of guards was required to hold the bridge.

The gorge was not the only challenge in approaching

the castle from the rear. At the top of the gorge lay a lengthy hillside that stretched from the gorge crest to the castle wall. The hillside offered no boulders, no trees, no structures to hide behind, only an open, barren slope. Beyond the slope stood the Pict castle, lording over the hillside with a single wooden door framed into its isolated north wall. The door was the single means of entrance along the wall—and it was usually guarded, especially at night.

From deep in the darkness of the gorge, Coric crept from the river, his soaked black outfit dripping with water as he emerged. He hastily concealed himself behind a large rock along the riverbank, then he lifted his head and peered up at the bridge spanning high above. The dull hue of the sparsely placed torches lit the long wooden bridge just enough for Coric to catch sight of two guards, who by appearances were oblivious to any threat of intrusion. Coric glanced back at Laise and Ronan. "Come on."

"Wait a moment. Ronan's foot is wedged in the rocks," Laise replied, as he rose from the water and pulled at his wet clothes. "This garb you had us wear sticks to my thighs, especially now that it is soaking wet. I hope it's worth it," Laise muttered. "I would have preferred my kilt."

"I'll take note of that," Coric remarked, looking down at his own feet and trying to find a footing. Then he heard a rock tumble and glanced over his shoulder.

"Ronan! You have to keep quiet," Coric whispered loudly. He peered back at the bridge and scanned its length, yet he saw no movement from the guards. Coric gained a footing and began his ascent up the rocky slope of the gorge.

Ronan stared at Coric's backside with a frustrated expression on his face. He rolled his eyes and moved forward to catch the two. When he reached Laise, he glanced back across the river at the elevated tree line. "Laise, are you sure the horses are secure?"

"Yes, Ronan, as I told you the last time you asked. Now, stop asking!"

Coric moved slowly up the gorge in the darkness. Maneuvering the rocky crags along the slope proved difficult, if not outright exhausting. A slippery algae film glazed the gorge's stones, and the nooks between them formed a natural wedge where a simple misstep would likely yield a broken ankle.

Coric steadied his pace and eased upward, frequently scanning the bridge and the small guardhouse at its far end. Keeping track of the guards would not be easy with only six torches lighting the eighty-foot expanse—two torches at each end of the bridge and two more in the center.

After negotiating the gorge and nearing its top, Coric drew close enough to spy the north wall of the castle. The stone monolith sat prominently on the crest of the hill. Coric took a moment to catch his breath as he gazed at the sight. Though the late summer nights had grown cooler, the climb had made him warm. Perspiration further moistened his already wet clothes and seeped into the black wraps that covered his neck and brow.

Coric moved ahead until eventually reaching the top of the rocky slope. Once there, he hid behind a large jagged boulder and peered around its side. Stooping in a crouch, he surveilled the castle and spotted two Picts guarding the lone door of the north wall. The enormity of the giant stone structure dwarfed the tiny wooden door. Coric slowly swept his gaze across the open landscape of the hillside, searching for more guards. He saw none.

When Laise and Ronan reached the top of the gorge, Coric waved his hand and signaled them. "Two guards," he said, holding up his fingers, hoping they could see.

He waited as they approached.

"Glad you could make it," Coric said. Laise glanced at Ronan and shook his head. Then the threesome took turns peering past the boulder at the large Pict castle. The two castle guards remained on watch beside the lone door with a single torch mounted above them. Under the glow of the torch, the guards' shadows stretched down the length of the hillside, forming dark giants in the night. Though only two, their shadowy presence was foreboding.

"Can you reach them, Laise?" Coric asked, hiding any sign of trepidation—if he had any.

The tall Scot smiled.

"Can you get them both?" he asked again.

"Not with the same arrow," Laise said and his grin widened.

"It's nice to know you're having a good time," Coric replied.

"He's not the one charging the castle," Ronan quipped.

Coric glanced at the bridge and pointed. "Looks like two more are standing guard at the far end of the bridge … but it's hard to tell."

"I know I saw three when I left the horses and marked the path. They were talking," Laise said. "I'm not sure where the other one is. Maybe he's in the guardhouse."

"Or probably taking a crap," Ronan said with a snicker.

"Alright, enough!" Coric replied. "We know the plan. Laise, after you drop the guards at the door, we wait. If the guards on the bridge don't notice and no one comes from the castle, then Ronan and I will head up the hill. Once we're at the door and in the castle, you'll have to take out the guards on the bridge and then get the horses."

Coric waited for a response.

"Right!" he insisted.

"Yes, we know the plan," Ronan groused.

"Well, I want to make sure. I don't intend to die here tonight, so I want to be certain." Coric glanced back and forth between the two, and his mind retraced to where he'd left off. "Once in the castle, Ronan and I are going to find Oengus—"

"That's the part I'm not sure about," Laise said. "That could take all night, and we don't have all night."

"We know his quarters are on the east side, and he'll have a guard outside his room. That's the room we'll look for," Coric replied. "We'll be quick, just have the horses waiting when we get out."

"Sure, no problem," Laise said. "I'll shoot the guards, stroll across the bridge, get the horses, and wait patiently until you two come out. Got it."

"I know this won't be simple, but we have to—"

"Coric—I've got it! I'll have the horses … you two just get out alive, alright?" Laise said, working to keep his wits.

The three nodded in unison.

Coric and Ronan peered back up the hill at the guards beside the door and prepared to move.

Laise extracted his longbow from the scabbard on his back. He attached its string to one end and placed the seated end on the ground. Then, leaning into the bow, he compressed it and seated the other end of the string. He lifted the bow and plucked its string like a skilled musician testing for tautness. Satisfied, he reached over his shoulder and pulled two arrows from his quiver. He turned to Coric. "Are you ready?" he asked.

"Ready," Coric said.

"Ready," Ronan added.

Laise paused, waiting for the breeze to settle. All was silent in the darkness, save the dull rush of the current passing below and the breathing of the three anxious Scots.

The wind died. It was time.

Laise set an arrow in his string and eyed his prey. Holding his breath, he aimed the bow. "I'm going for the one on the left," he uttered. "The one on the right looks to be asleep."

Coric and Ronan stared at the guards, waiting for the *twang* of the recoiling bowstring.

Twang … thump.

Even across the distance, the three could hear the arrow's impact as it hit the guard's chest. They watched the man stagger and collapse. His giant shadow shrunk up the hillside and was gone.

The second guard abruptly turned to his fallen comrade. *Twang.* A second arrow flew. *Thump.* The man released a cry of pain as the arrow drove deep into his shoulder.

Coric's head swiveled toward the bridge. The guards on the bridge were staring up the hill at the castle. "Laise, take the two on the bridge, I've got the one on the hill," Coric exclaimed.

Coric never looked back. He broke into a sprint and charged the hill as if launched from a catapult. Ronan quickly followed.

The wounded guard staggered to the castle door and pounded with his fist.

The guards on the bridge dashed across the eighty-foot wooden span. One held a crossbow. Both sported swords. Reaching the end of the bridge, the Picts spotted the two Scots rushing the hill. The guard with the bow stopped and cocked his weapon while the other stormed forward in pursuit.

The crossbowman lifted his weapon and aimed his arrow at Ronan's back. But it was another arrow, a long arrow, that flew first. Laise's long arrow soared toward the bridge and clipped the crossbowman's side. The man let out a yelp and stumbled forward. Another arrow followed, and the man was finished.

The guard at the castle continued to pound the wooden door. Coric advanced toward the man, leaping up the hill with long strides and knife in hand. Suddenly, a frightening image flashed through his mind—an image of an army of Picts standing behind the door, preparing to descend upon him.

Coric never slowed.

He tightened his grip on his knife. It begged for release. He would need to make it count. He waited and closed the distance. Then he raised his hand with his blade perched between his forefinger and thumb, and he flung the weapon forward. The knife spun end over end through the air and sunk into the base of the man's skull. The pounding stopped, and the man's body slumped to the ground.

Coric and Ronan reached the door, waiting for it to

open—expecting it to open. Then they heard footsteps ascending the slope behind them.

The sprinting guard raced up the hill with sword drawn. Laise steadied his aim and tracked his target.

The guard neared the Scots and lifted his sword.

Laise released his draw. The arrow swooped along the hillside like a bird of prey and nested in the guard's backside, piercing his left lung.

The guard tumbled backwards down the slope, his body flipping over and over until it came to rest twenty feet from the bridge. The man was dead.

Laise stepped from his hidden lair and moved through the darkness toward the two dead Picts at the foot of the bridge, never noticing the movement at the opposite end of the bridge.

Coric and Ronan paced outside the door, watching and waiting—swords drawn and hearts pounding.

The door never opened.

"Do you see that?" Ronan asked.

"See what?" Coric said.

"The door has no handle," Ronan said. "It only opens from the inside."

They stepped to the door. There was no handle, no latch, nothing but the rectangular slab of the wooden door.

"Do we knock?" Ronan groused sarcastically. "Or do we wait for the guards to invite us in?"

"Can you save the humor for later?" Coric said with a grimace before turning to scan the door. "Well, I know this, we aren't waiting. We have to get in there now." He stepped to the door and pressed his hands against it, then he gave a hard push.

"You're not going to run at it?" Ronan said, not sure if he was asking Coric or telling him. "Coric, you can't run through the door."

"I'm not going to run through it … give me a moment to think." Coric knelt beside the guard he'd slain, and he removed his knife, wiped the blade, and returned it to his belt. "No wonder he kept pounding … he couldn't get in," he muttered to Ronan. He lifted from his stoop and approached the door. Sizing the door a second time, Coric pushed on its sides, then the top, then the bottom. He pulled his knife from his belt and wedged the blade into the jam. "I wonder …," he said aloud without finishing.

Laise removed his arrow from the first of the fallen Picts. The shaft was cracked and the arrow was worthless. He broke off the tip, discarded the shaft, and placed the tip in his quiver. Then he walked to his other victim and retrieved a second arrow. He inspected the shaft—straight, still good. After returning the arrow to his quiver, he glanced to the far end of the bridge and then turned to view the hillside. Instantly, his head spun back to the bridge. His eyes had nearly missed a small detail at first glance—a single torch remained in its mount on the far side of the bridge, but the second torch mount was now empty. He scanned the two guards on the ground beside him. Neither held a torch.

Laise seated an arrow in the string of his bow. At this range, he would have preferred his short bow, but his longbow would have to do.

Click. From the outside, Coric lifted the latch on the

inside of the door. He removed his knife from the jam and eased the door open with a gentle push. Grabbing the torch mounted beside the door, Coric crept across the threshold and poked his head into the entryway. He met no resistance, save the deep darkness of the castle hallway. He extended the torch at arm's length and his eyes combed the hall, tracing the array of rectangular stones forming its walls. He glanced back at Ronan, "Follow me." The two stepped inside and disappeared into the bowels of the Pict castle.

The first room they reached had a large opening extending from floor to ceiling, but no door. Coric held the torch inside the entry and the dark room brightened. It appeared to be a sort of storage area, or armory, for the guards. A dozen crossbows lined the back wall and several shields and quivers sat on the floor below the bows. Along the adjacent wall, roughly thirty swords stood aligned in a row within a wooden rack, their blades worn and scarred.

"Grab a bow," Coric whispered.

Ronan stepped to the back wall and grabbed a crossbow and a quiver of arrows. Then he followed Coric out of the room and down a long corridor. Several perpendicular halls intersected the corridor as the two pressed deeper into the castle. Its black rock walls were dimly lit with distantly spaced torches mounted six-feet high. The flickering flames filled the walls with dancing shadows as the two crept forward.

"Coric, how are we going to locate Oengus in this maze?"

"I don't know, but let's keep moving until we find something. Follow me and keep quiet."

The two shuffled down the corridor, keeping their steps silent and swift.

"We should look for a bright hallway," Ronan said. "I'd guess Oengus keeps his end of the castle well lit."

"Sssshhh!" Coric whispered, turning to Ronan with a finger over this mouth. Then his hand shot upward and he motioned to Ronan to halt as the two reached another intersecting corridor. Coric peered around the corner and his eyes bulged through the black wrap that covered his cheeks and brow. He pointed down the shadowy hallway and shifted his body to allow Ronan to see.

Within the hallway, a large candle sat mounted outside a door, shining its light down upon a sleeping guard. The guard sat on a stool next to the door with his back pressed against the wall and his chin bent to his chest. He showed no movement, except the slow cadence of his chest rising and falling as he breathed. On the far side of the guard, a dull glow emanated from a square opening framed shoulder-high in the door.

Coric handed his torch to Ronan. "I'm going down there," he whispered. He gripped his knife tight in his fist, then eased down the length of the hall until he reached the guard. A quick inspection of the Pict confirmed that he was sound asleep.

Coric stepped past the guard and peeked through the square opening in the door, then he quickly ducked his head. He glanced back at Ronan and shot a puzzled glare before lifting to peek again. Again, he ducked then paused for a moment. After double checking the guard, he shuffled back to Ronan.

"What'd you see?" Ronan asked.

"A girl!"

"Did she see you?" Ronan whispered.

"No."

"Was she pretty?" Ronan asked.

"I don't know."

"Well, was she?"

"I couldn't tell—she was sleeping!"

"Are you sure?"

"Yes, I'm sure … now shut up! We've got to find Oengus."

Laise eased slowly along the bridge past the center-mounted torches, his longbow drawn and ready. He eyed the lone torch fluttering in the breeze at the far end of the bridge, then his focus moved past the torch toward the forest. Searching for movement, he saw none, except the slight sway of the tree branches. He quieted. The night hum of the forest and the passing water below were the only sounds. He glanced over his shoulder at the castle, hopeful the two were coming.

Nothing.

He took another step toward the far end of the bridge.

His forearm shook under the draw of his flexed bow. Slowly, he released his pull and allowed the tension to ease from the weapon. As his muscles recovered, he replayed the plan is his mind: *Cross the bridge, get to the forest, and retrieve the horses … but where is the third guard?*

An owl hooted in the woods and Laise stopped. He lingered a moment then crept forward. His shadow stretched in front of him as he stepped along the wooden planks. Then something caught his eye. Something like the figure of a man appeared to be leaning against the far post of the bridge, but the figure wasn't moving. The dull light of the lone torch made it difficult to tell what his eyes were seeing. Laise leaned into his bow, drew back the string, and leveled his weapon. He stepped forward, and the plank below his foot released a loud creak. He stopped.

The figure didn't move.

He stepped again.

As he drew closer to the man-like figure, its form grew more discernible. It was not a man but rather a bucket hooked on a tall wooden stand, apparently water for the guards.

Laise inched ahead and the bridge creaked again. He stilled and gazed into the darkness.

Suddenly, a shadow appeared from behind the guardhouse. Then a guard burst from the darkness, running with a torch lofted above his head and yelling a battle cry. The man rushed forward, undaunted—and he was heading straight toward the hanging bucket.

That's not water in the bucket! The realization hit Laise like a punch to the gut. *It's oil for the torches! One touch of that torch and flames will shoot high enough for all Perth to see!*

Laise released his arrow. It soared through the night air and planted itself below the guard's right clavicle. The torch dropped from the man's hand, and he fell forward. In his descent to the ground, the guard's head slammed into the bucket stand. The stand responded with a rocking, teetering motion, slopping its oil down the side of the hanging bucket. As the guard landed, the swaying stand gave way and toppled over with the bucket crashing beside it. In moments the overturned bucket emptied its content onto the bridge. The black goo slowly oozed over the planks and seeped into the wood.

Laise lowered his bow and raced past the unconscious

guard and the empty bucket. He headed into the darkness of the forest and disappeared—time was burning away.

"This could be it," Coric said. The glow of the intersecting hall ahead appeared brighter than the other halls.

"Do you think Oengus is down there?" Ronan whispered.

"We're about to find out."

The two inched closer to the brightly lit corridor. Coric eased his head past the corner and peered down the hall. A large Pict guard stood beside the lone door in the hallway. The man held a five-foot polearm glaive with a twelve-inch blade that shimmered in the bright hall light. The guard was statuesque, gripping his glaive with both hands as if propping himself up.

Coric studied the Pict and prayed he was asleep. He leaned toward Ronan and lifted his index finger to signal a single guard. Then he pointed at the crossbow and gestured for Ronan to shoot the man.

Coric pressed his body against the wall and let Ronan pass.

Ronan stepped forward and leaned around the corner. He raised the bow and took aim. Easing his finger through the trigger, the arrow released. It flew down the hall like a silent dart and struck the guard square in the neck.

The big man dropped to his knees, sputtering and gagging.

Coric and Ronan rushed forward. When Coric reached the guard, he delivered an angry kick to the man's chin. The Pict's teeth chomped together, and his body spun and collapsed to the floor, motionless.

Coric turned to the door. There was no square opening

as before, but only a heavy iron latch. He pressed the latch. It didn't move.

"You'll need this," Ronan said, kneeling beside the guard. He tossed Coric a key.

Coric inserted the key into the lock and gave it a turn. The bolt unlatched. Coric raised his hand to his face and pulled his black wrap over his cheeks and nose. Satisfied, he reached to his belt and checked for his knife.

He glanced at Ronan and nodded, then he slung the door open.

The man in the bed stirred.

Coric stormed toward the bed and held his torch aloft. The man was still sleeping—and the man was Oengus. His graying hair was matted and disheveled, and the wrinkles around his eyes were thick and distinct. He turned in the bed and reached for a blanket that covered his midsection.

Ronan moved to the foot of the bed and reloaded the crossbow before lowering it from sight.

Coric nodded to Ronan and then shook Oengus. "My lord, I have news. I have news!"

Oengus fought to lift from his slumber. His head rose from his pillow, and he gazed up at the man in black.

"I have news. We have killed Alpin of Dalriada!" Coric said, attempting to mimic the Pict accent. "As you have asked, he's dead!"

"What, what are you saying?" Oengus replied, shaking his head to dispel the fog of sleep. "What are you doing here, where is my guard?" he demanded. "Guard!" Oengus called to the hallway.

Ronan began to lift the bow.

Coric glanced in his direction and shook his head, *no*.

Ronan lowered the bow.

Coric glimpsed an empty torch mount on the wall beside the Pict lord's bed. He deposited his torch into the mount, then he turned and gazed down at Oengus. "We've come to tell you the news of Alpin. You wanted the news, yes?"

"Of course I wanted the news, but not at this hour, you fool!" Oengus rubbed his face. "Guard!" Oengus called again. He set his feet on the floor and lifted from the bed. He had expected Coric to move, and a puzzled expression appeared on his face when Coric didn't.

Coric shoved his hand against Oengus' chest and pushed the Pict lord back to the bed. In a blink, Coric's knife lay pressed against Oengus' throat. "So it's true! You wanted Alpin dead. *You* sent the men clothed in black." Coric pulled down his black wrap to reveal his face.

Oengus' eyes burned as he studied the features of the young Scot. The resemblance was uncanny—it was though he was staring at Alpin, thirty years younger. "The son of Alpin," Oengus sneered.

"You were behind this, weren't you?" Coric exclaimed. "It was you! You sent the men who tried to kill us." He locked eyes with Oengus as his knife pulsed in his grip, ready to sever flesh.

Oengus slowly lifted his hands in front of his chest as if to stay his executioner.

At the same moment, Ronan lifted his crossbow and pointed it at Oengus.

Oengus glared at Ronan and then back at Coric, gaping at the two with the maniacal gaze of a caged animal. "I knew the Britons were after your father! And yes, I admit, I would not stop them if their intent was to put an end to his madness!"

"*His* madness! This is *your* madness!"

"It was the Britons—"

"Shut your mouth!" Coric yelled. "It was your men, in these black wraps. Their painted arms prove it."

"Mercenaries," Oengus said. "They were someone else's mercen—"

Slap! The sound echoed in the room as Coric's hand landed hard against the Pict lord's face. "Your lies will be your end, old man!"

Oengus glared at Coric as he lifted his hand to wipe the blood from his lip.

"Tell me what I want to hear. I know you were behind the men hunting me and my father. It was your men. You gave the orders to kill my father!"

Oengus offered no response.

"You were also behind the Viking raid on Renton, weren't you? Weren't you!"

Ronan aimed his bow at Oengus' head.

Oengus held his tongue.

"Where are they? Where are my people?" Coric demanded.

"Your people? I don't know what you are talking about."

"Yes you do, you've conspired with the Vikings. You had them raid Renton. You carried out your threats against my father. You'll regret the day you gave the order. Now I am going to ask you again, where are they?"

"I do not know!"

The butt of Coric's knife swung swiftly, and Oengus never saw it coming. The blow to the temple knocked Oengus from the bed to the floor.

Oengus reeled in pain. He shook his head, wincing and gasping for breath. Sweat formed on his brow, and his heart thumped in his chest. He blinked his eyes rapidly and then widened them to focus.

Coric grabbed the crossbow from Ronan and stepped to Oengus and kicked him in the gut. Oengus doubled over, and Coric pointed the bow at the Pict lord as he groveled on the floor at Coric's feet. "You know where they are, now tell me!"

Oengus slowly rose to his knees and lifted his head. The razor tip of Coric's arrow hung inches from his eyes. Oengus stared past the silver arrowhead and up the bow to the young man holding its trigger. Oengus then realized that he wasn't sure if Alpin truly was dead or alive—and if Alpin was dead, the young Scot had little to lose. "I do not have your people. The Vikings do. Is your father dead?"

The question surprised Coric. He turned to Ronan, who was now standing guard at the door. His eyes swung back to Oengus. "Do not speak of my father. I want to know about my people. Where have the Vikings taken them?"

"I only know what my scouts have told me," Oengus said.

"Then tell me what you know!"

"I have been told that they are far to the west."

"Coric, we've got little time," Ronan interjected from the doorway.

Coric peered at Ronan.

Ronan glanced down the hall, then motioned with his eyes for Coric to hurry.

"Where in the west, Oengus?" Coric insisted, spitting as he spoke.

"I don't know."

"You're lying!" Coric yelled. He moved the tip of the bow to Oengus' leg and pressed it against his thigh. "I swear to

Almighty God, I will release this arrow into your leg—as you did to my father!" He jammed the arrow tip into the meat of Oengus' thigh. "Now tell me where my people are!"

Oengus released a loud groan. "My scouts report that they are far west of Loch Lomond, toward Ardmucknish Bay, near the Inverawe Woods. Now leave me!" Oengus gasped.

"Coric, I hear someone coming. Let's go," Ronan said.

Coric glared at Oengus. The thought of killing him entered Coric's mind—he was angry enough to start a fight, but smart enough to avoid a war, at least at this moment. "You better pray I find them!" Coric said, and he ground the sharp metal tip farther into Oengus' leg. "I do not fear you, old man, or your painted soldiers … and this is for my father!" Coric raised the bow and slammed the head of the arrow deep into the Pict lord's thigh.

Metal pierced muscle. Oengus howled in pain.

Coric withdrew the bow and its bloody arrowhead, then darted out the door only moments behind Ronan.

Oengus collapsed to the stone floor, wailing and gripping his leg. "Damn you, Scot! Damn you and your father," Oengus yelled as the two Scots vanished down the hall.

Coric rushed down the corridor trailing Ronan, the footsteps of approaching men echoed behind him. When he reached the corner, he glanced back. Three guards rounded the corner at the opposite end of the long hall. Coric wondered if they saw him, yet he didn't wait to find out.

He turned the corner and ran as fast as his feet would carry him.

"We must hurry!" Ronan said, reaching a second corner. He turned and disappeared.

Coric rounded the corner and flew forward to catch up with Ronan. Passing by one torch after another, the pathway down the corridor began to look familiar, but at the same time the pathways in every direction looked familiar. The two slowed to a jog, not completely certain they were moving in the right direction.

As they neared an intersection of hallways, a sudden shadow appeared from the adjacent hall. Then a Pict guard materialized and filled the intersection. The guard flinched when seeing the Scots, and a woman behind the guard screamed. Ronan shoved the man, and the guard lost his balance and stumbled backward, crashing into the woman and sending them both to the stone floor.

The woman's screams echoed through the maze of hallways as Coric and Ronan sprinted ahead.

Elsewhere in the castle, Aiden stirred and rose from his bed. Several guards rushed past his doorway. He grabbed his sword and quickly followed. He tried to run, but the lingering sting of his burns slowed his pace. Determined, and curious, he ignored the pain and pressed ahead.

When Aiden arrived at Oengus' room, he found the Pict lord's quarters lined with guards. The men had surrounded their leader and were helping him to his feet.

"Are you alright, my lord?" Aiden heard a guard ask.

"Do I look alright? Get Mathe!" Oengus ordered the man and then he turned to the other guards. "You three! There are two men dressed in black. Find them! I want them caught—dead or alive!"

"Yes, my lord!" the response came, and the guards hustled from the room.

Aiden watched as Oengus hobbled to his bed and began wrapping a sheet around his bloody thigh.

Ronan and Coric raced down the long hallway. Ahead, the hall ended and turned a corner.

"This is it!" Ronan called, recognizing his whereabouts. "The weapon room is ahead to the right, and so is the way out of here."

Ronan reached the corner—and froze in his tracks.

At the end of the connecting hall, a single Pict guard stood at the threshold of the castle doorway. The man was waiting for the Scots. He stood ten paces away and was the only thing standing between Ronan and his freedom.

Aiden stepped into Oengus' quarters, gazing at the Pict lord as he feverishly tended his leg. "Who were these men?" Aiden asked.

Oengus' eyes shot upward. When he saw Aiden, he paused and glared at him. "The men who attacked me were savages. They were mercenaries, sent by the Vikings. They have killed your father, and now they've tried to kill me!"

"If they are the men who killed my father, then you won't need your guards. I'll hunt them down and kill them myself!" Aiden declared and departed in a blur.

Coric closed on Ronan. As Coric reached the corner, he showed no signs of slowing. He raised his crossbow and rounded the corner. Flying past Ronan, he sighted the guard in the doorway and pulled the trigger. The arrow shot from the bow and ripped through the Pict's sternum. Coric charged forward, lowered his shoulder, and struck the waning guard. The man tumbled backwards, and Coric broke into the dark night.

Coric slowed to a stop and regained his balance. He peered back through the doorway at Ronan, still standing in the dimly lit hall. Coric lifted his black wrap over his nose. "Are you coming?"

Ronan hurried to the door. He bent down, grabbed the sword from the fallen Pict, and followed Coric down the hill.

Laise held the reigns of his horse in one hand and the leads of Coric's and Ronan's horses in the other. Traversing the forest, he kept the two horses in tow. When he reached the clearing, he was fifty yards from the bridge. The guard at the foot of the bridge lay where he had fallen, face down and unmoving.

Laise peered across the gorge and up the hill at the castle. The open door of the castle still held a dull glow emanating from its inner hall, but the doorway was empty. His eyes quickly moved along the length of the bridge. The torches continued to burn, but the bridge was empty.

Suddenly, the glow in the castle doorway grew brighter. Voices echoed in the distance, and Laise squinted to scan the dark hillside. Two figures were descending the hill, and in the same moment, three figures burst from the castle door.

Coric and Ronan were halfway down the hill when an arrow from a Pict crossbow nicked Ronan's leg. Ronan stumbled and dropped to a knee.

Coric turned to help his friend.

Another arrow came and flew past the two.

"You alright?" Coric asked, lifting Ronan to his feet.

Ronan felt his leg. "Yeah, I'm okay. It's not bad."

Coric glanced up the hill. The three guards were closing in, and a fourth appeared in the castle doorway.

Laise watched as one figure on the hill dropped and the second turned to help. Jerking his reigns, he rode for the bridge, bringing the other two horses behind him.

When Coric and Ronan reached the base of the hill, they were thirty yards from the bridge. The pursuing Picts were close behind and coming fast.

Coric turned to engage the Picts. He then realized his crossbow was empty, and he tossed it aside and drew his knife.

Ronan turned beside him and gripped his newfound sword with both hands.

The first guard sized Coric and then charged, swinging his blade at Coric's head.

The second guard eyed Ronan. He raised his sword and inched forward.

As the first Pict came at Coric, Coric dodged sideways. Then he lifted, spun on his heels, and shoved his knife into the guard's back. He removed the blade, and the guard fell. The third guard stood ten feet away, glaring at Coric and ready to attack.

Ronan swung his sword at the second guard. Their swords made a loud clang as the two blades met. They volleyed back and forth, lunging and blocking, striking metal on metal.

Coric stepped toward the third guard. The two moved in a half-circle, measuring one another from head to toe. Hoofbeats approached, but neither man turned—it was the guard's last mistake. The weight of the giant animal knocked the man off his feet. The horse plowed ahead and trampled the Pict as Laise spurred the beast and snuffed the life from his enemy.

The second Pict, contesting Ronan, heard the wail of his comrade and turned to glimpse the horse. Ronan saw his opening, and he lunged forward and buried his blade in the man's chest.

"Mount up—we've got to go!" Laise yelled, turning his steed toward the bridge where he had left the other horses.

Ronan ran to his horse and mounted the animal.

Coric gazed over the three dead men. In the darkness, he caught sight of a fourth figure at the foot of the hill charging toward him, not twenty feet away.

Bloodthirsty and vengeful, Coric sprinted toward the figure. The two collided at top speed, and Coric's larger, heavier mass toppled the man, knocking him to his backside.

The man let out a bellowing groan as his body hit the ground with a thud. He slowly rolled sideways and gripped his shoulder in pain.

Coric regained his footing and stared down at the man. He gazed at the bandages that wrapped the man's cheek and neck and extended below his shirt.

"Let's go! Now!" Laise yelled again.

Coric glanced at Laise and hesitated.

"More will be coming, let's go!" Laise repeated.

Coric left the man and sprinted to his horse. He mounted and stared back at his foe. "Not tonight, but your time is coming too, Pict!" Coric yelled. The three turned their horses and rode onto the bridge.

Aiden lifted to a sitting position, wheezing and laboring to suppress the pain that surged through his body. He rose to his feet and hurried after the three riders in a hobbled sprint.

At the center of the bridge, Laise slowed his horse. He leaned in his saddle and grabbed a torch from its mount. Coric and Ronan rode past and Laise followed.

Once across the bridge, they stopped, spun their horses, and stared back at the castle. The fourth man was still coming. The three Scots watched with indifference as the man struggled onto the bridge.

"Did you get what you came for?" Laise asked.

"Yes, I got enough," Coric replied, breathing heavily and working to catch his breath.

Laise raised his arm and threw his torch at the black goo that covered the nearby planks.

A burst of flames erupted when the torch hit the oil-soaked wooden bridge, completely engulfing the near end of the structure. The three watched in awe as a hot orange fire shot upward from the planks and a thick black plume of smoke rose into the night sky.

Aiden slowed and stared past the lofting flames. He panted for air and squinted through the blaze at the riders in black. The fire and heat blurred their silhouettes. "Your time is coming, you bastards … your time is coming," Aiden muttered to himself.

The three Scots turned their horses and rode into the night.

Aiden stepped back from the fire and drew a deep breath. Pain surged through his arm and shoulder. The fight on the hill had opened his wounds and set his burns ablaze. And the heat of the nearby fire only added to the sting. He suddenly felt as though he were trapped in an oven. His vision went black, and there, alone on the burning bridge, he fainted.

CHAPTER 12

BOOM! THE LARGE PINE CRASHED TO THE EARTH. Its branches cracked and snapped on impact, then the beast recoiled and sprung a foot off the ground before coming to a rest. There, the fallen mammoth lay silent. Once a beacon of strength in the Dalriadan forest, the massive tree now lay severed and dead on the damp forest floor.

"Ahh!" Dorrell let out an exuberant shout.

Kenneth's brow lifted in disbelief, amazed at the large Scot's ability to drop a tree.

Dorrell smiled at Kenneth. "Someday, when you grow up big and strong, you'll be able to drop'em like this!" He laughed and wiped the moisture, a mixture of sweat and mist, from his eyes.

Kenneth snickered, shaking his head with envy. Then he picked up his axe and began stripping the branches from the trunk of the fallen pine. The wet axe handle slid in his hands as he cut, in spite of his now calloused palms.

Kenneth stripped the first limb. The aroma of fresh pine filled his nostrils. He inhaled the evergreen scent. It carried the smell of strength, robust and pungent. He exhaled and levied his axe on a second limb. The thumping of his blade against the raw meat of the tree formed a syncopated rhythm with the axes of his fellow Scots cutting beside him. Dorrell's blows were the most prominent. His axe cut the deepest.

"Grisson, when you finish tying the first log, I want the other log tied to the horse as well," the fiery Viking with golden hair shouted to an older Scot harnessing the fallen logs. "The stallion will pull them both," the Viking finished. *Grisson* was a favored term of the Vikings for old and feeble men, and it was especially derogatory if the man wasn't all that old or feeble.

The older Scot, Nicol, acknowledged the Viking and finished tying the first tree to the tugs of the animal.

"Hurry with the stripping. I want that log tied up! And I want it done while it's still daylight!" the golden-haired Viking barked while waving a two-foot rod above his head.

The Viking's sarcasm annoyed Kenneth, for the day was not far past noon. Kenneth paused for a moment and glanced at the Viking guards standing watch. He had developed the habit of surveying his surroundings. If a chance for escape came, it would only last a moment and then vanish. Fighting would be another avenue of escape, but the guards' crossbows served as an adequate deterrent against such notions of insurrection.

Kenneth returned to the rhythmic swinging of his axe, dismembering one limb after another from the torso of the large pine. He didn't inform Dorrell that he was keeping count of the limbs that each removed, but he kept an eye on the larger Scot and worked with earnest to outpace him.

The collective thumping of the axes dismantled the tree in moments. The once great tree, with its towering height and boastful girth of green branches, was reduced to nothing more than a lifeless log, soon to be placed beside countless other logs forming the walls of the Viking fort. It would no longer stand proud among the Dalriadan forest, displaying its strength, rather it would stand stripped and bare amid an ignoble wall, displaying the strength of another.

"Fourteen!" Kenneth said triumphantly. He stood upright and gazed down the length of the fallen pine. Dozens of nubs, raw and coarse, protruded from its trunk.

Dorrell finished his last limb and straightened his frame. He lowered his axe head between his feet. "Fourteen what?" he asked.

"Fourteen limbs," Kenneth replied. "Sorry you couldn't match me."

"Match you? On the limbs?"

"Right. I cut fourteen and you cut twelve. Someday, when you get a little stronger and quicker, you may stand a chance of keeping up," Kenneth boasted, wearing a grin.

"Get the log up here. Tie it to the horse beside the other log," the Viking with the golden hair shouted at the Scots.

The men leaned their axes against the base of a standing pine and then grabbed the lifting ropes from the wooden cart. In groups of two, the men slid the ropes under the large limbless trunk, spacing themselves along the length of the tree. A dozen ropes were needed to lift the tree and place it behind the stallion to be hauled away.

Kenneth reached under the trunk and pulled half of the rope through to his side. He glanced at Gavin, his partner, and made sure he was holding his end. Gavin wrapped the rope around his forearm and held the end tight with his free hand, then he nodded at Kenneth. The two waited for the call.

"Set to lift?" Dorrell shouted to the men from the end

of the log. He and a heavyset Scot were standing at the rear to lift the base.

"Set," the men echoed.

"Lift!"

The ropes tightened, and the fallen giant slowly rose from the ground. The small army of men grunted and groaned as they wrestled the massive beast forward. The mist in the air made the ropes damp, and the dampness helped their grip. Yet too, it made it difficult to shuffle under the tree's great weight without encountering a slip on the slick, sludgy floor of the rain-soaked forest.

Step by step, the men inched forward, moving closer to the stallion and the previously secured log. The older Scots stood to the side, waiting to tie the two logs together for hauling. Moving the log grew more painful as the ground gradually sloped upward near the drop point. Kenneth huffed and heaved and felt as if his thighs were on fire. They burned with each step.

Upon ascending the incline and nearing the awaiting log, Gavin yelled to the back, "I think we're there." He glanced at Kenneth and muttered, "We better be."

"Drop on my call," Dorrell yelled to the men. "SET. DROP!" The heavy trunk hit the ground and rolled a foot to the right. Kenneth jumped to avoid the monstrous mankiller. The Scot behind him snickered. "Careful, it'll bite ya!"

Gavin released his rope and Kenneth pulled it through. Then the tree haulers rested.

Nicol, who'd been waiting for the log, motioned to two older men and signaled them to begin the tie-off. He turned to the golden-haired Viking and asked, "You're sure you want them together?"

"That's what I said. Isn't it, Grisson?" the Viking chided.

Nicol returned to his ropes. He and the two men began to weave the heavy cord around the thick trunk, intertwining the ropes and binding the two trunks together. As the three men hunched over the logs, forming their knots, one murmured to Nicol, "This one's enormous. With the slope of that hill, I don't think the horse can make it up with both of them." The man scanned the large logs again and frowned at Nicol. "It's not going to work."

"What's your problem?" the golden-hair Viking shouted.

"No problem. Just …," the man elected not to finish this thought and instead returned to his knot.

"Just what? Do you have a problem?" the Viking asked, taunting the man with his rod.

The three stopped and stared up at the golden-haired Viking.

"Get up here, Grisson!"

Nicol released his rope. He glimpsed at the two older men and then at Kenneth and the others resting nearby. His expression showed concern—concern of what was to come. The Scots knew firsthand of the golden-haired Viking's fiery temper. It was though the man had been denied the gift of self-control and instead had received a double-portion of the unsavory trait of poor temperament.

Nicol stepped away from the log and walked toward the stallion where the Viking was standing.

As Nicol approached, the Viking began his tirade, "Grisson, why must you always cause me problems? How hard is it to tie a knot? I want to know why you seem to have a problem!"

"We were simply noting that the second log is rather large—"

"And so, it's large? Is that a problem? Are Scots unable

to tie knots around large trees?" the Viking asked, pounding his rod into his open palm as he spoke.

"The men think the load may be too heavy for the horse to clear the hill."

"Your men think this, do they? Do I give a damn what your men think? Grisson, do you believe as they do? Do you believe I'm wrong, having both logs pulled together? Do you, Grisson?"

Nicol hesitated, choosing his words carefully. "I am not sure if the—"

"You're not sure of what, Grisson!" The man's golden hair flung across his shoulders as he lurched forward, thrusting his face inches from Nicol's. "Not sure of what!" Without a pause, the Viking slammed his rod against Nicol's thigh.

Nicol stumbled backwards into the hindquarters of the stallion. The horse spooked, and Nicol fell beside the animal.

The stallion reared up, hopping on its back legs, and then leapt forward, tugging the logs behind him. The heavy load incensed the beast and the horse lunged again, fighting its harness. Desperate to break free, the stallion moved at an angle, dragging the timber sideways across the incline. The logs jerked behind the animal and twisted to the side.

The two Scots tying the ropes leapt from the shifting load. The rear of the larger log began to slide down the hill, traversing the wet ground.

Again the stallion lurched forward, and the ropes of the big log snapped. The long, nubby trunk twisted away from its bindings and started to roll. It moved with pace, picking up momentum and bucking over rocks and bumps while descending the soggy slope.

The Scots gazed in amazement from the hilltop. The event was terrifying and fantastic at one and the same time.

A band of Vikings, stationed midway down the hill, caught sight of the tumbling log. They shuddered with terror in their eyes as the unwieldy giant rumbled toward them, boasting all the fury of an unleashed monster. Three ran to the left to avoid the angry behemoth. Two others leapt to the right, and the spinning timber missed the leg of the slower man by a measure of inches. A single Viking, caught in the middle, found no route of escape. He dropped behind a rock roughly two feet high and ducked into a crouch, cupping his head in his hands. The lumbering giant continued its violent descent, bucking and twisting down the hill. When the base of the log hit the dwarfed rock, it lifted in the air. The men above watched in awe as the mighty timber danced aloft in a soundless rage. At one particular moment, the massive pine hulk seemed to pause in time as it crested its ascent, then it dropped like a mallet on the powerless Viking crouched below.

The log continued onward without sympathy. For more than fifty feet it twisted and tumbled unabated, snapping and cracking small trees and saplings standing in its path. At the bottom of the hill, it crashed into two pines large enough to catch and keep their fallen brother. There, the big tree rested.

The forest fell silent.

The men above stood in shock at the terror of it all, while the Viking struck by the log lay motionless and bloody beside the small rock. Only the frustrated stallion dared to make a noise. The animal's bucking had ceased, but the beast continued to bristle and wheeze under the harness of the remaining log.

Midway down the hill, the Vikings rushed toward their fallen comrade. As they approached the body, they eased forward with hesitation. Then they glimpsed the gore of the crushed man and turned in revulsion. One Viking yelled up the hill to the leader with the golden hair, "Orroff is dead!"

The golden-haired Viking erupted, "You fool! You bloody fool!" His anger overtook him. He stormed Nicol and began striking him again and again with his rod.

Nicol covered his head and hunched to protect himself, but the rod struck hard and its tassels whipped across his flesh, tearing the skin on his arms. Nicol retreated and then tripped and fell as he backed away. He curled into a ball and the beating continued.

"You old fool! Do you not know how to tie a bloody rope! Your ignorance, your insolence did this!" the Viking screamed, feeding his rage with a torrent of blows.

The rod's whipping tassels shredded Nicol's clothing and tore open his flesh. Several blows struck his neck and shoulders. His cheeks began to bleed as the tassels lashed across his face, lacerating his skin.

Kenneth and the others watched, stunned, as the Viking released his vile-induced wrath on the old Scot. The beating was both cruel and excessive. Kenneth glanced at Dorrell and then at Gavin. He knew Nicol wouldn't survive if the beating continued.

"You—will—pay—for—this," the Viking shouted perversely, his words booming with each blow.

"You—stupid—stupid—"

A sudden blow to the backside of the golden-haired Viking sent him forward, and he tumbled over Nicol. He fell to his knees and caught himself before his face hit the ground, then he lifted his arm and reached for his blood-covered rod.

As the Viking rose to his knees, Kenneth leapt on his

back and jammed his face into the dirt. Kenneth grabbed his long golden locks and jerked his head upward. Then Kenneth twisted to his side and punched the Viking's face with one hand while gripping his hair in the other. Three punches landed before the Viking broke free.

Kenneth rolled sideways, and both men sprung to their feet. In a blink, the Viking swung his rod and struck Kenneth's arm. The tassels found Kenneth's back and delivered a biting sting. Again, the man swung. Kenneth blocked the rod and jumped into the Viking, crashing his head into the man's face. The Viking's nose broke with a loud *crack*. Kenneth threw a punch and thumped the Viking's eye. He punched again, but a Viking guard caught his arm. A second Viking spun him, and a third came from behind. The third man wrapped his arms under Kenneth's and placed Kenneth in a headlock, allowing the second Viking to release a round of pummeling fists to Kenneth's abdomen.

Kenneth fought for air between punches, but his lungs wouldn't fill. A sharp pain splintered along the left side of his midsection, likely the cracking of a rib.

Dorrell rushed forward, but Gavin grabbed the large Scot around the waist and fought with all his might to wrestle the big man back.

"Enough!" the golden-haired Viking shouted as a stream of red poured from his nostrils. His nose was bleeding and his eye was nearly swollen shut—and a thirst for revenge sat etched upon his face. He glared over his shoulder at a guard standing behind him. The guard held a crossbow. "*Drepe ham*," the golden-haired Viking uttered in his native tongue.

The man binding Kenneth released his headlock hold and shoved Kenneth forward.

Kenneth bent and coughed to catch his breath.

The Viking crossbowman elevated his weapon as Kenneth straightened and stood erect.

"Kill him!" the golden-haired Viking shouted.

Kenneth gaped at the crossbowman and the arrow aimed at his chest. A sneer formed on the man's face as he stared back at Kenneth. Kenneth held his ground, no remorse, no regrets—save one.

The Viking placed his finger on the trigger of the bow.

"Noooo!" A chilling, guttural war cry erupted from Dorrell's throat, and he swung his heavy axe over his head and hurled it into the air.

Thump.

The sound of the axe sinking into the Viking's back sent a shiver down Kenneth's spine. The man's eyes widened and then slowly rolled back in his head. He fell forward, limp, and hit the ground with a thud. The large axe handle protruded from his back like a slim wooden dorsal fin.

In an instant, a dozen Viking crossbowmen fixed their sights on Dorrell. Each man stood ready, eager for the golden-haired Viking's next command.

"Létta!" A loud shout bellowed from the hilltop.

Every head turned.

"Stop!" Fox, as Kenneth called him, yelled a second time, this time speaking Dalriadan. The Viking crossbows lowered. "I have no intention of losing more men or more slaves on this day." The angry bald Viking steered his horse off the path and moved down the hill.

The golden-haired Viking removed his hand from his nose and cursed the blood dripping from his fingers as he marched toward Fox. "These Scots are responsible for the deaths of two of my men. They must pay for their deeds!"

He motioned at Nicol and Dorrell then turned back to Fox, insisting consent.

"Alrik," Fox called the golden-haired Viking by name, "these are not your soldiers, though you will surely answer to Halfdan for their deaths. As for the Scots responsible, they will receive their due payment."

"And what of him? I want him for myself," Alrik seethed, pointing at Kenneth.

"He'll pay with the others. Now cut the rope from the horse and get the men back to camp. As for these three, I want their hands bound," Fox gave his orders, singling out Kenneth, Dorrell, and Nicol. "Bring them to me once you've returned to camp."

When Fox had finished, he peered at Alrik, "I want to see you once we've returned." He spun his horse without saying anything more, and he rode back up the hill.

⑨

A large ring of men stood in the center of the Viking courtyard and encircled Kenneth, Dorrell, and Nicol. Two dozen Vikings formed the circle, each brandishing a sword or axe—and all hungry for blood.

When Halfdan entered the circle, he stopped and glared at the three Scots. Kodran and Jorund stood behind him, shadowing him, teetering back and forth on their heels like bodyguards itching for a fight. The remaining Vikings, anxious for retribution, mobbed the courtyard outside the ring.

Kenneth, Dorrell, and Nicol stood with their condemnation before them. They stood facing Halfdan.

Their hands and feet were bound in chains, and their hearts were bound in doom. As the low western sun cast down upon their tattered faces, their well-beaten frames formed long, crooked shadows on the muddy ground behind them. Next to the three Scots sat a large oval-shaped stump.

Halfdan spoke in a loud, booming voice, "You three. I've been told of your crimes against my men. This is a very unfortunate day for those two men, those two dead men ... and a most unfortunate day for you. You and your foolishness are a stench in my presence. Such foolishness will not be tolerated. Your actions have led to very grave events, and such actions demand a costly payment in return." Halfdan glanced at Alrik, who stood among the men forming the ring. The golden-haired Viking nodded in affirmation, all the while wondering if he too would feel the wrath of Halfdan's heavy hand.

"As slaves, you must be taught the lesson for committing such crimes ... your fellow slaves would do well to learn from your poor decisions rather than suffer the misery of repeating them." Halfdan's dark eyes moved back and forth among the three prisoners as he spoke. "I am a just man, you should know this, and if not, then you will learn this. You shall receive precisely what you deserve for your actions."

Halfdan's gaze locked on Nicol. "Grisson, your questioning of my men's decisions cost a man his life today. Yet, too, I understand the incident was brought about by one of my own. I will deal with that in due time."

Alrik glared at Fox in resentment—and concern. He had seen, and even experienced, Halfdan's wrath in times past.

Halfdan continued, "Grisson, twenty lashes with the whip will be your punishment. If you survive, you'll carry out your days in the quarry."

Halfdan then peered at Kenneth. "Kenneth, that is what they call you?"

Kenneth gave no reply.

"You have been a misery to me from the beginning. Your chains have not been enough to teach you who is master and who is slave. We shall remedy that today. You, as well, will receive twenty lashes for your defiance. And know this, should you strike one of my men again, it'll be the last time you do. This is not a threat, it's a guarantee."

Halfdan's scowl tightened as he turned to Dorrell. "You chose your fate today, slave. A decision you will not live long to regret. My promise to you is to make your actions a memorable example of what the others should never repeat. You have chosen to take a life with your axe, so too, your life shall be taken by an axe. The same axe you used to kill my soldier will be used to take your head."

All eyes fell to Dorrell. The large Scot had no response. His expression was empty. His gaze lowered to the ground, and his eyes closed.

Kenneth took a single step forward and spoke, "This man killed another man, but only as a means of defending me. I would have been unjustly slain if it were not for him. Punish him as you must, but do not kill him."

Halfdan glared in disbelief, "You foolish Scot. Do you not see you are a slave? As a slave, you have no rights. You will not question me. You are nothing to me. You are as a roach. I have no need of you, or of this man," Halfdan seethed as he pointed to Dorrell.

"You are a leader of men," Kenneth responded, "Surely, you see the justice—"

"Shut your mouth, slave! Do not presume to tell me of justice. You are a man stripped of everything—you should plead daily for my mercy, that I might bring you the very food you require to live! You will NOT speak to me of justice! You are nothing!"

Kenneth brazened and spoke again, "If that is how you see justice, then take my life for his. He preserved my life from being wrongly taken. I will stand in his stead and pay the punishment due him."

"Kenneth, don't do this," Dorrell uttered. "I have no desire to live my days as a slave to these men. I willingly took the man's life. And I would do it again—"

"But you won't!" Halfdan exclaimed. "You will no longer have the pleasure of wielding an axe. Dead men don't wield axes."

Shouts of approval and vengeance rang out from the men of the mob.

Halfdan turned slowly on his heels, gazing over his men. His mind twisted in contemplation. And a thought made him grin.

"Maybe I have found something better. Seeing your affections for one another … and knowing how the other prisoners regard you both, I believe I have a punishment that may be more meaningful … more *just*." Halfdan turned to Kenneth. "If you are so eager to come to the aid of this man, I will let you. You shall receive your lashes, forty in total—yours and *his*," Halfdan said, motioning to Dorrell. "You shall work the quarry after your lashes. There you shall bring a double portion from the quarry. Yes, double—your share and the axeman's share. Should you fail to deliver your double portion of rock, it will be a sign to me that you no longer regard the life of the axeman. And as a just man, I shall see to his execution on that day."

"And for you," Halfdan said and peered at Dorrell,

"you shall never again carry, throw, or wield an axe … the craftsman shall lose his tool of craft. And you shall live your next thirty days in the pit." Halfdan pointed to the hole at the northeast corner of the fort. The pit wasn't dug as a well, it was never intended for such use. Rather, it was dug as an earthen prison, a den of solitude, for any poor soul that Halfdan sought to make miserable. Dorrell would be the first to know the miseries of the Viking pit.

"Men of Norse, I hope today you see your lord as a wise and just man … that Odin himself has poured out his favor on both you and me. With strength, we conquer. This is how we honor the great Odin. And with the wisdom of Odin, we enlighten the conquered." Halfdan held his hands aloft and turned in a circle before his men.

An eruption of cheers echoed among the brutes.

Halfdan lowered his arms and quieted the celebration. He addressed Dorrell, "Before you are taken to the pit, we must first ensure that you never commit treason with the axe again." Halfdan turned to his left and gestured with an open palm, "Jorund … the axe."

A Viking stepped into the center of the ring holding Dorrell's axe. The man extended the weapon to Jorund. Jorund grabbed the handle and ran his finger down the edge of the iron blade. He signaled two guards, and they escorted Dorrell to the stump in the center of the circle.

"Wait!" Kenneth shouted, fighting his chains, "You said he would not be put to death!"

"He shall not die … but he shall forever be reminded of his error," Halfdan replied. "He shall be capable of touching an axe, but never capable of using it—his great love shall be forever beyond his grip. And this shall serve as a reminder to him, and to all who should ever lay eyes upon him, that it is a fool's errand to challenge Halfdan the Black!"

Halfdan turned to Jorund, "Remove his thumbs!"

A lump formed in Dorrell's throat as he tried to swallow. His heart drummed against his chest, ready to burst. Two guards appeared on either side, clutched his arms, and muscled him to the stump. A sudden kick to the back of his legs dropped him to his knees.

Dorrell knelt before the stump and stared into the sky as if searching for intervention. Nothing. He closed his eyes, and his chest collapsed with an exasperated breath.

The Viking guards took his hands and placed them on the stump. They positioned his palms flat on the face of the wood and overlapped his thumbs at the lower knuckle. When finished, each guard placed a boot on Dorrell's wrist to prevent him from moving.

Dorrell opened his eyes and peered long at his hands. A thousand memories of swinging the axe, strong and swift, rushed through his mind. Then his eyes shut and his teeth clenched like a vice.

Jorund lifted the axe high in the air.

The weapon fell swiftly and stopped with a hideous thud. The heavy blade cut deep into the white wood, and a horrific yell exploded from the large Scot, piercing Kenneth's ears and etching its sound upon his soul. Kenneth turned his head and resisted the urge to vomit.

Dorrell lifted his hands and stared at the bloody nubs that had once been his thumbs. He closed his eyes and collapsed beside the stump. His body convulsed, and he faded into a slow rocking motion. As the pain surged, the large Scot spasmed and shock overtook him. Soon after, he lost consciousness.

⑨

Kenneth stood comatose, watching helplessly as Nicol
received his lashings. Jorund delivered blow upon blow to
the bloody back of the older Scot. After the last lash, Nicol
was untied from the whipping post. He slumped to the
ground and groaned in agony as drool dripped from his
open mouth and his body fell numb with pain.

"Take him away," Jorund barked the command.

Two men dragged Nicol from the post.

"Your turn," Jorund said, and he pointed to Kenneth.

Kenneth resisted, muscling against the guards as they
marched him to the whipping post. He was no match for the
overpowering brutes. They pressed his wrists together and
wrapped them with a rope, tighter than his chains, and they
secured him to the post.

"Remove his shirt," Jorund ordered.

When the two finished tying Kenneth, one stepped
behind him, grabbed his shirt, and yanked it from his body.
Kenneth stood as a spectacle before the Viking crowd, half
naked and leaning forward with his hands bound and his
head pressed against the wooden post.

"Wait!" Halfdan ordered, and he stepped toward
Kenneth. "What is this?" Halfdan extended his hand to the
gold cross dangling from Kenneth's neck. The cross settled
in Halfdan's palm, and he closed his hand. With a quick tug
he snatched it away. "You won't be needing this anymore,"
he said, grinning and admiring his new treasure. "Carry on,"
he barked. Then he turned and stepped away.

Kenneth heard Jorund's heavy footsteps behind him. His
body tensed. The sudden slap of the whip against his back

shot a blistering sting over his frame. His muscles seized at the sound of the whip recoiling behind him. The second lash came like fire to his skin. He agonized, awaiting the third.

Crack! The whip struck Kenneth's backside once again and his body shuddered. He gritted his teeth and tried to block the pain. Each successive strike came like a scalpel peeling away flesh, one layer at a time. The last words Kenneth heard were those of the guard shouting the count, "Twenty-three."

After that, everything went dark.

CHAPTER 13

ALPIN OPENED HIS EYES. HE STARED AT THE wooden ceiling and blinked several times to focus. The pitter-patter of rain tapped on the roof above. He cleared his throat and rubbed his eyes, working to shed the haze of slumber that clung to him like a moist garment.

"Good to see you've rejoined us," Luag said, moving through the room with a mug of hot cider. "You've been away for some time. We were wondering if you'd ever return at all." Luag chuckled as he spoke, hoping to lighten the air. He approached Alpin and set the cup of cider on the table beside the makeshift bed.

"Luag, where am I?" Alpin asked. He pushed back his blanket and shifted his weight to rise from the bed. "Ugh," he grunted, realizing his leg wasn't ready to move.

"Rest, Alpin. Rest." Luag placed his hands on Alpin's shoulders and coaxed him back to the bed. Then he lowered himself to the stool beside Alpin. "You're in Renton. You've been fading in and out of consciousness for several days. You're weak. You'll need food and rest before you can do much good for yourself or anyone else."

"Where's Coric ... and the other boys? Where's Ena?"

"Coric, Ronan, and Laise came back to Renton with you.

You were badly injured from the arrow you took in your leg. They nearly didn't get you back in time. Latharn's physician, Seamus, has been tending to you. He treated your wound to fight off infection." Luag lifted a jar of brown liquid from the table. "How is your leg?"

"The pain is bearable. I suppose it's healing," Alpin said, trying to dismiss the ache of the muscles throbbing in his thigh.

"Here, take this." Luag offered the mug of cider.

Alpin took it and drank.

"Alpin, it's good that you woke." Luag's tone turned serious. "Much has happened that requires your attention. The men are ready for war, but there is discord among them." Luag stood and turned. He thought carefully of his next words. "Alpin, there are other things that I must tell you."

Alpin lowered the mug to the table. He would force his body to obey. He shifted in the bed, pulled off the blanket, and set his feet on the floor. Pain surged through his injured leg. He grimaced and sat on the edge of the bed, pausing for a moment and peering at Luag. "What is it, Luag? By the look on your face, it isn't good."

"You're right, Alpin. It isn't good. Let me start by saying our men are at odds. As a people who must be united, we are divided. Right now, over five hundred men fill every square foot of Renton. Dalriadan men from across the countryside have come to fight the Vikings. They have come to protect our lands. Constantine and I both agree that we must move now to strike the Vikings if we hope to have any chance of rescuing our people. Guaire and that arrogant son of his insist we must join the Picts to ensure victory. And I should say, Taran speaks with a silver tongue, and many are swayed by him."

"Where is Constantine? Can he not convince the men otherwise?"

"Constantine is speaking to several of the men now. He will return shortly, I should guess. But Alpin, understand ... Constantine's position is weakened. When you were gone, he kept the men in Renton, insisting we wait for your return. And now you're back, but he cannot ... he ...," Luag stammered. "Frankly, you are not ready to lead the men, not in your condition. And Taran, he uses this as justification to seek aid from Oengus and the Picts."

"Damn him! We do not need Oengus and the Picts fighting our war. Taran is a fool to think Oengus would help us without demanding our very souls pledged to him. Why can't he see this? I grow weary of that boy," Alpin said, angry at Taran and even more so at his own incapacity to lead. He shook his head and stared at the floor. "What does Latharn say?"

"He agrees with Constantine, that we must keep our focus on the Vikings. But at times he has given ear to Guaire. It will help now that you are able to speak to the men."

"And Coric?" Alpin asked. "I assume he is Constantine's right hand in this. Yes?"

"Alpin, Coric is adamant that we not seek the help of the Picts. He's convinced that the men who ambushed you were sent by Oengus. Constantine tried to reason with him, but Coric wouldn't hear it. He's certain he's right. And now he has left, along with Ronan and Laise. We're not sure where they went. Coric only said that he could prove Oengus was involved in the attack on Renton. When we found that they had left, we sent scouts to find them. But we've yet to hear back." Luag studied Alpin, watching his brow furrow and the muscles in his arms and face tighten. "Do you believe the men who attacked you were Picts, Alpin?"

"I do not trust Oengus for a moment, but I believe in the end he knows he has too much to lose if he sides with the Vikings." Alpin lifted his head and stared at Luag. "I can't see Oengus doing this."

"Nor I, Alpin," Luag replied. "Nor I."

"Now I understand your concern. Coric, Ronan, and Laise have gone missing, possibly looking for clues, and Guaire and Taran remain here, stirring up trouble and dividing the men. I need to speak to Constantine."

Luag straightened his frame and began to pace. "Alpin, there are other things I must speak of." He paused and took a deep breath. "Nessa escaped from the Vikings and made it back to Renton. She arrived before you did, but we weren't able to tell you until now."

"Nessa's home!" Alpin exclaimed. "Is she with her mother?"

"She is with Ena. They are at Coric's house with Ceana," Luag said. "But there's more, Alpin. Kenneth was the one who freed her, but he was caught by the Vikings during their escape."

Alpin stared long into Luag's eyes. "There's something else you're not telling me, Luag. What is it? Tell me what happened to Kenneth, and what did Nessa say about Aiden? Tell me, Luag. Tell me—"

"Alpin, stop," Luag replied, lifting his hands to settle his friend. "As I said, Kenneth was taken captive. But Aiden … Alpin, he died during the escape."

"What? No. That can't be right?" Alpin rose to his feet, then swayed sideways and caught his balance. "There must be a mistake. He's got to be alive! Do you know this for certain?"

"Alpin, Nessa saw it happen. She saw it all. Aiden fell from high on a ridge. He and another man, a Viking … neither survived. I'm sorry, Alpin. I'm sorry."

Alpin ran his fingers through his hair. He scrubbed his scalp over and over, as if the scrubbing would subdue his nightmare. His shoulders hunched, and he buried his face in his forearms and pulled at the hair on the back of his head. "DAMMIT!" he yelled. He grabbed the mug of cider and hurled it across the room. The brittle vessel hit the wall and shattered, raining broken shards across the floor.

"I'll kill those bastards," Alpin seethed through clenched teeth. "I need your scouts to find Coric, Ronan, and Laise. We must leave at once! I will not lose Kenneth to those savages!"

"I understand, Alpin. But please, remain here and gather your strength for now. Let me fetch Constantine and the physician," Luag said, peering into Alpin's eyes. "I'll be back shortly," he muttered. Then he spun and hurried from the room.

Alpin returned to kneading his scalp, fighting to make sense of what he had heard. He moved from the bed and wandered about the small room, fighting his aching thigh and limping as he moved.

"I will find you, Kenneth. I will find you," he mumbled to himself.

⊚

"Constantine, we tire of inaction. And you know, as I do, the men tire as well. Certainly you agree?" Guaire said, standing under the tent that sheltered him and a half-dozen others from the drizzling rain.

"I understand, Guaire. Now get to your point," Constantine replied.

"For the sake of the men, the captives, and every Scot, we have to move forward. We cannot wait for Alpin to receive some divine healing to save us. We must move ahead," Guaire repeated.

"This is why you've called me here?" Constantine said. "You have some enlightened fix for all this?"

"We know you want the Scots to pursue the Vikings without aid. That is, if our men are still willing to stand as one. You believe that we alone can stop the Vikings. Constantine, these are not Britons, and this is not Ae. We need more men, and we need them now!"

"We have been over this Guaire. I will not, and these men will not, pledge fealty to a pompous Pict who wishes to be king!"

"We are not pledging fealty to Oengus," Taran interrupted. "We are asking him to help in a time of need. He will see likewise, that we are his aid against the Vikings, or else he'll be their next victim."

"What do you mean when you say, 'we are asking him to help,' Taran?" Constantine replied.

"My father and I have spoken to the men. The men of Dumbarton, as well as those from some of the other villages, have agreed that adding the Picts assures our victory," Taran replied. "We've sent five men from Dumbarton to Perth. They left this morning to speak to Oengus and relay our terms."

"Terms? I don't recall any terms," Constantine replied.

"Terms that state that we as a people will fight beside

the Picts in battle against the Vikings … they are enemies to both Pict and Scot," Taran said.

"Did you think that possibly Luag or I, or Alpin, would have liked to have known your *terms* before you sent these five men?" Constantine sneered, turning and glaring at Guaire.

"Alpin! You begged us to wait for his return," Taran accused. "Now he has returned, and he is so frail he cannot even get out of bed. He is not fit to lead!"

"Son, you would be wise to give your words more thought before you allow your tongue to speak. I assure you, Alpin is more fit to lead from bed than you are with wings, soaring high in the sky above." Constantine's ire grew and he fought to remain composed. "I am uncertain if it is your pride or your impetuous thinking that worries me most, but if your five men—"

"Constantine, Constantine!" Luag shouted, traipsing through the falling rain toward the men.

Constantine paused and waited for Luag to reach the tent. He shot an angry glance at Taran before turning his attention to Luag. "What is it, Luag?" he called out as Luag approached.

"Constantine, Alpin is awake. He's awake and he's walking," Luag said, as he entered the tent and took a moment to catch his breath.

"He's out of bed? When did he wake?"

"Not long ago. But he's up, I assure you. I should say too, I told him of Aiden. He is angry … very angry. We should get Seamus to look at him, but he likely needs a moment first … I'd give him some time."

A hush fell over the group and they gawked at one another, wordless.

Luag stared at the men huddled under the tent, his eyes moving from one man to the next, catching their furtive glances. Their silence—and posturing—was deafening. "What's been going on here?" Luag asked suspiciously, and he peered at Guaire and then at Taran and Constantine.

"Another incident, one that will only serve to feed Alpin's anger," Constantine replied. He glared at Guaire, "I'll let you be the one who explains this." Constantine lowered his head in disgust and walked from the shelter into the dreary rain.

CHAPTER 14

ARABELLA STOPPED BEFORE ENTERING THE LARGE dining hall. She half considered chiding Oengus for keeping her locked in her room for the day. After deliberating briefly, she concluded that diplomacy would serve more suitably if she hoped to persuade the Pict lord with her plea to aid the Scots.

Loitering moments longer in the corridor, Arabella heard the clanking of dinnerware and the dull tones of conversation coming from the dining hall. She adjusted her blouse and pulled at her hair, using her fingers to comb her long locks to one side. She took a deep breath and practiced a smile. Then she stepped around the corner into the hall.

"Good evening, gentlemen," Arabella said to the two men at the large table.

The two rose as she entered. "Arabella, I'm thrilled you have chosen to join me this evening. I have asked Deort to dine with us as well," Oengus said. "I was uncertain whether you would attend, so we began."

Deort nodded to Arabella and returned to his seat.

Oengus offered Arabella an armless chair adjacent to his seat at the head of the table, while masking his limp as he stepped. "Please sit and help yourself. I had the cooks prepare a course for you in the event you agreed to dine with us," Oengus said and returned to his seat.

Arabella sat. "Thank you, sir." She smiled and looked down at the moderate portion of ham and potatoes prepared on the plate in front of her. "I must admit, I thought twice about attending." She glanced at the two to see if they had taken the comment as she intended. "You've been kind in receiving me, so I must ask, why the sudden need to keep me behind locked doors? I am beginning to feel somewhat like a prisoner," she said, throwing her punch but not too hard.

"Do forgive me for the sudden constraint of your otherwise rich freedoms here in my home. But because of the breach of the castle last night, Deort and his captains agreed that we needed to secure the area and systematically ensure the grounds are safe for our people, including you, Arabella."

"You do understand that the intrusion left eight of my men dead and a ninth man injured," Deort said, sitting across from Arabella. "I take this quite seriously, I assure you. All guests and attendants were asked to remain in their quarters."

"Asked to remain, or forced to?" Arabella replied.

"Arabella, this was done for your safety. Nothing more, nothing less," Oengus remarked, extending his hand and placing it on her forearm.

"Forgive me, I understand. Indeed, it was awful seeing those men in black racing down the hall with their weapons and torches. I was quite frightened." Arabella glanced at Deort. "And I am sorry about your men," she said. "The ninth … is he going to make it?"

"He was in pretty poor shape to begin with. He'd been recovering from several burns. He didn't help himself by fighting those mercenaries, and he tore apart much of what had healed," Deort said before glancing at Oengus, who wore an unhappy frown. "He'll recover," Deort finished.

"This is the man burned from the fire, yes? I saw him that day in the courtyard with the other soldiers. I am sorry to hear he was hurt."

"He'll live. You needn't worry with him," Oengus assured her.

"Have you captured the men who broke into the castle? Who were they and what were they after?"

Oengus glanced at Deort before answering, "We did not capture them, but based on their black garb, they were likely mercenaries. They could have been hired by the Vikings. Our men confined them to the north wing of the castle and pushed them back before they obtained anything of value. They may have been coming directly for me, but they were unsuccessful, if that was their goal." Oengus took a bite of his ham, chewed, and swallowed. "We are tracking them, and we expect to apprehend them soon. Isn't that correct, Deort?" He turned and peered at Deort.

"Yes, my lord, that is correct."

"If these men were Vikings, or sent by the Vikings, doesn't that incline you all the more to join the Dalriadans? If they are attacking us both, would we not fare better together?" Arabella asked.

"Certainly, *if* they were Vikings, or sent by the Vikings, then it does seem reasonable to fight against them with the Dalriadans on our side," Oengus replied.

"Then are you willing to reconsider an agreement with the Dalriadans?"

Oengus set his knife and fork down beside his plate. He looked directly at Arabella, "I have no heartache in joining the Dalriadans against the Vikings. I simply asked that they pledge fealty to me, to my lordship. Then they will immediately have every sword in Pictland leading the charge against the Vikings. Remember, won't you … it was Alpin, that prideful and stubborn man, who believed he could take on the world with a single pathetic clan … and now look at Renton. The man must be humbled before he will ever see clearly." Oengus picked up his utensils and took another bite.

"But there are others in Dalriada who do see clearly … others who can reason with Alpin. It is not his decision alone. By his own words, he has no desire to be king over the Dalriadan people. I urge you, please reconsider my request for help." Arabella's eyes moved back and forth, glancing between the two men. "I believe in the end, it will be a benefit to you and to your people … to your own families."

Oengus dropped his napkin on his plate and he repeated the word 'families' under his breath. He lifted from his chair in an abrupt, agitated fashion and stepped away from the table.

Arabella glimpsed at Deort, puzzled. His expression bore an irritated grimace. She turned to Oengus. He was facing away, standing beside a small table at the end of the dining hall, pouring a cup of water. "My lord, was it something I said?"

"Nothing that I care to discuss," Oengus replied, remaining with his back turned.

Arabella sat silent for a moment, then spoke, "My lord, you mentioned 'families,' do you not believe that fighting against the Vikings would be a protection for the families of Pictland? I have seen firsthand what savages can do to families. You know that, my lord."

"Young lady, I regret to inform you that others too have felt the misery of losing those who are close," Oengus said, his tone cynical. "I'm sorry for your loss, but I would rather not discuss the matter beyond that."

"I understand … I apologize for misspeaking," Arabella placed her napkin on the table and stood. "I thank you for your hospitality. I came here to ask for your assistance in helping the Scots. It is desperately needed. I have done that, and now I pray you will consider it and act with favor." Arabella glanced at Deort and nodded politely. "Thank you, gentlemen. I shall gather my things and depart." She turned to leave the hall.

"Arabella," Oengus called out as she was walking away.

Arabella stopped and slowly turned her head.

"Don't misread my frustration as an irritation of your company. There are simply things in the past that are better left in the past. As for your attendance here, you are welcome to stay as long as you wish."

"I … I'm not sure what to say. I appreciate your kindness … however I came here for a specific purpose. I came in hopes of convincing you to help the Dalriadan people, my people. I have asked for your help … I can only hope that you have heard."

Oengus eased his cup of water back to the small tabletop. "I still find it amusing that you consider them 'your people,'" he noted inquisitively and feigned a grin. "You are a Pict. It is in your blood. You cannot change that."

"Maybe one's blood cannot be changed, but one's heart can be. There are many people whom I love, who stand to suffer and lose much if you do not intercede. That is why I've sought your help."

"Much is at stake for me to risk Pict lives to save a people who seem to care very little for the Picts themselves. Surely you can see that," Oengus said.

Arabella hesitated. "I believe that we see what we want to see, my lord," she replied and turned to leave the room.

"Where will you go, Arabella?"

"I think it's best if I depart. I will return to Cashel, or to Renton."

"Arabella, I have asked you to stay." Oengus looked at Deort and then back to Arabella. "It is quite dangerous beyond these walls. With the threat of the Vikings and the recent attack on the castle, traveling back to Dalriada at such a time would be a fool's errand. It would not be safe."

"I understand the risks. I considered them before I came."

"Well, it's not a risk that I am willing to take," Oengus replied. "You desire the relationship between the Picts and Scots to be strong. How angry would your father, Constantine, be with me if something were to happen to you after leaving my care?" A wry grin arched across his lips as he finished.

"Respectfully, he will be more angered if he believes me to be held up in this castle as your prisoner."

"As a man who has been a father, I'll take my chances with Constantine by ensuring your safety. If a Scot entourage were to visit Perth, I would gladly release you into their care. Or should a company of my men find an opportunity to visit Renton or Cashel, then you may proceed with them." Oengus held out his hands as a show of sincerity. "Until that time, please make yourself at home."

"I see," Arabella said. She turned and briskly departed the dining hall, leaving the two men to their meal.

❦

Arabella reclined on her bed, alone in her room deep within Oengus' castle. A single candle sat on the table beside her. She stared up at the dimly lit ceiling, lost in thought. *How wise was it to come to Perth?* Oengus had not mistreated her, but now she was somewhat of a prisoner within the castle's stone walls—free to walk about, to eat, and even to inquire, but not free to leave. *Had it been a mistake to come?*

She tried to dismiss her doubts but continued to second-guess her decision, even chastening herself for her sharp tongue in the dining hall with Oengus. Speaking to him in such a manner had not drawn him closer to helping her cause. *Maybe leaving Cashel was a poor idea? But surely, it was the right thing to do.*

Arabella pictured Kenneth and remembered the terrible men that had attacked them in Renton. She envisioned Kenneth in chains, pulling heavy ropes and digging muddy trenches while the Vikings mocked and likely beat him. *No one would last long in such cruel hands. There has to be a way to help,* she thought. With the men in Renton bickering over who would lead or how to lead, she settled that coming to Perth was the right thing—that Kenneth's life may be depending upon it.

She sat up in her bed. She stared at the walls of her room and wiped the moisture from her eyes as she thought of the man she loved and how their lives had been violently torn apart. She remembered how he'd asked her to marry him, and she allowed herself to muse for a moment, then a small laugh escaped.

She thought of their ride to the mountains before he had proposed. How she had held to him tightly as he spurred his horse toward the high hill to share his secret surprise. She remembered in times past of her giddiness, when she would romanticize of having children and building a home with Kenneth near Coric and Ceana. Life was designed to be lived and enjoyed. How quickly the dark side of the world could overtake and overwhelm those wishing for peace and simplicity. She thought of Kenneth and wondered if he was thinking of her. She loved his heart and his courage. She prayed he would hold on to both.

Arabella laid her head onto her pillow. Slowly, her solitude faded to depression. How long would she stay? Would Oengus force her to remain if she tried to leave? She asked herself these questions, yet the silence of the four walls provided no answers.

Only moments passed before the silence was interrupted.

Arabella was sure the noises had come from the hallway she now occupied, but the castle's maze of crisscrossed halls began to sow seeds of doubt. The sound had been much like that of a person groaning. She stood in the shadows of the long hallway, and her mind began to race. She wondered if someone was being tortured or beaten. She remained still, waiting and listening for the sound to return.

Silence.

She stepped forward and inched farther down the stone-walled hallway. Two rooms lay ahead. The door of the nearer room was half open, while the door to the far room was closed shut.

The groaning came again, more subdued this time. It came from the room with the open door. She was sure of it.

Arabella approached and stood just outside the half-open door. More groans. She closed her eyes and considered retreating to the security of her chambers. *No*, she had to see.

Opening her eyes, she leaned forward to peek through the doorway and winced as a gory image conjured in her mind.

She expelled the thought and leaned farther into the dimly lit room and glimpsed the leg of a man lying on a bed. The man's limb was poking out from the covers near the edge of the bed.

Arabella eased through the doorway and accidently bumped the door as she entered. A shrilling creak crept from the door's iron hinges.

"Who's there? Mathe, is that you?" The voice came from the young man in the bed.

Arabella stepped into the room. "No, I'm sorry. I shouldn't be here. I only came to see if you were alright."

"Did Mathe send you to check on me?" the young man asked, his voice faint and tired.

Arabella scanned the young man's covered frame as he rested in the bed. Sheets draped his body up to his chest. He neither lifted his head nor moved his limbs. Bandages wrapped his left shoulder and arm, as well as his neck and cheek. Brownish-pink splotches stained much of the bandaging. His eyes and forehead were covered by a damp beige cloth, leaving only his mouth and nose exposed. Arabella thought of the young man's question and was reticent to offer an answer. "No, Mathe did not send me. I ... ah, I heard your groans, and I wondered if you needed help. So I came."

The young man chuckled and then groaned from his laugh, "I guess you can see I need help. I wouldn't turn it down."

"The noises sounded like you were in pain, or that someone was ... well, that you were hurting."

"Yes, it's fair to say, I was hurting." The young man's

words slurred as he finished. He remained silent for a moment and then spoke again, "Mathe finds pleasure in making it painful when he changes my bandages. He swears the medicine … will heal the burns." His words faded off as he finished.

The young man took a deep, relaxed breath.

"Mathe gives me medicine to drink. It's supposed to kill the pain, but it still seems to hurt when he's … when he's bandaging …"

"I saw you the other day in the courtyard training with the other men. Oengus told me that you had been badly burned."

"I … I saw you too … I saw your hair. I wish I could see you now. You seem pretty. I know a girl like you, but she …," the young man tried to finish. The medicine had brought its intended comfort, and his voice diminished.

"I am going to let you sleep now. I wanted to make sure you were alright. I'm glad you're getting better. I'll visit again when I can," Arabella said. "Would you mind if I visit again?"

No response came.

"Would you mind?" she asked again and wondered if he'd fallen asleep.

"Why did you leave …," the young man said with a slur, as if fading into a dream.

"I'm still here. And I'm sorry that I didn't ask sooner, but what is your name?"

No answer came.

"Can you hear me? I said, what is your name?"

"Dros…"

The young man wandered off into a drug-induced slumber before the word completed on his tongue.

Arabella stared at her new acquaintance. She kept silent

and remained standing transfixed in the middle of the room. Something felt familiar. Her curiosity grew. She glanced at the open doorway and then slowly approached the bed. She moved closer, catching the pungent odor of the medicinal balm hovering in the air, and she stared at the young man. The cloth wraps appeared tight against his skin, and a clear fluid seeped from beneath the edge of the bandage wrapping his face. The site and smells caused her to gag, and she looked away.

She pitied him. She pitied his burns and his pain. She considered that Oengus must be proud of how he had fought off the intruders.

Returning her eyes back to the young man, she noticed his foot now dangling from the bed. She gently pushed it underneath the covers. Then she stepped back, gazing at him. Her eyes wandered over his frame and up to the bandages around his neck and shoulder. Her heart skipped a beat when her eyes locked onto a tiny sliver of silver hiding below the strips of cloth near the nape of his neck. Hearing the sound of footsteps, she spun and glanced toward the hallway. Someone was coming. She hurried to the young man's bedside and reached to lift the edge of his cloth wraps. She had to see.

She lifted the bandage—and gasped.

"What are you doing here?" Mathe demanded. The wiry-haired physician stood in the doorway with a condemning glare in his eye.

Arabella placed her hand over her mouth and rushed past the physician and out the door. She didn't stop until she reached her room. She quickly shut the door and ran to her bed. There, she collapsed and buried her face in her pillow—sobbing for Aiden.

Her heart was breaking, and she had no one to hold it or mend it back together. With tears she pleaded aloud, "Kenneth, where are you? If only you were here ... oh Kenneth, tell me everything will be alright. Tell me, Kenneth!"

Arabella lay in her bed, weeping, unaware of the key clicking in the metal lock of her door.

CHAPTER 15

THREE DAYS HAD PASSED SINCE KENNETH watched the metal axe cut across Dorrell's hands—three days had passed since the Viking whip lashed forty times across his very back.

The sting of the lacerations still lingered, plaguing Kenneth's waking hours. Sleep brought little relief. His dreams were nothing less than nightmares, dark realms where he relived his horrors with each closing of his eyes.

The thick sky that had released its deluge, that awful evening three nights prior, still remained above. It refused to depart and continued to spew down its wet dread upon Kenneth. The gray gloom hovered over the Viking fort, and the days passed with no warmth. For Kenneth, the external mirrored the internal, where a dreadful doom lined his veins like a venomous plaque.

Kenneth rotted in the solitude of the courtyard, chained between two posts. Miserable thoughts stirred his mind. His father, his family, his countrymen—were they not coming to free their brothers? Should they not have come already? Were they to be left to die as slaves?

Kenneth lifted his head and stared beyond the tall wooden posts forming the front wall of the hated Viking fort. He peered at the distant hill, the same hill he had crested so many countless days past when the Vikings first brought him to their wretched den. He stared into the distance as if to see the first soldiers of a long procession of Scots, marching over the hill to come and save and conquer.

The drizzling mist beaded on his brow. The drops fell one after another before his eyes. He stared past the thin curtain of water, fixing his gaze on the hill, waiting and wondering, yet fearing to hope.

His soldiers never came.

Mist continued to pool on his skin and course over his haggard frame. Drops streamed down his neck and torso and soaked the cloth around his waist. Kenneth's head eased downward, and his eyes fell to his bare chest. His heart sank when he recalled the missing cross that once dangled from his neck—and how the heirloom had once graced Arabella's sweet skin on a better day than this day. He tugged his chains and cursed as images of Halfdan, ripping away his brother's gift, replayed in his mind.

Kenneth relented and relaxed his arms. He succumbed to the rains and the dreary reality of the dismal day. Closing his eyes, he wanted to let go.

With summer now gone, the penetrating moisture of the steady rains brought the hollow chill of fall. The chill was an enemy. Kenneth had shivered through the past several nights where the cold had robbed him of any meaningful sleep. The only good the rains offered, if one could call it good, was a brief respite for his wounds to heal. The rains meant a reprieve from the rock quarry for the captives. But when the rains stopped, how would he deliver enough rocks for two men? The men in the quarry were worked to near death. How would he double their portion? And what would become of Dorrell if he didn't?

Kenneth gazed toward the Viking pit and the heavy logs lying over it, sealing it like an immovable hatch. He wondered if Dorrell was still alive in the muddy dungeon. Seeing Dorrell collapse and heave in shock under the falling axe gave Kenneth no assurance that his friend would survive. He imagined Dorrell and his mutilated hands, wasting away in the wet bowels of the pit with an incessant drip of rainwater seeping through the log covering.

In the three days that had passed, no sounds or stirrings ever came from the pit, only the guard's daily lowering of a food bucket into its black belly. This was Kenneth's only shred of hope that his friend was still alive.

The price Dorrell paid for saving Kenneth became an ever-growing weight upon Kenneth's soul, a very heavy weight—but then again, the burden of guilt is always heavy. In his mind, Kenneth wanted to deny it all, but deep down the reality was undeniable—the once vigorous Scot was now rotting away in a dark and miserable hole while Kenneth remained alive on the earth above.

⑤

The dawn of the fourth day brought with it an auspicious Dalriadan sunrise. The early morning air held a cool crispness that promised to dry the sodden ground, as well as Kenneth's saturated body. Kenneth stood to take in the warmth of the sun's light. He peered again at the distant hill, this time with a renewed hope that his father and brother would soon appear with an army of Dalriadans behind them.

Kenneth's stomach roared. He glanced at the prison

pen and the men inside moving about. They had stepped out from under the small thatch roof that offered shelter from the rains. With the showers now past, the men would be taken to the forest and the rock quarry, and the Vikings would bring a ration of bread as a morning meal. Kenneth craved the bread.

Kenneth gazed toward the pit. He prayed the sunshine might offer Dorrell some semblance of relief from the ceaseless moisture. That maybe the rising sun would pierce through the cracks in the log covering—anything to give his friend a modicum of warmth and a hopeful glimpse of medicinal light.

The guards soon arrived at the pen. There, they began throwing bread to the prisoners through the openings between the posts. The Scots rushed for the bread and devoured the scraps like starving dogs tearing into raw meat.

Kenneth's hunger erupted inside as two guards approached him. Each held a single piece of bread.

"Today's your day," the taller guard said. Then the man glanced at the second guard and smirked.

Kenneth peered at the two with a haughty glare, unamused and eager for his meal.

"I said, it's your day!" From nowhere, the tall guard's hand struck Kenneth, smacking his cheek. "Now wipe that look off your face, Scot!"

Kenneth straightened himself after his head finished its sideways swivel. He licked the edge of his lip and slowly glared upwards at the guard. "My day for what?"

"Your day to gather rocks … a good many rocks," the man said.

"Rocks," Kenneth muttered.

The guard lifted his hand with a sizable hunk of bread lodged between his fingers, and he took a bite. "Damn fine bread," he said.

Kenneth mockingly acknowledged with a single nod of his head.

The man took another bite. Then the second guard bit into his own piece of bread. The man began to chew the morsel slowly in his mouth.

"You'll get hungry carrying the rocks today," the tall man said. He swallowed and ripped another bite with his teeth. "Halfdan said that we should hold off on giving you any bread. He says you'll be working hard today and doesn't want you getting sick on a full stomach."

"Thoughtful," Kenneth murmured under his breath.

The two stared at Kenneth, amusing themselves as they finished their delicacy. Upon consuming the last of the bread, they unlocked Kenneth from his post. The shorter guard stepped behind Kenneth, and then Kenneth received a hard shove on his backside. The man's hand dug into Kenneth's open flesh and a crippling surge of pain shot through his torso. Kenneth stumbled forward and then slowed himself to gain his balance.

"Move it, Scot," the guard barked.

Kenneth ambled toward the two lines of captives forming outside the pen. He saw Nicol standing in the line to the left. The older Scot had recovered from his beating, but his movement was sluggish and labored.

The two guards escorted Kenneth to Nicol's line, the quarry line. There he was given a metal stake and a large iron mallet. A Viking shouted an order, and the Scots began their procession to the rock bed. Kenneth was last in line.

He purposed to keep pace and refused to let his raw back or chained limbs slow him.

⊚

Over the four days that followed, Kenneth found the task of breaking rock both physically grueling and mentally numbing. He much preferred the dropping of pines to the chiseling of rock. Though both chores exhausted the body, at least the felling of a tree brought a measure of achievement. At the quarry, a man could pound rock for an entire day, and still the massive granite walls never seemed to diminish. Kenneth endured the task and pushed himself to deliver twice the rocks of the others, though it came at a cost. By the middle of the fourth day, Kenneth found himself fighting exhaustion under the toiling labor that drained his strength like the desert sun on a shallow pool.

The fifth morning hit hard. The lack of food was crushing. The small portion of pasty bean mush given nightly to the captives hardly sustained him. The others had the benefit of a ration of morning bread, but Kenneth received no bread.

Morning call came. The Viking men lined up beside the captives and the march to the wall of rock began. Another day of quarry work had arrived.

Kenneth swung the heavy iron mallet, but his tired arms were all but robbed of strength. He felt powerless to break the rocks free. The returning gray skies only accentuated his misery. Despondency had shadowed him and now was taking root, penetrating deep and slowly sucking his will to press on.

Kenneth stared up at the dense, gloomy blanket of clouds. He lamented life—all things precious were being stripped from him, even the light of the sun.

The gloom continued as the hours crept by.

At midday, the prisoners were granted a moment of rest from their labor. Kenneth stopped where he stood. He wiped the sweat from his brow and surveyed the pile of rubble at his feet. His portion of rocks was running even with that of his fellow captives. He would need to do better.

The other prisoners took rest and sat beside their piles. A guard brought a sack of water and allowed the Scots to pass it among themselves. Not waiting for the water, Kenneth picked up his mallet and gazed at the monolithic wall of rock. He pressed his metal stake against the stone and swung his mallet.

"Sit, Scot!" a guard shouted.

Again, Kenneth lifted his mallet above his head.

"I said, sit." The guard drew his sword.

The sound of the sliding steel echoed in Kenneth's ears. He swung and landed his mallet a second time, loosening a large stone. Without looking back, he eased his hands open and dropped his mallet and stake at his feet. Then he lowered his frame and sat beside the large cracked stone, yearning to strike it again and set it free.

Nicol approached and offered a drink from the water sack. Kenneth took the water and drank. The tepid liquid refreshed his throat but could not quench his fear—his haunting fear of failure. He sat silent, staring at the loose stone still fixed in the rock wall.

"You alright?" Nicol asked and lowered to sit next to Kenneth.

Kenneth wiped his mouth and gazed at Nicol. "I should

guess I am," Kenneth replied. "Though I'd be lying if I said I'm doing well at getting the rocks I need."

The two looked at Kenneth's pile and then at the other piles.

"You're struggling," Nicol said. "You're far from a double portion."

"I don't understand it. I'm swinging the mallet and hitting the rock, but my strength … it's gone."

Nicol glanced over his shoulder at the guards. The men stood clustered in a group, bantering with one another. Nicol slid his hand to his waist and dug into his pocket. "I brought this for you," he said. He held out two portions of bread. "Take them and eat."

Kenneth gazed back at the older Scot. "You brought these for me? But you need them?"

"Some of the other men and I have rationed our bread, and we want you to have this." Nicol put the bread in Kenneth's hand and stood to leave. "The others have noted that the stone has gotten harder, looks to me that we'll be much slower than you this afternoon," Nicol said in a lowered voice. He offered a smile and walked away.

"Thanks," Kenneth said. It had been a long time since Kenneth had seen kindness. It had been a long time since he'd had bread. He tore at the first piece of bread and shoved a wad in his mouth. Its flavor overwhelmed his taste buds. The morsel was delicate and fine, and it danced on his tongue as he chewed. His mouth flooded with saliva, and he devoured the bite.

The delectable sustenance stirred his spirit and strengthened his resolve.

That afternoon, Kenneth's mallet was lighter and the

rocks were less defiant. He worked with earnest and added to his pile. And it grew quicker than the others.

The sun was now low in the western sky.

With his large rock pile complete, Kenneth began the first of his treks up the hill. He carried two, sometimes three rocks with each trip. At the top of the hill, he loaded the stones into the carts as the others did, and each time he hurried back down the hill for more.

Kenneth picked up a large stone on his fifth trip and moved up the hill.

"Stop there, Scot," Magnus said, stepping in front of Kenneth. The hairy brute had been given duties over Kenneth and a dozen others for the day. "You'll have to hurry if you plan to get the rest of your rocks in the carts by the time we pull away."

"I see that," Kenneth replied.

"Good, I'm glad you understand," Magnus responded.

"If you'll allow, I should move ahead."

Magnus stepped aside. "Then move, Scot!" he barked.

Kenneth climbed up and down the rocky hill, carrying his stones to the carts and passing the others coming and going with their loads. The company of Scots moved busily along the hillside, trekking back and forth like irritated ants toting rubble to a mound.

Kenneth stood beside his pile at the base of the quarry. Reaching down, he grabbed two rocks that were sizeable and jagged. The muscles in his hands throbbed as he wrapped his fingers around their rough edges and pulled them to his chest. With the rocks tight against his frame, he started up the hill.

Partway up, Kenneth passed under Magnus' shadow. The Viking was watching over the Scots from his perch atop a large grayish-brown boulder beside the path. Kenneth glanced upward.

"Move it!" Magnus called out. He was staring down the hill, apparently addressing someone behind Kenneth.

Kenneth cocked his head to steal a glance. Two Scots were kneeling beside their rock piles, claiming a moment of rest. The two picked at the stones in their piles and began to busy themselves. Kenneth turned and moved ahead to the carts.

When Kenneth reached the rear cart, he dropped his two rocks. They hit the ground with a thump. He bent over and grabbed the rocks one at a time. A spasm splintered across his lower back as he lifted the second rock up and over the sidewall of the cart. He heaved it onto the mounting pile, then stood erect, drew a deep breath, and stretched his arms as far as his chains allowed.

"So, Magnus has watch over you today?"

Kenneth stiffened when he heard the voice. He knew the voice. He closed his eyes. He took another deep breath and eyed peripherally over his shoulder. "Yes. Magnus has watch today," he said reluctantly.

"I should make sure he keeps a close eye on you. I would hate for you to fall short," Alrik said, sporting his typical pompous grin.

Kenneth rotated slowly on his heels. He stood square and peered at the Viking. Alrik's golden hair was ratty, and his nose was mildly disfigured from where his face had encountered Kenneth's fist only days prior. "I don't plan to fall short," Kenneth said. He didn't await a response. He stepped past Alrik and hurried down the hill as quickly as his shackled feet allowed.

"Magnus. Magnus, I must speak to you," Alrik's voice rang out from the top of the hill as Kenneth descended to his pile.

Kenneth grabbed a single large stone and headed back up the path. With his head tilted down, he peered through the matted hair that hung over his eyes, surveilling Alrik like a hawk. Alrik stood beside the large boulder claimed by Magnus, engaging the brute in the Norse tongue. Kenneth heard an exchange of words and then a collective laugh. He cursed them both under his breath as he passed.

The thick gray sky was a villain. The gloomy veil stole the evening remnants of sunlight, bringing an early closure to the day. Soon the Vikings would call the captives to form their lines and begin the hike back to the fort. Kenneth gazed at his pile. Five rocks remained. They were too large and too heavy to carry in a single load. It would take two trips. He picked up three of the rocks and left the other two.

Kenneth balanced the three stones in his arms and headed to the carts. As he neared the large boulder where Magnus perched, he spied Alrik still hovering beside the boulder with his eyes prowling over the Scots as they passed. Kenneth kept his head low and moved forward.

He neared Alrik.

The golden-haired Viking stepped into the path. "It doesn't look like you'll make your count today, Scot."

Kenneth neither lifted his eyes nor opened his mouth. He moved passed Alrik and continued up the hill.

"Magnus, did you see that? Has your boy gone deaf?"

"No, Alrik, I don't think he's gone deaf. I think he simply doesn't like you," Magnus said and then laughed aloud.

"Well, it appears it is time for your carts to pull out. The day has grown old and night is near. You should consider having your carts return to the fort," Alrik claimed.

Kenneth reached the carts and dumped his rocks. He paused for a brief moment before heading back for the last two. Yet there was no avoiding it—he would have to pass Alrik again.

Kenneth began his descent and glanced ahead at the hot-tempered Viking. He walked briskly along the far side of the path and stared down the hill, trying to appear distracted.

Alrik straddled the path. "Scot, the carts are leaving. You don't have time for any more rocks."

Kenneth ignored his foe and stepped to the edge of the path as he drew closer to Alrik.

"I said, you don't have time for any more rocks."

Kenneth glanced at Alrik. "I'll try," Kenneth replied without slowing. As he passed Alrik, the Viking grabbed his shoulder.

The words came again, "You are out of time!" Alrik finished his declaration and shoved Kenneth.

Kenneth stumbled forward, clumsily descending the path. As he fought to regain his balance, his foot clipped the chain binding his ankles, and he tripped and fell to a knee.

Magnus stood on the boulder, idly watching the two with amusement.

Kenneth turned and glared back at Alrik. The Viking stood in the middle of the path, shaking his head at Kenneth like a king to a fool.

Kenneth wanted to storm the hill and fight the man—he wanted to kill the man. Then he remembered his friend. He remembered Dorrell. Kenneth rose to his feet and hurried to retrieve his two remaining rocks. Alrik turned up the hill and strolled toward the carts.

Reaching his pile, Kenneth quickly gathered the last two rocks. He ignored his tightening muscles, his sore hands, and his now bloody knee. The rocks were heavy and odd-shaped, making them difficult to carry. Kenneth steadied himself and righted the load in his arms. Then he started up the hill.

Halfway up, Kenneth saw the first two carts pulling away. He saw Alrik speaking to the driver of the third and final cart. When the two finished their exchange, they peered down the hill, eyeing Kenneth as he approached.

Kenneth quickened his pace. As he neared the grayish-brown boulder, he tried to expand his stride. Yet his chains pulled tight, forcing him to lurch as he stepped. The larger rock twisted in his arms and dropped to the ground. When he bent to lift it, the second rock tumbled from his grip.

Kenneth peered up the hill. Alrik was standing beside the lead horse of the last cart. He struck the animal with his tasseled rod, and the horse jerked and the wheels of the cart began to roll. Kenneth grabbed the large rock with both hands and hurried to catch the cart as it pulled away.

Striding quickly, Kenneth passed Alrik and followed the moving cart to the crest of the hill. He closed on it and threw his rock forward. The rock landed with a crash on top of the pile and then rolled down over the other rocks until it settled on the edge. And there it rested, moving away with the cart and its rubble.

Kenneth gazed back at Magnus. The Viking had left his perch and was now standing where the cart had been parked. "Double portion," Kenneth said with labored breath.

"Double portion?" Magnus questioned.

"You're short! And the carts are gone," Alrik declared. The golden-haired Viking stepped beside Magnus and pointed back at the small rock that sat alone in the path. "Doesn't look like you finished. Magnus, you heard Halfdan … the Scot didn't meet his double portion."

"I suppose you're right, Alrik," Magnus replied.

"I usually am," Alrik responded smugly. Then he placed his hand to his jaw and began kneading the skin of his chin with his thumb and forefinger. "Kenneth, my dear Scot, your friend will be most disappointed to hear of this news … to hear you couldn't keep him alive for—"

"You bastard!" Kenneth shouted. "You wanted this!"

"Come now, don't be naïve. Didn't we all?" Alrik grinned and glanced at Magnus. He placed his hand on Magnus' shoulder. "Didn't we all."

"You bas—" Kenneth's tongue stopped when he felt the tip of a sword press into his back.

Magnus eyed the guard behind Kenneth and then glanced at each of the others, "We're done here, round up the prisoners and return to the fort."

"You heard him, move!" the voice behind Kenneth growled.

Kenneth turned and twisted in his chains through the night, wrestling in and out of sleep and wakefulness, yet never quite finding one or the other. His thoughts ran in a thousand directions, though none were settling. Thoughts of Arabella brought only misery, with the memories feeling more like regrets. In his chains, he could do nothing for her, nothing but leave her broken, much like he had Dorrell. He thought of Aiden and how he had left him in Renton, and how he had stood by helplessly on the cliff and watched him fall to his death. An image of his father sitting on a horse appeared in his mind. He considered how his father had raised his sons to be strong and courageous. Yet Kenneth couldn't help but feel that he had grown to nothing more than a worthless shell of weakness and shame. He recalled the awful day that Drostan came home lifeless in the wooden cart. What was left of his family? Only Coric, the warrior. Could even Coric stand against the evil that now darkened their world? And Dorrell, how could Kenneth look into his eyes when they pulled him from the pit? How could he gaze upon his friend knowing his friend was doomed to die— knowing Dorrell's blood was on his hands? The black night inched on, mocking Kenneth as it passed.

The sun broke across the eastern mountain ridge. Its brilliant, bright light burned away the morning clouds of dawn, filling the skies with an empty blue.

The sun's light fell on Kenneth's soiled skin. He opened his eyes, sadly, to another day. His back wrenched with aches, and his shackles weighed heavy on his limbs, though his physical afflictions were the least of all that tormented him.

Horrannn!

The blast of the sound sent shock waves through Kenneth's body. The terrible Viking horn filled his ears, and his head shot upwards. Guards rushed back and forth across the courtyard, churning a dreadfulness that stirred and lifted in the air like a cloud of invisible poison.

Two Vikings hurried past Kenneth, one carried a long rope looped over his shoulder. Kenneth locked his gaze on the two, and his stomach twisted as he helplessly envisioned the moments to come.

When the two men reached the pit, they circled its log covering and then stopped beside one another. After speaking for a moment, they split up and began to roll the logs to the side. One by one, they removed the logs and exposed the pit to the light of day.

With the covering removed, one guard took the rope and tied it to a post then threw the remainder of the line into the hole. Kenneth watched as the second man grabbed the rope and slowly disappeared into the pit.

Kenneth's eyes shut and images of Dorrell flashed through his mind. He half hoped his friend had already passed. Maybe in God's mercy Dorrell had moved from this world to the next, far away from this earthly hell. *Would it not be better to live in that distant paradise than to survive another moment in this misery?* he asked himself, though he suspected he knew the answer.

Kenneth shuddered at what he saw next.

Dorrell's limp frame lifted from the earthen dungeon and appeared as a lifeless carcass. The Vikings untied the Scot and released him. Devoid of all strength, Dorrell collapsed to his knees. Nothing was left of the man but mud and grime and a large, hollow, frail frame.

Dorrell slowly lifted his head.

Kenneth exhaled.

The two Vikings stood on either side of the beleaguered Scot. They grabbed his arms and hoisted him to an upright stance.

Dorrell released a groan as he rose from his knees. He

swayed as he stood, and his posture formed a crooked hunch. After several labored breaths, he lifted his gaze toward the sun inching above the horizon. There he remained, mesmerized, as if in a world of his own.

Suddenly, one of the Vikings shouted at Dorrell and slapped his face. Without awaiting a response the two men grabbed him and placed his arms behind his back and shackled his wrists. The Vikings convulsed at the sight of the bloody nubs on Dorrell's hands, remnants of where his thumbs once had been. After the two had finished binding Dorrell, they released his chains and dropped his locked wrists, leaving his bound arms to dangle behind his back.

He offered no resistance.

Horrannn!

The horn blew again.

A commotion stirred in the pen. The Vikings clanged their swords and shields against the wooden posts of the prison, barking orders to silence the prisoners and threatening them with their blades.

The prisoners ignored the threats and only shouted louder. Several took hold of the prison posts and violently heaved and pushed to tear them down. Their eyes pooled with anger and vengeance and hate. Had they the means of escape, their rage would have turned to riot—likely to their death. Yet the deep-seated posts stood fixed, containing the imprisoned Scots and their fury.

"Men of Dalriada!"

The booming voice echoed above the chaos.

The Viking guards stepped back from the prison and turned to face the voice.

Again, the voice boomed, "Men of Dalriada!"

The prisoners settled, stirring among the pen and muttering curses at the guards.

Kenneth twisted his body and cocked his head to look behind him. There, high on the platform in the middle of the courtyard, Halfdan stood, a dozen paces from where Kenneth was chained. Kodran and Jorund took positions on the ground, standing like guardians in front of the wooden structure.

"Men of Dalriada ... a day of reckoning has come to you. You once had the freedom to serve yourselves. But as you will see today, that freedom has been stripped away." Halfdan held out his hands and cast his gaze toward the prisoners.

"You once perceived yourselves as a strong people, a free people. Look around you ... that time has passed. And just as you now serve me, so too shall your wives, your sons, and your daughters, serve me in the days to come."

Kenneth glanced back at Dorrell, now standing beside the pit and staring listlessly into the sky.

Kenneth closed his eyes and lowered his head.

"Among you are those who have chosen to resist. This, I assure you, was a costly choice. In my mercy, I granted reprieve, a compromise." Halfdan glared down at Kenneth. "Yet you were unable to keep your part in the compromise." Halfdan walked to the edge of the platform and turned toward the prison pen. "Your beloved Kenneth, once a spirited man among you, seems to have lost his spirit. He no longer finds the strength to fight against the might of the Vikings. In a sense, he has grown wiser. His decision to relinquish his end of the compromise is a testimony to his wisdom—wisdom that sees that the weak shall always submit to the strong."

Kenneth turned his head and forced himself to look at Halfdan once again. His hatred for the man consumed him. He etched every detail of the man's face into his mind—his beard, his eyes, his thick brow, and his bony, rigid jaw. Kenneth seethed. He swore he would war with every ounce of strength to rid the earth of the animal. He wanted to kill the man and bring upon him a miserable and bitter death.

"It is time." Halfdan raised his hand and motioned to the two Vikings on either side of Dorrell.

Kenneth could only watch as the two men half dragged the ragged Scot past him to the edge of the courtyard. From the backside, Kenneth could see Dorrell's rib cage protruding against his sagging skin.

The three were twenty feet from Kenneth when Halfdan called for them to stop. They halted. The two men released Dorrell and waited for Halfdan's orders. Dorrell remained slumped with his back to Kenneth for several moments and then slowly straightened his frame but never turned.

Kenneth eyed the ground at Dorrell's feet. His gaze slowly moved up Dorrell's muddy legs to his torso. He stared at the crusty stubs on Dorrell's hands, the cruel reminder of his missing thumbs. It was then that Dorrell turned to face Kenneth.

Their eyes met, and a chill ran over Kenneth's body. He felt cold and naked. He wanted to say something, yet his tongue was paralyzed.

"Kenneth," he heard his name crawl from Dorrell's mouth.

"I'm sorry," Kenneth uttered. "You saved my life, Dorrell. I should be the one standing where you are."

Dorrell didn't speak. Instead, his eyes shifted from his friend to the barbarian on the platform.

Halfdan descended the planks of the wooden stage and slowly strode across the courtyard, stopping beside Dorrell. He dismissed the two guards and motioned for Kodran and Jorund.

Kenneth eyed the two as they approached, marching toward Dorrell like demons of death. Kenneth burned inside. He was bound, with all the passion to fight and kill, but without the freedom to do either. His jaw clenched. "Halfdan, you are a madman. You have no right to do this!" Saliva sprayed from his teeth as the words leapt from his mouth. He tore at his chains, yet his struggle was futile, the iron bindings would not yield.

Dejected, Kenneth turned his gaze toward Dorrell and surveyed the once virile Scot for a long, timeless moment. Then he spoke, "Don't let this happen, Dorrell."

The look in Dorrell's eyes severed Kenneth's heart. It was not a look of anger or blame, but one of empathy and affection. Kenneth had seen it before, but only in the eyes of his father.

Dorrell swallowed, then his mouth slowly moved, "Kenneth, destiny chooses as it pleases. This path has been chosen for me. You, my friend, have been destined for a path unlike mine. Destiny has a different plan for you, and a man cannot stay the Hand of Providence." The words fell from his lips like a portentous utterance from God.

Dorrell blinked several times, drew a deep breath, and then exhaled. "Kenneth, do not let your fury bring your demise, rather may it grant you wings to fly and carry you to a distant place, where you live again among a free people, beyond the misery of savage men."

"Enough!" Halfdan yelled. "End this!" He swept his hand through the air in a swift cutting motion.

Kodran drew his sword.

Dorrell stared at Kenneth with eyes portraying a dying wish. He nodded with a certain finality, and he pressed his last words deep into the young Scot's soul, "May the death of one ignite the freedom of many." Then Dorrell twisted his wrists behind his back, and his iron chains fell from his thumbless hands. He lifted his palms heavenward as if to grasp the hands of Christ.

In a blur, Kodran swung his angry sword and sliced the midsection of the large axeman.

For a moment, time ceased. Kenneth screamed to a world without ears, gazing on as Dorrell's entrails released from his open torso and poured onto the ground below.

Dorrell dropped to his knees, and with his arms still extended, he cried, "Lord God, grant me—"

Halfdan's four-inch, jewel-handled knife ripped across Dorrell's throat, cutting off his last words and stilling his tongue. Halfdan paused and then lifted his foot and pushed the Scot's bent frame to the ground. The axeman's body crumpled to a lifeless mound.

Halfdan rushed toward Kenneth. He grabbed a wad of Kenneth's hair and stuck his bloody blade an inch from Kenneth's eye. "This is on you, Scot! This is on you." He shoved Kenneth's head sideways and stormed away.

Every nightmare Kenneth had prayed against had now been fulfilled. The man he had hoped to save lay dead before him. Kenneth shut his eyes, and his heart. He despised all that made up the world, even life itself.

The courtyard was empty. An eternity had passed. No sound could be heard except the rush of the wind, blowing in an unseen direction. Despite the agony and regret, Kenneth summoned his spirit to gaze upon his fallen friend. There on the ground before him lay the broken body of the axeman, his cold blue eyes open and peering back at Kenneth. Dorrell's earlier words echoed in Kenneth's ears, piercing his heart like a spear thrown from heaven. In courage, his friend had saved his life and had willingly bore the consequences. It was then that Kenneth understood something he should have understood long ago—that courage is not borne in the hands of the mighty who oppress the weak, but rather in the hearts of the weak who dare to stand against the mighty.

He would not allow it to end here.

He prayed for courage—courage beyond his own.

CHAPTER 16

THAT DAY WAS THE MOST MISERABLE OF DAYS. IT was a day that refused to end. It lingered endlessly, festering like a wound with no cure. Morning had brought the misery of death. Kenneth had watched Dorrell die, robbed of life at the hands of the Vikings. Agony ate at Kenneth's insides like a caustic acid. He begged for the hours to pass, yet the sun stood still, stuck in the sky without end.

Kenneth wiped his brow across his bicep and released an exasperated breath. He surveyed the courtyard for the hundredth time. It was all there. The pit was there, the logs beside the pit were there, and looking down, his chains were there—but Dorrell's body was gone. Kenneth envisioned the butchery over and over in his mind. It was all so surreal.

Kenneth felt dazed. Lack of food and extreme fatigue had drained his strength. He wondered if he was hallucinating or even losing his mind, but the reality of that awful day was not simply some distant dream.

Kenneth shook his head and tried to piece together his thoughts. He scanned the courtyard one more time, looking for the Vikings, or the prisoners, or anything that stirred. They were all gone. The Vikings had taken the prisoners for another day of labor in the forest and quarry, and they had left Kenneth to rot in his chains.

Kenneth lowered his head in a dejected silence. His thoughts blurred and wandered aimlessly. He envisioned Dorrell's open body and Halfdan wielding his bloody blade. The image struck deep as he opened his eyes and peered at the dark red dirt where his friend had been slain.

It was all real, painfully real.

A commotion stirred in the rear of the fort, and more than a half-dozen men on horseback emerged and rode into the courtyard. Halfdan and Kodran rode lead. Magnus rode behind them, along with five others.

The pack of men stopped their horses at the nearly-completed front gate of the fort. Jorund appeared from the Viking barracks and approached the riders.

"Keep the men busy while I'm gone. And finish this," Halfdan said to Jorund as he pointed toward the front entrance.

"I'll see to it," Jorund replied.

"And while I'm away, if a single Scot lifts a finger in opposition, kill him. I tire of their ungrateful hearts."

"And him?" Jorund asked, glancing at Kenneth.

"I don't expect him to be around much longer. Leave him chained to the posts until I return—and cut his rations."

"And if he dies?"

"If he dies … then remove his carcass and throw it in the forest for the wolves," Halfdan groused.

The Viking leader then turned and glared at Kenneth. He leaned forward on his horse and spoke in a clear, deliberate tone, "Kenneth of Dalriada, you are a pitiful man, whom I despise and who comes from a people that I despise. Soon, your end will be upon you."

The words burned Kenneth's ears like a hot brand. "Why not kill me now? Why not take my life and end your madness?"

"Oh, you will give your life, Scot—and sooner than you know. But for now, you'll wait. You see, I prefer to have you die a slow, grueling death … in this way, you'll be a reminder for the other prisoners—a reminder of my hell." Halfdan sneered at Kenneth, holding his gaze for a long moment and daring him to respond.

Kenneth held his tongue. He had nothing to say.

Halfdan shook his head in disgust and turned from Kenneth. Then he pulled the reigns of his horse and pounded his heels into the animal's ribs. "Hayaa." The horse startled and sprinted forward in a gallop.

The others followed.

They headed east.

Ena and Ceana approached the small wooden house on the outskirts of Renton. Constantine and Luag stood conversing just outside the door.

"Constantine, Luag," Ena called out.

"Ena, Ceana," Constantine replied. Luag nodded and smiled cordially, eager to finish his words with Constantine.

"We brought bread and cheese. How is Alpin?" Ena asked.

"He's awake. And he is recovering … his leg more than his spirits," Constantine replied. "We've given him a staff to help him move, but he fusses about it more than he uses it."

"He wants to find them," Ena said somberly.

"We all do," Constantine echoed. He stepped toward the door and opened it. "Come in," he said, holding the door for the two ladies. They entered and Constantine followed, but Luag remained outside, giving a nod as the women passed.

Ena surveyed the walls of the musty stale dwelling before settling her eyes on Alpin. He was sitting in a chair beside the bed, lacing his boots. "Alpin, you're finding your strength again?"

"Ena, yes, I'm fine. Is everything alright?"

"Certainly," Ena said, ignoring Alpin's tone of concern. "We've baked fresh bread. It will lift your spirits." Ena uncovered the loaf and set it on the table.

"It smells good … the smell alone is enough to make a hungry man fight," Alpin replied.

"It's all yours, there's no need to fight," Ena responded. She distracted herself in her basket of food and unpacked a bowl of wild berries and set it down next to the bread.

"We brought cheese too," Ceana said, following behind Ena. She placed the white goat cheese on the table and tried to smile at her father-in-law.

"Thank you, darling," Alpin responded, "I'm sure it's delicious." He looked at her, and by the pink swelling near her eyes, he knew she had been crying. He stood and set his hand on Ceana's shoulder. "What's the matter?"

"It's nothing," Ceana replied. She turned away and began arranging the food, placing the cheese beside the berries and bread.

"It seems something must be wrong?" Constantine remarked, and he stepped to the opposite side of the small table and stared at the two women.

"Nothing's wrong, we have a war to fight and you men are worried about a young girl who is perfectly fine," Ena said, scolding the men.

"Well, clearly something's wrong," Alpin replied. "She's been crying. Anyone can see that."

Ena ignored the comment and poured a cup of water.

"I've been here at the camp with the men. But that doesn't mean I haven't noticed the changes," Alpin said. He peered at Ceana.

No one spoke.

"You're with child. Is that right?" Alpin asked.

Ceana nodded. "Yes," she replied softly.

"Does Coric know?"

"I haven't had the courage to tell him," she said.

"Why would you keep this from him?"

"He would go mad," Ceana blurted out abruptly. "He's consumed with finding Kenneth and the others. Nothing will stop him. If I tell him I am pregnant, it will tear him apart. He wouldn't stop his pursuit. He would only continue in guilt, knowing he's left his wife and his child."

Alpin peered at Ena, trying to measure her involvement. Ena said nothing.

"It's better this way," Ceana said and began cutting the bread, not wanting to cry.

"Ceana, I'm sorry. I am happy to hear of the baby— our first grandchild. But I am sorry Coric is gone. He's headstrong, but he's smart. He won't get into anything that he can't get himself out of. He'll be back," Alpin reassured her.

Ena stepped beside Ceana and gently rubbed her hand on Ceana's back. She turned to Alpin and spoke, "Maybe you should come home. We can feed you and tend to your—"

"No. I must remain here with the men, Ena. And Ceana, I truly am sorry. I'm sorry for Coric not being here."

"Alpin, you need hot meals and someone to tend to your leg. We can help you at home," Ena replied. "Now stop being stubborn and let Constantine stay with the men."

"The men sought me as their leader. I will not turn my back on that responsibility."

"If you're ready to lead, then why do you wait here in this dismal village with all these wandering souls—while our sons are missing!"

"Enough, Ena!" Alpin exclaimed, then paused to temper his anger. "Your words have come in haste. Much is at stake here … dare I say, even more than our sons. Look around, you see what this enemy is capable of. We must strike with a deadly blow, and our first chance may be our only chance. Or else, not only our homes, but our families, our land, and even our way of life could be taken. There is much more to this."

"Five men from Dumbarton have left for Perth," Constantine added, addressing Ena and Ceana. "Guaire believes Oengus and the Picts will join our fight against the Vikings. We have agreed to remain in Renton until they return—we expect two days, three at the most."

Ena stared at her husband. "Do you believe the Picts will fight with us?"

"We are doubtful," Constantine replied. "However, they may, if they believe we are their best chance for defeating the Vikings … and it does buy a few more days for Alpin to recover."

"As I've said to both of you, I am here and I am standing," Alpin rebutted. "I do not wish to lose any more days. We should leave immediately. I don't trust Oengus … I never have."

"I don't like it any more than you, Alpin." Constantine replied. "But we may have no choice this time."

The room fell silent.

Ena returned to her basket and busied herself by removing the bread crumbs from its wicker bottom. "You all should eat," she said aloud, yet to no one in particular.

Ceana occupied herself at the table, cutting the bread and laying each slice one by one on a small wooden plate.

"Ceana," Constantine broke the silence, "I plan on sending some of my men back to Cashel to check on Arabella—"

Thump. Ceana's knife dropped from her hand and hit the table. Her eyes lifted briefly, glancing at Constantine.

"Is there something wrong?" Constantine asked.

"Oh, no, nothing's wrong. The knife is just slippery, it fell from my hand ... what were you saying?" Ceana replied, feigning a smile as she picked up the knife.

"I was saying, some of my men will be returning to Cashel to check on Arabella and our home, as well as other things," Constantine said. "Maybe you would like to join them and stay with Arabella in Cashel. I know she enjoys you. Her company would be good for you, and it would be good for her, too. She'll be delighted to hear of the baby."

"She knows of the baby," Ceana said, blushing. "We talked before she left Renton. But you're right, I think spending time with Arabella would lift my spirits."

Ceana set the knife down beside the plate and turned to Ena, "Would you mind if I left to stay with Arabella for a bit?"

"No, darling. You should go to Cashel," Ena said. "Rest your mind, visit with Arabella. You'll be safe, and you'll be more at ease."

"Then it's settled, my men will leave in the morning. I shall see to it that you are personally escorted to Cashel." Constantine nodded and smiled at Ceana.

She returned his smile graciously.

◎

"Your burns appear to be healing once again," Mathe said as he removed the bandages from Aiden's neck and exposed the wound. "Soon you'll go without bandages, as long as you stay out of fights," the old physician chided.

"So they look better?" Aiden replied. "They still seem to sting when I raise my arm."

"You're lucky to have an arm. Infection could have taken it," Mathe replied, and he laid the soiled bandages on the table and grabbed a clean cloth to start a fresh wrap.

"Why won't you tell me her name?" Aiden asked.

"Whose name?" Mathe muttered, distracted as he cut the cloth into strips.

"The name of the girl who came to my room the other night."

"My duty is to make sick people better, not play matchmaker for young romances."

Aiden grinned and straightened his posture on the edge of the bed. "I am not asking you to arrange a courtship. I'm only curious who the girl was."

"That's not my business," Mathe replied.

"Can you take me to her? I'll introduce myself. You won't have to do anything."

The older man paused from his work and peered at the young Scot, "All I know is that she is a guest of Oengus. If you want more than that, you'll have to take it up with him. I have no more to offer."

"And I thought your duty was to help people," Aiden fussed. He grabbed his pillow and laid it in his lap. Then he rested his arms on it and stared up at the wooden beams framing the ceiling. "She sounded pretty," he murmured, more to himself than to the old physician.

⟐

Coric eyed the faraway figure. Though the distance was great, the signal was clear. He turned to Laise, "It's Ronan. He sees something. We have to get off the path. Let's head to that patch of trees ahead." He pointed to a grove of short evergreens.

Laise responded with a nod.

The two rode from the path and headed toward a dense patch of evergreens standing at the edge of the forest. There they dismounted and led their horses on foot through the brush, weaving deep into the trees. Then they stopped and stared back at the path.

"We'll wait here for Ronan," Coric said, patting his horse to relax the animal.

"Alright, I'll keep an eye out for him," Laise replied.

"The Vikings, they're coming!" Ronan hollered in a hushed voice as he tugged his horse through the trees.

"How far?" Coric asked.

"I was probably a quarter-mile back when I spotted them, and they were a good quarter-mile from where I was. I counted eight of them. They weren't coming at a full clip, but they're moving fast enough," Ronan said. He looked past

Coric, examining the forest behind him. "I think we should head farther back."

The other two agreed, and the three wove deeper into the security of the thickening woods.

After several paces, Coric stopped and peered back toward the path. He bobbed his head up and down, trying to gauge his view. "Let's stop here. I want to be able to see them."

"But, I don't want them seeing us," Ronan replied.

"They won't be able to see us here," Coric said. "Just keep the horses quiet."

The three young Scots settled in the hilly woods of northwest Dalriada, concealed in the forest's dense foliage. They kept silent, with the pounding of their hearts the only sound. Their minds raced and their veins pulsed as each moment passed. The riders would be coming soon.

Clip-clop. Clip-clop.

The faint sound of horse hooves crept into earshot.

"It's them," Coric said. His hand lowered to the handle of his sword. He squeezed its grip then glanced to his left where Laise had drawn an arrow and was seating it in the string of his bow. Glancing right, Ronan was kneeling on one knee, frozen like a stone statue with his crossbow chest high—he only lacked a target.

The sound of hoofbeats grew louder. Distinguishing the number of horses was difficult, but Coric was certain there were more than five and less than ten. He figured Ronan was about right when he had spoken of eight riders.

Coric turned toward Ronan and whispered, "Don't

shoot unless they come at us." Then he turned to Laise and whispered the same.

Coric's gaze returned to the path. Through a small gap in the branches, he saw the leg of a rider pass. He froze. Then a second and third rider passed, nearly at the same time. The shapes were difficult to distinguish from his narrow line of sight.

Three other riders passed in succession.

Then the snout of another horse appeared in view.

Crack.

The three Scots spun their heads, scanning the trees behind them—one of the horses had caught its lead on a twig. Ronan gazed at Coric, his eyes as round as saucers.

The clip-clop sound of the Viking horses stopped. Everything fell silent.

Coric peered back through his small window in the trees. The horse he had seen moments prior was now standing in place, filling his viewing gap between the branches.

The three dared not move, they dared not breathe.

Several voices volleyed back and forth on the path beyond the tree line.

Coric stared at Ronan, and Ronan at Coric. Coric lifted his finger to his mouth and shook his head, gesturing to keep quiet.

Moments passed. The voices died, and the clip-clop sound of the hoofbeats began to echo again through the trees.

The sound of the horses slowly faded and eventually grew faint until only the quiet of the forest remained. The three young Scots sat motionless in the concealment of the trees. No one moved. No one spoke.

After convincing themselves that the Vikings were gone,

the three scrambled on foot through the woods toward the path. Standing at the edge of the forest, they peered east along the path in the direction the Vikings had traveled. In the distance, the path crested and disappeared over a hill. There were no signs of the riders.

Laise left the protection of the trees and moved to the path. "Come here," he said. Kneeling down, he pointed to the fresh hoofprints. "I count eight, Ronan. You were right."

Coric studied the prints, puzzled. "Why eight, and why east?"

"Not sure I know the answer," Ronan muttered. "But if we backtrack and follow their tracks west, I'm guessing we'll find where they came from."

"I'd say they'll end somewhere near Inverawe Woods, and I bet that's where we'll find Kenneth and the others," Coric said. "Lord willing, they're still alive."

"Trust, Coric, trust," Ronan remarked. He peered east, staring down the path. Then he turned and headed toward the trees. "Come on, we need to get the horses," he shouted to the two as he vanished into the woods.

CHAPTER 17

A LONE PICT GUARD DARKENED OENGUS'
doorway and fought to catch his breath. "Lord Oengus,
riders approach from the west," the guard reported. "Eight,
my lord."

"Scots?" Oengus replied, lifting his gaze from a large
parchment on the table in front of him.

"Vikings, my lord."

"Vikings?" Oengus questioned. A single eyebrow raised
on his forehead. He stood from his seat beside the wide
square table and stared down at the parchment, a map of
northern Britannia. "Are you certain there's only eight?"

"Yes, my lord. No other riders, or foot soldiers, appear
to be following," the guard replied. "Should we permit them
to enter the castle—"

"Have you informed Deort?" Oengus interrupted as he
began to move across the floor.

"I have, my lord."

"I want Deort to gather two dozen men. He is to meet
these riders and escort them to the castle. When he returns,
he is to bring them to the dining hall. I will await their
arrival."

"As you wish, my lord." The guard turned and rushed from the doorway.

Oengus continued to pace about the room, massaging his temples as he moved.

Deort stepped through the entryway of the grand dining hall. "My lord, I present to you, Halfdan the Black." Halfdan and seven other Vikings entered the great hall behind Deort, followed by an entourage of Pict guards.

Oengus rose to his feet at the far end of the dining table. "A rather pleasant surprise to see you, Halfdan. What brings you to Perth so unexpectedly?"

Halfdan removed his horned helmet and placed it on the table. He gazed about the room as if Oengus' words had been uttered in silence. "Do you not offer your honored guests food and ale?" After tendering his indictment, Halfdan smirked and his haughty eyes settled on Oengus.

Oengus cocked his head toward a second entryway to his rear. "Baker, food and ale!" he shouted.

"Yes, my lord," a frantic, mousy voice responded from the connecting quarters. "Coming, my lord."

"You and your men are welcome to sit. Some items are being prepared for you," Oengus addressed his visitors and then motioned toward the large dining table in the center of the room. Twelve chairs sat tucked below the ornate oak table, while several more lined the perimeter of the expansive hall. Halfdan and Kodran took seats at the table. The six remaining Vikings found chairs along the wall. Oengus and his men remained standing.

Oengus returned to the head of the table and slowly lowered to his seat.

A small man carrying an oblong wooden plate scurried

into the room. The plate boasted a large portion of boiled chicken and hunks of broken bread piled in a heap. After the servant presented his offering, he set the plate on the table and vanished from the hall. A moment passed and the man reappeared, this time toting a tray of crafted iron steins brimming with ale.

"I trust you will find the food and ale pleasing," Oengus uttered.

"I grow weary of the bloody Scots," Halfdan growled. "For doing the work of slaves, they are a miserable lot. They're more trouble than they're worth. I should slaughter them all."

"You have dealt the Scots a significant blow, Halfdan," Oengus said. "They are broken and weak. I know they gather in Renton, camping among the ruins you left behind. Maybe now is a good time to deliver the next blow … a final blow."

Halfdan grabbed the stein that awaited him. He guzzled the frothy ale and clanged the near empty mug on the tabletop. A remnant of the dark brew perched on his mustache for a moment before slowly seeping into his whiskers and disappearing. He wiped his mouth across his sleeve. "Do you take me for a fool, Oengus?" Halfdan asked. "Do you think I am blind to your charade?"

Oengus chuckled. "I must confess, Halfdan … I miss your point. Enlighten me."

"How is it you know so much about the Scots and Renton, and yet you make no effort to run them through yourself … while they are 'broken and weak,' as you say?" Halfdan stood from his chair and ambled beside the table. "And why is it that I found five Scots on the outskirts of Perth … heading toward this castle?"

"Five Scots, coming here?" Oengus questioned as he rose from his seat. He shot a glance at Deort.

"They're no longer coming. My men saw to that. We came upon them as they watered their horses. And … let me say, they were ill prepared for the encounter," Halfdan noted. "I am certain of one thing—these Scots were no war party. They looked to be coming for a different reason … to make peace with the Picts, I presume."

"Halfdan, you know of my hatred for the Scots. It was I who provided you the time and place to attack them, without this knowledge your attack would have failed."

"Oengus, we both know that in the midst of war, a lie can often bring a man more benefit than the truth." Halfdan glared at Oengus. "Only a fool trusts a man who is not his brother … and the same blood does not run through our veins, old man. So I will say this one time, and one time only—END THE LIE!"

Deort ripped his sword from his metal sheath and leveled it at Halfdan. A loud shrill of scraping metal filled the hall as his men did the same. The Vikings quickly found themselves pinned below the sharp tips of the Pict swords—all except Kodran. His sword hovered neck high, with its point pressed against Oengus' throat.

Halfdan glared at Oengus and then swept his gaze toward Deort, peering into his eyes as if daring him to thrust the Pict blade into his Viking heart. "Ha," Halfdan broke the silence with a laugh. He eased his hand to Deort's blade and pushed it from his chest. "Your men are eager to defend your honor, Oengus. You should be proud." Halfdan surveyed the Pict soldiers, and the smile slowly faded from his face. "Have them withdraw their swords."

"Enough, Deort," Oengus commanded, staring at Kodran's blade and fearing to move.

The Picts lowered and sheathed their weapons. Yet Kodran's sword did not budge. His cold eyes locked on Oengus as the razor-thin tip of his blade teetered inches from the Pict lord's throat.

Oengus took a step backwards and sidled to face Halfdan. "Deort, escort these men to the gathering hall. I would like to speak to Halfdan ... alone."

"Yes, my lord," Deort replied.

Halfdan nodded to his men. The Vikings rose from their seats and departed with the company of Picts. "Magnus," Halfdan called out, "see that the horses are watered. Our stay will be brief."

⊙

Arabella heard a single set of footsteps moving down the stone hallway. The steps made the familiar clacking sound of a Pict guard. Arabella hurried to her bed and sat as the sound of a key clicked in the lock of her door. She leaned sideways and grabbed the hairbrush sitting on the dresser beside her bed. She righted her frame and began to comb the strands of her long brown hair.

When the door opened, a Pict guard stepped inside. The man was carrying a tray of fruit and cheese and a clay pitcher filled with water. The guard was the same guard who'd brought the same meal at the same time for the last six days.

"You come here each day with food. I am perfectly capable of getting my own. Why am I not free to eat outside this room? Why does Oengus insist on keeping me locked up?" Arabella demanded. "I feel as though I'm a prisoner, and yet I've done nothing wrong?"

"Nothing wrong?" the guard replied. "You were snooping about the castle, prying into things that you should have left alone," he said in a cold, terse voice, not looking for a response. He moved across the room to a small table and set down the tray.

"That's not true. I was checking on the young man, he was calling out as if he needed help. Keeping me locked in here isn't right. I want to speak with Oengus." She paused and thought for a moment, then chose a less confrontational approach. "The young man is not a Pict, is he?" she inquired with a softer tone.

"You'll need to ask Lord Oengus these questions," the guard replied. "I'm leaving your food here. You may eat as you will, when you'd like." He stepped from the table and turned to leave.

"Sir," Arabella said. "I'm sorry. I'm tired. I didn't mean to be harsh. Could you please place the tray on the dresser over here?"

The guard's lips pursed as his patience thinned. He lifted the tray and carried it to the dresser.

As the guard lowered the tray to the dresser, Arabella extended her hand, pointing with her hairbrush. "Would you pour—"

Crash. The clay water pitcher tumbled from the tray and smashed on the stone floor.

"Oh, my. I'm so sorry. I should've been more careful," Arabella exclaimed. "I've made such a mess."

The guard stood still, staring down at the broken members of the shattered pitcher. He bit his tongue to resist his urge to reprimand Arabella, then he stooped and began to gather the scattered shards.

Arabella squatted beside him. "Here's a large one," she said, grabbing a sizable fragment of the broken pitcher in one hand and a certain item she was pursing in the other. She stood and placed the jagged piece of hardened clay on the dresser. "I feel awful about this."

The guard, not offering a response, did his best to ignore her. He continued to collect the splintered pieces and piled them in his hand as he knelt on the floor.

Arabella quietly backed away with a single key clasped in her palm.

"I can't believe this," the guard muttered under his breath. He rose from his knees and placed a handful of shards on the tray beside Arabella's bed.

Click.

The lock on the door fastened tight.

The guard spun toward the closed door—and cursed.

۞

Oengus waited in silence as Deort and his men escorted the Viking brood from the dining hall. "You'll have to forgive Deort. He's as loyal as they come," Oengus said to Halfdan and then he walked toward a tall wooden cabinet at the far side of the hall.

"Kodran, as well … loyalty is hard to come by," Halfdan replied, "as is honesty."

Oengus felt the dart but resisted a response. Instead, he continued toward the cabinet and opened its long wooden doors. A small metal box sat on a shelf inside. Oengus pushed the box aside and found the narrow glass vase he was looking for. The slim-necked vessel was half full, boasting a red wine so dark that it appeared black inside the muted vase. He poured a portion and then another, and then he offered a glass to his visitor.

Halfdan took the offering and lifted it above his eyes. He slowly turned the glass, inspecting it in the light of the chandelier's luminance. Then he nodded at Oengus and waited before consuming the crimson nectar.

"It is customary in my culture to propose a toast when partaking of such a fine delight," Oengus said and smiled. "A toast … to the demise of the Scots and to a land free of their misery."

"To the demise of the Scots," Halfdan replied, and he lifted his glass and swigged its contents. The gesture was nothing more than a profane placation. After the red drink emptied into his mouth, Halfdan lowered his glass to the table. He swallowed with a smug grin and spoke, "I trust you're prepared to prove your toast of demise with your sword. Certainly you realize that I did not come here to drink your wine. I came to see that you're ready to fight."

"Picts, Halfdan, are always ready to fight."

"I am glad to hear it, for my patience with the Scots is over. Their time has come. Together, we shall storm their villages and bring their end."

"Yes, we shall," Oengus replied. "And then what? What is your plan once we have crushed the Scots?" Oengus stood arm's length from Halfdan, peering into his cold black eyes. As he gazed at the Viking leader, he realized how little he trusted the man—afraid to call him "enemy" and unwilling to call him "friend."

"My plan? Why must I plan what I have already purposed to do? Surely, you understand that a man must do what a man must do?" Halfdan replied. "I will kill the Scots, and after that, I will do as I please … that is my *plan*."

Oengus, still nursing the wine of his half-empty glass, sidled along the edge of the dining table and separated himself from Halfdan. He paused and peered at the Viking. As if giving a salutary toast, Oengus lifted his glass. "Then we shall kill them together," he proclaimed.

"Kill who together?" a woman's voice came from the large central entryway of the dining hall.

"Arabella, what are you doing here?" Oengus said in startled surprise. A surge of adrenaline raced through his veins, and he eased his glass to the table.

Arabella stepped forward and entered the large room. "Who? Who do you plan to—" She froze as a large figure filled the corner of her eye.

"Your daughter, Oengus?" Halfdan asked, keeping his gaze fixed on the beautiful girl who now occupied his presence.

"No, I am not his daughter," Arabella snapped. "I am more of a … a prisoner, or so it seems." She glared at Oengus, daring him to deny the charge.

"A prisoner?" Halfdan said, amused.

"No, she is not a prisoner," Oengus replied. "She is my guest."

Arabella clasped her hands in front of her waist to keep her poise. "Then why is it you've chosen to lock me away? And who is the young man in bandages that you're keeping? I've spoken to him."

"You have chosen a poor time and place to have this discussion," Oengus said, working to hide his exasperation. "For your own good, you should leave us."

"I don't like what's—" Arabella stopped mid-sentence when she glimpsed the horned helmet sitting at the edge of the dining table. A wave of confusion rushed over her, and her mind went numb. She swallowed hard and took a deep breath as her lungs struggled for air.

She glared at Oengus. "You took Aiden! You took him from Renton! You burned Kenneth's home in Renton, and you took Aiden!" she screamed. "You're not protecting me from the Vikings, you're helping them!"

"Quiet, woman!" Oengus exclaimed. "You know nothing of what you say. My men found that boy half dead on the riverbanks. I had nothing to do with the burning of Renton!"

Halfdan removed his jewel-handled knife from his belt. "Come now, Oengus. Would you truly say *nothing*?" He pulled an apple from the basket in the center of the table, cut a sliver from the green fruit, and shoved it in his mouth. "You should tell the young lady of your little secret."

"Halfdan, please," Oengus insisted.

Halfdan swallowed his mouthful and then chomped a second bite without cutting it. Dribbles of the apple's juice beaded on his beard. He gazed at Arabella and smiled. "You mentioned this *Kenneth*. Would this be Kenneth the Scot?" His smile faded to a sneer.

Arabella stared into the Viking's eyes, dumbstruck. She wanted to speak but her lips were incapable of forming words.

"Kenneth the Scot, son of Alpin … a son of Renton," Halfdan restated. "Yes. By your silence, I assume we speak of the same Kenneth."

Halfdan bit again into the apple. He tossed the half-eaten core on the table and approached Arabella. "Indeed, you are a pretty little thing. Is this Kenneth your brother …

no, a relative … no, a lover," Halfdan said with a smirk. "Yes, yes, a lover. Your tongue is still, yet your heart exposes you. He is your lover. Or should I say … he was your lover."

"Halfdan, please. She is my guest. Please, let her be." Oengus glared at Arabella with a stern frown carved upon his face, "Arabella, please go."

"Wait, let's not have her leave just yet," Halfdan said and then glanced down at the pouch hanging from his belt. "I have something to show her. A surprise for her." Halfdan dug into his pouch and removed a gold cross tied to a cord of leather. With the cord draped over his finger, he lifted the necklace into the air, dangling the gold trinket in front of Arabella like a small prized pendulum swinging back and forth.

"Where did you get this?" Arabella asked and reached for the cross.

Halfdan snatched it back and grinned, "I ripped it from the little runt's neck, before I left him to die. I suppose the crows are now feasting upon his rotting flesh."

"Oh God, no!" Arabella placed her hand over her mouth and dashed from the room.

"Arabella, wait!" Oengus shouted and he rushed toward the corridor.

Halfdan grabbed the Pict lord by the arm. "She is not your concern right now, old man. We have more important things to pursue—"

Oengus ripped his arm from Halfdan's grasp. "I will not be told what I may or may not do in my land and in my castle."

"You act as a fool, Pict."

"You've been the fool. She's the daughter of Constantine. He—"

"He what? Who is Constantine and why should I care?"

"Letting her know about us was foolish," Oengus said. "She knows too much."

"Then kill her."

"I will not kill her … is that your answer for everything, kill everyone?"

"You are weak, Pict."

"I know this land. I know these people. Only a fool would—"

"Choose your next words wisely, Pict … choose them wisely," Halfdan warned.

Oengus gazed down the empty hallway and then set his eyes on Halfdan. He shook his head and began to pace, rubbing his forehead as he thought. He stopped and stood for a moment and then broke his silence, "Halfdan, it's best that you leave."

Halfdan glared at the Pict. "And the Scots?"

"They're yours to kill … kill them if you wish," Oengus replied, and he waved his hand in the air as if to relinquish his conscience.

"I will go … and I will kill them. And when I'm done, I will take their land—and any land I please." Halfdan ripped his helmet from the table and departed the hall.

Arabella found the outdoor air of the courtyard. She staggered several steps and clutched a stone pillar at the perimeter of the yard. She bent and heaved as her stomach convulsed. She didn't want to believe the man's words. They couldn't be true. Kenneth couldn't be dead. He'd promised he'd return. Dread pervaded her every thought. She tried to convince herself that the man with the gold cross was a liar—and that Kenneth was alive.

Despair overwhelmed her as vivid, horrific images stormed her mind, images of Viking men beating Kenneth and stripping the necklace from his dead body. He would never give it up—not alive.

She placed her palms on the stone pillar for strength, then straightened herself and lifted her eyes. She stared up at the sky, looking to Heaven for even the smallest glimmer of understanding. But the chilly gray sky offered no sign, no promise, no hope.

She remained silent, wondering—wondering if Kenneth had suffered. Question after question tumbled through her mind. *Why was the Viking with Oengus? Who did they plan on killing? Why does Oengus have Aiden?* Nothing made sense, only now she knew she could trust no one.

She stood alone, dazed, angry, and broken.

A hand suddenly grabbed her arm.

She spun quickly, expecting Oengus or a Pict guard. The hand belonged to no guard and to no Pict.

The Viking was massive and covered with hair. From his head to his neck and down his shoulders and arms, his skin appeared as wool. The beastly, hirsute brute gazed at her with excitement, amused by her reaction. His lips snarled through his beard and mustache and he chuckled. "Quite the pretty little Pict," he muttered.

"Don't touch me," she shouted. "Keep your hands off me!"

"I know women like you. You play as though you want to resist, but you enjoy the attention," Magnus said. Then he pulled Arabella toward him and reached for her other arm.

Arabella flailed and slapped his chest as he grabbed for her.

"You're a playful one, aren't you?" he said. His hand shot

forward again, this time successfully grasping her free wrist. Her arms were now tightly locked in his grip. "Come here you. You're a pretty little lassie … I want a kiss."

Arabella craned her neck to turn away.

Magnus pulled her close and puckered his lips. His hairy mouth touched her skin and he kissed her cheek, his tongue flipping and turning in search of her lips.

She shook her head violently side to side. "Stop, stop!"

Magnus stood upright and eyed Arabella's comely frame, surveying her from head to toe, "You're special, little lady. I could eat you up." He tightened his grip and forced himself on her a second time.

"No, stop!" Arabella screamed as she fought her assailant.

The more she fought, the more aggressive he became. He let go of her wrists and grabbed her blouse. With a yank, he tore off her sleeve, exposing her arm and shoulder. Magnus held his cloth prize aloft and smiled proudly.

Arabella screamed and then heard a *thump*.

Magnus stood stone-cold with a blank look filling his eyes.

Thump!

A second blow landed.

Magnus released his hold. His hearing dulled, and his vision blurred with dots of black. He stumbled forward, swaying side to side. Then he fell backwards and struck the ground, unconscious.

"Arabella!" Aiden exclaimed, holding a large rock in his hands. He threw the stone to the ground beside the oversized Viking.

"Aiden, it's you!" She wrapped her arms around his waist and hugged him. "Your bandages," she said. Releasing Aiden, she inspected the cloth wraps around his neck. "You've been badly injured … I knew it was you."

"Yes, I was burned when the Vikings raided Renton … but I'm getting better now," Aiden replied. "What about you, what are you doing here? I thought you were dead?"

A puzzled expression formed on Arabella's face. "You thought I was dead?"

"Searc told me how the Vikings came back to Renton and raided again, that they returned to finish what they'd started, that only my mother survived. I thought you, too, were killed when they returned."

"Searc? When did you see Searc? And how did you survive, Nessa said she watched you fall from the ridge?"

"Nessa!" Aiden exclaimed. "You saw Nessa? And Kenneth?"

Hearing the name nearly killed Arabella. A flood of sadness poured over her. She gazed at Aiden and shook her head back and forth, "Nessa's alright … but Aiden … I don't think Kenneth made it."

"No, Arabella, don't say that. Don't say that."

Arabella's eyes closed and a tear streamed down her cheek. "Aiden, they killed him. They have his cross. They told me they watched him die."

"Who did, Arabella? Who?"

"The Vikings. They're here … I think he's one of them," Arabella said, and she pointed at Magnus.

"Does Oengus know? We have to find him."

"No, Aiden, you don't understand—he's with them."

"What do you mean, 'he's with them?'" Aiden replied. "Oengus hates them. Arabella, he saved my life. It was Oengus, it was his soldiers, who found me lying on a riverbank nearly dead. I owe them everything for saving me."

"Aiden, you don't owe the Picts, you don't owe Oengus. He's a part of all this. He ...," Arabella stopped herself and quickly glanced about the courtyard. "Aiden, we need to leave this place. We're not safe here."

"Let me speak with Oengus. He'll explain all this."

"No, Aiden, you have to trust me." Arabella pointed again toward Magnus, "Do you see this man, do you see his clothes, Aiden? Do you recognize them? He is a Viking. Please trust me, we have to leave now!"

"Alright, alright, I trust you. Let me go and get my sword and—"

"Aiden, we can't go back. We must go now!"

Aiden peered at the Viking and the puddle of blood pooling beside his head. "I'll take his sword," Aiden muttered, and he stooped and removed Magnus' weapon. Then he lifted and paused to scan the walkways exiting the courtyard. "Come with me," he said, taking Arabella's hand. "I know a way out."

CHAPTER 18

UNDER THE HIGH NOON SUN THE COOL TOUCH OF water falling upon Kenneth's lips felt as though an angel from heaven had come to take him home. He opened his eyes and beheld the silhouette of a woman—*Arabella*?

She was radiant. She extended a cup and offered another sip.

"Bella." A smile formed on Kenneth's cracked lips as he spoke. He blinked to clear the haze from his sight, but a fog remained, clouding his mind. He wanted to hold the angelic being, to feel her, to touch her. Speaking in a broken, hardly intelligible voice, a desire-laden utterance spilled from his tongue, "kiss me."

The woman shifted in her stance, yet did not bend or reach to extend her lips to his.

Kenneth shook his head and widened his eyes. The blurry image of Arabella faded, and the form of a young redhead appeared.

"It's alright," Rhiannon said. "Go ahead, drink."

"I'm sorry … I thought you were someone—" he couldn't finish.

"No … it's only me," Rhiannon responded, her

expression veiling a hidden frown. She placed the cup to Kenneth's lips and he drank.

"Thank you ... thank you for the water," Kenneth said. A single drop of the precious liquid dripped from his chin as he lowered his head.

Rhiannon stared at his chains. Her eyes inched from his bound wrists to the trim muscles of his arms and up to the fleshy sores on his shoulders, where the Viking whip had left its marks. She dared not to gaze upon his back. Her heart broke for him as he knelt before her, tattered and shackled like a tortured criminal. She extended her fingers to touch his hand. Yet, hovering above his skin, she withdrew.

Kenneth lifted his brow and settled his eyes on her. "Rhiannon, I never meant for it to happen. Dorrell was a good friend, a good man. I'm sorry for his death. Please forgive me."

Rhiannon nodded, her countenance now unable to conceal her sadness. "I'm sorry, too." She withdrew from Kenneth, still gazing at him, and then she slowly turned and stepped away.

Kenneth's frame sunk, and his eyes lowered to the ground.

⊚

Coric stopped midstride. He raised his hand and gave the signal to halt.

The three Scots froze in the thick forest, listening to the loud boom still echoing through the trees.

"The cracking sound and then the *thump*. That was a tree falling," Laise whispered.

"It's hard to say where it came from, but it sounded as if it was over there," Ronan said and pointed south.

"Shhh," Coric muttered in a low voice. "Can you hear that?"

"Hear what?" Ronan asked.

Coric waited a moment. "That," he said. He cocked his head and cupped his hand behind his ear. "That *thunk, thunk, thunk* sound."

"I don't hear anything," Ronan replied.

"Try cleaning your ears next time you bathe," Coric said. He glanced at Laise, and the two smiled at one another.

"Shut up. I don't hear the *thunk, thunk* you're talking about. Maybe it's you. Maybe you're hearing things."

"I hear it," Laise said. "It's faint, but it sounds like an axe."

"That would explain the falling tree," Coric noted.

"We could be closer to the Vikings than we think," Ronan said. "We've been off the path for some time."

"It wasn't safe, and any riders would have spotted us," Coric replied. "But you're right, we may be nearer than we think." Coric scanned the forest. The ground sloped upward to the south and crested a hundred yards ahead. "I agree. I think the sound came from that direction." He stepped forward slowly and waved his arm for the two to follow.

The three ascended the incline, sidestepping the fallen branches and dead logs strewn across the forest floor as they proceeded in silence.

"Alright, I hear the *thunk* sound now," Ronan whispered loudly as the three neared the crest of the hill.

"Good to know your ears are working," Coric chided.

The threesome stopped at the top of the hill and ducked

to lower themselves. One by one, they lifted to peer over the hill.

"Coric, do you see that? There, through those trees, do you see someone moving?" Laise said, pointing as he spoke.

"Yes, I do. I see movement."

"Look over there, there's more of them. I hear the axes again, too," Ronan added as the sound of the chopping blades returned.

"I see people moving, but I can't see enough to make out who they are," Coric said. "The trees are too thick."

"I think I can. Look, right there." Ronan pointed. "That one's wearing a helmet. I see the horns too—it's a Viking."

Laise hunched and ambled to his left, keeping behind the hill as he moved. He stopped and peered again through the trees. "I can see more men from over here. The men with the axes aren't Vikings, they're Scots!"

"Can you see Kenneth?" Coric hurried toward Laise. "Where do you see Scots? Wait, I see them … Kenneth must be near, we've got to get closer."

"We can't get any closer without them seeing us," Ronan warned.

"We have to. If we move north, we can go around them and get closer."

"Are you trying to get us killed? Even from here, I'd say there are at least a dozen Vikings."

Coric peered at Ronan. "Are you saying I'm going alone?" *Crack … crack … crack … BOOM!*

The shearing of a great pine and its subsequent smashing to the earth was enough to startle the three. "Damn, that scared me," Ronan said, anxious and edgy. He glared at Coric, "I wasn't saying you have to go alone. I'm saying you're bloody mad!"

"Coric, look at the sky. Dusk is near," Laise said. "With darkness coming, they'll be finished soon. When they leave, we can follow them … they'll lead us to their camp."

"And then what do we do, ask them to surrender and tell them to burn everything?" Ronan quipped.

"We're going to do something. We didn't come here to stand in the distance and watch."

"What do we do with the horses?"

"We'll have to leave them here. The risk is too great to bring them with us," Coric replied. He glanced at Laise and then back at Ronan. "We'll wait 'til dusk … and then we'll follow them on foot."

"That's the final cart of logs, and the prisoners are being led away," Coric whispered and then pointed to a man in the distance. "That one over there is the last of the Vikings from what I can see. We should go now." He glimpsed over his shoulder but found only Laise, who was crouching with his back turned and staring into the forest. "Where is Ronan?" Coric exclaimed. "He was just here."

"He needed to find a tree," Laise said with a lopsided grin. Then he glanced back at the forest, "Hurry up, Ronan. We've got to go."

Ronan stepped from behind a large oak tree. "Finished," he stated proudly.

"Couldn't you have done that earlier?"

Ronan smiled. "I'm done. No worries, let's go."

Coric shook his head. "Get your things, we're heading out. We must keep them in our sights." Coric lifted to his feet and moved over the hill. He kept his eyes locked on the horned helmet of the last Viking rider. From afar, they followed the procession of men.

As dusk settled, the distant sun broke through the western clouds and sat on the horizon like a dull pink globe. Soon after, the blanketing clouds swelled and darkness crept into the evening sky.

A small remnant of sunlight lingered as Coric and the two followed the Vikings west. The patchwork of trees among the dipping valleys and lofting hills gave the three ample means of hiding as they trailed their enemy. They followed the Vikings, carts, and captives from a distance, silent and unseen. When the procession reached a particularly large hill, several of the Vikings broke right and separated from the others.

"What are they doing?" Coric said.

"Looks like they're splitting up. The prisoners and the carts are going over there," Laise said and gestured with his hand. "Yet most of the Vikings on horseback are heading that way." He then motioned northward.

"Maybe their camp is on the other side of the hill," Ronan added.

"Then maybe Kenneth is there," Coric replied.

The captives and carts vanished beyond the hill, and the last Viking disappeared behind them.

"It'll be dark soon," Laise said. "We've got to see what's on the other side."

"See the large evergreen where the hill crests?" Ronan said. "If we could get to it, its branches are near enough to the ground that we could hide under them."

"Yes, that's good. Let's go!" Coric leapt forward and ran across the opening toward the evergreen.

"He's absolutely mad," Ronan grumbled aloud.

Laise stood and pulled his bow off his back. He glanced left and then right before staring square into Ronan's eyes,

"It's now or never." Ronan nodded, and the two burst into the opening and dashed up the hill behind Coric.

Reaching the evergreen, Coric leapt and slid headfirst below the sweeping green branches of the broad-based tree. His face brushed across the ground, and a handful of pine needles stuck to his lips. He lifted his head with a grimace and spat the needles from his mouth. He quickly found he wasn't alone. His sudden intrusion beneath the tree had caused a stir, and an angry dove fluttered in the branches above his head. The bird chirped and chattered, then flew from the evergreen.

A moment later, Ronan and Laise slid in behind him.

Coric glanced at the two while still wiping debris from his mouth. "I was hoping you'd follow."

"Did we have a choice?" Ronan groused.

After brushing off their hands and shoulders, the three rearranged and sat up under the thick green branches.

Coric parted the limbs and peered into the distance. "Look at that thing," he uttered in amazement.

Laise and Ronan crawled forward and gazed through the branches across the hill. They beheld something they had never expected to see in Dalriada.

"It's unbelievable," Ronan muttered.

"It's massive," Laise said. "Appears they expect to stay."

"Look over there, next to the creek. The Vikings are taking their horses to that fenced corral. Follow the fence … can you see where it—my God, there must be a couple hundred horses in there," Coric said, half dazed, half astonished.

"And down there, the prisoners are heading through that opening in the front of the fort," Ronan said. "They're turning left as they enter, but I can't tell where they're going."

"Coric! Do you see that!" Laise said, pulling Coric's shoulder to align his sight.

"Yes ... I see."

"Do you think that is—"

"Kenneth?" Coric said, finishing Laise's thought. "Yes, that's him. I'm sure of it."

"He seems to be in bad shape. Looks nearly dead."

"I'm guessing he wouldn't be chained to those posts if he was dead," Coric snapped.

"Well, if he is still alive, we'd better get him soon," Ronan said.

"I intend to," Coric replied. "I intend to."

"How do we want to do this and keep ourselves and the others alive?" Ronan asked. "The sun is gone, and soon there won't be a trace of light."

"Here's what we know. We've got to free Kenneth and the others. Once they're free, we've got to get out of there without them chasing us ... or catching us," Coric said.

"I know that's *what* we want to do. I'm asking, *how* are we going to do it?"

"You and I are going in there, Ronan."

"Why is it always me that has to go with you? What's Laise going to do?"

"He'll do what he does best," Coric replied.

Ronan rubbed his face and exhaled. "Coric ... never mind." Ronan said nothing more. He took another deep breath and retreated back to rubbing his face.

"I know this won't be easy, but Ronan, I have no other choice. I have to save my brother—"

"And if you can't?" Ronan asked.

Coric glared at him. "Then I'll die trying."

Moonlight gleamed through a thin slit in the low-hanging clouds. The sun rested for the night. Coric glanced down at his dim reflection in the creek's glassy black water. Then he looked back to find Ronan. With his body submerged, Ronan's wet matted hair appeared as a smooth black helmet floating on the water's surface.

Coric swiveled his head to survey his surroundings. The corral stood forty yards away. The snorting of the penned horses was the only disturbance in the silence of the night. Coric sunk deeper in the water and began crawling with his hands and feet toward the bank of the creek.

When he reached the shallows of the bank, he remained buried below the water with only his eyes and nose exposed.

He waited.

Ronan snuck beside Coric and then stopped and lifted his head to see.

"Shhh," Coric whispered. His hand slowly rose from the water. He held up two fingers and pointed to the side of the corral where it connected to the fort.

Ronan's eyes followed Coric's fingers. He shifted his head sideways to see under the horses. Past the legs and bellies of the animals, Ronan spotted the feet of two men. "Any others?" Ronan whispered.

"No, not that I can see," Coric replied. He glanced back at the far side of the creek, then slowly combed his eyes over the water and back to the rear of the corral before returning his gaze to the men inside the pen.

Quietly, he inched from the water. Droplets dribbled off his clothes and fell back into the black pool from which he emerged. The night air was cool on his skin.

Ronan followed.

The two crept toward the outermost edge of the corral. When they reached the pen, they slipped between its horizontal beams and slowly twisted their way through the labyrinth of horses, hunching as they moved and keeping their distance from the Viking guards. Coric couldn't recall seeing this many horses in one place. They numbered well into the hundreds.

The two continued their silent weave through the large animals, advancing toward the fort. Ronan stayed lockstep with Coric until a small mare stepped between the two. Ronan paused and then nudged the mare's hindquarters, attempting to move by her. The horse nickered at Ronan's unwelcomed shove.

Coric heard the animal's complaint—and the murmuring of the guards that followed. He stopped in his tracks and kept low, his heart pounding in his chest. He glanced back, scanning to find Ronan. Lowering to a squat, he panned in a circle and saw Ronan's feet not far behind. Then he spied ahead to sight the guards. The murmuring had stopped, but only one set of feet remained.

Where is the second guard? Coric's thoughts ran wild. He scanned below the horses again, studying every movement. There, fifteen feet ahead, were the feet of the second guard— and they were coming straight toward him.

The Viking traversed between the few remaining horses that separated the two. Then the man stopped.

Coric could hear the guard speaking, but he couldn't understand the words. Coric ducked below the belly of a tall black gelding, and his eyes locked on the guard's feet. The man began to move again, still heading toward Coric.

Coric's breathing accelerated and adrenaline coursed

through his veins. The man shuffled toward the large horse, stepped behind the animal's back end, and stopped close enough for Coric to touch him.

The man slowly bent to peer below the gelding.

Instantly, Coric sprung from the side of the beast and cleared the animal's rear in a single bound. When the Viking lifted, Coric reached for the man's head and cupped his hand over the man's mouth. In a blink, Coric's wet blade severed the Viking's soft throat.

Coric clutched the Viking to his chest as the man shuttered. Then he eased the Viking's dying frame to the ground. Coric squatted next to the body and wiped his blade on the Viking's sleeve. The horses stirred and began pressing in on him. He scooted to an opening and surveyed below the horses in search of Ronan. Seeing only hooves in the shadowy darkness, he lifted and peeked over the horses to locate the second guard. The guard was gone.

Coric lowered his head and stared back at the dead man and the puddle beside the man's neck. Coric closed his eyes tight and shook his head for a single moment.

Abruptly, he snapped from his trance. He had to find Ronan—he had to find Kenneth.

Coric eased up and poked his head above the horses.

"Olaf … Olaf?" a husky voice called out.

Coric ducked. The voice was close.

Unff.

Coric tensed. The sound was distinct. It was the chilling, unforgiving sound of a man's last gasp of breath.

Coric's heart thumped like a pounding hammer inside his chest. He squeezed his knife and leapt forward, passing three horses before his pelvis rammed unexpectedly into the railing of the corral. He doubled over and fought to right himself, exposed under the dim moonlight. Out of the corner of his eye, he caught the figure of a man.

Coric spun, knife in hand, ready to fight.

"Coric," the voice said.

"Ronan, it's you. You nearly scared me to death." Coric stepped away from the pen railing, rubbing his hip.

"At least this one's dead." Ronan whispered, glancing down at the lifeless body at his feet. "Tell me you got the other one?"

"Yes, but it wasn't pretty," Coric replied as he seated his knife in his belt.

"Come with me, I think I found what we're looking for." Ronan turned toward the fort and motioned for Coric to follow.

Ronan led Coric to an eight-foot-wide opening on the side wall of the fort, the means of access between the fort and the corral. A single pine log, suspended chest high, spanned the opening.

"Let's take this off before we go in. I don't want to get blocked inside the fort if we need to escape with the others," Coric said, and he grabbed one end of the log.

"What about the horses? What if they follow us?"

"We better not be in there that long … we'll set it down here. That'll keep them from coming behind us," Coric replied, pointing to the ground at the opening.

"I don't know, Coric."

"Just lift the damn log!" Coric grabbed his end and glared at Ronan.

Ronan grabbed the opposite end, and the two lifted the log from its braces.

Coric laid his end on the ground. "I've got another idea

that will help," he said and hurried past Ronan to the corral railing.

Ronan set the log down and followed.

"Let's remove some of these beams in the railing," Coric said.

"I don't think …," Ronan started, then he glimpsed Coric's irritated frown and held his tongue. "Forget it," he mumbled to himself.

The two removed enough beams to satisfy Coric, and then they disappeared into the shadows of the fort.

Kenneth kept his eyes closed. He would force himself to sleep. Maybe sleep would come. It was his only escape. Often, he wished he would sleep and never wake. He hated himself for wishing such things. It was shameful, and the shame ate at him.

He twisted in his chains, trying to relieve his back of the crick that throbbed between his shoulder blades. Night brought his muscles the ills of sleeping upright, pain that wouldn't ease no matter how he altered his posture. As he lifted his chin to stretch the knotted muscles in his neck, he heard the guards stirring at the entrance to the prison. Kenneth opened a single disinterested eye and gazed at the two.

One of the guards had stood and was walking away from his seat beside the prison door. Kenneth opened both eyes. *Looking for a place to piss,* Kenneth guessed. The second guard remained slumped on his stump, half asleep.

Kenneth shut his eyes. The pain between his shoulders bit again. He rolled his head to either side in search of relief. None came. *God, crush me now and end this.* He took a deep breath and released a miserable sigh. Then he lowered his head.

His muscles continued to burn.

More footsteps. Kenneth opened his eyes again. He gazed at the prison entrance. The two guards sat like statues in the dull moonlight.

The footsteps? He knew he'd heard them. He looked left, Dorrell's pit lay somewhere within the dark shadows of the fort's front wall. Kenneth stared into the darkness. It was empty and black. Kenneth envisioned Dorrell emerging from the shadowy pit and a chill ran down his spine. He blinked his eyes and squinted. Something in the darkness was moving.

Kenneth quickly glanced back toward the prison guards. Neither budged.

He peered again at the pit and stared into the darkness. Someone was watching him.

Coric remained in the shadows, gazing at the figure tied to the post. *It's Kenneth.* Emotions flooded over Coric's soul like a crashing tidal wave. He inhaled to catch his breath. He thought of his father—and how he would treasure the sight of his son, alive.

Kenneth was alive, but barely. Even the dim ambience of the cloudy night couldn't hide Kenneth's worn, beleaguered frame and his gaunt appearance.

Coric glanced at the two guards sitting in near slumber beside the prison. "Ronan, I'm getting Kenneth," he whispered. Coric stood straight, clutched his knife, and stepped out of the shadows. He brazenly walked the Viking courtyard toward his brother as if the sun lit the sky above and the two were the only people left on earth. He dared any man to stop him—he had found his brother, and he was going to take him home.

A silhouette materialized and moved toward Kenneth.

Kenneth studied the figure as it approached. The movement of the body, the gait of the stride, they were familiar.

Kenneth wondered if his eyes were playing tricks on him. *Coric? His heart leapt. It can't be! It can't be!* Kenneth's mouth opened, and he uttered a hopeful whisper, "Coric?" He thought he was hallucinating. Again, he uttered, "Coric?" The urge to laugh and weep swept over him in delirium.

"Yes, Kenneth it's me, Coric. I've come to get you out of here." Coric placed his hand on the back of Kenneth's head and cupped it like a father would a child. His eyes traced up and down Kenneth's haggard frame—he looked awful, but he was alive. A smile spread across Coric's face. He gripped Kenneth's soiled hair and peered into his eyes, "We're going home."

"Coric … I never thought I'd see you again … I thought I would die here."

"No Kenneth, you're not going to die here. Not here. Not tonight."

As Kenneth beheld Coric, his heart fell. "Coric … Aiden is dead."

Coric stared long into his brother's eyes. "I know, Kenneth. I know." Coric drew a deep breath, "Kenneth, we've got to get you out of here."

Kenneth gazed down and lifted his hands, "But these chains … and the guards?"

Suddenly, the sound of footsteps emerged behind Coric.

Kenneth peered past his brother. "Coric! The guard, he's coming."

Coric glanced at his knife, then he gazed at Kenneth and nodded.

"What are you doing?" the guard called as he approached. Then the man lifted his sword.

Coric didn't turn, he didn't move.

Kenneth's eyes widened. "Coric!"

The whisper of an arrow hummed in the darkness. It came quietly through the night air from a distant longbow and entered the Viking's back. There the arrow rested with its bloody tip poking out from the man's chest. The man gaped down at his severed flesh and slowly collapsed beside the two Scots, dead.

Kenneth's mind spun in a daze.

Coric turned the Viking over and grabbed the iron key from the man's belt. "Nice shot," Coric muttered to Kenneth. "Glad he's on our side."

"Laise?" Kenneth asked.

Coric nodded and unlocked his brother.

Kenneth rubbed his wrists and ankles. "Freedom. I never thought I'd feel it again. Thank you, Coric."

"I'm happy you're alive. Let's get you—"

"Stop there, Scot!"

Coric slowly turned. The guard held his crossbow locked on Coric's heart.

"Where did you come from?" the guard said, then a confused expression appeared upon his face, and he glanced back at the prison door.

A second arrow streaked through the night and found its target. A brittle *crack* of wood sounded when the Viking hit the ground and snapped the arrow that protruded from his forehead.

"Hurry, Kenneth, we've got to go. Follow me," Coric said, and he led Kenneth to the fort entrance. The two reached the fifteen-foot front opening and moved past it to the shadows near Dorrell's pit.

Ronan stepped from the darkness. "Kenneth."

"Ronan?" Kenneth said in disbelief. "Are there others here, too?"

"Only Laise, Ronan, and me. We tried to come sooner with Father, but we were ambushed, and Father took an arrow in the thigh. It got him good. He'll limp for a while, but he'll recover," Coric said. He gazed about the dark fort, surveying the large courtyard. Ten low-burning torches sat mounted along the fort walls. "I saw the prison over there. Is that where the others are?"

"There are a few dozen men in the prison," Kenneth said, and he motioned to where the guards had been. "And over there, that's where the women are being kept." Kenneth pointed past the prison. Then he turned toward the north wall and pointed again, "Those quarters are where the Vikings are. The bastard Halfdan, their leader, left with several others. I'm not sure where they were heading."

"We saw eight Vikings on the path as we came … I suspect that was them," Ronan said, then he peered at Coric. "What do we do now?"

"We free our people and we burn the place," Coric answered.

Coric unlocked the prison door. The three stepped into the pen and woke the captives. Under the sparse clouds of the dark Dalriada night, they devised a plan.

Kenneth left the prison first. He left to free the women.

After Kenneth departed, the weakest of the captives were led from the prison to the carts where the men began hitching the horses. They were the first to escape the miserable fort.

The last to exit the pen was Gavin. He joined several of the prisoners, and together they headed to a pile of extinguished torches. There the men scattered and lit their torches from those burning along the fort walls. Scampering the fort perimeter, they set fire to the pine-built fortress. Then a handful of Scots broke from the group and dashed to Halfdan's platform and set it ablaze. The Vikings' quarters were the last to be lit—the Scots final salvo would be the lighting of the hornets' nest.

Kenneth entered the women's quarters holding a torch in one hand. He woke the first woman. She startled, and he placed his hand to her mouth. "Shhh," he whispered. "It's alright. It's me, Kenneth. We're escaping tonight. Help me wake the others. We have to get out of here!"

Once the women were up, Kenneth gathered them to the door. He quietly poked his head outside and then turned and addressed the ladies, "You need to stay together and head to the corral. The men will get you in the carts and take you away from here. Go quickly."

The women fled the small lean-to and hurried toward the corral. Only Rhiannon stayed behind. She gazed at Kenneth, "How did you do this?"

"It wasn't me. It was my brother. He's come with some others. Now, you must go."

"Will I see you again?"

Kenneth stared at her, puzzled, "You must go … please hurry."

Rhiannon placed her hands on his cheeks, and she leaned forward and kissed him.

Her lips were soft and tender against his. He thought of pushing her away.

He pulled back. "You should go."

She peered into his eyes and then spun and vanished through the door.

A dozen Scots were all that remained inside the fort walls. The small group seized an empty cart and wheeled it to the entryway of the horse corral. Once positioned, the men flipped the cart on its side and set it on fire to hinder any attempt to access the corral. Then the group split in two. Half of them headed to the Viking quarters, while the others hurried to the fort's front entrance.

Reaching the Viking's sleeping quarters, the Scots hurled their torches onto the thick thatch roofs. In moments, the thatch ignited in flames. Light danced upon the men's faces as they watched the fire consume the rooftops. They joyously cursed the devils inside before hurrying to the fort entrance.

Jorund and several dozen groggy, disoriented Vikings scurried from the burning structures. Jorund yelled an order to one of his men. The man tore through the courtyard and grabbed the large brass war horn from its post. The man puffed out his chest and blew.

Hoorrraaannn.

Seconds passed before the blazing fort was crawling with Vikings scrambling about like a crazed colony of ants traversing a freshly crushed mound.

Jorund barked at the men, but his shouts fell on deaf ears amidst the chaos of shadows and fire. He rushed back into his quarters, ignoring the scorching flames, and reappeared with axe in hand. A lone Scot heading to the fort entrance ran past. The large Viking swung his weapon and struck the man, waylaying the poor soul in a single blow.

Jorund turned and strode with quick, angry steps toward the corral. There he found the toppled cart, ablaze and sealing the entryway. He spat on the flames in disgust and headed to the front entrance of the fort. In the distance, a mob of Scots surrounded a cart filled with the day's lumber. Jorund moved with pace toward the mob.

The Scots worked the log-filled cart back and forth, steering it across the opening of the front entryway.

"You men, push from the rear." Kenneth shouted. "Coric, you and I will pull from the front. We've almost got it."

As the men pushed and pulled, the tall white pines forming the fort walls burned like a furnace in the black Dalriadan night.

Kenneth stepped back and sized the fort opening while the others gave a final push to the slow-rolling cart. "Stop, that's good—let's go," Kenneth called to Coric and the men.

The two brothers stood side by side, watching as the men ducked below the cart and lifted to freedom on the opposite side.

Out of nowhere, Nicol appeared from the shadows, winded and excited. "We got'em Kenneth. We got'em. The entire fort is going up in flames!"

"They get what they deserve," Kenneth said with a notable tone of spite. "Now, drop below the cart and get out of here."

As Nicol began to stoop, Kenneth grabbed his arm. "Wait, where's Gavin?"

"He was right behind me. He should be coming."

Kenneth nodded and turned back to scan the courtyard. His eyes locked on the posts where he'd been chained. "Good riddance," he muttered. Then something caught the corner of his eye. He spun his head and stiffened. It was Jorund. The beastly Viking was approaching fast, with several men behind him. "Coric, Nicol, we have to go."

Gavin instantly materialized in front of the three, sprinting with a torch in one hand and a bucket of oil in the other. Without stopping to speak, he doused the log-filled cart with the oil, threw his torch onto the logs, and swiftly slipped below the undercarriage. In an instant, he popped up on the other side and dashed toward the waiting horses.

As Gavin's torch came to rest on the pile of logs, it teetered momentarily before dropping between the lumber into the belly of the cart. Within moments, billowing fingers of fire rose from the bed, licking the logs and lifting high into the air.

Nicol rushed to the cart and grabbed a rope from the sidewall. Then he lowered to the ground and crawled under. On the other side, he jumped to his feet and peered back at Kenneth and Coric through the flames.

Kenneth glanced at Jorund, now forty paces away. "Let's go, Coric," Kenneth said and he moved to the cart. He squatted to duck under then suddenly realized something wasn't right. He paused and peered back at Coric.

"Coric, no!"

Coric was ready—ready to fight, knife drawn and wild-eyed, glaring at the fast-approaching giant.

"Coric, don't do this! Not now!"

Coric stepped toward Jorund.

"Coric!"

Coric glanced at Kenneth, still squatting beside the cart. "Not now, Coric. We have to go!"

Coric wanted Jorund. He wanted him badly. The Viking was twenty paces away and closing quickly. A buzzing sound zipped past Coric's head and lodged in the ground at Jorund's feet. The large Viking stopped in his tracks, staring at the long vibrating arrow shaft as it slowed to a rest.

Coric smirked and shoved his knife in his belt. He hurried toward Kenneth, and the two dropped to the ground and slipped below the flaming cart.

From the shadows of freedom, Ronan rode to Coric, Kenneth, and Nicol, towing three horses behind him. "Take the horses," he said. "We've got to get out of here."

Coric and Kenneth mounted up and followed Ronan away from the blazing fort. Kenneth slowed after several paces and glanced back, searching for Nicol. The old Scot had left his horse and was pulling a rope through the side wheels of the cart.

"Nicol, come on," Kenneth shouted. Then he noticed the cart slowly rolling away from the entrance of the fort.

"They're pushing it," Nicol yelled. He finished knotting the rope and ran back to his horse. "Haw!" he yelled as he slapped the hindquarters of the beast. The horse bucked and charged forward. The rope tightened, and the wheels lurched, yet the cart stood. Again, Nicol slapped the animal. This time the impulse of the horse's sudden tug ripped the two side wheels from the cart's boxy frame. The cart toppled, and the burning timber dumped into a heap on the ground, sealing the Vikings inside the fiery inferno.

Nicol mounted his horse and darted up the hill past Kenneth, dragging his rope and the two wheels behind him.

Kenneth stared back at the furious, red-hot flames. It

was a place where much had been learned and much had been lost, and both had come at a cost. He would forever despise the men and the miseries of that place, the place where he had entered Hell.

He peered down at his unbound hands and the ring of callouses circling his wrists. A sliver of hope sprung in his heart. Now that he was free, there was someone he had to find. And he would not stop until he held her.

He turned his horse and raced to catch the others.

CHAPTER 19

"WE SHOULD HUNT THEM DOWN," MAGNUS grumbled. "We should've gone after them in Perth." He placed his hand on the back of his head and pulled at the dried blood caked in his hair.

"I told you then, we aren't going after them. Don't speak of it again," Halfdan muttered.

"You're lucky you're alive, Magnus. I'm not sure you want to see the girl again. She may kill you next time," the rider beside Magnus jeered. The others snickered.

"Shut up," Magnus growled.

"Forget the woman. She's not the problem," Halfdan demanded. "Oengus is the problem. He's a liar and a coward. I want him dead."

"And the Scots?" Kodran asked.

"Their time will come soon … but I will not be lied to or threatened. Oengus' days are numbered. Playing him has run its course. He's no longer of use."

"He never was going to fight the Scots, was he?" Kodran said.

"He feigns bravery, but he's weak. I see it in his eyes. He'd rather have others do his fighting."

"Afraid of a fight," Kodran remarked to no one in particular. "Coward."

"Be sure of this, he'll get his chance to fight—whether he wants it or not." Halfdan cleared his throat and spat a wad of phlegm into the air. "Soon, Perth will have hell to pay … as will the Scots."

❧

"How does it look?" Aiden asked. He sat on a rock and stared at Arabella as she leaned toward him. The morning sun had pushed through the early fog, and Aiden took notice of how its rays lightened Arabella's long brown hair. His eyes then focused on hers, and he followed her gaze as she studied his neck and slowly removed his bandages.

"The burns are red and tender … though your skin appears to be healing," Arabella said. "Does it hurt?"

"It always hurts, but the pain is less than it was."

"Take off your shirt and I'll remove the bandages from your shoulder. When we get them off, I'll soak them in the creek," Arabella said, and she stepped back from Aiden and allowed him to disrobe. As she waited, she gathered the soiled bandages she'd removed and wadded them in her palm.

Aiden unbuttoned his shirt, grimacing as he undid each button. "This arm becomes stiff if I let it sit, and it doesn't want to move sometimes."

"I know it must hard," Arabella replied. "Do you need help?"

"I'm alright. I think I've got it."

Arabella stood silent as Aiden finished unbuttoning his

shirt. Then she spoke, "Aiden, how long do you think we have before they come looking for us?"

"I'd guess they're already looking. We covered a good distance last night, and we may be hard to track since we're on foot," Aiden replied. "They may not even know if we went south or east. But to be safe, we should head out again soon." Aiden unfastened the last button and let his arms drop to his side. He slumped over to rest, and his shirt hung open, exposing his chest.

"Sit here. I'll get it for you," Arabella said and she stepped behind Aiden as he lowered to a sizeable rock. "Lift your arms a little." Arabella gently pulled his shirt from his frame and laid it on the rock beside him. "I'm going to undo the bandages from your shoulder. Tell me if it hurts and I'll stop."

"It already hurts," he said and chuckled.

"Well, tell me if it hurts badly." Arabella grinned and then slowly began to remove the bandages. "The skin on your back looks irritated and sore ... I'm so sorry this happened."

Aiden peered over his shoulder and gazed at Arabella. He watched as she delicately pulled the soiled cloth from his skin. She was beautiful.

"Arabella, can I tell you something?"

"What, Aiden?"

"When I think of Kenneth, I—"

Arabella's eyes fell. "Aiden, I don't know if I can talk about this."

"No, please, I have to say it." He glanced at her, anticipating a response. She didn't refuse. He continued, "When Nessa and I were taken by the Vikings, I thought we were both going to die. We had nothing. We had no hope at all. Then, I was lying there in the middle of the night, surrounded by Vikings, and Kenneth suddenly appeared in the darkness. I can't believe he came for us. I think of how he fought to free us, and now he's …" Aiden paused. "Maybe I can't say it … I can't even believe it. He was my brother … I loved him."

Arabella stepped in front of Aiden. "I loved him too, Aiden."

"But that's what I'm trying to say, Arabella."

She lowered her head and busied herself with his bandages.

"You two had everything, everything that was special. Kenneth never wanted your heart to break. He was so in love with you. He knew it would tear you apart when he left to fight. He never wanted to hurt you." Aiden stared at Arabella, watching her petite fingers ease the bandages from his burns. "I don't want to see you hurt either. I want you to know, I'm here for you, Arabella. I'll do whatever I can to make sure your heart doesn't break again." He searched her eyes. "I mean that, Arabella."

Arabella lifted the last bandage. "Aiden, I don't know if I—" She froze as she removed the dressing and caught sight of the silver cross pressed against Aiden's skin.

"What is it?" Aiden asked.

"Your cross," Arabella said, stepping away from Aiden and gaping at him. "It reminds me of Kenneth." Tears welled in her eyes. "Why did this have to happen? I just can't believe it."

Aiden lifted from his seat on the rock and gazed at Arabella for a long moment. "I don't know what to believe myself."

The two stood in silence, staring at one another. Then a light breeze cooled the air and blew against their bodies.

The gust was cold on Aiden's chest, and a chill rushed over his skin. He lifted his arm and ran his hand through his hair. "I'm sorry, Arabella. I'm sorry for saying all that. I must be going mad." He paused and rubbed his palms together, not knowing what to say next. His thoughts turned. "This is all unbelievable. I can't believe it … I can't believe any of it. I can't believe Searc lied to me—what the hell was he doing? Why did he tell me the Vikings raided again and killed everyone? It doesn't make sense."

"It doesn't, Aiden."

"I suppose I can believe Oengus lied, he's a Pict. My father was right. I should have never trusted the man. I guess that after he saved my life, I was willing to believe anything he said. But why did Searc come to him, why did he lie to me?"

"I don't know, Aiden. But I know that after your father left with Coric to find you, the men in Renton were lost without a leader." Arabella's lips trembled. "My father and several others wanted to take the men and follow after him, but the men from Dumbarton saw what the Vikings had done to Renton, and they wanted the Picts' help if we were to fight those animals."

"Why didn't Constantine refuse and leave with the men? That was the whole reason they gathered in Renton."

"They just kept arguing, Aiden. They couldn't agree. There were many who wanted to leave Renton and go after the Vikings, but others kept speaking of the Picts," Arabella said. The conversation made her bitter as she thought of Kenneth and how he was forced to face the Vikings alone. "The men were doing nothing, nothing but bickering. I could only imagine how Kenneth and the others must have been suffering at the hands of those savages. That's why I had to come to Perth. I thought I could reason with Oengus. Maybe if he was told about the raid on Renton, then he would see that the Picts were in danger as well, and he would be forced to join the fight against the Vikings."

"Well, that question has been answered."

"It wasn't supposed to happen like this, Aiden." Arabella lowered her head, not wanting to give in to her sadness. She turned. She couldn't stop herself. She held her hands to her face and wept.

"Arabella, don't do that. Everything's going to be alright." Aiden stepped beside her, put his arms around her frame, and held her.

"Nothing's alright, Aiden. Kenneth is dead, your father and Coric are gone, and the men in Renton—"

"Shh, shh, stop." Aiden lifted Arabella's chin and peered into her eyes. "You're alive. I'm alive. We'll make it back to Renton and we'll see—"

"We'll see what?" Arabella blurted out. "What is there to see? A bunch of men, arguing over what to do next?"

"Arabella, for all we know my father and Coric have returned. They may have an army of men moving out to fight the Vikings. We can't give up now."

Arabella stepped away, lost, gazing listlessly at the grass-covered ground. "I'm sorry, but it all seems so hopeless."

"Yes, from here it does. We are standing somewhere in the middle of Pictland. I see that. But we'll make it back to Renton … it'll be alright." Aiden gestured with his hands, "Here, I'll take those bandages. I'll clean them in the creek, and then we'll head to Renton."

Arabella's eyes abruptly widened, and she stood stone still. "Do you hear that?"

Aiden quieted and swiveled his head to either side,

glancing at the creek and then toward the woods behind him. "Hear what?" he whispered.

"Horses!"

⊚

"We can't stay on this path all the way to Renton. With the sun rising, the Vikings will round up enough horses to come after us. When they do, they'll come with a vengeance, and they'll follow our trail straight down this path," Coric said to Kenneth and Ronan. He looked over his shoulder at the three carts moving sluggishly behind them, and at Laise and Gavin who were riding rear. Coric lifted his hand in the air to signal Laise.

Laise returned a lifted fist, gesturing no sign of trouble.

Coric turned to Kenneth, "We've covered a good distance, but the carts are overloaded and they're slowing us down. At this pace, the Vikings will eventually catch us."

"Maybe we should leave the path and find our way through the woods back to Renton."

"The carts would only move slower through the trees," Coric replied.

"And we need to get to Renton before the Vikings do," Ronan added. "We have to warn the others that they're coming."

"The way I see it, we've got two options," Coric said. "We could send the carts with the women and older men through the woods and let Gavin and Nicol lead them. They could head south away from Renton to keep safe, and we could ride to Renton, which would get us there faster. Or, we could have Gavin and Nicol lead them on foot through the woods, and we could take the empty carts to Renton to make sure the Vikings followed us and not them."

"I like the second idea," Kenneth replied. "The older men and the women are weak, but they are strong enough to move through the woods to safety … especially now that they're free. I'd hate to send them on their own in the carts, only to have the Vikings follow their tracks and capture them again. That can't happen, Coric. They wouldn't survive."

"But the carts will slow us, if we take them," Ronan said. "We need to get to Renton to tell our fathers that war is coming … and for all we know, the Vikings may not be far behind."

"Let's take the chance. We can take the carts far enough to lure the Vikings into following us, then we can abandon the carts when we have to," Kenneth said, glancing back and forth between his brother and Ronan.

"Alright, the older men and the women will head south through the woods on foot with whatever horses we can spare. We'll take the carts and head to Renton," Coric said. "I'll tell Laise."

Coric turned his horse and broke from the two. He headed to the rear to see Laise.

"We've stopped here to split up," Coric said in a loud voice, addressing the haggard band of absconding Scots. "The Vikings have likely gathered their scattered horses, and I'm sure they're coming after us. I'd suspect they'll be moving as fast as their horses can carry them. They'll likely catch us before we make it to Renton at the rate we're moving."

"What are you saying?" asked an older Scot, sitting in the lead cart.

"I'm saying for your safety, we're going to have those of you in the carts leave from here on foot and head south through the woods. We don't want you to go to Renton, the Vikings will be heading there. We want you to keep moving south until you are far enough from here that you're out of danger," Coric said. "The rest of us will take the empty carts and the horses, and we'll ride the path to Renton. The Vikings will track our path and will follow us there. If you head south through the woods, you'll be safe."

"I don't like the sound of that," the older man said. "What if the Vikings follow us through the woods? We have no swords, and we have no horses. We'll be as good as dead."

"No, that won't happen," Kenneth said. He sat up straight on his horse and spoke, "My brother is right. You must head south on foot through the woods. You will be safe that way. The Vikings will surely catch us if we keep moving as we are."

"How can you be sure?" the man asked.

Kenneth gazed at the man for a long moment, "Do you trust me?"

The man stared back at Kenneth and nodded his head. "Yes … I trust you."

Kenneth nodded in return. "Good, then you and the others need to head south."

Coric's eyes met his younger brother's, and he smirked. Then Coric turned to the men and women filling the carts. "We're able to spare a few horses for you as you head south. I'm going to have Nicol and Gavin lead you. Also, I am going to ask for three volunteers to drive the carts as we head back to Renton. I'll warn you, this could be dangerous. If our plan works, the Vikings will come after those of us heading to

Renton. If we get far enough, we can leave the carts behind and ride to the village."

A host of disheveled faces stared back at him, but no one spoke.

"Do I have anyone willing to drive—"

"I will," Gavin said. "I'll take a cart."

"Gavin, you need to stay with the group heading south," Kenneth replied.

"Whichever man goes with you will be fighting the Vikings, right? Either on the path, or at Renton," Gavin said. "I want to be one of those men. Would you deny me that?"

Kenneth thought for a moment and then shook his head. "No. No, Gavin, I wouldn't." He glanced at his brother. "Coric?"

"Fair enough," Coric said. "Gavin, you'll take a cart. Nicol, you'll lead the others heading south on foot. I trust you're up to that?"

"Yes, I can do it," Nicol replied.

"Alright, we need two more for the carts," Coric said.

The beleaguered man driving the second cart raised his hand. "I've come this far with this thing. I suppose I'm up to finishing it."

The man driving the third cart lifted his hand as well. "Count me in, too."

"Very good," Coric replied. "Gavin, looks like you've got the front cart." Coric turned to Ronan. "You and Laise help them out of the carts. We've burned enough time here. We need to get moving."

⟲

"Let's hide here, beside this tree. They shouldn't be able

to see us from the other side of the creek," Aiden said in a voice barely above a whisper.

Arabella lowered to the creek's moist bank and Aiden scooted beside her. The two tucked themselves into a four-foot earthy embankment formed at the water's edge and hid beside a large willow growing sideways toward the creek.

Aiden quickly surveyed their surroundings and then nudged Arabella closer to the crooked tree.

"How many do you think there are?" Arabella asked.

"I can't be sure. Four or five, maybe," Aiden said, and he motioned with his hand to keep low. He took a deep breath then pushed aside a gnarly willow root that dangled next to his face.

After sitting for several moments, Aiden lifted his head and peered up the gradually sloping hill, looking for an escape route. Visibility was poor. A morning fog hovered in the air and sat like a thick mist, making it difficult to see for any measurable distance. Aiden lowered and turned back toward the creek. "I can hear them, but I can't see them," he said. "We'll stay here. Hopefully, they'll pass without spotting us."

The sound of horses drew nearer. Voices followed, muttering to one another somewhere in the fog.

Arabella clutched Aiden's arm, "We can't be caught—"

Suddenly, a splashing sound echoed from the creek. The mist began to move and Arabella tightened her grip on Aiden.

"Don't say a word, even if you see them." Aiden cautioned, trying to remain calm.

The creek instantly came to life. Its waters thrashed violently, erupting as though a stampede of beasts were emerging from its depths.

Aiden gripped his sword and shot a piercing glance at Arabella. "Stay behind me!"

The sound of thrashing water subsided, but was quickly replaced by the drumming of hooves beating upon the muddy bank.

Arabella held her breath.

"Keep moving," a voice called through the fog. "They've got to be out here somewhere."

A horse suddenly appeared, storming along the bank in the mist. The rider paused, then rode past the far side of the willow and leapt onto the ledge of the four-foot drop.

Aiden and Arabella sunk deeper into the earthy wall beside the dangling roots of the large tree.

The horse and rider continued up the hill, away from the ledge and the willow. Five more horses moved in a line behind the first, passing the willow and ascending the hill one by one.

Aiden loosened his grip on his sword and exhaled. He faced Arabella. Her eyes were shut as tight as a vice, and her lips were moving in a silent prayer. "Are you alright?" he whispered.

Arabella nodded.

The beat of the horses' hooves faded, and Aiden lifted his head and peered beyond the ledge, watching as the last horseman reached the hillcrest. He glimpsed the rider's Pict garb before the horse disappeared into the white mist.

The Scots, ragged but free, rode their pilfered horses and carts along the western banks of Loch Lomond. Dalriada's air never felt so fresh, so crisp, so pure—like a healing balm, soothing their wounds as much as their spirits.

Ronan gazed over his shoulder down the long stretch of path behind the procession. "Still no sign of Vikings, Coric. Should we dump the carts? We would get to Renton sooner."

Coric glanced at Kenneth, riding beside him, and then back at Ronan. "The others should have made it well south by now. I suppose we're far enough that it would be safe to leave the carts and head to Renton with just the horses," Coric replied. He pointed in the distance, "There's a spot beyond those trees. Let's hide them there."

Coric rode ahead and guided his horse off the path. He quickly scanned the thick grove of evergreens and found a site that suited him. Then he signaled Kenneth and Ronan.

The two veered from the trail with the caravan of riders and carts behind them.

Coric circled his horse and then stopped to address the group. "You men in the carts, pull ahead and untie your horses. We're leaving the carts here." Coric turned to the four riding horseback, "I need you to help the others with the horses."

Kenneth nodded and began to dismount.

"No you don't," Coric said. "I'm not letting you out of my sight. Ronan, you and Laise help the men with the carts. And make sure they're hidden well ... we don't need to leave any extra clues for the Vikings. Kenneth and I will watch the path."

Kenneth righted himself on his horse and waited for his brother to finish, contemplating how he'd deliver his next words to Coric.

"Come with me," Coric said, motioning to Kenneth. The two rode to the path and stopped to watch for riders.

"Hope we've put enough distance between us and them," Coric said. "We'll need to get to Renton soon to warn Father."

"Coric, I'm not going to Renton."

Coric jerked his head sideways and shot Kenneth a disbelieving glare. "What did you say?"

"I said, I'm not going to Renton."

"What are you talking about, Kenneth? Are you mad? Where else would you go?"

"To Cashel."

"Cashel?"

"I'm going to Cashel, Coric. I told Arabella to wait there—I told her I would return for her."

"You're going to Cashel to get Arabella? That's not an option, Kenneth. You're not leaving my sight."

"Coric, you and the others can go to Renton and tell Father. I'm going to Cashel, then I'll head straight to Renton. I'll only be a few hours behind you."

"I can't let you do that, Kenneth."

"Coric, I am going to see Arabella … I am not going with you to Renton."

"Dammit, Kenneth, I need you to stay with me. With Aiden dead, Father has to see you. I can't return without you!"

"Then come with me. Come with me to Cashel. We'll get Arabella and we'll go to Renton."

"She's not going to be safe in Renton, Kenneth."

"And how do I know she'll be safe in Cashel? For all I know, the Vikings could hit Cashel before they hit Renton. She'd be killed or taken for sure if that were to happen, and I'm not going to let it happen!"

"You're a fool, Kenneth. You're a crazy fool. Somehow, I think I'll have to kill you to get you to Renton. And I really shouldn't do that. Not after I risked my life to save your skin."

Kenneth smiled. "So you'll come with me to Cashel?"

Coric shook his head, cussing himself.

Ronan approached and adjusted in his saddle. "Did I hear you say, Cashel?"

"That's right. He said, Cashel" Coric replied, half perturbed and still wondering if it was such a good idea.

"Coric and I are going to Cashel. We're going to make sure Arabella is safe, and we're going to bring her back to Renton," Kenneth said. "You, Laise, and the others should ride ahead to Renton and warn our fathers of the Vikings."

"Is he kidding, Coric?"

"No, he's not kidding," Coric replied. "I don't know that I can convince him otherwise. We'll do this, and we'll meet up in Renton. We won't be long."

"But Coric, that's insane. We've got to get to Renton."

"Don't you think I know that! He's going to Cashel whether I go or not, and I'm not letting him out of my sight— I'm going to Cashel with him."

Ronan stared at Kenneth and shook his head.

"I don't want to hear it, Ronan," Kenneth barked. "For weeks, even months, I've lived through hell, not even knowing if I would survive to see the light of another day. I don't need your permission or anyone else's to go to Cashel."

Ronan's lips pursed, and he gawked at Coric.

"We're ready," Laise called out as he rode from the brush, heading toward the path. When he reached the three, he found an awkward silence. "What's going on?"

"I'm going to Cashel," Kenneth said. "Coric has agreed to come with me. We'll be in Renton by nightfall. You, Ronan, and the rest of the men will head to Renton ahead of us to tell the others."

"Is this true, Coric?" Laise asked with a perplexed gaze.

"Yes, that's the plan." Coric said nothing more.

"Alright then," Laise replied. "We're heading to Renton. And you two are heading to Cashel. I trust you know what you're doing."

"Coric, if you're going to Cashel, then I'm going with you," Ronan said. He turned to Laise, expecting a measure of protest. "Are you good with taking the others to Renton?"

Laise glanced at Gavin and the six other men. They had hidden the carts and were mounting the horses. He nodded. "I can do that. But if we're going, I want to go now. Those devils will be coming soon … and I don't want to be sitting here when they do. So yes, I'll head to Renton with the others."

"Thanks, Laise," Coric said. "Tell my father that Kenneth is safe. Tell him that we'll be in Renton by nightfall." Coric turned to Kenneth, "We need to get back to Renton before the Vikings do. This visit to Cashel had better be quick."

Laise slid his horse beside Kenneth's. "Glad you're alive, Kenneth. Stay that way … and keep your brother out of trouble, too."

"I can't thank you enough, Laise. I appreciate you coming after me with Coric and Ronan. I owe you."

"Likewise," Gavin said, riding up next to Laise. "I owe all of you."

"Well, I was told several lovely ladies had been taken captive. That's who I was trying to save. You two were extra, I guess," Laise said with a smirk, then he removed his sword. "Here, Kenneth. I want to give you this … just in case you need it."

Kenneth extended his hand to receive the weapon. "I'd rather have your bow," he said with a smile.

"I'm not sure you'd hit much with it," Laise replied.

They laughed. It felt good to laugh.

"Well, if you want a bow, then take this," Gavin said, offering a crossbow to Kenneth. "One of the men swiped it from the Vikings during the escape. It may be easier for you to hit your target."

"How about I take that," Coric remarked. "Kenneth looks to be a little slow on the draw in his condition."

"Sure, but now that you're taking it, you better not miss," Kenneth replied.

Coric accepted the crossbow and a quiver of arrows and thanked Gavin. Turning to Laise, he extended his arm. The two locked forearms. "You'll look after Ceana until I return, yes?"

"Yes, I'll look after her," Laise said with a nod. "She is my sister, remember."

"I remember." Coric held Laise's eyes in a familial gaze. "Thanks for everything, brother. I'll see you in Renton."

"See you in Renton," Laise replied.

Laise, Gavin, and the others rode south to Renton.

Coric, Kenneth, and Ronan turned their horses and headed east across the southern rim of Loch Lomond.

Cashel would be waiting.

CHAPTER 20

SEARC CROUCHED IN SOLITUDE BESIDE HIS DYING campfire. He stoked its flames with a half-rotten stick. A myriad of unwanted thoughts stirred in his head—thoughts that refused to quiet despite the noiseless ambiance of the surrounding forest. He cursed and forced his mind to focus on the present, on the fire, on the camp, anything that would provide a momentary distraction.

His focused act of denial was beginning to work, and then a distant noise crept into his ears. He cocked his head to listen and suddenly stiffened like a corpse.

His chest heaved and he trembled.

Silently, he eased to a stance and peeked above the shoulder-high underbrush.

Riders!

Furiously, he kicked at the ground, using his foot as a veritable shovel to extinguish the fire. Then he dropped to his knees and dug his fingers into the soil, ripping at the earth and tossing fistfuls of dirt onto the flames, praying the smoke would cease.

He stopped abruptly and held his breath to listen again. His mind raced. The riders were drawing near to him, maybe even coming for him. He threw a final handful of soil on the fire and stomped the dirt into the smoldering embers.

The thicket surrounding his tiny camp was sufficiently dense to conceal him from passersby, but the fear of being seen overwhelmed him. He grabbed his bedroll and fled his snuffed-out campfire. After several paces, he ducked behind a large oak tree and squatted to the ground.

The pounding hoofbeats reverberated in his ears, and their rapid pattering verified they were moving quickly—quickly toward him.

Searc waited in his hiding spot then slowly peeked beyond the tree, spying for movement between the small gaps in the brush that separated him from the riders.

The advancing riders approached, and then they passed as quickly as they came, moving through a clearing less than thirty yards away.

As the sound of the horses faded, Searc stepped from behind the oak and peered over the brush. He counted three riders—and though he saw only their backsides, he recognized them immediately.

His hideout on the outskirts of Cashel had gone unnoticed, but curiosity had found him. He hurried to his horse and pulled himself up.

⑨

When the three arrived at Constantine's home in Cashel, Kenneth was the first to dismount.

"How are you so sure she's still here, Kenneth? You've been gone a long time," Coric said as Kenneth left his horse and scrambled to the door.

"Because I told her to wait here. I told her I'd come for her," Kenneth replied without breaking stride.

Coric dismounted and waited for Ronan to do the same.

Kenneth reached the door and pounded with a rapid fist. A wave of exhilaration swept into his heart. "Arabella. Arabella," he called out.

The latch lifted and the door opened.

Kenneth paused when he saw her face.

"Kenneth, you're alive!" Ceana exclaimed. She reached forward and hugged him.

"Ceana ... yes, I'm alive," Kenneth said, still locked in her embrace. "Where is Arabella?"

"Ceana," Coric called, quickening his steps. "You're here?"

Ceana released Kenneth and rushed to Coric. She wrapped her arms around his waist, and her stomach pressed against his. "Coric, how did you find him?"

Coric's arms tightened around her frame, and he allowed the warmth of her body to seep into his. "It wasn't easy. He was far away, but we found him—"

"Ceana, where is Arabella?" Kenneth interrupted.

"Come inside, all of you," Ceana said. "Let me get you something to eat." She released Coric and hurried past Kenneth.

"Ceana, where's Arabella?" Kenneth repeated, traipsing behind her into the house, impatient for an answer.

"Ceana, where is Arabella?" This time it was Coric asking the question. "We need to know where she is."

Ceana stopped beside the dining table. She removed a cloth that covered a loaf of bread and scooted the loaf toward the edge of the table as an offering. Her eyes lifted first to Coric and then to Kenneth. "Arabella is not here."

"Where is she?" Kenneth said, trying to veil his anger.

"She's gone—searching for a way to save you, Kenneth."

"What do you mean? Is she in Renton?"

"No, she's not in Renton. She left several days ago—for Perth."

"Perth?" Kenneth's mind reeled as the words sunk into his ears.

"She left for Perth. She said she had to see Oengus."

Kenneth closed his eyes, dumbstruck.

Coric could only watch as his brother sunk under Ceana's words, as though his newfound freedom had vanished into an abyss of hopelessness. "Ceana, tell us, why did she go to Perth?" Coric asked. "Oengus is a madman. What did she hope to find there?"

"Coric, you saw the men in Renton. They were paralyzed without your father to lead them. As he recovered in that bed, they sat by their campfires biting at each other's throats. Arabella was powerless. She felt that maybe in some way she could convince the Picts to help. She did it for you, Kenneth. She was afraid for you … afraid you were going to die."

Kenneth's brow furrowed and his jaw tightened. "I told her to wait for me here. I can't believe she's gone. Why didn't she wait!" He dropped into a seat beside the table and ran his palms across his cheeks. "Have you heard any word from her since she left?"

"No, Kenneth. I haven't."

Kenneth lowered his head and placed his hands over his face, appearing as though he was working to solve an unsolvable riddle.

"Ceana, why did you leave my mother?" Coric asked. "Why did you come to Cashel?"

Ceana stared down at the floor, rubbing her belly slowly. Her eyes lifted, "I came because I knew you'd find Kenneth."

"And so you came to Cashel?" Coric questioned, confused by the response.

"I came because I knew the first place Kenneth would look for Arabella was here, in Cashel. I knew he would come for her."

"But Ceana, I—"

"Coric," Ceana interrupted, not letting him finish. She paused and tried to calm herself. "You're a dedicated man. You are relentless in your stubborn, unending dedication to your father and your family. That is who you are. I know that. And I know Kenneth. I knew his heart would not stop until he found Arabella, that he'd come straight to Cashel to find her … and I knew that's where I'd find you."

Coric melted. His mind twisted. His heart wrenched.

"Ceana, I couldn't leave Kenneth." Coric grasped for words to fight back. "We came here to get Arabella, and we were planning to return to Renton this evening. I was coming home to you … I had to make sure Kenneth stayed alive."

"Coric, I need *you* to stay alive," Ceana said. She hesitated. "Your child needs you to stay alive."

"My child?" Coric uttered.

"Yes, Coric, your child."

"You're pregnant? You're going to have a baby? I'm going to be a father?"

"You are a father, Coric. I wanted to tell you before you left," Ceana said as tears formed in her eyes. "I wanted to tell you, but I was afraid it was something you wouldn't want to hear."

Coric stepped to his wife and lifted her chin, "Why would you say that I wouldn't want to hear? Of course, I want to hear. You know I love you. I would do anything for you."

"But I see how you regard your father. There is nothing you wouldn't do for him. You would go to the end of the earth for him."

"Ceana, this is not about my father. You should have told me about our child."

"Would you have stayed if I did?"

Coric pulled away. He couldn't help his reaction, or deny it, even though he tried. "Our people were dying, Ceana. Somebody had to do something. The Picts are against us, the Vikings—"

"What about me? What about our child? What about us, Coric?"

"Ceana, this is not just about us. All of this … it's bigger than us. If we don't do something, there won't be an 'us' … there won't be a Dalriada."

"And that is why I came here, Coric. I know who you are. I know how driven you are. You won't let yourself stop until you've saved the world!"

Coric drew a deep breath and stared silently at his bride. He gazed at her stomach, and his eyes slowly traced her frame upward until his eyes met hers. He wanted to tell her she was wrong. He wanted to justify himself, exonerate himself. He wanted to reassure her. He wanted her to know that he loved her. What could he say? His words were lost. He turned from Ceana and walked out the door.

She let him go.

She stood mute as tears ran down her cheeks.

"I'm sorry, Ceana," Kenneth said. He stepped to her and placed his hands on her shoulders. She trembled in his grasp. Several moments passed before he eased his eyes toward Ronan.

Ronan shook his head. "What do we do?"

"I know what I've got to do," Kenneth replied, his tone cool and resolute. "Ceana, I am sorry. I'm happy to hear you are expecting a child … and I'm sorry for all that has happened to our family."

Ceana lifted her head. Sorrow etched her face like the sculpture of a forgotten angel. She nodded and closed her eyes.

Kenneth stepped away and walked past Ronan toward the door. "I have to see Coric."

"She needs you, Coric," Kenneth said as he approached his brother. He paused and stared at him.

Coric glimpsed toward Kenneth and then looked away without speaking.

Kenneth shook his head and stepped past his brother.

"Where are you going?" Coric asked.

"The horses … after that ride, they need water." Kenneth slowed his pace and gazed back. "Coric, she's concerned about you. She needs you."

Coric heard the words. He rubbed his brow and then turned and faced the house, not sure of what he'd say if he walked back through the door. He snapped from his trance and called to his brother, "Kenneth, what about Arabella? What about you?"

Kenneth stopped and spun on his heels. "Coric, I am forever grateful to you for what you did for me, but I think it's time to stop worrying about me. You've got a wife and a child to think about."

A long pause passed and Kenneth waited for Coric to concede. Concession never came. Kenneth was wordless. His head lowered, and he turned and moved toward the horses.

Coric gazed at his brother as he walked away, his brother's words still echoing in his ears. Some things came easy for Coric, yet other things did not. He wrung his hands and took a deep breath, then he stepped toward the open door to return to his wife.

Ceana remained in her chair next to the small wooden table. Ronan had found a stool and was now stooped beside her. He was comforting her with a calm, steady voice. When he heard footsteps behind him, he quieted and turned to see Coric entering the doorway. Coric motioned to him with his eyes and Ronan stood.

"Thank you for the bread, Ceana," Ronan said. He glanced at Coric. "I think I'll get some air."

Coric waited for Ronan to depart. The door closed, and the two were alone. Coric crossed his arms and gazed silently at the table and the broken loaf of bread. He searched carefully for the right words. "I shouldn't have gotten angry, Ceana. We are expecting a child. That is a blessing." He stared down at her sandy-brown hair and thought of what she meant to him. "I want to be a father, a good father. I want to be a good husband. I want you to understand that."

Ceana lifted her head and gazed into his eyes. "I understand, Coric. This child could not have a better father. I am certain you will be his greatest hero. Coric, that is what you are to me … a hero. It's only that sometimes … sometimes, I need a husband."

"I'm not a hero, Ceana. I'm a man, like every other man. I've tried to be a good husband. Ceana, I love you. No matter what I do or what you think of me, I love you."

"Coric, I believe you love me. I believe—"

Suddenly, the door to the house flung open, swiveling on its iron hinges and slamming against the wall behind it. Ronan leapt into the room. "Coric, I know you don't want to hear this, but it's Kenneth. He said he was taking the horses to get water, and he headed down the path to the well. But I just saw him on his horse, riding east through the field!"

"Our horses, where are they?" Coric exclaimed.

"I don't know. I'll check the well," Ronan said, and he vanished out the door.

"I'll be right behind you," Coric shouted toward the empty doorway. He turned to Ceana one last time, "I've got to go. We'll get him, and we'll be back." He left her and hurried through the door without awaiting a response.

Coric surveyed the field. No sign of Kenneth. He turned in the direction of the well and darted down the path in an open sprint.

Nearing the well, Coric spotted Ronan chasing the horses along the tree line. Coric continued his sprint. After closing the gap of nearly forty yards, he approached the two horses opposite of Ronan and together they corralled the animals.

"How far ahead is he?" Coric asked as Ronan mounted.

"He got a pretty good jump on us. I lost him when he disappeared through the trees over there," Ronan replied, pointing to a tuft of trees several hundred yards away.

Coric mounted and the two rode back to the house.

There in the darkened doorway, Ceana stood alone, watching and waiting—and knowing.

Coric slowed his horse and gazed at her. "I have to go after him."

"Don't go, Coric. Ronan can get him. I need you. Don't leave again."

"Ceana, he'll die out there by himself. I have to go."

"Don't leave me, Coric," she begged, her lips quivering as she spoke.

"He's my brother, I have to get him," Coric replied. He glanced at Ronan, "Go after him, I'll catch you."

Ronan nodded, snapped his reigns, and shot into the field toward the distant tree line.

"Ceana, stay here. I'll be back, but you must stay here. Don't go to Renton. It won't be safe." Coric's horse spun in a circle beneath him, and he swiveled his head to keep his eyes on Ceana. "I will come back for you."

"But what if you don't come back?"

"I'll be back, Ceana … I promise. I'll be back." Coric jabbed his heels into his horse, and the animal leapt forward.

"Coric, don't leave."

"I'll return soon," Coric yelled back as his horse opened the gap between the two.

"No, Coric. No," Ceana cried aloud, with no one left to hear. Her petite frame slowly crumbled, and she fell to her knees. Staring at her husband's fleeting silhouette, she lowered her head, wrapped her arms around her swollen stomach, and wept.

◎

In Renton, Alpin, Constantine, Luag, and Latharn

hovered beside a round pine table below the meeting tent. Guaire, Taran, and three others stood opposite them. A map occupied the tabletop between the parties, and the men were bantering back and forth.

Alpin leaned forward and pressed his finger on the map. "They have to be in this area," he said, pointing to the mountain region of western Dalriada.

"Alpin, Alpin!" a young man yelled from the distance, running toward the men. Upon reaching the tent, the young man paused and panted with excitement, "Laise has returned! He's brought Gavin and several others that escaped the Vikings. The men are bringing them now."

Alpin peered past the messenger to see Laise and a small pack of riders approaching on horseback. He quickly stepped from the tent and craned his neck to peer through the pack, searching for his boys.

Laise and the other riders stopped their horses and dismounted.

Latharn rushed to greet his son, with Alpin only steps behind.

"Laise, you're back. It's good to see you," Alpin said loudly, above the hum of the gathering. "Where are Coric and Ronan?"

The crowd hushed, and Laise responded, "They're alright. And, Kenneth is too. We found him at the Viking camp. We were able to free him and several more. He was in bad shape, but he'll live."

"You found Kenneth alive? Praise God, it's a miracle!" Alpin exclaimed with an exuberance that stole his breath. "Where are Kenneth and Coric now?"

"They're with Ronan. The three of them went to Cashel. They'll be here by nightfall. We freed roughly two dozen other prisoners. They headed south on foot once we reached the northwest edge of Loch Lomond. They were to head south on foot and find safety."

"That's good news, Laise. Truly, it is. You young men never cease to amaze me. But, I don't understand. Why did Coric, Kenneth, and Ronan go to Cashel?"

"I'm not sure you're going to like the answer, Alpin, but it was Kenneth. He insisted he had to go to Cashel and see about Arabella. Coric and Ronan weren't happy with him, but he was determined. And Coric wasn't going to leave him. They promised to be home by nightfall."

"Foolish boy. Why does he do this? That girl will get him killed one day, he's lucky he isn't dead already." Alpin shook his head in frustration. "I suppose the Vikings didn't let you walk out of there—"

"No, sir," Laise said. "That's what I need to tell you. The Vikings had a large fort, far to the west, close to Ardmucknish Bay in the Inverawe Woods. We struck in the middle of the night. Once we had the prisoners free, we burned the fort."

"You burned the fort!" Luag exclaimed in disbelief.

"We burned the whole bloody thing. We scattered their horses, and we blocked the exits of the fort with the Vikings inside."

"Did they come after you?" Alpin asked.

"Frankly, I don't know, and we didn't stick around to find out. We took three carts and several horses, and we left as fast as we could. I'd guess they found a way out, but they still had to round up their horses. We've been watching behind us, but we've seen no sign of them yet. We left Coric, Kenneth, and Ronan on the south side of the loch, and the eight of us rode here as quickly as we could."

"Constantine, Latharn, Guaire, get your men ready," Alpin ordered. "The battle may be coming to us."

"Wait," Taran interjected. "Our scouts haven't returned from Perth. They could be coming with the Picts as we speak."

Alpin glared at Taran. "We've waited long enough for your damn scouts. It's been well over a week since you sent them on this dream of yours. For all we know, they're locked in Oengus' dungeon, or worse, they're hanging from his gallows. There is no time to wait!"

Taran spun and faced his father, glaring at him and expecting support. Guaire said nothing. Taran peered back at Alpin, "How long did we wait for you on your rescue mission? How long have we waited for you to recover? Now you groan about waiting for the Picts. They'll double our numbers."

"If you are so dead set on having the Picts join us, then you wait for them. The rest of us have a battle to fight," Alpin fumed. He shook his head with disgust and turned to Luag. "Send three men north. I want eyes on the road ahead. I want to know what we're up against. I want to know where the Vikings are and when they're coming."

"Yes, sir," Luag replied.

"Constantine, Latharn, Guaire … as I said, ready your men."

The men dispersed—and Taran cursed beneath his breath.

⑨

Searc emerged quietly from behind an overgrown hedge of blackthorn bushes. He had watched Kenneth ride away.

He had watched Coric and Ronan follow. He had watched Ceana break down and cry.

Mounting his horse, Searc moved up the path to Constantine's home. There, he dismounted, secured his lead to a post, and shuffled to the house.

Searc stood at the door and paused to scan the field where he had seen the others ride away. He took a deep breath and then opened the door and stepped inside.

Moments later, the door swung open and Searc rushed back into the light of day. Shame tore at his gut like a flesh-eating poison. He ran to his horse, untied the animal, and mounted. He rode as fast as the beast could carry him—south toward Renton.

෧

Halfdan and his horde of seven moved along the northern rim of Loch Lomond. Halfdan's bitterness with Oengus had yet to subside. As the eight reached the western trail to Inverawe Woods, a dull rumble rose in the distance.

Kodran slowed and motioned to Halfdan.

"Halt," Halfdan shouted to the men.

The eight slowed to a stop.

The rumbling grew louder.

To the west, a dark wave emerged far down the path.

"What the hell is that?" Kodran said, squinting to make out the figures.

"An army, it appears," Halfdan replied.

"A large army," another man said.

"Get off the path," Halfdan commanded. "I want to see who this is."

The small band of eight turned their horses and tucked themselves into the shadows of the forest along the path.

They waited.

The advancing army moved forward like a swarm of angry bees.

The swarm drew closer.

"Jorund! Halfdan, it's Jorund!" Kodran exclaimed.

"What is he doing here?" Halfdan muttered. "Follow me." Halfdan jerked his reins and rode from the trees. He moved to the center of the path and sat erect on his horse, facing the oncoming army. His seven men stopped beside him, aligning their horses side by side and forming a virtual wall across the path.

They waited for Jorund.

Jorund tugged the reins of his horse and stopped the large steed fifteen feet from Halfdan. The army of Vikings halted behind him.

"I don't like the looks of this, Jorund. Tell me you have good news," Halfdan said. A large vein swelled on his forehead as he glared at Jorund.

"I'm afraid the news is not good, Halfdan," Jorund replied.

"Go on." Halfdan braced himself.

"We were attacked in the night. The fort was burned and the prisoners were taken."

"Scots?"

"Yes, Scots."

"Dammit, you ox! I left you there to make sure this didn't happen!" Halfdan's jaws crushed together and his lips tightened around his teeth. "How could you let them do this?"

Halfdan elevated in his saddle and peered over the mass of men behind Jorund. His head turned to the south as a dozen thoughts twisted in his mind. He lowered his frame and slowly gazed at Kodran. "We have two enemies to destroy ... the question is, which one first?"

CHAPTER 21

"HALT! HALT!" A SCOT POSTED AT THE NORTH edge of Renton called out. The rider slowed and stopped next to the man. A second Scot stepped in front of the horse, cocked his crossbow, and pointed it at the rider. The Scot beside the horse lifted his torch to illuminate the rider's face. "Searc!" the man exclaimed. "What are you doing here at this hour?"

"Where is Alpin? I must speak to him," Searc said, gulping for air as he spoke.

⊚

"Any news from your scouts?" Alpin said to Luag in the confines of his recovery quarters. The small building proved useful for meetings of confidence.

"Alpin, they only left at dusk. They've yet to return," Luag replied.

"Are the men ready? I don't want to be surprised. We need to attack as planned, we don't know their numbers."

"Yes, the men are ready. Constantine and Guaire both report that their men are in position and are prepared to move on your orders."

"Very good. We must stay alert." Alpin peered out the small window of the room. Night had come and a half-dozen torches dotted the village, emanating a dim hue of amber light in the darkness. "Where could they be?" Alpin muttered. "Laise said that Coric and the others would return by nightfall. Isn't that what he said?"

"By nightfall, yes," Luag replied, recalling the words and stroking his beard as he spoke. "I'm as concerned as you, Alpin. But those boys have proven themselves. They'll be back … give them time."

"There may not be much time," Alpin said, still gaping out the window.

A loud knock rapped on the door.

Luag shot a quick glance at Alpin.

"Enter," Alpin said.

The door opened and a messenger filled the entryway. "Alpin, it's Searc. He's come from Cashel, and he asks to speak with you. He says it's urgent. He seems somewhat out of sorts, so I have a man watching him."

"Searc? Take me to him," Alpin replied and stepped forward to follow the messenger. Luag trailed behind him and grabbed a torch mounted outside the door as the two departed the dwelling.

Searc stood in the distance beside his escort.

"We thought you'd disappeared, Searc," Alpin said as he approached the boy. "I was told you've come from Cashel, that you had news. Is there something you know?"

"Yes, Alpin, there is," Searc said nervously. "There's something I have to tell you."

"Well, I'm here. Go ahead."

"I need to speak to you ... alone," Searc uttered, glancing first at Luag and then at the other two.

"Very well." Alpin gestured to the messenger and the escort. The men acknowledged and departed. "Luag, please stay," Alpin insisted. "Anything Searc has to say, I'm sure you'll need to hear as well."

Searc glanced to his left and right, searching the darkness beyond the dim glow of Luag's torch. "Alpin, everything's gone wrong. It wasn't supposed to be like this. The Picts, the Vikings, everything."

"Slow down, son. What are you talking about?"

"Oengus, he was supposed to help. But he's a liar. He hates you. He doesn't mean to help us. He's against us."

"I know that, Searc. I've always known that. Get on with it, what does Oengus have to do with Cashel?"

"I went to see Oengus," Searc said, twitching as he spoke. "Weeks back, I went to him. We thought the Picts could strengthen us, so I went to him for help. At first, he acted as if he was willing. He asked that you pledge your loyalty to him. I told him of our plans to assemble the Scots to fight the Vikings. Alpin, I think he used it against us. He wants you dead."

"Dammit, Searc! You went to Oengus. What were you thinking? You should've never done this. You conspired with our enemy. That's treasonous!"

"Others wanted Oengus' help as well. It wasn't just me. I was the only one willing to go to him. With his men, we could have destroyed the Vikings. We could have destroyed the Britons."

"You've gone mad, Searc. You're babbling like a fool. This is not about the Britons, when will you let that go?"

Searc stared blankly at the two, stumbling for words

before a sudden declaration erupted from his lips, "He's got Aiden!"

Alpin winced at hearing his son's name. His emotions exploded—disbelief, confusion, rage. He stepped within striking distance of Searc with fire in his eyes, piercing the boy with his gaze. "What did you say?"

"Aiden is alive. Oengus found him. He was badly burned, and Oengus had him in a bed inside his castle. He was bandaged and very weak. Oengus is keeping him even now. He made me tell Aiden that everyone in Renton had been killed by the Vikings. I didn't want to do it, Alpin."

"You saw Aiden alive? Why didn't you come to me!"

"He made me do it, Alpin."

"I should cut you down where you stand. You're a fool, Searc. A damn fool!"

"You don't understand. You've never understood!" Searc shouted, his lips quivering. "I came here to tell you that your sons, Ronan too, were in Cashel, and they left to ride to Perth … but you don't care what I say—you've never cared! You watched my father die on the fields of Ae, and you've never given a damn about me, or avenging my father since that day!"

"What do you mean, our sons rode to Perth?" Luag said. "Tell me, Searc. I'm listening."

Spit hung on Searc's lips as he gazed back and forth between the two. "Coric, Kenneth, and Ronan rode from Cashel around sunset. Coric found Kenneth, he freed him from the Vikings, and then they rode to Cashel. I was outside of Cashel when they passed, and I followed them. I saw them leave, and Ceana told me that Kenneth went to find Arabella. She said Arabella went to Perth some time back. I never saw her there. But when Kenneth left Cashel, Coric and Ronan followed after him." Searc finished and slowly melted in a groan with tears streaming from his eyes.

Alpin stared into the night sky, grimacing in anger at the stars and fighting a fury that boiled inside.

"Alpin! Did you hear me!" Searc screamed. His face fell flush and his chest heaved in and out.

"I heard you," Alpin said in a bitter, unsympathetic tone.

"Then what are you going to do?" Searc yelled.

"I'm going to do nothing. You have woven your deception and your hatred, and now I can only respond to what lies ahead. You never should have done this, Searc."

"Me! I was only doing what you were too stubborn to do. And there were others—others that said you were too prideful to join the Picts ... and they were right."

"I should slay you where you stand, you fool. But that would be too kind for the punishment of treason," Alpin uttered, reeking with disgust. He turned and peered at Luag, then he shook his head and walked away.

"Then kill me! Kill me if you're so righteous ... you coward!"

Alpin's steps slowed. He resisted the urge to turn back to the boy.

Searc slid a hand to his backside and pulled a small-bladed dagger from his belt. He lifted the weapon and ran at Alpin.

Luag lunged for the boy but missed. "Alpin!" Luag shouted.

Alpin swiveled on his heels, but only to watch as a silent arrow suddenly plunged into Searc's chest.

The knife fell from Searc's hand. He stared wide-eyed at the arrow protruding from his sternum. "No. No," Searc muttered, his voice quiet and helpless. Fright swept over his pitiful face. His body drew limp, and he dropped to the ground at Alpin's feet.

Alpin bent and hovered over the boy. "Searc, Searc." He grabbed Searc's arm and shook him. No response. Alpin gazed at Luag and then startled at the sound of footsteps.

A figure emerged from the darkness.

"Taran?"

"He was going to kill you, Alpin," Taran said, lowering his crossbow as he approached.

"He wouldn't have killed me, Taran," Alpin muttered. He turned and attended Searc, checking his neck for a pulse. The boy's hollow eyes stared up at him. "He's dead," Alpin said, and he stood and fixed his gaze on Taran. "How long were you standing there?"

"I was checking on the men. When I heard shouting, I headed this way. That's when I saw him pull the knife and come after you." Taran glanced at Luag, then back at Alpin. "Who was he? Why was he trying to kill you?" Taran asked curiously.

"His name was Searc. He was from Renton, and he was an angry, fatherless boy," Alpin said, glancing at Luag with a look of suspicion. "He's been in Renton during our meetings, Taran. I would have thought you would have known him, or at least met him."

"No. The name isn't familiar." Taran shook his head, staring at the body. "There are a lot of men here ... I don't recall seeing him before."

"He was upset, but he didn't have to die," Alpin said, and he bent down and folded the boy's arms across his chest. Then he removed the arrow and set it on the ground. "Taran, get your father. Luag, get Constantine and Latharn. We need to talk," Alpin said. "And Luag, send some men to help bury the boy."

"Thank you for coming," Alpin addressed the five men gathered in the small room. "I know your men are anxious. We've yet to hear from our scouts. Our hope is that they return in time to prepare us for the Vikings. We assume the attack will come from the north. The loch will hinder them from the east. However, they may flank us and strike from the west if they think we're waiting for a northern attack. We will hold our position until we hear more, but that's not the only reason I've gathered you. As you may have heard, Searc, whom some of you know, or knew, returned to Renton tonight—and he is now dead."

Reaction to the news differed among those in the room, varying from man to man, but it was Taran's apathy that surprised Alpin the most.

"Unfortunately, it did not have to happen," Alpin finished.

"But Alpin," Taran objected.

Alpin lifted his hand to silence the fiery redhead, then he motioned for him to sit.

Taran glanced at his father with an indignant frown, and Guaire returned an open palm, subtly cautioning his son.

"Taran did what he thought best. Searc had gone mad. He came at me with a knife, and Taran shot him with a crossbow. I may have done the same, had I seen Searc running to down a man. This isn't about Taran. Luag was there, he tried to stop the boy, but Searc was determined. As I said, it was unfortunate." Alpin paused and began to pace. "Searc brought troubling news when he arrived. Before he lost himself, he told me and Luag about his involvement with

Oengus. Evidently, he had visited Oengus in Perth some time ago."

Alpin peered at Guaire. "Do you know anything about his visit to Oengus?"

Guaire shook his head and glanced at Taran and then at the others. "No, I have no idea who this Searc is. And I have certainly never spoken to him about Oengus. What are you getting at, Alpin?"

"Before Searc died, he said that I should have conceded to the Picts, that I should have sought Oengus and his men to help fight the Vikings. You and your son have been keen on this idea for some time. Have your men given any indication that they've spoken to Searc about the matter?"

"Alpin, this is nonsense. Yes, I encouraged you to seek the Picts. And yes, five of our men were sent to Oengus. They were to inquire of his help, to tell him of the attack on Renton and inform him that the Vikings could attack Perth as well … but you knew this, Alpin. You speak as if the Dumbartons have been conspiring against you. I assure you, this is not the case."

"And have your five men returned?" Alpin replied. "They've been gone over a week."

The room fell silent.

Guaire wrung his hands and delayed before responding. "No. They've not reported back."

"Doesn't that give you pause?"

"I don't like it," Guaire conceded. "They should have been back by now. But they could walk through that door in the next moment for all I know."

Alpin turned and stared at the door. He peered back at Guaire. "That's my point, we don't know. My suspicion is, if what Searc said about Oengus is true, then Oengus may have taken them prisoner. If Oengus is against us, worse yet, if he's conspiring with the Vikings, then he would be a fool to send your men back to Renton."

"This is insane, Alpin. Why would Oengus side with the Vikings? They're savages. They'd kill him the moment they met him. They have no need of the Picts."

"Do not underestimate Oengus. He's not to be trusted. He's never been a friend, and only a fool would trust a liar. I would not put it past him to make a truce with the Vikings and deliver us into their hands as a means of achieving his desires."

"Are you saying that the Picts could attack as well?" Constantine asked.

"I'm saying anything is possible."

"How do we know this boy, Searc, was telling the truth?" Guaire replied. "You yourself said he'd gone mad."

"Mad, yes, but he was a close friend of Alpin's son, Aiden," Luag said.

"Alpin, I am sorry for your son, Aiden," Guaire lamented. "But what does your son have to do with Searc and the Picts?"

"Searc told us that Aiden is being held by Oengus. He said that Oengus had found Aiden, burned and nearly dead from the fires in Renton, and that he tricked Aiden into thinking the Vikings had returned to Renton and killed the remaining survivors," Alpin said. "Searc was not himself, but he wouldn't tell me these things about Aiden if they weren't true. In fact, it may have been the guilt he carried of Aiden that drove him mad."

"And possibly his anger over the death of his father," Taran added.

Alpin peered at Taran, "I didn't think you'd heard that much."

"He was shouting, Alpin," Taran said.

"Yes. He was shouting," Alpin responded, the suspicion in his voice was hardly discernable.

Luag stepped to the center of the room. "I agree with Alpin. The boy was mad, but I believe enough of his story that we should prepare for the worst—we may be facing the Picts as well." His gaze swept over the men before his eyes settled on Alpin. "If that's true, we should reinforce our positions to the east. And we'll need more scouts."

Alpin ambled to the window and peered up at the moon, palming his chin in contemplation. "We will hold here in Renton until we know more. Each of you prepare your men, it will be a long night. And Luag, the scouts you noted … send out three more, and send them east."

CHAPTER 22

"SLOW DOWN, KENNETH. SLOW DOWN," CORIC shouted as he closed on Kenneth.

Kenneth lifted his reigns and tugged to slow his horse, knowing his brother was too stubborn to quit.

Coric and Ronan trotted alongside Kenneth, and the three came to a stop under the cold, starry sky.

"Coric, you shouldn't have followed me."

"You shouldn't have left. How long were you going to ride?"

"I made it this far. I figured I could reach Perth by sunrise," Kenneth replied.

"You're reckless, Kenneth. I know you want to rescue Arabella, you've proven that. But you shouldn't have left Ronan and me back in Cashel, having us chase you halfway across Pictland."

"You should've turned back. You should've stayed with Ceana. She needs you, Coric. Your child needs you."

"I don't need you telling me how to run my family. I'm trying to help you and *our* family, while you're running reckless like some star-crossed lover. There's a war going on! Did you think of that, Kenneth?"

"I had plenty of time to think, Coric. I know there's a

war, but I also know the woman I love risked her life to save me … and now the Picts have her, doing who knows what to her."

"Well, others risked their lives to save you, too, brother. Seems you require a lot of saving."

"Coric, I can never repay you for saving me, nor Ronan or Laise. I knew you wouldn't let me go after Arabella, and I know Ceana needs you with her. I wasn't about to ask you to come with me and rip you away from her. I've torn up enough lives already. Couldn't you have just let me go?"

"No dammit, I couldn't. Father was nearly killed trying to find you. Don't you see, Kenneth? When we lost Drostan, a part of Father died—he watched our brother die in his arms. And with the loss of Aiden, how much more do you want to cripple him? I'm not about to let you run off to Perth and get yourself killed. You don't know Oengus. He'll kill you. I swear, he'll kill you."

"Good for him. Halfdan wanted the same, yet here I am," Kenneth replied, spreading his arms wide in a righteous gesture.

Coric gave no response save an incredulous glare, peering silently at his brother. There Alpin's sons remained wordless for a long moment, locked in a silent stalemate. Ronan, annoyed by the entire exchange, trotted his horse away from the two to gather his wits.

Coric's eyes weighed heavy. He continued in his silence, sitting on his horse and gazing at Kenneth. He was fatigued and exhausted. Even emotionally, he was drained, aggravated by his decision to leave his wife and child once again.

Kenneth studied Coric as the seconds continued to pass—and then it struck him. In Coric, he saw a brother who was tired and spent, yet at the same time Coric was his own flesh and blood, and his brother's determination and endless drive would not be denied. It was clear now that Coric had taken up the mantle, the weighty mantle, of being the oldest son. Whether or not Coric had purposed to do so, he now bore the heavy weight that Drostan had laid down.

Kenneth replayed the events of the last day in his mind, recalling his brother's courage—entering the enemy's lair, stealing away their prisoners, and burning their dwelling to the ground. Coric's admonishment that 'Oengus would kill him if he went to Perth,' echoed in Kenneth's ears. Kenneth recounted his boastful reply, that 'Halfdan wanted the same.' He regretted his words, wishing he could take them back.

"You're right," Kenneth conceded. "Halfdan wanted me dead, probably still does. So Oengus will have to wait his turn, I suppose." He grinned at Coric as a brother would grin.

Coric eased. He rubbed his fingers through his hair and sighed. "Well thanks to me and Ronan, we saved your skin … so now, they'll both have to wait if they want you dead." Coric returned the grin.

"And don't think saving you was easy, either," Ronan added, rejoining the two. "Your brother is just as crazy as you are, maybe worse."

"I guess I owe you both for risking your necks for me," Kenneth relented. "And Laise, too. I suppose I shouldn't forget the marksman."

"Him too," Coric agreed. "So you see, truly, we don't want you getting killed."

"Now that you two have settled things, I should probably mention that these horses are all but done," Ronan noted. "Can we agree to bunk here for the night? We can rest the horses and plan for tomorrow."

"I guess I don't have much choice," Kenneth muttered.

"No, you don't. And on top of it all, I have to take a leak before my bladder bursts," Coric groused and dismounted his horse.

"Maybe we should tie him down while we sleep tonight, Coric. We don't need to wake to an empty bedroll," Ronan said and then smirked at Kenneth.

☺

Morning came early in Renton. Alpin and his leaders were up before sunrise after a short and sleepless night. The group collected themselves under the meeting tent to rehearse their battle plans. Alpin was peppering the men with possible counterattack scenarios when a single scout entered Renton from the north.

Luag noticed the fast approaching rider and stepped from beneath the covering into the drizzling rain. "Have you found the Vikings?" he addressed the beleaguered scout as he dismounted.

The scout brushed a fistful of rainwater from his brow and nodded. "Yes, we spotted them."

Luag motioned the man to join him and the others under the tent. There the scout addressed the group, "We saw Halfdan and his men on the northwest corner of Loch Lomond. They were moving east, along the north rim of the loch in the direction of Perth. The other scouts are still tracking them."

"That doesn't make sense," Luag said, staring at Alpin. "If they were going to attack us, why would they travel the longer path east around the loch? They'll burn supplies and allow us time to prepare."

"They may not be coming for us ... not yet. From the direction they're moving, they may well be heading to Perth," Alpin said. "Considering Searc's news, it may make sense. They could be heading to Perth to join Oengus, and from there, they'd bring a swell of men on Renton."

"I don't like this Alpin," Constantine replied. "We've amassed hundreds of men ready to fight. But I don't like our odds facing the Vikings and Picts together."

"No, you're right. We stand little chance against a force that size. I believe our only chance is to attack them before they attack us."

"Attack the Picts and the Vikings?" Taran questioned. "We don't even know for sure they're aligned."

"Everything points to it, Taran," Alpin said. "And the—"

"Wait, this is absurd!" Taran exclaimed. "You're going to trust a madman?"

"Enough, Taran," Guaire demanded. "Let Alpin finish."

Alpin acknowledged Guaire and continued, "I'm not saying we attack the Picts. I'm saying we attack the Vikings before they reach Perth."

"If that's even where they're headed," Taran replied.

"I said that's enough, Taran," Guaire insisted. "Oengus has made his bed. We have no choice. We must stop the Vikings, whether in Renton or on the fields of Pictland—"

"We do have a choice, Father!"

"Taran, don't go there," Alpin cautioned. "We're not seeking the Pict's help. That path is a dead end. Leave it alone."

"Stay out of this, Alpin. I'm speaking to my father!"

"Taran, you're out of line," Guaire warned.

"Dammit, Father! Why won't you listen to me? You stand

here like a coward listening to these old men wax and wane, pondering every little decision, treating us as puppets—"

"Taran," Luag uttered as he tapped the young man on the back.

Taran turned, "What!"

The punch came so quickly that Taran saw only the knuckles of Luag's fist before they thumped against his eye. Instantly, Taran buckled like a broken barley stalk and crumpled to the ground.

The men stared white-faced at Luag.

"Somebody had to do it," Luag stated as a grin inched upon his lips.

"Well, Guaire?" Alpin said. "Are you good?"

Guaire gazed down at his son reeling in a half-conscious daze. "I'm good," he replied.

"Now that we have that behind us, where were we?" Alpin said.

"I think you were saying we're headed to Pictland."

"Yes, Constantine, I believe you're right." Alpin eyed his comrades. "Gentlemen, rally your troops. We're heading out."

᠀

"I wish there was another way," Kenneth said to Coric as the two finished filling their water sacks beside the creek, their bodies still stiff from the night's rest.

"I do, too. But we both know there's not," Coric replied. "Not with Oengus being as mad as hell with me—and with Father. There's no way he'd see you … not without killing you first. And we don't know for sure that Arabella is even there."

"I'm certain she's there, Coric."

"We don't know that ... not for sure," Coric said. He adjusted the two water sacks hanging from his shoulders. "When we get back to Ronan and the horses, we'll pack the bedrolls and leave for Renton. We don't need to be out here in the middle of Pictland ... not without more men." Coric glanced at Kenneth. "Father needs us in Renton. He'll be glad to see you. I only hope we're not too late."

"It'll be good to see Father ... and Mother and the others. But the first chance I get, I'm going to find Arabella. Agreed?"

"Agreed," Coric replied. "And I promise I'll help you find her."

"After you tend to Ceana, right?"

"Yeah, she's been weighing on my mind. I'll get her and bring her back to Renton when this is over. Then I'll make sure you find Arabella," Coric said. He sidestepped a rock and then slowed to glance up at the sky. He mused to himself for a moment and then spoke, "I can't believe I'm going to be a father."

"And me an uncle. Doesn't seem real." Kenneth remarked, smiling at his brother.

"Did you get the water?" Ronan called as the two approached.

"Yes, we found a creek not far over the hill," Coric replied. "Are the horses ready?"

"They're ready."

"We'll head back that way," Coric said, pointing west toward a treeless hillcrest.

Ronan and Kenneth both nodded in agreement.

When Coric reached his horse, he secured his two water sacks and then gazed east at the rising sun. "I figure we should make it to Renton by midday. Pray we get there before the Vikings do. Hopefully, Laise and the others made it and told them about the Vikings."

"I'm sure he did," Ronan said. He lifted from his seat on a log and double-checked the bedroll tied to his horse. "Knowing him, he told the men and then found the highest perch to pick off the Vikings one by one."

"Wouldn't surprise me," Coric replied and mounted up. Ronan and Kenneth mounted behind him.

"To Renton," Coric called in a sure voice.

"To Renton," the two replied.

The sun lifted into the blue sky as the three moved southwest. For several miles they followed the winding creek until it emptied into a small loch nestled amid a hilly collage of juniper and aspen trees.

"The forest is thick ahead. The trees will slow us down. If we move due west, away from the loch, we may find open land to ride," Coric called out to Ronan as the three wove through the trees. Coric glanced back at Kenneth, riding rear.

Kenneth agreed with a nod.

Ahead, Ronan nudged his horse past an ancient river birch and moved up the sloping ground, steering his way through the maze of trees and the glinting beams of sunlight that pierced the forest's dense canopy. Nearing the top of the hill, he slowed and studied the woody surroundings. Then he glanced back at Coric with a puzzled expression.

Coric's brow rose.

Ronan lifted his finger to his lips, "Shhh." He placed his hand to his ear, listened a moment longer, and then signaled the two to halt. "Do you hear that?" he mouthed, his voice hardly audible.

"What is it?" Coric whispered.

"I think someone is talking?" he said, exaggerating the movement of his mouth so Coric could read his lips.

Coric slowly dismounted. "Stay here, I'm going to have a look." He untied his crossbow, moved past Ronan, and snuck up the hill.

Ronan and Kenneth eyed the woody terrain as Coric crested the hill and ducked behind a bolder. Then Ronan dismounted and motioned for Kenneth to follow.

Kenneth slid from his horse and ascended the hill behind Ronan.

"What do you see?" Ronan asked, and he dropped to lay prone next to Coric. Then Kenneth lowered beside him, and the three peered down the far side of the hill.

"Remember the guard we saw at the Pict castle, the one with bandages?" Coric said.

"Yeah, he chased us across the bridge," Ronan replied. "I remember."

"He's down there and I saw his bandages. But now he's moved behind the willow. I think he's sitting on that rock," Coric said. "Kenneth, he's the guard who came after us when we raided Oengus' castle."

"I can't see anyone." Kenneth said. "That tree is blocking my view."

"Wait. In a moment, he'll move and you'll see him better," Coric whispered.

"How many are there?"

"I can't tell. He seems to be talking to someone near the water, past those large rocks."

"I don't see any horses," Kenneth said.

"Keep an eye out behind us. If they're part of a patrol of Picts, I don't want them spotting us here."

"He's standing!" Ronan whispered. "It is the one from the castle. What's he doing out here in the middle of nowhere? There's not a Pict village for miles." He lifted his head and quickly scanned the trees. "I don't like this, Coric. There has to be more Picts nearby. We should leave."

"Or maybe we should take them out while we have the chance," Coric said. He peered down the sights of his crossbow and aimed at the man.

"Coric, we can't do this. There may be a hundred more over the next hill," Kenneth exclaimed. "What if they shout or yell for help?"

"They can't shout if they're dead," Coric replied, with the man now locked in his sights.

"Wait, he's moving. And somebody's coming up from the loch. They're saying something."

"Get ready. This could happen quickly," Coric muttered, tracking the man as he moved.

"Are you just going to shoot him?" Kenneth quipped. "We could take them as prisoners and see what they know about Oengus' plans. Maybe they know about the Vikings."

Coric pulled away from the bow with a frown on his face. "That guard has already tried to kill me once. I don't intend to give him a second chance. Not to mention the bastards nearly killed Father."

"Shh," Ronan whispered and pointed. "Look there, behind the willow, another Pict. Can you see 'em?"

"Not clearly," Coric replied.

The three stared down the hillside at the two figures veiled behind the tree's leafy foliage—and then a woman stepped beyond the drooping willow branches into the sun's clear brilliant light.

Kenneth gasped, and his heart skipped in his chest. "Good God, it's Arabella!" he exclaimed and lifted. "Cover me, Coric."

"Get down, Kenneth! Get down!"

Kenneth sprung to his feet and drew his sword in a single motion then darted forward.

"I'll kill that Pict bastard if he moves," Coric said, sighting his target.

"Coric, your brother is as mad as you!" Ronan exclaimed, rising to a stance. "I'm going. There may be more." He ripped his dagger from his belt and rushed down the hill.

"Dammit," Coric muttered and jumped up and descended behind Ronan with his finger still gripped on the crossbow's trigger.

The three were halfway down the hill when Arabella's eyes lifted. The cloth in her hand slid from her fingers as a wave of numbness fell over her. Her face flushed white, and she gaped as if seeing a ghost. "Kenneth!"

"Arabella, get down," Kenneth yelled, motioning his hands in a flurry. He glanced back over his shoulder.

Coric flew down the hillside and closed on the bandaged man, itching to release his arrow. "You're a dead man, Pict!" Coric yelled. His finger surged against the bow's trigger.

"Coric, no! It's Aiden!" Arabella screamed.

Aiden? Coric's mind spun.

"Don't shoot. Don't shoot," Arabella yelled, moving to shield Aiden.

The bandaged man turned—and his eyes met Coric's.

"Aiden!" Coric gulped and tossed his bow aside. "It's you!

You're alive!" He hopped headlong down the hill, moving with such exuberance that he nearly tumbled in his descent.

"Arabella! It's a miracle," Kenneth gushed. In a single swoop of his arms, he picked her up and pulled her close. "I can't believe this," his strong, welcomed voice poured into her ears. Then he pressed his lips to hers and squeezed her to him, and her body warmed him.

"You're alive, Kenneth," Arabella gasped, catching her breath. "I thought you were dead. I thought for sure you were dead."

"No, I'm not dead. I'm right here. Right here with you." He lifted his hands and cupped her face in his leathery palms, and he kissed her hard. The suppleness of her lips felt like the kiss of an angel. Her tears smeared across her flesh, salty and sweet, like honey from a hive. He released her lips and stared into her eyes, gushing in exhilaration. Then he brushed his fingers through her hair and spoke, "I can't believe I found you. I have dreamt of holding you a thousand times ... and now it's come true."

"Kenneth," Coric shouted. "Did you see who else we found?"

Kenneth turned to Aiden, and a wide smile lifted on his cheeks. Kenneth let go of Arabella's hand. "I'm not going anywhere," he said to her softly, and then he stepped toward his brother.

"I thought you'd been killed, Kenneth. The Picts found me after I fell from the ridge. I never thought I'd see any of you again."

The memory of the fall flashed through Kenneth's mind. The burns, the Vikings, the cliff—all his brother had suffered. Kenneth's guilt was heavy. "Aiden. I'm sorry. I'm so sorry. All this happened because of—"

"Kenneth," Aiden stopped him. "I don't blame you. This wasn't your doing. It was the Vikings. And the Picts. They did this."

"But I left you in Renton. I should've never left you there alone."

"Kenneth, I was the one who said you were foolish for staying in Renton. This isn't your fault." Aiden gazed at his brother, and a smile arched across his face. "Heck, you nearly got yourself killed trying to save me and Nessa."

Kenneth stood motionless, combing his eyes over Aiden. "I'm glad you're alive ... I missed you," Kenneth said. "Me too," Aiden uttered as Kenneth hugged his brother's head.

"Alright, enough of the mush," Ronan piped.

"I agree with Ronan. I should kick both of you in the rear for getting caught and making us hunt you down," Coric said. "But I do have to say, it's good to see you, Aiden. Father won't believe it."

"Is the family reunion almost over?" Ronan muttered. "We're in the middle of Pictland, and we've got to get back to Renton ... and it won't be as pretty there."

"Ronan's right," Coric replied. "Let's head home. They're going to need our help." Coric turned with Aiden and Ronan, and the three headed back up the hill, striding shoulder to shoulder.

"I'll be right there, Coric," Kenneth called out. He turned to Arabella and took her hand.

She traced the curvature of his face, studying the stubble on his cheeks and his dark soiled hair before settling her gaze on his tired blue eyes. "I've missed you, Kenneth, son of Alpin." A happy smile appeared on her lips. "I love you," she said.

"I love you, too, Arabella. And I will never leave you again."

CHAPTER 23

THE FIVE RODE UNDAUNTED THROUGH THE OPEN Pictland valley, Aiden with Coric and Arabella with Kenneth. Ronan rode solo. The noon air was moist, and the sun slept behind the clouds as the group moved toward Renton.

"You doing alright?" Coric called back to Aiden.

"Besides having to hold you close, I'm doing fine," he replied.

Ronan, riding beside the two, snickered aloud.

"Hold your laughter, Ronan," Coric said. "You get him next."

"He doesn't want to hold me close, I assure you."

A cool wind blew against their faces. They were glad to be heading home, even if it meant having to fight.

"We lost a lot of time back at the loch," Ronan said. "Think we'll make it home by sundown?"

Coric eyed the lofted ridge lines bounding the five on either side. "The horses aren't as fast riding double, and we've got a lot of valley ahead. But if we stay clear of the forest, I'd say we'll make it home before the sun sets."

⊚

"Lord Halfdan," the Viking scout called as he approached the advancing horde, "I have news." The scout slowed and rode his horse alongside Halfdan and Kodran.

"What have you found?" Halfdan barked.

"From the ridge ahead, I spotted three horses—"

"Picts?"

"I don't think so, they appear to be Scots. They're heading west. Two horses had double riders. And one of them looks to be a girl."

"Ha," Halfdan laughed. "Oengus must've never found his lassie. Serves him right."

"But sir, that's not all. If my eyes weren't fooling me, I would swear one of the riders was Kenneth. He was riding double with the girl."

"I'll be damned. The little bastard went straight to Perth and somehow found his darling, Arabella," Halfdan mocked and peered at Kodran.

Kodran smirked and shook his head.

"How far are they?" Halfdan asked the scout.

"Maybe an hour ... and with only three horses, they weren't moving quickly."

"Lead the way," Halfdan replied, and he turned and glared at Kodran. "I want them dead—and Oengus next."

⑨

"How long until we hear from Luag's men?" Latharn asked, riding next to Alpin.

Alpin glimpsed back at Luag and Constantine riding several paces behind. "We are expecting a scout to report back shortly after noon, with or without news of the Vikings. We should hear something soon."

"If we don't find the enemy, how long do we ride before heading back to Renton? I don't like that we left the village unprotected."

"We had no choice, Latharn. We know the Vikings are out here. And we know they're heading east. Once we find them, we'll set our ambush." Alpin glanced at Latharn. "How are your men?"

"Ready to fight," Latharn replied.

"And their longbows?"

"Very ready."

⑨

"Lord Oengus," Deort said anxiously, hurrying into the large Pict hall.

"Deort," Oengus replied as he sat molded to his cushioned chair, staring out a tall narrow window. "I hope you've come to tell me that you've found Aiden and our lovely Arabella?"

"No, my lord. Our patrols have found no sign of them, but—"

"But what! I want them found. And now!"

"Lord Oengus, please … there is something more urgent that I must tell you. A boy from a small village northeast of Loch Lomond claims he saw an army of men riding east towards Perth. A messenger just arrived with the news."

Oengus leapt from his seat, "An army, coming north of Loch Lomond to Perth—Halfdan! Curse the savage. He's coming here and bringing his army of animals with him," the words spewed from Oengus' lips as he tried to sort his thoughts. He clasped his hands and strode across the room.

"He's not wasting any time in making good on his threats," he murmured to himself.

Oengus thought a moment longer and then shot a furtive glance toward Deort. "Prepare your men."

"They are prepared, my lord."

"Well done, Deort," Oengus said, relishing his newly conceived plan with a sinister sneer. "We leave at once!"

⑨

"Here come the pathetic fools now. Look at them … they have no idea," Halfdan grunted, sitting high on his horse in the shadows of Torrie Forest. "Let them draw a little closer."

Halfdan turned to his left and spoke with a calm, casual demeanor, "Jorund, I know you're set on killing our friend, Kenneth. I insist you make sure I'm there to enjoy his miserable death … I will not miss it."

Kodran leaned forward and eyed Jorund. "If you reach him first, make sure I'm there to see it too."

Jorund's brow furrowed, and then a scowl formed on his face. He stared in a trance at the oncoming riders, watching, hungry for a kill. His eyes locked on Kenneth like a hawk on a rat. "I'll make sure you're there," he muttered.

"Coric, do you have any venison in your food sack?" Aiden asked. "The apple was good, but apples alone can keep a fellow hungry."

"Sounds like Pictland didn't ruin your appetite. You were probably getting fat eating from Oengus' table. I don't have any venison, but I can take you back to Perth and we can ask the Picts."

"On second thought, I'll wait until we get home," Aiden

replied. "I'm looking forward to Mother's mutton potato stew."

"Don't talk about that," Coric groaned. "You're making me hungry now."

"Men, our moment has arrived. The fools are riding straight into our hands," Halfdan mused. "Kodran, Jorund, split your men and surround them. No one is to escape."

The two nodded in unison and broke from Halfdan. Within moments, Torrie Forest erupted under the thunder of hooves.

The trees moved and swayed a hundred yards ahead. Ronan rubbed his eyes and looked again. "What is that?" he shouted and pointed at the forest.

"No ... no!" Kenneth yelled, seeing a sight he refused to believe—the sight of the Viking horde emerging from the timberline like a herd of wild beasts.

Arabella shrilled in terror, nearly bursting Kenneth's eardrums. She lowered behind Kenneth and clutched his torso.

"Turn the horses. We'll return the way we came. Split up if you have to," Coric shouted. The three spun their horses, snapping their reigns and spurring the animals in retreat through the valley. "We've got to find a gap in the ridge, we'll never outrun them."

"There, up ahead, we passed the gap earlier," Kenneth shouted.

"It's too far, we won't make it," Ronan replied.

"Ronan, ride ahead. We'll come behind you," Coric yelled.

Ronan lowered on his horse and kicked his heels into its

ribs. The animal pulled away, and he raced toward the gap in the ridgeline.

The roar of the Viking horses loudened. Aiden peered back at the horde and recognized Kodran's face as the Viking warrior drew nearer with an army of riders behind him. "This isn't good, Coric," Aiden said. "If we don't make the gap, I want the crossbow. I aim to kill as many of those bastards as I can before I go."

"You're not going anywhere, Aiden. We'll make it through this. I'll see to that."

The rumble of the advancing riders shook Arabella's insides. Instinctively, she pressed herself against Kenneth and buried her face in his back, praying the five would survive the ambush. Then she mustered her courage and pried open her eyes. "Kenneth!" she exclaimed.

Kenneth glanced to his right and glimpsed the bobbing snout of a Viking horse, not twenty feet away. Kenneth snapped his reigns, hoping to pull ahead. But the Vikings kept coming.

Coric eyed Ronan as his friend raced ahead in the distance and drew within sixty strides from the small gap in the ridge. Then Coric glanced at Kenneth. The two were side by side, yet on the far side of his brother the Vikings were pulling ahead and passing him—heading for Ronan and the only way out. "Go, Ronan, go!" Coric shouted.

Coric slapped his horse, willing the creature forward. But the animal refused. Insistent, Coric jammed his feet into the side of the beast, demanding more, yet the horse had none to give and Coric knew it. He could only watch as his friend disappeared through the distant gap—with three Vikings vanishing behind him.

A dozen more Vikings funneled toward the gap. Reaching the opening, they stopped and turned their horses to form a wall and seal its entrance. There was no escape.

Both Kenneth's and Coric's horses slowed. The creatures moved in a spent, dispirited trot, as if they knew their fate, as if they accepted it.

Coric jumped to the ground and drew his sword. Aiden slid off behind him and grabbed the crossbow. Kenneth stopped his horse beside Coric's and dismounted. He reached for Arabella, pulled her down, and pinned her between him and the horse. "Don't move," he said to her, and he turned and brandished his sword.

Kodran savored the moment, sitting on his steed thirty feet from Coric and Aiden, with half an army mounted behind him.

On the far side of the four Scots, Jorund and his men had already dismounted. They paced the ground and formed an arc, closing off any path of escape for Kenneth and Arabella. Jorund glared at Kenneth with a lust for blood.

Halfdan trotted his stallion through the sea of men while a path formed to clear his way. He stopped and gazed down at the Scots. Then he smiled. "You boys have been busy. And you have been bad. I don't like that," he said, and his smiled faded into a scowl. "And you Kenneth, won't you please die? I grow so tired of you. You made Jorund very angry with your mischief at the fort … the fort you and your beloved Dorrell worked so hard to build. I'm disappointed."

Kenneth secured Arabella behind him and waved his sword. "Sorry to disappoint you, Halfdan."

"I'm sure you are. Soon, you'll be very sorry," Halfdan

replied. "Now let's see, I've met your lovely lady friend before—so nice to see you again, Arabella—but I haven't had the pleasure of meeting your other friends. Wait, I do recognize the one with the bandages. Yes, that's right, he was the badly burned one that we took from Renton when we destroyed your village."

Halfdan peered at Kodran, "I thought he was dead. Isn't that what I was told?"

"He went over the cliff with one of my men. He's supposed to be dead ... I can make it happen," Kodran replied and instantly dismounted.

"Oh, patience, patience, Kodran. In due time." Halfdan returned his gaze to Kenneth, "So, I know the three of you, who's the fourth one at our little party?"

"He's my brother—"

"Coric, son of Alpin. I've been waiting for the day I'd meet you," Coric said, and he took a step forward.

"Ahh. Coric, son of Alpin. That's got a nice ring to it," Halfdan mocked. "Are you the roach that scurried into my home and decided to release all the other little roaches?"

"I burned your fort to the ground, if that's what you mean."

"Good to know, all the more pleasure I'll have when I watch you die," Halfdan sneered. Then he glanced ahead at his men guarding the gap in the ridge. "And the other rider, the one my men are hunting as we speak ... is this yet another, 'son of Alpin?'"

"Ronan, son of Luag," Coric replied. "And you'll need more men if you plan on hunting him down."

"We'll see about that. Vikings make fairly good hunters, especially when hunting human prey," Halfdan scoffed. He glanced at Kodran and then at Jorund. "I believe we've had our share of pleasantry here, let's have some sport."

"Stay behind me, Arabella," Kenneth whispered. "If I go down, take the horse and head to the gap."

Arabella placed her hands on his waist. "If I die, I'm dying here, with you," she whispered.

Jorund and his men approached. Kenneth lifted his sword.

"Take as many as you can with the bow, Aiden. We're not going down without a fight!" Coric exclaimed.

Kodran and four others moved toward the two.

"Just say when," Aiden replied.

"Now!"

The arrow released like a lightning bolt and buried itself into Viking flesh. The man dropped like a rock, and Aiden hurried to reload the bow.

Coric slapped his horse hard, and the animal reared on its haunches and released a shrilling cry. It came down in a clamor, turning and bucking through the Vikings.

Kodran leapt sideways to avoid the beast and reflexed to a striking position, swiveling his sword and sizing Coric.

Aiden shot again and dropped a second Viking.

"I want a piece of you, you little runt," Jorund grunted. He lifted his double-bladed axe and eyed Kenneth. Then he came fast.

Kenneth clutched his sword in his hands and lifted it overhead.

Jorund's axe crashed down and collided against Kenneth's blade. The blow hit hard, stunning Kenneth and knocking him to the ground. Instantly, he rolled and jumped to his feet. With the big man looming, Kenneth flicked his sword side to side, working to lure Jorund away from Arabella. "If you want me, you bastard, then come and get me!"

Jorund growled and swung his axe again, shredding the air in front of Kenneth's nose.

Suddenly, a loud guttural cry echoed from the gap in the ridge. Every man turned.

In a blink, Ronan's horse burst from the gap and charged the Viking blockade. He careened against the wall of beasts and wedged a hole large enough to escape. Once free, Ronan steered his horse toward the mass of animals and men in the distance and targeted the man sitting high on his steed— Halfdan. Like a deranged killer, Ronan raised his blood-tipped sword into the air and rode headlong with the rage of a madman.

"Stop him!" Halfdan shouted, and he reached for his sword.

Kodran rammed his shoulder into Coric, knocked him backwards, and continued his run to intercept Ronan's oncoming horse. When he reached the spot he was looking for, he stopped. He tightened his grip on his sword and waited for the horse and its rider.

As the horse advanced, Jorund left Kenneth and dashed toward the animal. He didn't wait for Kodran to make his play, he would have the honor of dropping the horse and its lunatic rider. Jorund lifted his heavy axe and hurled it at the animal. The weapon lumbered through the air as if waiting for the horse to arrive. In an instant, the two moving objects collided, and the axe lodged into the front shoulder of the beast, missing Ronan's leg by inches. The horse whinnied and veered sideways before collapsing. Ronan tried to separate from the animal but the ground came too quickly. The horse landed with a thud, wedging Ronan's leg beneath its frame.

Halfdan lifted his sword high above his head. "I want them dead! All of them! Dead!"

For a moment, time stood still.

Before the Viking army could prepare its strike, something in the valley changed. A shadow from heaven crept over from above. The whisper of arrows filled the air, and the sky darkened as though a thousand birds had lofted into flight.

The Viking warriors lifted their eyes and a rain of Dalriadan arrows poured down upon them like a deadly ocean wave.

Halfdan could only watch as the torrent of arrows fell and found his men. Dozens stumbled and collapsed to the ground. Halfdan surveyed the high ridgeline bounding the southern edge of the valley. A multitude of Dalriadan archers lined the ridge, sending down their iron-tipped killers unimpeded.

The arrows had fallen fifty feet from where Halfdan stood. The gap in the ridge had stopped the archers from getting close enough to reach him. He watched as a second volley of arrows rose and fell over his men.

Without warning, a battle cry broke out from the southwest floor of the valley. The cry was loud and angry.

Halfdan twisted on his heels and gazed at the sight—an army of Scots stampeding forward like the hounds of Hell. Halfdan called to his gods of war and cursed the God of

Heaven. The Scot attack was coming from above and below, enveloping the Vikings where they stood.

The Vikings were left reeling, and their casualties grew countless. Those still standing mounted their horses—some rode to battle, some rode to retreat.

⑨

Oengus trotted his horse to the edge of the ridge and stopped beside Deort. The two sat horseback with a half dozen Pict soldiers on either side. Oengus stared long, surveying the calamity in the valley below. "What have we here, Deort?"

"Lord Oengus, the Scots attack from two fronts—their archers from the opposing ridge and their horsemen from the south. Your orders, sir?" Deort asked, awaiting Oengus' command.

Oengus watched the battle rage from the security of the ridgeline. He found no displeasure in what he saw. "We'll let them fight themselves until both are weak. If the Vikings look to have the upper hand, then we attack. And we rid the earth of them!" He rubbed his chin in thought before continuing, "Our aid to the Scots would then end the battle, making us the hero and … indebting them … if you will."

"And if the Scots are the last standing?"

"Alpin is a stubborn fool, and I'm not certain his men have the heart, Deort," Oengus said. "But should they make me a liar, I will grant them mercy on this day. And when the Scots see my mercy, then all the more will they be swayed … and inclined to embrace the goodness of my hand."

"Very wise, my lord," Deort said with a nod.

"That, Deort, is how kingdoms are built," Oengus said. He chuckled to himself and mused over the battle below.

⑨

Ronan struggled to free his trapped leg, still wedged beneath his horse.

A husky, barrel-chested Viking caught sight of him and rushed at him with an axe leveled in the air above his helmet.

Ronan glanced at his fallen sword. Its handle lay just beyond his reach. The tips of his fingers crawled forward, inching toward the weapon, yet to no avail. He squirmed and fought to extend his arm.

The Viking closed.

"Ronan, look out" Coric yelled and threw himself into the man's side. The man flew from his feet and toppled to the ground. Coric lifted his sword and plunged it into the man's abdomen. Without a thought, he removed the blade and darted to Ronan.

"Here, I'll lift," Coric said. "Can you get loose?"

"It's coming … I got it, thanks." Ronan rubbed his knee and stood, testing his leg for strength.

"You're welcome." Coric turned and found another Viking. The two clashed blades and another fight began.

Kenneth's eyes never left Jorund. The large Viking had dropped the horse and was moving toward Ronan and Coric to retrieve his axe. "Jorund, over here … we're not finished," Kenneth shouted.

Jorund spun, glaring at Kenneth. Fire burned in his eyes, and he pulled an eight-inch knife from his belt.

Kenneth lifted his sword and charged forward. The brute

stood his ground and twirled his knife, waiting for Kenneth. Kenneth didn't wait. He swung his blade with deft precision and knocked the knife from Jorund's hand.

Jorund's head swiveled toward his double-bladed axe still buried in Ronan's dead horse. Then Jorund broke for the horse.

Kenneth rushed after him.

"Kenneth!" Arabella screamed.

Kenneth's head jerked, and he scanned the battlefield. Arabella cried again, and Kenneth spotted her in the clutches of a burly, muscular Viking. The man was lifting her onto a horse, and she was fighting him. Kenneth turned from Jorund, and he sprinted toward the two.

The burly Viking whirled when he heard the stomping of Kenneth's footsteps. Arabella took the opening and pushed away and the Viking stumbled. Before he could right himself, Kenneth's blade sliced from overhead. The blade severed flesh and split the man's clavicle, breaking the bone in two. The Viking dropped to his knees, and a pained growl crawled from his throat. Kenneth recoiled and hammered the butt of his sword against the man's jaw. The man spiraled on his knees and fell limp to the ground.

Kenneth reached for Arabella. "Are you alright?" he said, panting as he spoke.

"Yes, I'm okay."

"Take this horse. Ride to those two trees and stay there," Kenneth said, pointing to a pair of oaks. "And do you see down there? Your father is coming with mine. Wait for them by the trees and stay out of sight."

"What about you, Kenneth?"

"Arabella, you have to do this. I have to help my brothers. They need me. Now go!"

Kenneth pushed her up onto the horse, and she rode toward the two trees that stood like ancient witnesses to the horrific battle of life and death.

Kenneth stared south for a long moment. The battle raged. The Scots warred, fighting hand to hand and blade to blade, with a thirst for Viking blood. In the middle of it all stood Halfdan. He was alone—and he was staring back at Kenneth. Kenneth caught his gaze and then turned and peered back over his shoulder in search of Jorund. The large Viking loomed in the distance, hovering over Ronan's dead horse, his axe now extracted and dripping with blood.

The Scot fighters progressed north along the valley floor as their longbow guardians, high on the ridge above, delivered their wooden-shaft manslayers upon the thickest pockets of the enemy. The Scots reaching the frontline of the fight quickly discovered that their advance had pushed them beyond the protection of their archers on the ridge. There at the front, the men showed their courage, engaging in a foray of hand-to-hand combat against the fiercest of Halfdan's soldiers.

Kodran kept watch on his prey. He surreptitiously moved towards Aiden, quietly, like a hunter, watching the young Scot expend his arrows one by one.

The hunter paused. From the corner of his eye, Kodran caught sight of a man disturbing his hunt. The Scot warrior rushed the Viking hunter. The warrior swung his sword. The hunter ducked. The warrior's blade sliced the empty air.

Kodran lifted and drove his elbow into the warrior's face, snapping the man's neck backwards and splitting his nose. Kodran spun and swung his leg across the back of his attacker's knees. When the Scot hit the ground, Kodran drove his sword through the man's ribcage, ventilating his lungs and robbing him of breath. Without pausing, Kodran pressed his foot on the Scot's chest and withdrew his red blade.

Kodran lifted his head and returned his gaze to the young Scot with the crossbow. And the hunt continued.

Aiden pulled the trigger of his bow. The arrow shot forward and found its victim. He reached for his quiver and extracted another arrow—his eyes quickly double-backed to the quiver.

"Last one," the voice said.

Aiden's head slowly lifted. Fifteen feet separated him from the Viking hunter, Kodran.

Aiden fumbled to set his arrow.

"I should have killed you myself on that ridge. I'll make things right this time," Kodran said and sneered.

Aiden locked the arrow and drew back the release. In an instant, Kodran's boot slammed against Aiden's hands, and the bow flew from his grip and tumbled to the ground. Aiden moved for his sword. A sudden backhand struck his bandaged face and sent him sprawling. A thousand splinters of pain flushed through his body.

"Get up!" Kodran shouted. "Get up!"

Aiden rose to his knees.

"Viking!" Coric yelled. "Looking for a fight!" Twenty paces separated Coric from the hunter.

Kodran turned.

Coric rushed forward.

The gap closed.

Coric never slowed.

Kodran reeled and swung his sword crossways, targeting Coric's gut.

Coric twisted his sword downward and blocked the blow. As he passed Kodran, he swirled his blade and cut into the Viking's hamstring.

Kodran dropped to a knee. Coric spun on his heel and kicked Kodran square in the jaw. The angry Viking toppled backwards and landed prostrate on the ground.

A second Viking appeared, coming from behind. It was Magnus.

"Coric!" Aiden shouted.

Coric turned as Magnus' dagger sliced deep across his forearm. Coric's sword fell from his grip. The brutish Viking peered at him and a maniacal grin slowly emerged through his heavy brown beard.

Coric's eyes twitched sideways, glancing toward a fallen Viking lying several feet to his right.

Magnus inched forward, waving his dagger at the Scot, eager to cut more.

Coric leapt toward the Viking corpse and performed an acrobatic roll, grabbing a wide-bladed sword resting atop the dead man's open belly.

Magnus rushed forward and Coric drove his foot into the brute's knee, folding it backwards and snapping the joint with a loud pop. Magnus gaped at his disfigured limb. When he lifted his eyes, it was too late. In a seamless motion, Coric's blade sliced his bearded throat, and Magnus slowly melted and sunk to the ground.

Coric gasped for breath and a sharp pain pulsed through his shoulder. He cursed and quickly gripped his arm to stop the blood seeping from his wound.

"That was close," Aiden said. He stepped beside Coric and peered down at Magnus' lifeless body.

"Yeah, thanks for the warning," Coric replied, working to hide the grimace tightening across his face.

Jorund held his axe low, letting its heavy head sway back and forth as he stared at Kenneth twenty feet away. "I'm looking forward to this, Scot!"

"Me too. I've been wanting you dead for a long time." Kenneth's heart thumped against his chest as he measured the big man. He'd watched him for a long time, long enough. He'd seen him fight, and he knew his tendencies—those that made him strong and those that made him weak.

With his hands clutching his sword, Kenneth lifted his blade head-high and pointed it at Jorund. "Aaaahhhh!" Kenneth yelled, and he leapt forward in a fury—the gap quickly shrunk between David and Goliath.

In a mad thrust, Jorund swung his axe to displace the oncoming metal blade—he took the bait.

Kenneth leaned, dipped his sword low, and shoved the cold steel blade through Jorund's chest.

Jorund gasped.

Kenneth released his sword and slowly stepped back, staring deep into the big Viking's mystified eyes.

Jorund lowered his head and peered down at the iron handle of the long blade. He grasped the sword with his hands and, inch by inch, pulled the weapon from his chest. He heaved for air. He gazed at Kenneth, and his brow slowly creased. His lips pulsed as if trying to speak, and a frothy, red saliva crept from the cracks between his teeth. Then he dropped, face first, to the ground.

Kenneth wiped the sweat from his brow and bent to remove his sword from Jorund's dead hands. As he lifted, he peered up at the gray sky and allowed a moment of relief to swell over him. Immediately, Arabella swept into his mind and he spun to find the two oaks.

He quickly spotted the large trees and then spotted Arabella. She was standing between them—and Halfdan was standing beside her, clutching her arm and pressing his sword against her midsection.

The two men locked eyes.

Halfdan waved his sword, inviting Kenneth to come—daring him to come.

Kenneth's rage trumped his cunning. Without a thought, he rushed the battlefield, straight toward his enemy. He neared and stopped ten paces from his opponent, gripping his sword in his sweaty palms. "You're not getting out of here alive, Halfdan."

"I still breathe, Scot," Halfdan exclaimed brazenly. "And you are hardly man enough to change that." He shoved Arabella aside, and he lifted his sword and charged Kenneth.

Kenneth leapt forward and swung his weapon. The two blades clashed, and a loud clang echoed in the air.

Halfdan stepped back, gained his footing, and then lunged forward with a jab of his sword.

Kenneth sidled left to avoid the blow and then swung his blade. The metal edge sliced across Halfdan's bicep. Blood gushed from the Viking's torn flesh, reddening his sleeve and igniting his anger. Halfdan lowered his chin and licked the gash. A deranged grin appeared on his face, and he leapt forward and caught Kenneth's hip with his sword.

A sharp sting shot down Kenneth's leg. Kenneth staggered backwards, waving his sword to keep his guard.

He glanced at his hip and pressed his fingers against the wound. The muscle was intact. Instantly, his eyes swept to Halfdan, and the two squared off and began moving in a circle, round and round, watching and waiting for a chance to strike.

"Kenneth!"

The voice was like a memory. It had been a long time since Kenneth had heard the once familiar tone—too long.

Halfdan sneered, and Kenneth dared a quick glance behind him. "Father!" Kenneth called.

Before Kenneth could close his mouth, Halfdan broke into a dash and grabbed Arabella. He clutched her waist and held the tip of his blade to her throat. "So the great Alpin has come to save his son," Halfdan shouted, with the crazed rage of a lunatic circling in his eyes.

"Halfdan, drop your sword," Alpin demanded. "Most of your men are dead, and the others are retreating. You're outnumbered. You don't stand a chance. Your only hope is surrender. Now drop your sword!"

Halfdan's gaze never left Kenneth, "I prefer to kill the girl and your son first, then we—"

Thump!

"Umff," Halfdan gasped as an arrow sunk into his shoulder. He stumbled backward under the impact and fought to keep his balance.

"Arabella, come to me!" Constantine yelled, standing behind Alpin with a spent crossbow in his hand.

Arabella fled and ran to her father.

Halfdan blinked several times as pain splintered across his chest. He dropped his sword and peered at Kenneth. Then, like a wild boar, he burst into a sprint and barreled into Kenneth, knocking him to the ground. He kept moving forward, rushing toward his horse thirty yards away.

Kenneth jumped to his feet in pursuit. His strides were unbound and his determination unfettered. He closed quickly on the Viking. As Halfdan neared his horse, Kenneth leapt and tackled him around the waist. The two hit the ground in a tangled heap.

"Damn you, Scot," Halfdan growled. He punched Kenneth's head and twisted to find his knife.

Kenneth lifted to his knees and threw himself on top of Halfdan. The two struggled several moments before Kenneth's palm brushed over Halfdan's weapon. He pulled the jewel-handled blade from Halfdan's belt, lifted the knife into the air, and shoved it into Halfdan's chest. "That's for Dorrell!" Without a blink, he removed the blade and jabbed it over and over into the lord of the Vikings' helpless flesh. "And that's for every other Scot you've slaughtered." The words poured from his lips in a psychotic rage with each thrust of the jewel-handled blade.

Halfdan stared up at Kenneth with a pale white face as blood trickled from his half-open mouth. Then his eyes turned dull and cold and slowly shut.

Kenneth rose and tucked the knife into his belt, ruminating as he peered down at Halfdan. The Viking lay stiff and dead. Kenneth studied Halfdan's mangled torso, and his eye caught a glimmer of gold. The edge of a small, corded trinket hung from a fold, a pocket, within Halfdan's dark leather garb. Kenneth stooped and lifted the trinket. Dangling from the thin black cord was a small gold cross— his cross, Coric's gift. A sneer of satisfaction formed on Kenneth's lips as he placed the cross around his neck. He tied it slowly, staring down at the would-be Viking king.

"Kenneth," Alpin called.

"Father!" Kenneth broke from his trance, half dazed. He paused and gazed across the battlefield then turned back to his father. "Have you found Coric and Aiden?"

"Our men have turned the battle, Coric," Aiden shouted, pointing south across the valley. "The Vikings are scattering. They're running scared."

Coric eyed the battle-bloodied wasteland. The Scots had come—and they'd come strong. "Where is Father, can you spot his horse? Where is Kenneth? And Ronan?"

"I lost Kenneth the moment we dismounted. I haven't seen either one since Ronan broke through the Viking wall at the gap."

Coric glanced at his arm and clenched his teeth, grimacing in pain. "Hand me your belt, Aiden," he said, and he pinched together the severed flesh on his forearm to slow the bleeding.

"That's bad, Coric," Aiden said, removing his belt from his waist. "Give me your arm."

Coric shoved his sword into the ground, standing it upright on its tip. He extended his arm to Aiden and tried to keep the wound closed with his other hand. "I could kill that bastard twice for slicing me open like this." Coric gazed down at Magnus' corpse and spat.

"At least you killed him once," Aiden said. He took Coric's arm and pulled his brother's sleeve over the injury. Then he cinched the belt above the area and wrapped it down Coric's forearm to keep pressure on the wound.

"Hurry, Aiden. This isn't over, and we don't need to get caught with our guard down."

"Almost got it."

Coric glanced south at the clusters of men still fighting, "Father's got to be here somewhere—" Coric winced as Aiden slipped the belt under the last loop and pulled it tight.

"That should do it," Aiden said. Then he peered up—and his mouth dropped open.

Coric saw the fright in Aiden's eyes and realized something wasn't right. Coric's heart accelerated and the muscles in his body constricted.

"I think you lost this," the voice said.

Coric slowly turned.

Kodran sat on his horse, staring down at the two and holding Aiden's crossbow. He pointed the seated arrow back and forth between the brothers. "One arrow, two Scots," he said, eyeing them both. "I've owed you this for some time now." He pointed the bow at Aiden and pulled the trigger.

"Aiden!" Coric leapt into his brother.

The arrow flew fast and hard. It hit Coric like a punch and drove deep into his chest above his heart. Coric swayed and dropped to the ground, then eased to his backside.

"You lucky little bastard," Kodran said and glanced over his shoulder at a handful of approaching riders. "I'll come again for you someday," he growled and hurled the bow at Aiden. Then he kicked his horse and the animal shot forward in a blur toward Torrie Forest.

"Coric, are you alright?" Aiden yelled. He lowered to his knees and propped Coric up.

Coric tried to speak but couldn't. His upper lip curled, and he fought to draw air in and out of his nostrils. His eyes lowered to the arrow, and he grabbed the shaft with this hand.

"Don't touch it, Coric," Aiden said. "Leave it. I'll get help." Then Aiden eased Coric to the ground.

Ronan sprinted to the two brothers as fast as his feet could fly.

"What happened?" Ronan exclaimed, catching his breath and staring down at Coric.

"He took an arrow to the chest. It's pretty bad, it's deep."

Ronan knelt beside Coric and studied the arrow-pierced wound. "Aiden, I saw Gavin with the men. I signaled him when I saw you waving. Keep an eye out, he should be coming with help."

Coric's eyes opened. He rolled his head toward Ronan and breathed in short shallow breaths, laboring to keep conscious.

"You better not die on me after all this," Ronan said and faked a grin.

"Shut up," Coric muttered, then he coughed and wheezed.

"Easy, Coric, easy," Ronan whispered.

"He's talking again," Aiden said. "That's a good sign."

Ronan stood and glared at Aiden, "Who did this?"

"The one they call Kodran. He surprised us, and he had a crossbow. He wanted to kill me." Aiden glanced down at Coric and then gazed at Ronan. "When he shot, Coric jumped in front."

"I should have guessed," Ronan muttered, shaking his head and staring down at his foolhardy friend. "Where's Kodran? I've got a score to settle."

Aiden pointed to the distant tree line. "He rode that way, toward Torrie Forest."

Ronan squinted and stared into the distance. A fleeting figure retreated far away, and a small group of Viking riders joined the retreat.

"Ronan," Gavin shouted, tugging his reigns as he

reached the three. "Your father is coming. What's happened to Coric?"

Before Ronan could answer, he heard his father shout his name. Ronan glimpsed past Gavin to see his father riding toward him with three other Scots not far behind. He motioned frantically to his father, urging him to hurry.

When Luag reached the boys, he leapt from his horse before the animal had stopped.

"Father, it's Coric. He's taken an arrow. He needs help."

Luag pushed the boys aside and knelt next to Coric. "Relax, son. Don't try to talk, relax. Nod your head if you can hear me."

Coric opened his eyes and gazed listlessly at Luag, then slowly nodded his head.

"You men," Luag called to two of the men arriving behind him. "Find Alpin, and tell him we need Seamus! We need him now! Go!"

The two Scots turned their steeds and raced across the field.

"Father, I'm taking your horse," Ronan shouted. "Gavin, come with me." Ronan had mounted before Luag could deny him.

"What are you doing?"

Ronan paused and stared at his father. "I'm going to avenge Coric!" Finishing his words, he spun the horse and burst forward—with Torrie Forest fixed in his sights.

"Dammit, take more men with you!" Luag yelled as Ronan and Gavin galloped away.

"Tell them to meet us as we ride," Ronan yelled back, racing for the forest.

Luag swore under his breath. He could only watch as the

ground stretched between him and his son. He bit his lip and returned to Coric.

Tearing open Coric's shirt, Luag exposed the bloody puncture wound with the arrow standing upright in its center. The torn skin lay severed and moist around the arrow's shaft. Luag pried open the wound and gaped into the wet hole. The arrow was deep.

Aiden gazed down at his brother's wound and pulled off his shirt, ignoring the sting of his remnant burns. He unwrapped a bandage from his shoulder. "I don't need this," he said, and he handed the cloth wrap to Luag.

"You boys are pretty beat up," Luag replied and he pressed the rag onto Coric's wound to restrict the oozing blood.

An uneasy feeling swept over Aiden. He turned and combed the battlefield for Seamus. The physician was nowhere in sight. He slowly lowered to his knees beside Coric, watching his older brother struggle to breathe. Lifting his eyes to Luag, he spoke in a quiet voice, "Is he going to make it?"

"He's a fighter, Aiden. He'll fight."

◎

Aiden lifted to his feet. "Here they come!"

"Hold on, Coric. We'll get you home," Luag said as Coric rested with his eyes closed. Luag wondered how Alpin would react to the sight of his son. He paused and said a prayer before standing to receive Alpin.

Alpin, Constantine, and Seamus arrived and descended their horses. Kenneth, Arabella, and a dozen more riders quickly followed and dismounted behind the three.

Luag stepped to Alpin. "He's asking to speak to you," Luag said. "Go slow with him, he's weak."

"Thank you, Luag," Alpin said. He peered past Luag, and his gaze settled on Coric for a moment before shifting to Aiden. "Aiden, you're alive. We had feared the worst. The Lord has been merciful." Alpin approached Aiden and the two embraced. "It's good to lay eyes on you again, Son. How is your brother?"

"Father, he's been badly hurt. He jumped in front of me and took an arrow in the chest. He's been struggling to breathe ... but he's talking now, though not much."

Alpin moved to Coric and knelt beside his son. Seamus followed and crouched across from him. Kenneth stepped behind his father, gazing over his father's shoulder.

Alpin peered into Coric's eyes. He composed himself and smiled. "Coric. It's over, Son. The battle is over. We've routed the Vikings. Halfdan and his men are dead. It's over."

A grin slowly formed on Coric's lips. "That's good, Father. I knew we could do it."

"Constantine told me you'd left Renton, mad as hell at the Picts and determined to find Kenneth and the Vikings. Laise said you and Ronan nearly killed Oengus in his own bed—you three are brave young men to take on Perth by yourselves."

Coric's grin grew larger, and then he peered past his father toward Kenneth and managed a wink.

Kenneth responded in kind. "I think he ticked off the Vikings worse than the Picts. He burned their fort to the ground," Kenneth added proudly.

Coric chuckled and then lifted his hand to his mouth to stop from coughing. "Yeah, they were surprised to see us," Coric forced out the words in a dry, raspy voice.

"You are a warrior, Coric—a brave warrior. Because of your courage, your brothers are with us again." Alpin glanced up at Aiden and Kenneth before peering back at Coric. "I'm reminded of the day you three stood along the path beside the barley field. You wanted to be warriors, you wanted to be men … you were but boys. I rode that day with Drostan. He told me how you'd wanted to trick me and hide among the men. I wish he were here now. He'd be proud of you, Coric … very proud."

Coric gazed up at the dull gray sky, searching the heavens with his eyes. "I miss him, Father."

"I do too, Coric. I do too."

"Father, how is Mother?"

"She's well, Coric. You'll see her soon. She misses you, you know. We'll get you home and have her prepare her finest feast. Does that sound good?"

"Yes, that sounds—" Coric wheezed and tried to catch his breath. He coughed hard, wincing and grabbing at the arrow as he coughed.

Alpin placed his hand behind Coric's neck and helped him to sit. As Coric lifted, he huffed and coughed again. "Seamus," Alpin said, glancing at the physician. "What do we need to do to help him?'

"Let's see if he can take a drink." Seamus removed the plug from his water sack and lifted it for Coric.

Coric eased his mouth forward and took a sip and swallowed.

"That's a start," Seamus said. "Let me check him." He placed his hand against Coric's forehead. Then he pressed his fingers against Coric's neck to find a pulse. "He's cool, and he's lost a lot of blood. Let's get him a blanket."

"Should we remove the arrow?" Kenneth asked.

Seamus' head lifted, and he stared up at Kenneth. "No, we don't remove the arrow. If we do, we'll rip him open and he'll bleed out. I'll have to cut into the wound to remove it, but I can't do that here. Alpin, can you have your men find a cart. We need to get him to Renton. He'll need to rest once I remove the arrow."

Coric lifted his hand and placed it on his father's shoulder. "No, Father. Take me to Cashel," he said, wincing as he spoke.

"Get a cart over here and make it quick," Alpin shouted to his men. He gazed back at Coric, "Son, we need to get you home. We'll take you to your place and—"

"No, Father, please. Take me to Cashel, to Ceana. I have to see her." His eyes shut and his body relaxed.

"Coric!" Alpin shouted. Coric's eyes opened narrowly, and he nodded his head before lowering his chin to his chest. Alpin eased him back to the ground.

"Father, he wants to see Ceana," Kenneth said. "She's pregnant and she's at Cashel."

"I know, Kenneth," Alpin replied, pushing aside Coric's hair and brushing his bangs from his eyes.

"We'll take him to my place, Alpin," Constantine said. "He can see Ceana while Seamus works on him. Then he can rest there."

Alpin nodded. "Very well, let's get the cart and we'll take him to Cashel."

※

"Luag, here comes Ronan," Constantine said, sitting horseback beside the cart.

"Gavin and several others are with him," Aiden added, mounted next to Constantine.

The men settled Coric inside the cart and waited for Ronan and the others to arrive.

"How's Coric?" Ronan called as he approached.

"He's stable for now," Seamus said, kneeling in the cart beside Coric with Kenneth stooped beside him.

"Did you find the men you were after?" Luag asked.

"No. They got away. We chased them to the forest and then headed deeper into the woods. That's where we lost them."

"It was Kodran. I think Alrik and Fox were with him," Gavin said, addressing Kenneth.

"Dammit," Kenneth cursed. "Those bastards deserve to die."

"How many were with this 'Kodran,' only two?" Alpin asked from the far side of the cart.

"I counted nine," Ronan replied. "But others may have retreated to the forest before we got there."

Alpin stared at the distant forest and then turned his eyes to the darkening sky. "Well, Coric is our first concern. We've got enough angry Scots that we can send after them." Alpin peered at Kenneth, watching him seethe at the news of the report. "Put it out of your mind, Kenneth. We'll get them in due time."

Seamus tapped Kenneth's leg. "Here, take this bedroll and use it as a pillow for your brother." He handed the bedroll to Kenneth.

Kenneth took the roll and placed it under Coric's head. Then he reached down to a blanket covering Coric, and he pulled it close to Coric's neck without disturbing the arrow.

Satisfied his brother was comfortable, he jumped from the cart and stared at his father. "He's ready," Kenneth said.

Alpin nodded.

Kenneth peered into the cart one last time. "Hang in there, Coric. We'll get you to Ceana." As Kenneth stepped away, he couldn't help but notice the scars in the cart's wooden sidewall, the scars Coric had placed there on a cold night long ago. Kenneth shut his eyes and shook his head before finally turning away.

"He's ready, Alpin," Seamus said. "We should go."

Alpin glanced at the others, "You heard the doctor. Let's move out."

The driver of the cart snapped the reigns, and the cart rolled forward.

⊚

As the cart moved from the battlefield under the cold, gloomy skies, a horn blew in the distance. It was a Pict horn. It was not the horn of battle, but the horn of retreat. Alpin had heard both in his days.

"Halt," Alpin called out. The cart and the riders stopped. Alpin turned his horse and stared up at the distant ridge, the ridge opposite the one held by the Dalriadan archers. High on the ridgeline stood an endless row of Picts mounted on horseback. They numbered more than Alpin cared to count.

Kenneth watched his father gaze motionless at his lifelong foe. Kenneth nodded to Arabella and then turned his horse from hers. He rode beside his father and stared up at the ridge.

In the middle of the row, a man lifted his hand high into

the air. The man extended his hand aloft for several moments and then lowered it.

Alpin's eyes sat fixed on the figure. "Oengus," he uttered. Then he lowered his head and turned his horse.

Kenneth followed.

Alpin rode his horse beside the cart and lingered momentarily, then he gazed over his men. "Move out," he said. "We're done here."

CHAPTER 24

THE RIDE TO CASHEL WAS LONG—LONG AND dreary. The Scots were spent, and the cold day had turned to a colder night. The clouds had passed, and the stars hung above, gazing down upon Dalriada's weary warriors below. Seamus remained by Coric's side. Coric coughed and groaned now and then, but spoke not a word. In fact, no one spoke much.

As the cart eventually reached Cashel, the Scots moved through the last field that separated them from the small home awaiting Coric. It was then that Kenneth noticed the tired barley wafting sleepily in the breeze of the dark, solemn night. The moon cast down its timid glow, but the barley refused to wake. Kenneth's thoughts faded back in time to the barley fields of Renton, where he had stood as a young boy with his brothers. Yet the land that once boasted a radiance of gold in his youth now seemed muted and tarnished under the colorless light of the sullen September sky. Kenneth stared at Coric's cart and closed his eyes. After a moment had passed, he opened them and looked ahead.

When the cart arrived at Constantine's home, Ceana was waiting at the door. Her father and brother had ridden ahead to bring news of Coric. She stood like a statue between the two men, cupping her hands to her face, waiting for her husband to come back to her.

As the cart and horses came to a stop, she glanced at the riders and their faces. They were dimly lit in the dull moonlight. Ceana gazed at the cart, hoping to find Coric sitting up, searching for her. Instead, she saw only a darkened cart and the bobbing head of an old physician. She sunk back from her father and brother and retreated inside.

Arabella dismounted when she saw Ceana flee into the shelter of the house. She hurried after her and disappeared through the door.

Kenneth left his horse and climbed into the cart beside Coric. He shook him gently. "We're here, Brother."

Coric opened one eye. "Ceana?" he said.

"She's here. We're taking you inside, hold tight."

Coric lifted his hand and grabbed Kenneth's leg. "Don't move me ... bring her to me," he muttered.

"Sure," Kenneth said. He rose, half standing, "Constantine, can you get a lantern? And have Arabella bring Ceana. Coric is asking for her." Kenneth stooped at Coric's side. "She's coming," he said. Then he glimpsed to see his father and brother hurrying to tie their horses. He lowered his eyes to Coric, "You're going to make it. Hang in there."

Coric grinned at Kenneth, peacefully, and spoke in a faint voice, "For the last many hours, I've stared up at the stars, watching them shine silently above, all the while wondering if my next breath would be my last. Kenneth, I was a fool. I suppose I figured I could conquer the world alone ... that I could save Dalriada with only a sword and bow. Yet here I lie … in a place where I can no longer even save myself."

"Coric, you were not a fool. You saved my life." Kenneth said. "I was the fool for taking you on an endless chase. Otherwise, this may have never happened."

"Your chase led us to Aiden, as well as Arabella … had I known Aiden was there, I would have gone with or without you." Coric released a small laugh and then pressed his lips together to keep from coughing. He took a deep breath to relax himself. "Look at the sky, Kenneth … it's enormous, spanning forever with ten thousand stars gazing down upon us. And Dalriada, it's like the sky, it spans for countless miles in splendor … filled with simple people searching for peace. We've stood in its sunshine since we were boys. It was a gift our fathers bled and died for. They gave all they could give that we could have a homeland … I don't want to lose it for my child, or for yours, Kenneth. Promise me, you will not let the Picts, or the Vikings, or any other man take our land. Do what you must to protect it." Coric grimaced, then reached to his wound and adjusted the arrow to ease his pain. "And Kenneth, look after Ceana and my child—he'll need a father."

Kenneth stared at Coric, shaking his head in disbelief. "I promise, Coric … but it won't matter, you'll get better."

"No, Kenneth, no … but it's alright," Coric whispered. He stared for a long moment at Kenneth. "I will see Drostan soon … but I will miss you, Brother."

A mountain of sorrow fell upon Kenneth. He felt the crushing of his heart as he stared back into his dying brother's eyes. "I will miss you too, Coric."

Coric nodded.

Kenneth's throat ran dry, and he tried to swallow.

He turned, hearing footsteps beside the cart. "How is he, Kenneth?" his father asked and leaned over the side of the cart with Aiden and Ronan standing behind him.

"Father ... he's struggling. He's speaking, but he doesn't want to be moved," Kenneth replied.

"You alright, Coric?" Aiden said, peering into the cart beside his father.

"Trying," Coric muttered.

Alpin reached his arm into the cart and clasped Coric's hand. "Son, we're concerned about you. How are you holding up?"

"I guess I've been better," Coric replied, strengthening his voice.

"You stood tall on the battlefield today, Son."

Coric's eyes warmed. "You taught us how to be strong, Father. I wanted to be strong. I wanted you to be proud. But now look what I've done."

"I am proud, Coric. You've always made me proud," Alpin said, gazing down at his son. "You brought Kenneth and Aiden back to us today. Without your courage—and your stubborn head—we may have never seen them again. I am grateful, Son, but I don't want to lose you. You have a beautiful wife and a child that needs a father. Stay strong, Seamus will mend you."

Coric lifted his head and gazed at Alpin. He tightened his hand around his father's, and a hidden tear sat in the corner of his eye. "I love you, Father."

"I love you, too, Son. Be strong for her." Alpin squeezed Coric's hand with a firm grip one last time, and then he let go of his son.

Arabella approached with Ceana. "Here's Ceana, Kenneth."

"Let me help you, Ceana." Kenneth took her hand and helped her into the cart. Before Kenneth jumped down, he knelt beside Coric. "I love you, Brother. Thank you for saving my life … I'll keep those promises, Coric." He tried to smile for his brother. Coric smiled back.

"Here's a lantern, I'll set it in the corner," Constantine whispered, trying not to interrupt. He placed the lantern in the cart and stepped away.

"Give them room, boys," Alpin said, and he walked to the rear of the cart next to Constantine.

Kenneth stepped from the cart and stood beside his father. He reached for Arabella's hand and pulled her to him. He held her. It felt good to hold her, it was the only comfort he found in his otherwise chasm of sorrow. Kenneth stood silent, gazing at Ronan and Aiden as they finished speaking to Coric.

Ronan peered down into the cart and met eyes with Coric, "You've been a brother to me all my life, Coric. You fought one hell of a fight today. Thanks for saving my neck. Fight the good fight, Brother. You're going to make it."

Aiden reached in the cart and patted Coric on the leg. "You know, Drostan was always my hero … after seeing you battle today, I guess I now have two. Make sure you hold still when Seamus fixes you up." He ended, and he stepped away with Ronan as a gentle grin formed and slowly faded from Coric's face.

Ceana knelt at Coric's side and placed her hand on his chest, wanting to touch him, to feel him. "Oh, Coric," she said, trying to find the right words. "I'm so sorry." She stared into his eyes, not willing to gaze upon his wound.

"Ceana," Coric said, taking her hand in his. "I told you I

would come back. I guess I didn't think it would be like this."
He steadied his breath. "How's the baby?"

"We're fine, Coric. The baby is fine. It's you that I'm worried about."

He looked over her sweet face and reached his hand up to touch her cheek. His thumb covered the scar below her eye, the scar that had always made her feel less than beautiful. "Did I ever tell you how perfect you are?"

Ceana's eyes fell from his, and she pressed his hand against her face, warming his palm with her skin.

"Did I ever tell you how much you mean to me? I'm sorry for leaving you. I'm sorry for leaving our child. I wanted to—" Coric paused and held his chest. He lifted his head, coughed, and then laid his head back on the bedroll. "I wanted to tell you that I was wrong for leaving you. I wish I had a second chance."

Ceana touched her fingers to the side of his face and softly stroked the rough skin of his cheek. "Coric, let me have them take you inside. Let Seamus work on you."

"No, Ceana … I'm not going inside," he said, laboring to find his breath.

Ceana gazed into his eyes, "Oh, Coric." Her voice trembled as she spoke. She felt his palm touch her swollen belly, and she placed her hand on top of his. Tears rolled down her cheeks and dripped to his chest beside his wound.

"Ceana, I think it's a boy. If it is, name him Duncan, after your grandfather … and make sure he grows up big and strong." He tried to smile but winced. "Tell him about me, Ceana. Tell him that I loved him … tell him that I loved his mother." Coric peered up into the starry sky above. "It's beautiful, Ceana. It's always been beautiful," he said. He turned to her and gazed long into her eyes. The light of the lantern cast its dim hue upon her soft skin. "Know that I loved you, Ceana," he said, and he closed his eyes and breathed his last breath.

◉

The Dalriadans gave much to keep their freedom, and Dalriada, for now, was free. The Viking tales they'd heard and told were no longer tales, they were memories. They were gruesome and sad memories. Their stories had once been colored with battles of glory and valor and courage, but in living out such stories, they found them to be colored much more with misery and bloodshed and loss.

Boys dream of becoming men. They thrive on testing their grit in battle, but the fires of war do more to a man than prove his strength. They burn and tear and twist the mind and spirit into scars that are not to be desired. Still, there are times when battles must be fought and wars must be waged. For often, those things held most dear can only be attained and safely kept in heeding the call of battle. It is a transcendent calling, a call that a man must be willing to live for—and die for. And in so doing, by the grace of God, may such a noble man inherit his prize and receive it with honor, as he gives himself for another.

End, Book II

EPILOGUE

YOUNG DUNCAN, SON OF CORIC: I, KENNETH, write this letter to tell you of your father, Coric, son of Alpin and brother to me. He was a remarkable man, much unlike most other men. He was strong, brave, and full of life. In knowing him, you would have proudly called him, *Father*, and he alike, would have proudly called you, *Son*. He was exceptional, giving all that he was to protect those he loved—not for glory, but for love and honor. There are many who esteem honor and seek honor with the tongue, yet not your father. Though he did not seek honor from others, through the living and giving of his life, he attained it in the highest of measures.

Your father was valiant in spirit, and as such, I suppose that I shall see this same spirit in you. Being young, you are bound to be daring and brave, hearty and foolhardy, at one and the same time. As you know already from life, you will find dark days where you struggle to overcome. And so I share with you a trace of wisdom gained in the years given me. I encourage you to move beyond your losses and live life fully, and in doing so, I urge you to find contentment in all things. You see, in the spring of life, a man pursues those things he prizes most dearly. He aspires to great heights. Whether want or need, whether right or wrong, he pursues them with all exuberance and fervor. The summer of life then follows and brings a man his challenges, the things that stand in the way of the desires of his heart. Here a man finds how earnestly he truly wishes to attain such treasures. Here his passions, his strength, and his ambition are refined—refined in the fires of struggle and adversity. Autumn, in turn, follows summer. Autumn is the season of life where a man comes to know what is strong, and what is weak, about his character and his heart, and often there is much of both. Along the way, treasures are won and others lost, not all that was pursued was obtained. Dreams are dreamt and hearts are broken. In the end, a man knows with much greater clarity what is worth treasuring, worth keeping, and worth fighting for, and he knows of the things which were meant to be let go of, or were never meant to be had. Though the virility of spring has faded, and the struggles of summer have passed, wisdom comes in autumn, and a man—be he a wise man, a kind man, a humble man—finds contentment in what he has, shedding all regard for that which he has not.

Young Duncan, how I wish with you that you could behold your father. That you could hear his voice, touch his skin, feel his angst and his laughter. Were he with you, he would teach you to fight for good, and fight hard for it, and to put all you have into life through good and bad times—for all men see both. Live free, and give what is called of you to preserve that freedom. For you are free this day because of what your father gave. Though losing him has left loss in your heart, and mine, he was the kind of man who would rather have you live in Dalriada's freedom with only his memory, than to live in bondage with him at your side. Thus, I adjure you, cherish freedom with all your might. And be assured of this in life, the things you find worth treasuring will require you to toil and fight to attain them. For it is the sacred value of such things that make them worth the fight. Love and faith, hope and freedom, these are things worth treasuring. Esteem them highly, for your father fought and gave so that we may know these treasures. Smile, young man, for you are strong. Keep the faith of your father, and in time, on that other side, we shall see him again.

GLOSSARY

Dalriadan Men:

Alpin – Leading Dalriadan in Renton; father of Drostan, Nessa, Coric, Kenneth, Aiden, and Donald

Drostan – Alpin's oldest son

Coric – Alpin's second oldest son

Kenneth – Alpin's third oldest son

Aiden – Alpin's fourth oldest son

Donald – Alpin's youngest son

Eochaid – Alpin's father

Malcolm – Alpin's grandfather

Constantine – Alpin's cousin who lives in Cashel; Senga's husband; adopted Arabella

Ronan – Coric's good friend; Luag's son

Luag – Alpin's right hand man; Ronan's father

Laise – Dalriadan from Milton; strong with a long bow; son of Latharn and brother of Ceana

Latharn – Leader of Milton clan; father of Laise and Ceana

Gormal – Dalriadan from Renton; father of Searc

Searc – Dalriadan from Renton; Gormal's son

Taran – Dalriadan from Dumbarton; Guaire's son

Guaire – Dalriadan from Dumbarton; Taran's father

Feragus – Blacksmith in Renton

Gilchrist – Cleric in Renton

Gavin – Young man from Renton, prisoner of Vikings

Dorrell – Dalriadan whose village is destroyed; uncle and cousin are killed by Vikings

Seamus – A man from Milton; a physician of sorts who tends to Alpin and Coric

Nicol – An older Scot, a prisoner at the Viking fort

Dalriadan Women:

Arabella – Pict by birth, adopted daughter of Constantine and Senga

Ena – Alpin's wife; Mother of Drostan, Nessa, Coric, Kenneth, Aiden, and Donald

Nessa – Alpin's daughter; sister of Drostan, Coric, Kenneth, Aiden, and Donald

Sorcha – Dalriadan woman from Milton, wife of Latharn, mother of Laise and Ceana

Ceana – Young Dalriadan woman from Milton; daughter of Latharn; wife of Coric; sister of Laise

Rhiannon – Young Dalriadan woman whose father and brother are killed by the Vikings

Picts and Vikings:

Oengus – Pict Lord

Deort – Oengus' right hand; captain of the Pict guard

Grogan – Pict who finds a Scot along a river bank

Mathe – Pict physician

Halfdan the Black – the Viking leader

Kodran – Viking warrior, second in command

Jorund – Large Viking; third in command

Gudrod the Hunter – a Viking king; father of Halfdan

Alrik, Magnus, and Fox – Vikings who serve Halfdan